Sons of the

Eden Phillpotts

Alpha Editions

This edition published in 2024

ISBN : 9789357962643

Design and Setting By
Alpha Editions
www.alphaedis.com
Email - info@alphaedis.com

Contents

BOOK I. ....- 1 -

CHAPTER I. THE BEECH TREE ....- 3 -

CHAPTER II. BEAR DOWN FARM ....- 12 -

CHAPTER III. A WISE MAN AND A
WISE WOMAN...- 20 -

CHAPTER IV. THE KISS...- 27 -

CHAPTER V. PAGAN ALTARS ....- 34 -

CHAPTER VI. ANTHEMIS COTULA ....- 43 -

CHAPTER VII. A BADGER'S EARTH ....- 50 -

CHAPTER VIII. OUT OF THE MIST................................- 58 -

CHAPTER IX. THE WARNING ....- 66 -

CHAPTER X. THREE ANGRY MAIDS ....- 76 -

CHAPTER XI. PARTINGS...- 83 -

CHAPTER XII. THE DEFINITE DEED ....- 92 -

CHAPTER XIII. SNOW ON SCOR
HILL ....- 98 -

CHAPTER XIV. THE WISDOM OF DR. CLACK ....- 104 -

CHAPTER XV. SUN DANCE ....- 109 -

CHAPTER XVI. A SHELF OF SLATE ....- 117 -

CHAPTER XVII. SPRING ON SCOR HILL ....- 126 -

CHAPTER XVIII. ROSES AND ROSETTES...- 132 -

BOOK II..- 139 -

CHAPTER I. THE SEEDS ....- 141 -

CHAPTER II. CHERRY GREPE'S SINS ....- 148 -

CHAPTER III. A SECRET...- 155 -

CHAPTER IV. THE WISDOM OF MANY ....- 159 -

CHAPTER V. IN SPRING MOONLIGHT ....- 166 -

CHAPTER VI. SORROW'S FACE.....................................- 174 -

CHAPTER VII. PLOTS AGAINST AN ORPHAN ....- 180 -

CHAPTER VIII. A NECKLACE OF BIRDS' EGGS..- 184 -

CHAPTER IX. AN OLD-TIME PRESCRIPTION ....- 190 -

CHAPTER X. OIL OF MAN ....- 197 -

CHAPTER XI. A CLEAN BREAST OF IT...- 206 -

CHAPTER XII. LIGHT.....................................- 214 -

BOOK III. ....- 221 -

CHAPTER I. VANESSA IO ....- 223 -

CHAPTER II. THE MEETING OF THE MEN...- 231 -

CHAPTER III. FLAGS IN THE WIND............................- 236 -

CHAPTER IV. DRIFTING ....- 242 -

CHAPTER V. A HUNTING MORNING ....- 249 -

CHAPTER VI. LOVE OF MAN ....- 255 -

CHAPTER VII. LAPSES ....- 261 -

CHAPTER VIII. THE ROUND ROBIN ....- 272 -

CHAPTER IX. RED DAWN............................- 280 -

CHAPTER X. A MAN OF COURAGE............................- 288 -

CHAPTER XI. THE ROAD TO PEACE ....- 293 -

CHAPTER XII. PEACE ....- 299 -

CHAPTER XIII. A SOUND OF SUFFERING...- 305 -

CHAPTER XIV. FROM WORDS TO BLOWS..- 307 -

CHAPTER XV. WATERN TOR ....- 314 -

CHAPTER XVI. THRENODY ....- 319 -

BOOK IV. ....- 323 -

CHAPTER I. THE PASSAGE OF TWO YEARS ....- 325 -

CHAPTER II. NO AFTER-GLOW ....- 328 -

BOOK I.

CHAPTER I.
THE BEECH TREE

Above unnumbered sisters she arose, an object noteworthy even amid these aisles, where, spun from the survival of the best endowed, fabrics of ancient forest enveloped the foot-hills of the Moor and belted heather and granite with great woodlands. A dapple of dull silver marked her ascension and glimmered upwards through the masses of her robe. From noble girth of moss-grown trunk she sprang; her high top was full of a silky summer song; while sunbeams played in the meshes of her million leaves and cascades of amber light, born from her ripening harvest, streamed over the dark foliage. She displayed in unusual perfection the special symmetry of her kind, stood higher than her neighbours, and fretted the blue above with pinnacles of feathering arborescence, whose last, subtle expression, at that altitude, escaped the eye. Her midmost boughs tended from the horizontal gradually downward, and the nether branches, rippling to earth like a waterfall, fashioned a bower or music-making dome of translucent green around about the bole. Within this arbour the roots twisted down their dragon shapes into the dark, sweet-scented earth, and fortified the beech against all winds that blew. So she stood, queen of the wold, a creation loved by song-birds, a treasure-house for squirrels, pigeons, and the pheasants that, at autumn-time, strutted gorgeous in the copper lake of her fallen leaves. Beneath her now, cool and moist in twilight of shadows, grew delicate melampyre that brought light into the herbage, stood the wan seed-vessels of bygone bluebells, and trailed grasses, with other soft, etiolate things that had never known direct sunshine. The pale trunk was delicately wrought with paler lichens, splashed and circled upon its bark; while mossy boulders of granite, lying scattered within the circumference of the tree's vastness, completed this modest harmony of grey and silver, lemon and shadowed green.

Woodland roads wound at hand, and in a noontide hour of late July these paths were barred and flooded with golden sunlight; were flanked by trunks of gnarled oak and wrinkled ash; were bridged with the far-flung limbs of the former, whereon trailed and intertwined festoons of ivy and wreaths of polypody fern that mingled with tree mosses. Through this spacious temple, seen under avenues of many a pillar, sparkled falling water where the sisters Teign, their separate journeys done, murmured together and blended their crystal at an ancient bridge. Henceforth these two streams sweep under hanging woods of larch and pine, by meadows, orchards, homesteads, through the purple throat of oak and fir-crowned Fingle, and so onwards, by way of open vales, to their sad-coloured, heron-haunted estuary. Hand in hand they run, here moving a mill-wheel, there bringing sweet water to a hamlet, and ever singing their changeful song. The melody of them deepens, from its first baby prattle at springs in Sittaford's stony bosom, to the riotous roar of waterfalls below; lulls, from the music reverberated in stony gorges, to a whisper amid unechoing valleys and most placid pasture lands. Finally salt winds with solemn message from the sea welcome Teign; and mewing of gulls on shining mud-flats; and the race and ripple of the tides, who joyfully bring the little stream to that great Lover of all rivers.

Leading from dingles on the eastern bank to interspaces of more open glades beside the great beech tree, a bridge, fashioned of oak saplings, still clothed with bark and ash-coloured lichen, crossed the river; and, at this sunlit moment, a woman stood upon it and a man shook the frail structure from his standpoint on the bank. His purpose was to alarm the maiden if he could; but she only laughed, and hastened across sure-footed.

Honor Endicott was two-and-twenty; of tall, slight habit, and a healthy, brown complexion. Her face betrayed some confusion of characteristics. In repose the general effect suggested melancholy; but this expression vanished when her eyes were lighted with laughter or her lips parted in a smile. Then the sad cast of her features wholly disappeared and, as the sky wakes at dawn or sunset, Honor was transfigured. A beholder carried from her not the impression of her more usual reserve, but the face, with its rather untidy black hair, pale brown eyes and bright lips all smile-lighted. Happily she laughed often, from no vain consciousness of her peculiar charm, but because she possessed the gift of a humorous disposition, in the modern acceptation of that word, and found the world, albeit lonely and not devoid of grey days, yet well stored with matter for laughter. This sense, than which heredity—that godmother, half fairy, half fiend—can bestow no better treasure on man or woman, kept the world sweet for Honor. Her humour was no paltry idiosyncrasy of mere joy in the ridiculous; but rather a quality that helped her to taking of large views, that lent a sense of just proportion in affairs, that tended to tolerance and leavened with charity her outlook on all things. It also served to brighten and better an existence, not indeed unhappy, but unusually lonely for a young woman.

She held up a pretty brown hand, and shook her head at the man.

"Christopher," she said, "supposing that your bridge had broken, and I had tumbled in?"

"I should have saved you, without doubt—a delicious experience."

"For you. What a subject for a romance: you, the last of your line; I, the last of mine, being swept to death by old Teign! And my farm would be desolate, and your woods and hills and ancestral hall, all bundled wretchedly into Chancery, or some such horrid place."

"On the contrary, I save you; I rescue you at great personal peril, and we join hands and lands, and live happily ever afterwards."

"There's a heron! You frightened him with your folly."

The great bird ascended from a shallow, trailed his thin legs over the water, then gathered speed, rose clear, steered with heavy and laborious flight amid overhanging boughs, and sought a lonelier hunting-ground elsewhere.

"Brutes! I always walk right on top of them when I'm not carrying my gun. I hate to think of the number of young trout they eat."

"Plenty left to grow big and be caught all the same," said Honor, as she peeped down to watch grey shadows, that sped up stream at sight of her and set little sandclouds rising under the clear water where they flashed away.

"Nothing like a Devon trout in the world, I think," she added. "I caught a half-pounder in the Wallabrook last night, just at the end of the evening rise, with that fly, like a 'woolly bear' caterpillar, you gave me."

Christopher Yeoland nodded, well pleased. He was a broad and tall young man of thirty, and he walked through woods and beside waters that had belonged to his family for years without count. Ardent in some things, sanguine in all, and unconquerably lazy, he had entered the world to find it entirely a problem. Succeeding upon several generations of shiftless and unpractical ancestors—men of like metal with himself—he stood the penniless possessor of a corner of Devon wherein Nature had exhausted her loving resources. He clung to the involved home of his fathers, and dreamed of retrieving the desperate position some day. He lived an open-air life, and spun courses of action, quite majestic in their proportions, for the succour and restoration of his property; but the taking of a definite step in any direction seemed beyond his powers. In theory he swept to action and achievement, and, if words could have done it, Godleigh had been freed from all encumbrance thrice in every week; but practically Christopher appeared content to live from hand to mouth at his old manor house, to keep one horse in the huge stables, two dogs in the kennels, a solitary old woman and one man in his echoing and empty house, where, aforetime, more than half a score of folk had bustled away their busy lives.

Godleigh, or Godbold's Leigh, as it was first called after its earliest Norman owner, may be identified among the Domesday manors of Devon; but it is almost beyond parallel to find possessions descending through a line of commoners so unbroken as in this case. To Yeoland's ancestors, none of whom had ever been ennobled, this place accrued soon after 1300 A.D., during the reign of the second Edward; but since that period the original estate had been shorn of many acres, and sad subdivisions and relinquishments from century to century were also responsible for its diminution. Now hill and valley immediately around Godleigh, together with those tracts upon which stood the village and church of Little Silver, with sundry outlying farms, were all that survived of the former domain, and even these pined under heavy mortgages held by remote money-lending machines with whom Christopher's father had been much concerned throughout the years of his later life. The present old fifteenth-century house, built on foundations far more ancient, peeped, with grey mullioned windows and twisted chimneys, from forest of pine on a noble hill under the eastern ramparts of Dartmoor. Granite crowned this elevation, and Teign turned about, like a silver ribbon, far beneath it.

Here the last of his line passed with Honor Endicott beside the river, and she mourned presently that the sole care of such noble woods rested with the Mother only, and that never a forester came to remove the dead or clear overgrowth of brake and thicket.

"Nature's so untidy," said Honor.

"She is," Yeoland admitted, "and she takes her own time, which seems long from our point of view. But then there's no pay-day for her, thank God. She doesn't turn up on Saturdays for the pieces of silver and bite them suspiciously, like some of your farm folk you lent to help save my hay last week; and she consumes all her own rubbish, which is a thing beyond human ingenuity."

This man and woman had known each other from early youth, and were now left by Chance in positions curiously similar; for Honor Endicott was also an orphan, also came of ancient Devon stock, and also found her patrimony of Bear Down Farm—a large property on the fringe of the Moor and chiefly under grass—somewhat of a problem. It was unencumbered, but hungered for the spending of money. Concerning the Endicotts, who had dwelt there for many generations, it need only be said that they were of yeoman descent, dated from Tudor times, and had of late, like many a kindred family all England over, sunk from their former estate to the capacity of working farmers.

Honor, who had enjoyed educational privileges as a result of some self-denial on the part of both of her parents, now reigned mistress at "Endicott's," as Bear Down Farm was commonly called. At first sovereign power proved a source of pleasure; now, blunted by nearly a year of experience, her rule occasioned no particular delight.

Presently Christopher led his companion beside the great beech and pointed to a leafy tent beneath it.

"Come into my parlour! I found this delicious place yesterday, and I said to myself, 'Mistress Endicott may take pleasure in such a spot as this.' Here will we sit—among the spiders with bodies like peas and legs like hairs; and I'll make you laugh."

"It's late, Christopher."

"Never too late to laugh. Just half one little hour. What are thirty minutes to two independent people who 'toil not, neither do they spin'—nor even knit, like your uncle? There—isn't it jolly comfortable? Wish the upholstery on some of my old-world furniture was as complete. By the way, you know that sofa thing with dachshund legs and a general convulsed look about it, as though the poor wretch had been stuffed with something that was not suiting it? Well, Doctor Clack says that it's worth fifty pounds! But he's such a sanguine brute. Yet this granite, with its moss cushions, is softer than my own easy chair. There are no such springs as Nature's. Look at heather, or a tree branch in a gale of wind, or a———"

"Now don't begin again about Nature, Christo; you've talked of nothing else since we started. Make me laugh if I'm to stop another minute."

"Well, I will. I was looking through some musty old odds and ends in our muniment-room last night and reading about my forefathers. And they did put me so much in mind of the old governor. Such muddlers—always procrastinating and postponing and giving way, and looking at life through the wrong end of the telescope."

"I've heard my father say that Mr. Yeoland was such a man."

"Yes; and money! He never paid anything in his life but the debt of Nature, dear old chap; and if he could have found a way to make Nature take something in the pound, he'd be here pouring his wisdom into my ears yet."

"We're all bankrupts to her, I suppose."

"He only made one enemy in all his long life; and that was himself."

Christopher reflected a moment, then laughed and drew a paper from his pocket.

"That reminds me of what I set out on. We are most of us Yeolands much like the governor. As I tell you, I rummaged in the archives to kill an hour, and found some remarkably ancient things, ought to send them to Exeter Museum, or somewhere; only it's such a bother. Couldn't help laughing, though it was a sort of Sardinian chuckle—on the wrong side of my face. We're always yielding up, or ceding, or giving away, or losing something. Here's a scrap I copied from a paper dated 1330. Listen!"

He smoothed his screed, looked to see that Honor was attending, then read:—

"'Simon de Yeolandde, s. of John Geoffrey de Yeolandde, gives to Bernard Faber and Alice his wife his tenement at Throwle'—that's Throwley, of course '*i.e.* my hall and my orchard called Cridland Barton, and my herb garden, and my piece of land south of my hall, and my piece of land north of my hall as far as Cosdonne, and the reversion of the dowry his mother Dyonisia holds.' There—the grammar is rocky, but the meaning clear enough. Here's another—in 1373. 'Aylmer Yeolande'—we'd given away one of our 'd's' by that time, you see—'Aylmer Yeolande releases to William Corndone 4*d.* (four pence) of annual rent, and to Johanna Wordel all his right in the hundred of Exemynster.' And here's just one more; then I'll shut up. In 1500 I find this: 'Suit between Dennys Yeolandde'—we'd got our 'd' back again for a while—'Gentleman, of Godbold's Leigh, and Jno. Prouze, Knight, of Chaggeforde, as to right of lands in Waye and Aller—excepting only 12*s.* (twelve shillings) of chief rent, which Dennys Yeolandde hath; and the right of comyn of pasture.' Of course my kinsman went to the wall, for the next entry shows him climbing down and yielding at every point to the redoubtable Sir John. We're always fighting the Prouzes, and generally getting the worst of it. Then their marriage settlements! Poor love-stricken souls, they would have given their silly heads away, like everything else, if they could have unscrewed them!"

"So would you," said Honor Endicott. "You laugh at them; but you're a Yeoland to the marrow in your bones—one of the old, stupid sort."

"I believe I must be. The sixteenth and seventeenth century chaps were made of harder stuff, and went to the wars and got back much that their fathers had lost. They built us into a firm folk again from being a feeble; but of late we're thrown back to the old slack-twisted stock, I fear."

"That's atavism," declared Honor learnedly.

"Whew! What a word for a pretty mouth!"

"I was taught science of a milk-and-water sort at school."

"Smother science! Look at me, Honor, and tell me when you're going to answer my question. 'By our native fountains and our kindred gods'; by all we love in common, it's time you did. A thousand years at least I've waited, and you such a good sportswoman where other things are concerned. How can you treat a Christian man worse than you'd treat a fish?"

She looked at his handsome, fair face, and lost sight of the small chin and mouth before a broad, sun-tanned forehead, curly hair, and blue eyes.

"You knew the answer, Christo, or you'd never have been so patient."

"On the contrary, how can I know? I hang on in a storm of agony."

"You look a miserable wretch enough—such a furrowed cheek—such a haggard gleam in your eyes."

"I say, now! Of course I don't wear my heart on my sleeve, or my awful suspense upon my face. No, I hide my sufferings, go on shaving and putting on my best clothes every Sunday, and worshipping in church and carrying the plate, and all the rest of the dreary round. Only the sunrises know of all I endure. But once refuse, and you'll see what despair can drive a man to; say 'No' and I fling everything up and go off to Australia, where lives the last relation I've got in the world—an old gentleman in the 'back blocks,' or some such dismal place."

"You must not dream of that. Men have to work there."

"Then you'll do the only thing to stop me from such an awful fate? You'll take me for better for worse? You'll join your fat lands to my lean ones? You'll——"

"Don't," she said, rather bitterly, "don't laugh at me and mine in the midst of a proposal of marriage. Somehow it makes my blood run cold, though I'm not sentimental. Yet marriage—even with you—has a serious side. I want to think how serious. We can't go on laughing for ever."

"Why not? You know the summing-up of a very wise man after he'd devoted his life to philosophy? Nothing is new, and nothing is true, and nothing matters. God bless my own—very own little brown mouse of an Honor! Somehow I had a sneaking hope all along that you would say 'Yes'!"

"I haven't yet."

"Kiss me, and don't quibble at a moment like this. You haven't kissed me since you were fifteen."

But Honor's humour for once deserted her. She tried to conjure thoughts proper to the moment and magnify its solemnity; she made an effort, in some measure pathetic, to feel more than she really felt.

"You'll be wise, clearest Christo; you'll think of me and love me always and——"

"Anything—anything but work for you, sweet," he said, hugging her to himself, and kissing her with a boy's rapture.

"Oh, Christopher, don't say that!"

"Then I won't; I'll even work, if you can steel yourself to the thought of such a spectacle as Christo labouring with a sense of duty—like an ant with a grain of corn. God bless and bless and bless your dear little warm heart and body, and soft hair and eyes and everything! Work for you! You wait and see."

"I knew this was coming," she said a little drearily. "Ever so long ago I saw it coming and heard it coming. And I rehearsed my part over and over. Yet the thing itself is an anti-climax, Christo. I should have said 'Yes' the second time you asked me."

"The first time, my pearl."

"Perhaps so. It's like flat cider now."

"Don't say that. We've been courting continuously, if you look back, ever since we were children. Then you had dear little tails down your back—two of them—and I used to get you birds' eggs and other useful things. When will you marry me, sweetheart?"

"Oh, I don't know," said Honor. "When I can afford a cake."

But there was a tear in her eye that he did not see.

"There speaks again my own brave, heroic Honor! We will have a cake; but why should you pay for it?"

"I must—there's nobody else to do so. You can't. Come, it is time, and more than time, that I went home."

"Wait," he said; "on a great, historic occasion like the present one marks the day with a white stone. This spot is henceforward sacred to every subsequent Yeoland or Endicott. It may become the shrine of family pilgrimages. So I'll set a true lover's knot upon this venerable beech bole, together with the initials H.E.—that's God's feminine masterpiece—and C.A.Y.—that's Christopher Aylmer Yeoland—not a divine inspiration, I grant you; but a worthy, harmless child of Nature, taking him all round. Hark to my best-loved poet:—

'And in the rind of every comely tree

I'll carve thy name, and in that name kisse thee.'"

He cut and chattered; then, his work completed, bid Honor inspect the conventional bow with their united initials staring white and naked from the bark.

"Nature will tone it down and make it pretty later on," he said.

"I hope she will make you wise later on."

They departed then and wandered upward by a woodland track to Godleigh. His arm was round her; her head rested against his shoulder, and her spirits rose a little. They laughed together, each at the other's slight fancies; and then a vision of death met them. In a glade beside the way, where honeysuckle hung pale lamps about the altar of sacrifice, appeared a fallen cloud of feathers that warmed from grey to golden-green. There a hawk had slain a woodpecker, and nothing remained of the victim save the under-down and plumage, with his upper mandible and a scattered feather or two from his crimson crest.

"That's unlucky," said Honor.

"Very—for the bird," admitted Christopher. "Poor beggar—I'm sorry. I like the green woodpeckers. They've such a sense of humour, and love a laugh as well as I do myself."

CHAPTER II.
BEAR DOWN FARM

The lovers passed through Godleigh, and then, entering the main road that ran from Little Silver to those high regions above it, pursued their way by Devonshire lanes whose lofty hedge-banks shut out all view of the grass lands extending upon each side. Here and there, however, gates opened into the hayfields, and from one, where two of Honor's ricks were slowly rising, came hum of voices. The scene was set in silver-green wisps of hay; a sweet scent clung to the air; two horses rested on the shady side of the rick; an elm or two whispered into the haze of summer; and, hard by, sat above half a dozen persons taking their midday meal under the hedge. Speech was hushed; the nearest men touched their hats, and a girl dropped a curtsey as Honor walked by at discreet distance from young Yeoland. And then, upon their passing, the haymakers broke into a new subject with ready tongue.

A man, smartly attired and apparently not of the working party, winked as Christopher and his lady moved out of sight.

"'Tis a case for sartain sure," he said.

"Have been this many a day, if you ax me," answered a young woman near him. She wore a sun-bonnet of faded blue, and a brown dress dragged up to her belt on one side over a rusty red petticoat.

"They've been tinkering arter each other ever since I can mind, an' I be nineteen," she added.

Another spoke. He was a tall labourer, clad in earth-colour, with a big nose, a long neck, large, sun-blistered ears, and black hair.

"Might be a happy thing belike," he said; and to him a smaller man replied—a man whose bristly beard was nearly grey, whose frowning, dark eyes and high, discontented forehead promised little amiability.

"'A happy thing'! A happy fiddlestick, Henry Collins! Godleigh's sea-deep in debt, an' so much a land of the Jews as Jerusalem's self, by all accounts. An' missis—better her bide a maid all her days than marry him, I reckon. She's a jewel tu precious for the likes of that gude-for-nothing. An' I've my doubts, but—Sally, give awver, will 'e, an' remember you'm a grawed gal!"

This sudden exhortation Mr. Jonah Cramphorn cast at his daughter, the maiden who had first spoken; and necessity for such rebuke appeared in the fact that Sally, a ripe and plump damsel, with red lips, grey eyes and corn-coloured hair, was now pelting the youth beside her with hay, while he returned the compliment as best he could.

Gregory Libby, in his well-fitting garments with neat gaiters and cap to match, though formerly a worker, enjoyed holiday to-day for reasons now to appear. He was a mean type of man, with sandy locks, a slight hare-lip, and a low forehead; but to Sally's eyes these defects were not apparent. Mr. Libby could sing charming songs, and within the past week he was richer by a legacy of five hundred pounds. On the previous day he had come back from London to Little Silver, and now, still putting off his return to work, stood among the folk of Bear Down and posed as a person of some consequence. Sally's conduct woke indignation elsewhere than in her father's breast. Mr. Henry Collins glared at the grey figure of Gregory. The big-nosed man was a new hand at Bear Down; but one fortnight in the company of Sally had served to enslave Henry's maiden heart. He was in love with Miss Cramphorn, but thus far had hidden his secret.

Beside the rising hayrick, sitting in sunshine with his face to the others, an old, bald labourer ate bread and onions and drank from a little cider barrel. His countenance showed a marvellous network of wrinkles; his scant hair, reduced to tufts above his ears, was very white; his whiskers were also white, and his eyes, blue as the summer sky, wore an expression of boyish frankness. His small, clean-shaved mouth was pursed like a young child's.

"'Tis pity," he said, resuming the former topic, "'tis pity as missis can't find a way to mate wi' her cousin, Maister Myles Stapledon, him what be comin' to pay a visit presently. A snug man they say, an' a firm-footed—solid every way in fact. I mind last time he comed here—more'n ten year ago. A wise young youth even then."

"Ban't purty Miss Endicott's sort by the sound of un," said Gregory Libby; then, accepting a drink of cider from a horn mug which Sally brought him, he drew forth a cigar from a yellow leather case. This he presently lighted, marched about, and puffed with great show of satisfaction, not oblivious to the attention he attracted.

"A strange fashion way to take tobacco," said the ancient, who was called Churdles Ash.

"So it is then," assented Mr. Cramphorn; "an' what's more, I ban't gwaine to allow 'tis a fit an' proper way of smokin' for the likes of him. What's five hunderd pound when all's said?"

"'Twill blamed soon be five hunderd pence, if the man's gwaine to broadcast it away 'pon fantastic machines like them, as awnly gentlefolks have any business with," said Samuel Pinsent, another labourer, who passed for a great wit, chiefly by reason of a Merry-Andrew power to pull remarkable faces. He was a red man with weak eyes; and his fellows alleged him impervious to all feminine attractions.

"For Sundays an' high rejoicings a cigar may pass now an' again," argued Henry Collins. "Not as I'm saying a word for Greg Libby," he added in violent haste, as he caught Sally's eye. "He'm a puny twoad an' always was—brass or no brass. What do the likes of him want wi' stiff collars 'pon week-days? Let un go back to his job, which was hedge-tacking, an' not done tu well neither, most times."

"He'm the monkey as have seed the world," said old Ash, lighting a black pipe and crossing his hands over his stomach.

Mr. Collins mopped his forehead, and looked up from where he sat. Then he tightened the leather thongs that fastened in his trousers below the knees and answered as he did so—

"Seed the world! Him! I knaw what he seed. He seed a cheap tailor in the Edgware Road, Paddington way; an' he seed a wicked back street or two; an' no doubt a theayter——"

"That'll do, if you please, Henery," said Mr. Cramphorn. "Me an' Ash, as weern't born essterday, can guess all the rest. I ban't in nature suspicious——"

Then in his turn Jonah was interrupted.

"Ess fay, you be, my son," declared Mr. Ash.

"Anyway," answered the parent, darkly scowling, "I see my darter pulling eyes at the fule an' I won't stand it—wouldn't for twice five hunderd pound."

"No need to fright yourself," said Churdles Ash, shaking his head. "Libby's not a marryin' man—tu selfish to marry while his auld mother's alive to slave for him an' kiss the ground he walks on. Besides, there's your other darter—Margery. He'm so set 'pon wan as t'other; but 'tis all philandering, not business."

"He'll end by havin' a sore back anyways if I see much more of it. Sally to marry him indeed! Shaw me a purtier gal than Sally this side Exeter an' I'll give 'e a gawlden sovereign!"

"An' I'll give 'e another!" declared Mr. Collins.

At this moment Jonah's second daughter, together with one Mrs. Loveys, housekeeper at Bear Down, appeared. The latter was an ample, elderly widow. She had a capacious bosom, bare arms, and a most kindly face. Her late husband, Timothy Loveys, after a lifetime of service at Endicott's, passed within a year of his master; and upon his death Mr. Cramphorn had won promotion and was now head man. As for Margery, a thin, long-faced girl, cast in mould more fragile than her sister, she worked as dairymaid at the farm. She too was personable, but her slimmer contour, reserved manner, and sharp tongue contrasted ill, in masculine opinion, with Sally's physical exuberance and good temper.

The women who now came to fetch empty utensils and baskets stayed awhile, and Mrs. Loveys asked a question.

"An' what for be you offerin' gawlden sovereigns so free, Henry Collins?" she inquired with a side glance.

"To find a purtier maiden than Sally, ma'am."

Margery laughed and blushed, with her eyes on Mr. Libby.

"What about missis?" she asked.

"Missis," answered Jonah, "be a lady. She'm built on a different pattern, though with like material. No disrespect to her, as I'd shed my life's blood for, but the differ'nce betwixt she an' my Sally's the differ'nce betwixt sunlight an' moonlight."

"Between a wind-flower an' a butivul, full-blawed cabbage rose," hazarded Mr. Collins.

"Yet theer's them as would liefer have the windflower," said Margery, who secretly believed herself very like her mistress, and dressed as near to Honor as she dared. Mrs. Loveys nodded approval of this statement; Mr. Cramphorn stoutly questioned it.

"What d'you say, Churdles?" asked Pinsent; "or be you tu auld to call home the maids you felt kind-like towards in last century when you was full o' sap?"

"I say 'tis time to go to work," replied Mr. Ash, who never answered a question involving difference of opinion between his friends. "Come, Collins, 'Thirty Acres' to finish 'fore sundown, an' theer's full work 'pon it yet! An' you, Tommy Bates; you fall to sharpenin' the knives for the cutter, this minute!"

He rose, walked with spreading feet and bent back across the road, then dipped down into a great field on the other side. There lay a machine-mower at the edge of the shorn hay, to the nakedness of which still rippled a russet ocean of standing grass. Colourless light passed in great waves over it; the lavender of knautias, together with too-frequent gold of yellow rattle, flashed in it; and the great expanse, viewed remotely, glowed with dull fire of seeding sorrels. Above, danced butterflies; within, the grasshoppers maintained a ceaseless stridulation; and soon the silvery knives were again purring at the cool heart of the undergreen, while ripe grassheads, flowers, sweet clovers, tottered and fell together in shining lines, where Churdles Ash, most just embodiment of Father Time, pursued his way, perched aloft behind two old horses. At each corner the jarring ceased a moment, and the old man's thin voice addressed his steeds; then an angle was turned, and he tinkled on again under the dancing heat. Elsewhere Tommy Bates prepared another knife, and sharpened its shark-like teeth with a file; Pinsent brought up a load of hay from a further field; Cramphorn ascended one rick, and took the harvest from the forks; while Sally and Collins turned the drying grasses at hand, and pursued the business of tossing them with dexterity begotten from long practice. Mr. Libby crept about in the near neighbourhood of the girl, but conscious that Jonah, from the high vantage of the rick, kept sharp eyes upon her, adventured no horseplay, and merely complimented her under his breath upon her splendid arms.

Meanwhile, Christopher Yeoland had seen Honor to her home and so departed.

Bear Down lay in the centre of hay lands immediately beneath the Moor. Above it stretched the heather-clad undulations of Scor Hill, and beneath subtended forest-hidden slopes. The farm itself was approached through a little avenue of sycamores, whose foliage, though it fell and turned to sere, black-spotted death sadly early in most autumns, yet made dimpled play of cool shadow through summer days on the great whitewashed barn beneath it. Then, through a grass-grown yard and the foundations of vanished buildings, one reached a duck-pond set in rhododendrons, and a little garden. The house itself was a patchwork of several generations, and its main fabric stood in shape of a carpenter's mitre, whose inner faces fronted east and south. Each portion had its proper entrance, and that pertaining to the frontage which faced dawn was of the seventeenth century. Here a spacious granite doorway stood, on one side of whose portal there appeared the initials "J.E.", set in a shield and standing for one John Endicott, who had raised this stout pile in the past; while on the other, a date, 1655, indicated the year of its erection. The fabric that looked southwards was of a later period, yet each matched with the other well enough, and time, with the eternal mists of the Moor for his brush, already began to paint modern stone and slate into tune with the harmonious warmth of the more ancient wing. Behind the farmhouse were huddled a dairy, outbuildings, and various erections, that made fair medley of rusty red tile, warm brown wood-stack, and silver thatch. A little lawn rolled away from the granite walls of the farm front, and the parterres, spread snugly in the angle of the building, were set with rough quartz and gay under old-world flowers. Here throve in many-coloured, many-scented joy martagon lilies—pale, purple, and lemon—dark monkshoods, sweet-williams, sweet-sultans, lavender, great purple poppies, snapdragons, pansies, stocks, and flaming marigolds. Along the streamlet, coaxed hither from Scor Hill to feed the farm, grew ferns and willow-herbs, wild geraniums of varied sorts, wood strawberries, orpine, and other country folks. The garden was a happy hunting-ground for little red calves, who wandered bleating about it in the mists of early morning; and for poultry, who laid their eggs in thickets of flowers, scratched up dust-baths in the beds, and hatched out many a clutch of chicks or ducklings under sheltered corners. Against the weathered forehead of its seventeenth-century wing Endicott's displayed an ancient cherry tree that annually shook forth umbels of snowy blossom about the casements, and, later, jewelled these granite walls or decorated the venerable inscription on the lintel with ruby-red fruit seen twinkling through green leaves. Elsewhere ivy and honeysuckle and everlasting pea climbed on a wooden trellis, and in one sheltered nook stood a syringa and a great japonica, whose scarlet brightened the cloud-coloured days of early springtime, whose pomaceous harvest adorned the spot in autumn.

Within doors the farm was fashioned on a generous plan, and contained large, low-ceiled rooms approached through one another by a method most disorderly and ancient. Once, in the heyday of Endicott prosperity, these chambers had been much occupied; now, as became practical farmers, the men—generation by generation—had gradually drifted from the luxuries of many dwelling-rooms. Their wives and daughters indeed struggled against this defection, but masculine obstinacy won its way, until the huge and pleasant kitchen began to be recognised as the house-place also, while other apartments became associated with Sunday, or with such ceremonious events as deaths and marriages might represent.

Almost to the farm walls each year there rippled some hundreds of acres of grass, for no other form of agriculture served the turn so well at that high altitude. Roots and corn they grew, but only to the extent of their own requirements. Of stock Bear Down boasted much too little; hay was the staple commodity, and at this busy season Honor watched the heavens with a farmer's eye, and personally inspected the undergrass, its density and texture, in every field.

A late, cold spring had thrown back the principal harvest somewhat during the year in question; yet it promised well notwithstanding. Mr. Cramphorn alone declared himself disappointed; but seldom had a crop been known to satisfy him, and his sustained discontent throughout the procession of the seasons counted for nothing.

Honor, despite education and reasonable gift of common sense, never wholly pleased her parents. Her father largely lacked humour in his outlook, and he had passed doubly sad: in the knowledge that the name of Endicott must vanish from Bear Down upon the marriage or decease of his daughter, and in the dark fear that one so fond of laughter would never make a farmer. Indeed, his dying hope had been that the weight of supreme control might steady the girl to gravity.

Now, Christopher gone, Honor entered her house, and proceeded into the kitchen. A little separate parlour she had, but particular reasons led to the spending of much time in the larger apartment. Nor was this an ordinary kitchen. You are to imagine, rather, a spacious, lofty, and comfortable dwelling-room; a place snug against the bitter draughts which often bulged up the carpets and screamed in the windows throughout the farm; a chamber warm in winter, in summer cool. Peat fires glowed upon its cavernous and open hearth, and, like Vesta's sacred brands, they never wholly died by night or day. Above the fireplace a granite mantel-shelf supported shining metal-ware—brass candlesticks and tin receptacles polished to splendour; a pair of old stirrups were nailed against the wall, with a rack of guns—mostly antique muzzle-loaders; while elsewhere, suspended in a pattern, there hung a dozen pair of sheep-shears. Oak beams supported the roof, and from them depended hams in canvas bags. At one corner, flanked by two bright warming-pans, stood a lofty clock with a green dial-plate and ornate case of venerable date; and about its feet there ranged cream-pans at this moment, the crust of whose contents matched the apricot tone of kitchen walls and made splendid contrast with the blue-stone floor where sunlight brightened it. The outer doorstone had yielded to innumerable steel-shod boots; it was worn clean through at the centre, and a square of granite had been inserted upon the softer stone. Beside the fire stood a brown leathern screen, and beneath the window, where light, falling through the leaves of many geraniums, was cooled to a pale green, there stretched a settle.

The kitchen was full of sound. A wire-haired fox-terrier pup worried a bit of rabbit-skin under the table, and growled and tumbled and gurgled to his heart's content; crickets, in dark caves and crannies behind the hearth, maintained a cheerful chorus; and from behind the screen came tapping of wooden needles, where sat an old man knitting yarn.

"Honor at last," he said, as he heard her feet.

"Yes, uncle Mark; and late I'm afraid."

"I didn't wait for you. The dinner is on the table. What has kept you?"

"Christo has been asking me to marry him again."

"But that's an everyday amusement of his, so I've heard you say."

"Uncle, I'm going to."

The needles stopped for one brief moment; then they tapped on again.

"Well, well! Almost a pity you didn't wait a little longer."

"I know what's in your head—Myles Stapledon."

"He was. I confess to it."

"If only you could see his photograph, dearest. Oh so cold, hard, inscrutable!"

"I remember him as a boy—self-contained and old-fashioned I grant you. But sober-minded youths often take life too seriously at the start. There's a sort of men—the best sort—who grow younger as they grow older. Mrs. Loveys told me that the picture he sent you makes a handsome chap of Myles."

"Handsome—yes, very—like something carved out of stone."

The blind man was silent for a moment; then he said—

"This shows the folly of building castles in the air for other folks to live in. Anyway you must make him welcome during his visit, Honor, for there are many reasons why you should. The farm and the mill, once his father's, down Tavistock way, have passed out of his hands now. He is free; he has capital; he wants an investment. At least you'll treat him as a kinsman; while as to the possibilities about Bear Down, Myles will very quickly find those out for himself if he's a practical man, as I guess."

"You don't congratulate me on Christo," she said petulantly.

"I hardly seem able to take it seriously yet."

Honor turned away with impatience. Her uncle's attitude to the engagement was almost her own, allowing for difference of standpoint; and the discovery first made her uncomfortable, then angry. But she was too proud to discuss the matter or reveal her discomposure.

CHAPTER III.
A WISE MAN AND A WISE WOMAN

Mr. Scobell, the Vicar of Little Silver, often said, concerning Mark Endicott, that he was as much the spiritual father of the hamlet as its parson. Herein he stated no more than the truth, for the blind man stood as a sort of perpetual palliative of human trouble at Bear Down; in his obscure, night-foundered passage through the world, he had soothed much sorrow and brought comfort to not a few sad, primitive hearts in the bosoms of man and maid. He was seventy years old and knew trouble himself; for, born to the glory of light, he had been blind since the age of thirty, about which period the accident of a bursting gun destroyed his right eye. The other, by sympathetic action, soon became darkened also; and Mark Endicott endured the full storm-centre of such a loss, in that he was a man of the fields, who had depended for his life's joy on rapid movement under the sky; on sporting; on the companionship of horse and dog and those, like himself, whose lives were knit up in country pursuits. He had dwelt at Bear Down before the catastrophe, with his elder brother, Honor Endicott's father; and, after the affliction, Mark still remained at the farm. He was a bachelor, possessed small means sufficient for his needs, and, when the world was changed for him, cast anchor for life in the scene of his early activities. Before eclipse the man had been of a jovial, genial sort, wholly occupied with the business of his simple pleasures, quite content to remain poor; since loss of sight he had fallen in upon himself and developed mentally to an extent not to have been predicted from survey of his sunlit youth. Forty years of darkness indeed ripened Mark Endicott into an original thinker, a man whose estimate of life's treasures and solutions of its problems were broad-based, tolerant, and just. If stoical, his philosophy was yet marked by that latter reverence for humanity and patience with its manifold frailties that wove courses of golden light into the decaying fabric of the porch, and wakened a dying splendour in those solemn and austere galleries ere the sun set upon their grey ruins for ever. Epictetus and Antonine were names unknown to him, yet by his own blind road he had groped to some of their lucid outlook, to that forbearance, fearless courage, contempt of trifles and ruthless self-estimate an emperor learned from a slave and practised from the lofty standpoint of his throne. Mark Endicott appraised his own conduct in a spirit that had been morbid exhibited by any other than a blind man; yet in him this merciless introspection was proper and wholesome. The death of his sight was the birth of his mind, or at least the first step towards his intellectual education. Seeing, the man had probably gone down to his grave unconsidered and with his existence scarcely justified; but blind, he had accomplished a career of usefulness, had carved for himself an enduring monument in the hearts of rustic men and women. He was generally serious, though not particularly grave, and he could tolerate laughter in others though he had little mind to it himself. His niece represented his highest interest and possessed all his love. Her happiness was his own, and amongst his regrets not the least centred in the knowledge that he understood her so little. Mark's own active participation in affairs extended not far beyond speech. He sat behind his leathern screen, busied his hands with knitting great woollen comforters for the fishermen of Brixham, and held a sort of modest open court. Often, during the long hours when he was quite alone, he broke the monotony of silence by talking to himself or repeating passages, both sacred and secular, from works that gave him satisfaction. Such were his reflections that listeners never heard any ill of themselves, though it was whispered that more than one eavesdropper had overheard Mr. Endicott speak to the point. His quick ear sometimes revealed to him the presence of an individual; and, on such occasions, the blind man either uttered a truth for that particular listener's private guidance, or published an opinion, using him as the intelligencer. It is to be noted also that Mark Endicott oftentimes slipped into the vernacular when talking with the country people—a circumstance that set them at ease and enabled him to impart much homely force to his utterances. Finally of him it may be said that in person he was tall and broad, that he had big features, grizzled hair, which he wore rather long, and a great grey beard that fell to the last button of his waistcoat. His eyes were not disfigured though obviously without power of sight.

Honor made a hearty meal and then departed to continue preparations for her cousin's visit. In two days' time he was arriving from Tavistock, to spend a period of uncertain duration at Bear Down. The bright afternoon waned; the shadows lengthened; then there came a knock at the outer door of the kitchen and Henry Collins entered. He had long been seeking for an opportunity to speak in private with Mr. Endicott; and now his face brightened from its usual vacuity to find that Mark was alone.

"Could I have half a word, maister, the place bein' empty?"

"You're Collins, the new man, are you not?"

"Ess, sir; Henery Collins at your sarvice; an' hearin' tell you'm ready to give your ripe judgment wheer 'tis axed an' doan't grudge wisdom more'n a cloud grudges rain, I made so bold—ess, I made that bold like as to—as to——"

"What is it? Don't waste breath in vain words. If I can give you a bit of advice, it's yours; an' take it or leave it as you mind to."

"I'll take it for sure. 'Tis this then: I be a man o' big bones an' big appetite, an' do handle my share o' vittles braavely; but I do allus get that cruel hot when I eat—to every pore as you might say—which swelterin' be a curse to me—an' a painful sight for a female, 'specially if theer's like to be anything 'twixt you an' she in the way of keepin' comp'ny. An' if theer ban't no offence, I'd ax 'e what I should take for't."

Mr. Endicott smiled.

"Take less, my son; an' don't swallow every mouthful as if the devil was arter you. Eat your meat an' sup your drink slow."

"Ban't a calamity as caan't be cured, you reckon?"

"Nothing at all but greediness. Watch how your betters take their food an' see how the women eat. 'Tis only gluttony in you. Remember you're a man, not a pig; then 'twill come right."

Mr. Collins was greatly gratified.

"I'm sure I thank 'e wi' all my heart, maister; for 'twould be a sorry thing if such a ill-convenience should come between me an' a bowerly maid like Sally Cramphorn, the out-door girl."

"So it would then," assented the elder kindly; "but no need—no need at all."

Collins repeated his sense of obligation and withdrew; while elsewhere that identical young woman who now began to distract the lethargic solidity of his inner life was herself seeking advice upon a deep matter touching heart's desire. Soon after five o'clock Sally escaped from the supervision of her jealous parent, and started upon a private and particular errand through leafy lanes that led northerly from the farm and skirted the Moor in that direction. Presently she turned to the left, where a gate marked the boundaries of common land and arrested cattle from straying on to the roads. Here, dipping into a little tunnel of living green, where hazels met over a watercourse, Sally proceeded by a moist and muddy short cut to her goal. It was a cottage that rose all alone at a point where the Moor rippled down to its hinder wall and a wilderness of furze and water-meadow, laced with rivulets and dotted with the feathers of geese, extended in front. A dead fir tree stood on one side of the cot, and the low breast-work of granite and peat that separated a little garden from the waste without was very strangely decked with the vertebræ of a bygone ox. The bones squatted imp-like in a row there—a spectacle of some awe to those who knew the significance of the spot. Upon the door were nailed many horse-shoes, and walls of red earth or cob, painted with whitewash and crowned by venerable and moss-grown thatch, formed the fabric of the cottage.

Upon fine days this mural surface displayed much magic of varied colour; it shone cool in grey dawns, hot at noon, delicate rose and red gold under such brief gleams of sunset light as the Moor's ragged mane permitted to reach it. Stone-crops wove mellow tints into the rotting thatch above, and the moss cushions of dark and shining green were sometimes brushed and subdued by a haze or orange veil thrown over them by the colour of their ripe seed-vessels. In the garden grew many herbs, knowledge of whose potency their owner alone possessed, and at one corner arose the golden spires of great mullein—a flower aforetime called "hag's taper" and associated with witches and their mystic doings. Here the tall plant towered, like a streak of flame, above pale, widespread, woolly leaves; and it was held a sign and token of this wise woman's garden, for when the mullein flowered she had proclaimed that her herbs and simples were most potent. Then would such of her own generation as remained visit ancient Charity Grepe in her stronghold; while to her also came, with shamefaced secrecy, young men and maidens, often under cover of darkness, or in the lonely hour of winter twilights.

"Cherry," as old Charity was most frequently called, had openly been dubbed a witch in times past. She recollected an experience, now near fifty years behind her, when rough hands had forced open her jaws to seek those five black spots observed upon the roof of a right witch's mouth; she knew also that the same diabolic imprint is visible upon the feet of swine, and that it indicated the point where unnumbered demons, upon Christ's command, once entered into Gadara's ill-omened herd. Since then, from a notoriety wholly sinister, she had acquired more seemly renown until, in the year of grace 1870, being at that date some five or six years older than the century, Mother Grepe enjoyed mingled reputation. Some held her a white witch, others still declared that she was a black one. Be that as it may, the old woman created a measure of interest in the most sceptical, and, like the rest of her vanishing class, stood as a storehouse of unwritten lumber and oral tradition handed on through generations, from mother to daughter, from father to son. The possessor and remembrancer of strange formularies and exorcisms, she would repeat the same upon proper occasion, but only after a solemn assurance from those who heard her that they would not commit her incantations to any sort of writing. In her judgment all virtue instantly departed from the written word.

At this season of her late autumn, the gammer was entering upon frosty times, for, under pressure of church and school, the world began to view her accomplishments with indifference. Yet the uncultured so far bowed to custom and a lustre handed down through half a century as to credit Cherry with some vague measure of vaguer power. Little Silver called her the "wise woman," and granted her all due credit for skill in those frank arts that pretend to no superhuman attribute. It is certain that she was familiar with the officinal herbs of the field. She could charm the secrets and soothing essences from coriander and anise and dill—with other of the umbel-bearing wild folk, whose bodies are often poison, whose seeds are little caskets holding carminative and anodyne. Of local plants she grew in her garden those most desirable, and there flourished peppermint, mother-o'-thyme, marjoram, and numerous other aromatic weeds. With these materials the old woman made shift to live, and exacted trifling sums from the mothers of Little Silver by preparing cordials for sick children; from the small farmers and credulous owners of live stock, by furnishing boluses for beasts.

Sally Cramphorn, however, had come on other business and about a widely different sort of potion. She was among those who respected Cherry's darker accomplishments, and her father himself—a man not prone to praise his fellow-creatures—openly confessed to firm belief in Mother Grepe's unusual powers.

The old woman was in her garden when Sally arrived. It had needed sharp scrutiny to observe much promise of wisdom about her. She was brown, wrinkled and shrivelled, yet exhibited abundant vitality and spoke in a voice that seemed musical because one expected the reverse. Her eyes alone challenged a second glance. They were black, and flashed in the twilight. Dame Grepe's visitor, a stranger to shyness, soon explained the nature of the thing desired. With blushes, but complete self-possession in all other respects, she spoke.

"'Tis 'bout the matter of a husband, Cherry; an' you'm so wise, I lay you knaw it wi'out my tellin' you."

"Ess—you be wife-auld in body; but what about the thinking part of 'e, Sally Cramphorn? Anyway I wonder you dare let your mind go gadding arter a male, seeing what fashion o' man your faither is."

Sally pouted.

"That's the very reason for it I reckon. What gal can be happy in a home like mine?"

"A man quick to think evil—your faither—a vain man—a man as scowls at shadows an' sees gunpowder treason hid behind every hedge—poor fule!"

"So he do then; an' ban't very nice for a grawed woman like me. If I lifts my eye to a chap's face, he thinks I be gwaine to run away from un; an' there ban't a man in Little Silver, from Squire Yeoland to the cowboy at the farm, as he've got a tender word for."

"I knaw, I knaw. Come in the house."

Sally followed the old woman into her cottage, and spoke as she did so.

"It's hard come to think on it, 'cause I'm no more against a husband than any other gal. 'Tis awnly that they'm feared of the sound 'pon theer tongues as gals won't awn up honest they'd sooner have husbands than not. Look at missis—she'll find herself a happy wife bimebye if squire do count for anything."

"Be they much together?"

"Ess fay—allus!"

The old woman shook her head.

"A nature, hers, born to trouble as the sparks fly upwards. Fine metal, but easy to crack by fire. She comed to me wance—years agone—comed half in jest, half in earnest; an' I tawld her strange things to her fortune tu—things as'll mean gert changes an' more sorrow than joy when all's acted an' done. Full, fair share of gude an' bad—evil an' balm—an' her very well content to creep under the green grass an' rest her head 'pon the airth come fulness of time."

"Lor, mother! You do make me all awver creepy-crawly to hear tell such dreadful things," declared Miss Cramphorn.

"No need for you to fear. You'm coarser clay, Sally, an' won't get no thinner for love of a man. An' why should 'e? Pray for a fixed mind; an' doan't, when the man comes beggin', begin weighing the blemishes of un or doubtin' your awn heart."

"Never, I won't—and my heart's fixed; an' I be so much in love as a gal can be an' hide it, Cherry."

"I knaw, I knaw. 'Tis Greg Libby you wants," answered the sibyl, who had observed certain hay-makers some hours earlier in the day.

"Ess, I do then, though you'm the awnly living sawl as knaws it."

"Doan't he knaw it?"

"Not a blink of it. He'm a wonnerful, dandified man since he come from Lunnon."

"Be he gwaine to do any more work?"

"Not so long as his clothes bide flam-new, I reckon. Ban't no call for un to. An' I love un very much, an' do truly think he loves me, Cherry. An', in such things, a little comin'-on spirit in the man's like to save the maid much heart-burnin'; an' I minded how you helped she as was Thirza Foster, in the matter of Michael Maybridge, her husband now. 'Tis pity Gregory should bide dumb along of his backward disposition."

"A love drink you're arter! Who believes in all that now?"

"I mind how you made Maybridge speak, whether or no, an' I'll give 'e half-a-crown for same thing what you gived Thirza."

It was growing dusk. Gammer Grepe preserved silence a moment, then rose and lighted a candle.

"Half-a-crown! An' I've had gawld for less than that! Yet times change, an' them as believed believe no more. It all lies theer. If you believe, the thing have power; if not, 'tis vain to use it."

"I do b'lieve like gospel, I assure 'e. Who wouldn't arter Thirza?"

"Then give me your money an' do what I bid."

She took the silver, spat upon it, raised her hand, and pointed out of the window.

"Do 'e see thicky plant in the garden theer, wi' flowers, like to tired eyes, starin' out of the dimpsy light? 'Tis a herb o' power. You'll find un grawin' wild on rubbish heaps an' waste places."

She pointed where a clump of wild chamomile rose with daisy-like blossoms pallid in the twilight.

"Ess, mother."

Then the wise woman mouthed solemn directions, which Sally listened to as solemnly.

"Pick you that—twenty-five stalks—at the new moon. Then pluck off the flowers an' cast 'em in the river; but the stalks take home-along an' boil 'em in three parts of half a pint o' spring watter. Fling stalks away but keep the gude boiled out of 'em, an' add to it a drop more watter caught up in your thimble from a place wheer forget-me-not do graw. Then put the whole in a li'l bottle, an' say Lard's Prayer avver it thrice; and, come fust ripe chance, give it to the man to drink mixed in tea or cider, but not beer nor other liquor."

With the ease of an artist Cherry improvised this twaddle on the spot, and the girl, all ears and eyes, expressed great thankfulness for such a potent charm, bid the gammer farewell, and hastened away.

CHAPTER IV.
THE KISS

Some days later Christopher Yeoland was returning from the village of Throwley to Little Silver, by a road that winds along the flank of the Moor. He carried a basket in which reposed a young collie pup. Himself he wanted no such thing, but the little beast came of notable stock, possessed a special value, and seemed worthy of Honor. Among those delights represented by his engagement was the facility it afforded for giving of presents. He had already sketched on paper the designs of many engagement rings. A circle of gold with diamonds and emeralds in it was his vague intention; while his visions of how he should come at such a jewel were still more doubtful. This man possessed great power in the direction of dreams, in projecting the shadows of pleasant things and winning happiness from these conceits despite their improbability. Love of beauty was a characteristic in him, but otherwise he could not be described as sensual. Beauty he adored; yet delight of the eye appeared to suffice him. His attitude towards the opposite sex is illustrated by an event now to be described.

The day was done and the hour of rest had come upon the workers. Labouring folk moved through the long July twilight upon their own concerns, as private pleasure or business led them; and now, under the huge shadow of the Moor, there unfolded a little drama, slight enough, yet reflecting sensibly upon the future concerns of those who played in the scene. Christopher Yeoland, his mind quite full of Honor, overtook Sally Cramphorn in the valley, and being upon friendly terms with all the countryside, marched awhile beside her. He allowed no social differences at any time to obtain between him and a pretty face. Sally was good to see, and as for Yeoland, of late days, chiefly by reason of an exceeding honour that the mistress of Bear Down had done him, he felt pliable, even reverential before all things feminine, for her dear sake. He was not of that sort who find all other women sink into shadows after the unutterable One has joined her fate with his for evermore; but, contrariwise, the possession of Honor heightened his interest in her sex. He might have been likened to a bee, that indeed loved clover before all else, yet did not disdain a foxglove or purple lupin upon occasion. So he walked beside Sally and contemplated her proportions with pleasure, watched her throat work and the rosy light leap to her cheek as he praised her.

In Sally's heart was a wish that Greg Libby might see her with such a courtier; but unfortunately a very different person did so. Mr. Cramphorn, with an ancient muzzle-loading gun at full-cock and a fox-terrier under the furzes ahead of him, was engaged in stalking rabbits a few hundred yards distant. His keen eye, now turning suddenly, rested upon his daughter. He recognised her by her walk and carriage; but her companion, in that he bore a basket, deceived Mr. Cramphorn. Full of suspicion and growling dire threats in his throat, Jonah forgot the rabbits for this nobler game. He began stalking the man and woman, skulked along behind the hazels at the common edge, and presently, after feats of great and unnecessary agility, found himself snugly hidden in a lofty hedge immediately beneath which his daughter and her escort must presently pass.

Meanwhile, she strolled along and soon recovered her self-possession, for Yeoland was in no sense awe-inspiring. The young woman had now come from securing a priceless thimbleful of water that bathed the roots of forget-me-nots. She carried this magic liquid concealed in a little phial; the rest of the ingredients were hidden at home; and she hoped that night to brew the philtre destined for Mr. Libby.

"Sally," said Christopher, "I'll tell you a great piece of news. No, I won't; you must guess it."

She looked up at him with a knowing smile on her red mouth.

"You'm gwaine to marry missis, sir—be that it?"

"You gimlet of a girl! But, no, you never guessed—I'm positive you didn't. Somebody told you; Miss Endicott herself, perhaps."

"None told me. I guessed it."

"How jolly of you! I like you for guessing, Sally. It was a compliment to us."

"I doan't knaw what you mean by that, sir."

"No matter. You will some day, and feel extremely flattered if people congratulate you before you've told them. If you simply adore one girl, Sally, you love them all!"

"Gude Lard! Ban't so along wi' us. If we'm sweet in wan plaace, we'm shy in t'others."

"Only one man in the world for you, then?"

"Ess—awnly wan."

"He's a lucky chap. Mind that I know all about it in good time, Sally. You shall have a fine wedding present, I promise you—whatever you like, in fact."

"Things ban't come to that yet; though thank you kindly, sir, I'm sure."

"Well, they will."

"He haven't axed ezacally yet."

"Ass! Fool! Dolt! But perhaps he's in mortal fear of you—frightened to speak and not able to trust his pen. You're too good for him, Sally, and he knows it."

"I be his awn order in life, for that matter."

"I see, I see; it's this hidden flame burning in you that made you so quick to find out our secret. I love you for it! I love every pretty face in Devonshire, because my lady is pretty; and every young woman on Dartmoor, because my lady is young. Can you understand that?"

"No, I caan't," confessed Sally. "'Tis fulishness."

"Not at all. At this moment I could positively hug you—not disrespectfully, you know, but just out of love—for Miss Endicott."

"It do make a man dangerous seemin'ly—this gert love of a lady."

"Not at all. Far from it. It draws his claws. He goes in chains. Did anybody ever dare to hug you, Sally?"

"No fay! Should like to have seed 'em!"

"You wouldn't have minded one though?"

"Caan't say, as he never offered to."

"D'you mean he's never even kissed you, Sally?"

"Wance he axed if he might."

"'Axed'! And of course you said 'No' like any other girl would?"

"Ess, I did."

"Fancy asking!"

"What should he have done then?"

It was a dangerous inquiry on Miss Cramphorn's part, and it is within the bounds of possibility that she knew it. Had she been aware that her sole parent was glaring, like an angry monkey, from a point in the hedge within six yards of her, Sally had scarcely put that disingenuous problem. The answer came instantly. Honor's pup fell headlong into the road and greeted its descent with a yell; like lightning a pair of tweed-clad arms were round Sally, and a rough, amber-coloured moustache against her lips.

"Sir—give awver! How dare 'e! What be doin' of? You'm squeezin' me—oh——!"

There was a crash in the hedge, the bark of a dog and the oath of a man. Then Christopher felt himself suddenly seized by the collar and dragged backwards. He turned red as the sunset, swore in his turn, then realised that no less a personage than Jonah Cramphorn had been witness to his folly. Trembling with rage, Bear Down's head man accosted the squire of Little Silver.

"You! You to call yourself a gen'leman! Out 'pon 'e—to rape a gal under her faither's awn eyes! By God, 'tis time your wicked thread was cut an' Yeolands did cease out of the land! Small wonder they'm come down to——"

"Shut your mouth, you fool!" retorted Christopher savagely. "How dare you lay a finger upon me? I'll have you up for breaking other people's hedges, and, what's more, I've a mind to give you a damned good hiding myself."

"You tell like that, you hookem-snivey young blackguard! I'd crack your blasted bones like a bad egg—an' gude riddance tu! Ban't she my awn darter, an' wasn't you carneying an' cuddlin' of her in broad day? 'Struth! I could spit blood to think such things can happen! An' me to be threatened by you! You'll hide me—eh? Thank your stars I didn't shoot 'e. An' if I'd slayed the pair of 'e 'twouldn't have been no gert loss to clean-livin' folks!"

"I'm ashamed of you, Cramphorn—reading evil into everything that happens," said Yeoland calmly.

"God stiffen it! Hear him! Hear him! Preachin' my duty to me. You lewd, stalled ox, for two pins——"

"Put that gun down or I'll break it over your head!" answered Christopher; but the other, now a mere maniac, shaking and dancing with passion, refused. Whereupon Yeoland rushed at him, twisted the gun out of his hands, and threw it upon the ground. The next moment Jonah had hit his enemy in the face with a big fist; Christopher struck back, Sally screamed, and Cramphorn spit blood in earnest. Then they closed, and Jonah's dog, grasping the fact that his master was in difficulties, and needed assistance, very properly fastened on one of Yeoland's leathern leggings and hung there, as both men tumbled into the road.

The girl wrung her hands, lifted her voice and screamed to the only being visible—a man with a cart of peat outlined against the sunset on the heather ridges of the Moor. But he was a mile distant and quite beyond reach of poor Sally's frantic appeal. Then both combatants rose, and

Cramphorn, returning to battle, got knocked off his feet again. At the same moment a man came round the corner of the road, and mended his steps upon hearing a frenzied announcement that two fellow-creatures were killing each other. A moment later he hastened between the combatants, took a hard blow or two from both, swept Christopher aside with no particular difficulty, and saved the elder from further punishment.

Sally wept, thanked God, and went to minister to her parent; while the new-comer, in a passionless voice that contrasted strangely with the rapidity of his actions, accosted Yeoland.

"What is this? Don't you know better than to strike a man old enough to be your father?"

"Mind your own business," gasped Christopher, brushing the dust off himself and examining a wound in his wrist.

"It's anybody's business, surely."

The other did not answer. His passion was rapidly cooling to shame. He scanned the speaker and wished that they might be alone together. The man was tall, very heavily built, one who would naturally move with a long and tardy stride. His recent energy was the result of circumstances and an action most unusual. He still breathed deep upon it.

"I'm sure you'll regret what has happened in a calmer moment, and pardon me for helping you to your senses," he said.

"So he shall regret it, I'll take my dying oath to that," spluttered Mr. Cramphorn. "Idle, lecherous, cold-hearted, hot-blooded beast as he be."

"Get cool," said the stranger, "and don't use foul language. There are remedies for most evils. If he's wronged you, you can have the law of him. Put some cold water on his head."

Sally, to whom the last remark was addressed, dipped her apron in the brook by the wayside, but Mr. Cramphorn waved her off.

"Get out o' my sight, you easy minx! To think that any cheel o' mine would let strange men put theer arms around her in broad day!"

"I'm entirely to blame—my fault altogether—not hers," said Christopher. "I felt in a cuddling mood," he added frankly. "I wouldn't have hurt a hair of her head, and she knows it. Why should it be worse to kiss a pretty girl than to smell a pretty flower? Tell me that."

"Theer's devil's talk for 'e!" gurgled Jonah.

"You miserable old ass—but I'm sorry—heartily sorry. Forgive me, and go to Doctor Clack and get a soothing something. And if I've hurt your gun I'll buy you a new one."

"Likely as I'd have any dealin's wi' a son of Belial Beelzebub same as you be! I'll put the law to work against 'e, that's what I'll do; an' us'll see if a woman be at the mercy of every gen'leman, so-called, as loafs 'pon the land because he'm tu idle to work!"

"That'll do. Now go off about your business, Cramphorn, and let us have no more nonsense. We ought both to be ashamed of ourselves, and I'm sure I am. As a Christian man, you must forgive me; I'm sure, as a Christian girl, Sally will."

"Leave her alone, will 'e! I won't have her name on your tongue. Us'll see if folks can break the laws; us'll see——"

He strode off, pulling his daughter by the hand, and entirely forgetting his gun beside the way; but after the irate father had departed, Yeoland recovered his weapon and found it unhurt. He then picked up Honor's pup, and overtook the stranger who was proceeding in the direction of Little Silver.

"How came you to get that man into such a white heat?" the latter asked him.

"Well, I kissed his daughter; and he was behind the hedge at the critical point and saw me."

"Ah!"

"I'm a chap who wouldn't hurt a fly, you know. But I'm particularly happy about some private affairs just at present, and—well, my lightness of heart took that turn."

The other did not smile, but looked at Christopher curiously.

"You said a strange thing just now," he remarked, in a deep voice, with slow, dragging accents. "You declared that to kiss a girl was no worse than to smell a flower. That seemed a new idea to me."

Yeoland opined that it might well be so. This was no woman's man.

"I believe it's true, all the same," he answered.

"Isn't there a lack of respect to women in the idea?"

The speaker stood over Christopher by two inches. His face had a cold comeliness. His features were large, regular, and finely modelled; his complexion was dark; his eyes were grey; he wore a moustache but no other hair upon his face. A great solidity, slowness, and phlegm marked his movements and utterances, and his handsome countenance was something of a mask, not from practised simulation or deliberate drilling of feature, but by the accident of flesh. A high forehead neither declared nor denied intellect by its shape; the man in fact showed but little of himself externally. One might, however, have predicted a strenuous temperament and suspected probable lack of humour from a peculiar sort of gravity of face. His eyes were evidently of exceptional keenness; his speech was marked by an uncertainty in choice of words that denoted he was habitually taciturn; his manner suggested one who kept much of his own company and lived a lonely life—either from necessity or choice.

CHAPTER V.
PAGAN ALTARS

The men proceeded together, and Christopher's companion made himself known by a chance question. He inquired the way to Bear Down, whereupon Yeoland, aware that a kinsman of the Endicotts was expected, guessed that this must be he.

"You're Myles Stapledon then?"

"I am. I walked from Okehampton to get a glimpse of the Moor. Came by way of the Belstones and Cosdon—a glorious scene—more spacious in some respects than my native wilds down West."

"You like scenery? Then you'll be joyful here. If Honor had known you were walking, I'll dare swear she would have tramped out to meet you; still, thank the Lord she didn't."

"You know her well to speak of her by her Christian name," said Stapledon slowly.

Christopher was but two years younger than his companion, but one had guessed that a decade separated them.

"Know her! Know Honor! I should rather think I did know her. She's my sun and moon and stars. I suppose she hoped to tell you the great news herself, and now I've babbled it. Engaged—she and I—and I'm the happiest man in all the South of England."

"I congratulate you. My cousin promised to be a pretty woman—just a dinky maid in short frocks when last I saw her. And your name——?"

"My name is Yeoland."

"The Squire of Godleigh, of course?"

"That proud personage; and there lies Endicott's—under the wind-blown sycamores where the whitewash peeps out. Your luggage is there before you, no doubt. This is my way: to the left. You go to the right, pass that farm there on your left, follow the road and so, after about five minutes, find yourself in the presence of the Queen of the Moor. Good-bye. We shall meet again."

"Good-bye, and thank you."

Stapledon moved onwards; then he heard a man running and Christopher overtook him.

"One moment. I thought I'd ask you not to mention that scrimmage on the hillside. Honor would quite understand my performance, but she'd be pained to think I had struck or been struck by that lout, and perhaps—well. She'll hear of it, for Cramphorn and his daughter are Bear Down people, but——"

"Not from me, rest assured."

"A thousand thanks. You might mention that you met me returning from Throwley and that the pup is a gem. I'll bring it along some time or other to-morrow."

Again they separated, and such is the character often-times exhibited in a man's method of walking, that appreciation of each had been possible from study of his gait. Stapledon appeared to move slowly, but his stride was tremendous and in reality he walked at four miles an hour; the other, albeit his step looked brisk, never maintained any regularity in it. He stopped to pat a bruised knee, wandered from one side of the road to the other, and presently climbed the hedge to get a sight of Bear Down, with hope that Honor might be seen in her garden.

But at that moment the mistress of Endicott's was welcoming her cousin. They greeted one another heartily and spoke awhile together. Then, when Myles had ascended to the room prepared for him, Mr. Endicott listened to his niece's description of the new arrival.

"Better far than his photograph," she said. "More expression, but too big. He's a tremendous man; yet very kind, I should think, and not proud. Almost humble and most austere in dress. No rings or scarf pin—just grey everything. He looks older than I thought, and his voice is so curiously deep that it makes little things in the room rattle. We were in the parlour for two minutes, and every time he spoke he vibrated one particular bass note of the piano until I grew quite nervous. He has very kind eyes—slate-coloured. I should say he was extremely easy to please."

"A fine open-air voice, certainly, and a good grip to his hand," said the blind man.

"Yet no tact, I fear," criticised Honor. "Fancy beginning about poor old Bear Down wanting attention, and hoping that he might put some money into it before he had been in the house five minutes!"

"Nervousness. Perhaps you surprised him."

But, later in the day, Myles endeavoured to repair a clumsiness he had been conscious of at the time, and, after collecting his thoughts—honestly somewhat unsettled by the sight of Honor, who had leapt from lanky girl to beautiful woman since last he saw her—his first words were a hearty congratulation upon the engagement.

"Endicott's stock is very nearly as old, but there's a social difference," he said bluntly. "'Tis a very good match for you, I hope. You'll live at Godleigh, of course?"

"It's all a long, long way off, cousin; and I'm sure I cannot guess how you come to know anything at all about it," said Honor.

Then the traveller told her, beginning his narrative at the point where he had asked Christopher the road to Bear Down. He concluded with a friendly word.

"Handsome he is, for certain, with the wind and the sun on his cheek; and a man of his own ideas, I judge; an original man. I wish you joy, Honor, if I may call you Honor."

"What nonsense! Of course. And I'm glad you like my Christo, because then you'll like me too, I hope. We have very much in common really. We see things alike, live alike, laugh alike. He has a wonderful sense of humour; it teaches him to look at the world from the outside."

"A mighty unwholesome, unnatural attitude for any man," said Mark Endicott.

"Yet hardly from the outside either, if he's so human as to want a wife?" asked Honor's cousin.

"He wants a wife," she answered calmly, "to take the seat next him at the theatre, to walk beside him through the picture-gallery, to compare notes with, to laugh with at the fun of the fair, as he calls it."

Mr. Endicott's needles tapped impatiently.

"Vain talk, vain talk," he said.

"It may be vain, uncle, but it's none the less true," she answered. "If I do not know Christopher, who does? The companionship of a congenial spirit is the idea in his mind—perhaps in mine too. He's a laughing philosopher, and so platonic, so abstracted, that if he had found a man friend, instead of a woman, he would have been just as content to swear eternal friendship and invite the man to sit and watch the great play with him and laugh away their lives together."

"I hope you don't know Mr. Yeoland as well as you imagine, Honor," said Mark Endicott.

"You misjudge him really, I expect," ventured Myles, his thoughts upon a recent incident. "Think what it would be to one of active and jovial mind to sit and look on at life and take no part."

"'Look on!'" burst out the blind man. "Only God Almighty looks on; and not even He, come to think of it, for He's pulling the strings."

"Not so," said Myles; "not so, Uncle Endicott. He put us on the stage, I grant you; and will take us off again when our part is done. But we're moved from inside, not driven from out. We play our lives ourselves, and the wrong step at the entrance—the faulty speech—the good deed—the bad—they all come from inside—all build up the part. Free-will is the only sort of freedom a created thing with conscious intelligence can have. There's no choice about the theatre or the play; but neither man nor God dictates to me how I enact my character."

Mark Endicott reflected. He was a stout Christian, and, like an old war-horse, he smelt battle in this utterance, and rejoiced. It was left for Honor to fill the silence.

"It's all a puppet-show, say what you will, cousin," she summed up; "and anybody can see the strings that move nine dolls out of ten. A puppet-show, and a few of us pay too little for our seats at it; but most of us pay too much. And you need not argue with me, because I know I'm right, and here is Mrs. Loveys to say that supper's ready."

A week later it was practically determined that Myles should concern himself with Bear Down; but the man still remained as unknown to Honor as in the moment of their first meeting. His money interested her not at all; his character presented a problem which attracted her considerably during those scanty hours she found heart to spend away from her lover. It happened that Christopher having departed on a sudden inspiration to Newton Races, Honor Endicott and her cousin set out together for an excursion of pleasure upon the high Moor.

The day was one in August, and hot sunshine brooded with glowing and misty light on hills and valleys, on rivers and woods, on farm lands and wide-spread shorn grasses, where the last silver-green ribbons of dried hay, stretching forth in parallel and winding waves, like tide-marks upon great sands, awaited the wain. Stapledon walked beside Honor's pony, and together they passed upwards to the heather, beside an old wall whose motley fabric glimmered sun-kissed through a blue shimmer of flowers, and faded into a perspective all silvery with lichens, broken with brown, thirsty mosses, many grasses, and the little pale pagodas of navelwort. Beech trees crowned the granite, and the whisper of their leaves was echoed by a brook that murmured unseen in a hollow upon the other side of the road. Here Dartmoor stretched forth a finger, scattered stone, and sowed bracken and furze, heather and rush and the little flowers that love stream-sides.

The travellers climbed awhile, then Myles stopped at a gate in the old wall and Honor drew up her pony. For a moment there was no sound but the gentle crick-crick-crick from bursting seed-pods of the greater gorse, where they scattered their treasure at the touch of the sun. Then the rider spoke.

"How fond you are of leaning upon gates, Myles!"

He smiled.

"I know I am. I've learned more from looking over gates than from most books. You take Nature by surprise that way and win many a pretty secret from her."

The girl stared as at a revelation. Thus far she had scarcely penetrated under her cousin's exterior. He was very fond of dumb animals and very solicitous for them; but more of him she had not gleaned until the present.

"Do you really care for wild things—birds, beasts, weeds? I never guessed that. How interesting! So does Christo. And he loves the dawn as much as you do."

"We have often met at cock-light. It is a bond we have—the love of the morning hour. But don't you like Nature too?"

"Not madly, I'm afraid. I admire her general effects. But I'm a little frightened of her at heart and I cringe to her in her gracious moods. Christo's always poking about into her affairs and wanting to know the meaning of curious things; but he's much too lazy to learn."

"There's nothing so good as to follow Nature and find out a little about her methods in hedges and ditches, where she'll let you."

"You surprise me. I should have thought men and women were much more interesting than rabbits and wild flowers."

"You cannot get so near to them," he answered; "at least, I cannot. I haven't that touch that opens hearts. I wish I had. People draw the blinds down, I always think, before me. Either so, or I'm more than common dense. Yet everybody has the greater part of himself or herself hidden, I suppose; everybody has one little chamber he wouldn't open to God if he could help it."

"Are you a Christian, Myles? But don't answer if you would rather not."

"Why, it makes a man's heart warm by night or by day to think of the Founder of that faith."

Again Honor was surprised.

"I like to hear you say so," she answered. "D'you know I believe that we think nearly alike—with a difference. Christ is much dearer to me than the great awful God of the Universe. He was so good to women and little children; but the Almighty I can only see in Nature—relentless, unforgiving, always ready to punish a slip, always demon-quick to see a mistake and visit the sins of the fathers on the children. Nature's the stern image of a stern God to me—a thing no more to be blamed than the lightning, but as much to be feared. Christ knew how to forgive and weep for others, how to heal body and soul. The tenderness of Him! And He fought Nature and conquered her; brought life where she had willed death; health where she had sent sickness; stilled her passion on blue Galilee; turned her water into wine."

"You can credit all that?"

"As easily as I can credit a power kinder than Nature, and stronger. Yes, I believe. It is a great comfort to believe; and Christopher does too."

"A beautiful religion," said Myles; "especially for women. They do well to love One who raised them out of the dust and set them up. Besides, there is their general mistiness on the subject of justice. Christianity repels me here, draws me there. It is child's meat, with its sugar-plums and whips for the good and naughty; it is higher than the stars in its humanity."

"You don't believe in hell, of course?"

"No—or in heaven either. That is a lack in me—a sorrowful limitation."

"Yet, if heaven exists, God being just, the man whose life qualifies him for it has got to go there. That's a comforting thought for those who love you, Myles."

The word struck a deep note. He started and looked at her.

"How kind to think of that! How good and generous of you to say it!"

The voice of him sent an emotion through Honor, and, according to her custom when moved beyond common, she fell back upon laughter.

"Why, we're getting quite confidential, you and I! But here's the Moor at last."

They stood upon Scor Hill and surveyed their subsequent way, where it passed on before. Beneath swelled and subtended a mighty valley in the lap of stone-crowned hills—a rare expanse of multitudinous browns. Through every tone of auburn and russet, sepia and cinnamon, tan and dark chocolate of the peat cuttings, these colour harmonies spread and undulated in many planes. From the warmth and richness of velvet under sunshine they passed into the chill of far-flung cloud-shadows, that painted the Moor with slowly-moving sobriety and robbed her bosom of its jewels, her streamlets of their silver. Teign wound below, entered the valley far away under little cliffs of yellow gravel, then, by sinuous courses, through a mosaic of dusky peat, ripe rushes, and green banks overlaid with heather, passed where steep medley and tanglement of motionless boulders awakened its volume to a wilder music. Here, above this chaos of huge and moss-grown rocks, scarlet harvests of rowan flung a flame along the gorges; grey granite swam into the grey-green of the sallows; luxuriant concourse of flowers and ferns rippled to the brown lips of the river; and terraces of tumbling water crowned all that unutterable opulence of summer-clad dingle with spouts, with threads, with broad, thundering cataracts of foaming light. Here Iris twinkled in a mist that steamed above the apron of mossy-margined falls; here tree shadows restrained the sunlight, yet suffered chance arrows of pure amber to pierce some tremulous pool.

Each kiss of the Mother wakened long miles of earth into some rare hue, where the Moor colours spread enormous in their breadth, clarity, and volume. They rolled and rippled together; they twined and intertwined and parted again; they limned new harmonies from the union of rush and heath and naked stone; they chimed into fresh combinations of earth and air and sunshine; they won something from the sky outspread above them, and wove the summer blue into their secret fabrics, even as the sea does. Between dispersed tracts of the brake fern and heather, and amid walls of piled stone, that stretched threadlike over the Moor, there lay dark or naked spaces brushed with green—theatres of past spring fires; rough cart roads sprawled to the right and left; sheep tracks and the courses of distant rivulets seamed the hills; while peat ridges streaked the valleys, together with evidences of those vanished generations who streamed for metal upon this spacious spot in the spacious times. Beyond, towards the heart of the Moor, there arose Sittaford's crown; to the west ranged Watern's castles; and northerly an enormous shoulder of Cosdon climbed heaven until the opaline hazes of that noontide hour softened its heroic outlines and something dimmed the mighty shadows cast upon its slopes. Light winds fanned the mane of Honor's pony and brought with them the woolly jangle of a sheep-bell, the bellow of distant kine, the little, long-drawn, lonely tinkle of a golden bird upon a golden furze.

"The Moor," said Honor; and as she spoke a shade lifted off the face of the man beside her, a trouble faded from his eyes.

"Yes, the Moor—the great, candid, undissembling home of sweet air, sweet water, sweet space."

"And death and desolation in winter, and hidden skeletons under the quaking bogs."

"It is an animate God to me notwithstanding."

She shivered slightly and set her pony in motion.

"What a God! Where will it lead you?"

"I cannot tell; yet I trust. Nature is more than the mere art of God, as men have called it. That is why I must live with it, why I cannot mew myself in bricks and mortar. Here's God's best in this sort—the dearest sort I know—the Moor—spread out for me to see and hear and touch and tread all the days of my life. This is more than His expression—it is Him. Nothing can be greater—not high mountains, or eternal snows, or calling oceans. Nothing can be greater to me, because I too am of all this—spun of it, born of it, bred on it, a brother of the granite and the mist and the lonely flower. Do you understand?"

"I understand that this desert is no desert to you, Myles. Yet what a faith! What a certainty!"

"Better than nothing at all."

"Anything is better than that. Our best certainties are only straws thrown to the drowning—if we think as you do."

"Bars of lead rather. They help to sink us the quicker. We know much—but not the truth of anything that matters."

"You will some day, Myles."

"Yes, too late, if your faith and its whips and sugarplums are true, Honor."

"The life of the Moor is so short," she said, suddenly changing the subject. "Now it is just trembling out into the yearly splendour of the ling; then, that done, it will go to sleep again for month upon month—lying dry, sere, dead, save for the mournful singing of rains and winds. The austerity and sternness of it!"

"Tonic to toughen mental fibres."

"I'm not so philosophical. I feel the cold in winter, the heat in summer. Come, let us cross Teign and wind away round Batworthy to Kes Tor. There are alignments and hut circles and ruins of human homes there— granite all, but they spell men and women. I can tolerate them. They cheer me. Only sheep haunt them now—those ruins—but people dwelt there once; Damnonian babies were born there, and wild mothers sang cradle songs and logged little children in wolf-skin cradles and dreamed golden dreams for them."

"Nature was kind to those early folk."

"Kind! Not kinder than I to my cattle."

"They were happier than you and I, nevertheless. Happier, because nearer the other end of her chain. They had less intelligence, less capacity for suffering."

"That's a theory of Christopher's. He often wishes that he had been born thousands of years ago."

"Not since you promised to marry him," said Myles, with unusual quickness of mind.

"Perhaps not; but he's a savage really. He declares that too much work is done in the world—too much cutting and tunnelling and probing and tearing Nature's heart out. He vows that the great Mother must hate man and resent his hideous activity and lament his creation."

"One can imagine such a thing."

"And Christo says there is a deal of nonsense talked about the dignity of work. He got that out of a book, I believe, and took the trouble to remember it because the theory suited his own lazy creed so perfectly."

For once Myles Stapledon laughed.

"I do admire him: a natural man, loving the wine of life. We have more in common than you might think, for all that I'm no sportsman. I respect any man who will rise with the birds for sheer love of a fair dawn."

"Your rule of conduct is so much more strenuous, so much sterner and greyer," she said, "The cold rain and the shriek of east winds in ill-hung doors are nothing to you. They really hurt him."

"Temperament. Yet I think our paths lead the same way."

Honor laughed in her turn.

"If they do," she declared, "there are a great many more turnpike gates on your road than upon Christopher's."

CHAPTER VI.
ANTHEMIS COTULA

As Myles Stapledon proceeded at the stirrup of his cousin their conversation became more trifling, for the girl talked and the man was well content to listen. She entertained him with a humorous commentary on the life of the Moor-edge and the people who went to compose it. She pointed to stately roofs bowered in forests and expatiated on the mushroom folk who dwelt beneath them.

"My Christo is not good enough for these! I'm a mere farmeress, and wouldn't count, though I do trace my ancestors back to Tudor times. Yet you might have supposed a Yeoland could dare to breathe the same air as Brown, Jones, and Robinson. Don't you think so? What are these great men?"

"Successful," he said, not perceiving that she spoke ironically.

"Ah! the god Success!"

"Don't blame them. Money's the only power in the world now. Birth can't give splendid entertainments and pose as patron of the local institutions and be useful generally and scatter gold—if it has no gold to scatter. The old order changes, because those that represent it are mostly bankrupt. But money has always been the first power. Now it has changed hands—that's all the difference. A few generations of idleness and behold! the red blood has got all the money; the blue blood has none."

"Poor blue blood!"

"They are nothing to you—these people. They pay proper suit and service to the god that made them; they know the power of money, the futility of birth. What is the present use of old families if they represent nothing but bygone memories and musty parchments? Rank is a marketable commodity to be bought and sold—a thing as interesting and desirable to many as old china or any other fad of the wealthy. That they can understand, but poor commoners!—why, it isn't business. Don't you see?"

"Christo's ancestors were a power in the land before this sort of people were invented."

"They *were* invented. If you look back far enough, you'll see that plenty of your ancient houses sprang from just this sort of people. Only their way to power and prosperity was more romantic then. Now they merely risk their health and eyesight grubbing for half a lifetime at desks in offices or in a bad climate; then they risked their lives under some Devon Drake or Raleigh upon unknown seas, or the field of battle. Our present methods of fortune-making are just as romantic really, only it will take another age, that looks at this from a bird's-eye point of view, to see it. Every dog has his day, and romance always means yesterday. It is summed up in that. I'll wager the neglect of the wealthy doesn't worry Yeoland."

"No, he laughs."

"They are too sordid to understand a man living his life and content to do so. It isn't business."

Honor laughed.

"No—they have the advantage of him there. Yet I do wish he wasn't so lazy."

But Stapledon felt that he could not speak upon that question, so the subject dropped.

They had now left the Moor and were descending to the valley and the river below. A magpie, like a great black and white butterfly, passed with slow flutter before them; there was a drone and gleam of shining insects in the air; and upon the sunny hedge-banks many oaks dripped with the fat sweetness of the aphides until the steep way beneath was darkened in patches as though by rain.

"D'you hear them?" asked Honor. "The twin Teigns! They meet at the bridge beneath us. They know they are going to meet, and they begin to purr and sing to one another. They will rush into each other's arms in a minute. I love to see them do it."

Forward went her surefooted pony, and Myles, striding now on one side, now upon the other, with his eyes in the rich fabric of the hedges, fell a little way behind. When he caught his cousin up again she saw that he had been picking wild flowers. A smile trembled on her lips, for the little blossoms looked out of place—almost ridiculous—in this stolid man's great hand. Honor thought there was a pathetic appeal in the eyes of the summer speedwells and dog-roses, a righteous indignation in the bristling locks of the ragged-robins that he held; but, assuming that the bouquet was designed for her, she concealed her amusement. Then her mind ranged to another aspect of this action, and she found the man's simplicity appeal to her. He did not offer Honor the flowers, but added others to them; named each hedge blossom; showed with frank interest how the seeds of the wood-sorrels sprang away and scattered at a touch; appeared entirely interested by the unconsidered business and beauty of a Devon lane. These concerns, so trivial to Honor's eye, clearly wakened in Stapledon an interest and enthusiasm as keen as any pertaining to humanity.

They proceeded through the valley woods, past the great beech of the proposal, whose secret inscription was discreetly turned away from the high road, and then travelled towards Chagford, hard by the ancient mill of Holy Street—once a happy haunt of artists, to-day denied to all men. Here Honor pointed out the broken head of an old religious relic that formed part of a hedge upon their right hand.

"Market Cross," she said. "It used to be in Chagford until a worthy clergyman rescued it and set it here."

The fragment was of similar character to the granite round about it and shared with the component wall a decoration of mosses, fern, nettle, ivy, and brambles. Upon the stone itself was a rough incised cross, and the whole appeared to occupy this humble place with peaceful propriety. Myles viewed the fragment closely, then, moved by an idea, thrust his bouquet between its arms and passed on.

"I thought they were for me," said Honor.

"No," he answered. "I picked them without a particular object."

They went forward again, traversed Chagford Bridge, and so, by dell and hamlet, hill and valley, returned towards Little Silver and began to breast the great acclivity to Bear Down.

At the foot of this steep climb one Doctor Courteney Clack met them. He was a plump, genial soul of five-and-forty, and love of sport with lack of ambition combined to anchor him in this remote region. He had little to do and so much the more leisure for rod and horse. But to-day he was walking, and his round, clean-shorn face showed him to be remarkably warm.

"Not at the races, Doctor? How extraordinary!"

"Sheer evil fortune, Miss Endicott. A most inconsiderate young person."

"Mrs. Ford?"

"Exactly so. Nature has no sympathy with sportsmen. Christo is to tell me everything. He also has charge of a five-pound note. So I enjoy the sport in spirit."

Hurried footsteps interrupted the conversation, and a boy was seen running at top speed down the hill.

"It's Tommy Bates from home!" cried Honor. "What on earth does he want to go at that pace for?"

"Me probably," said Doctor Clack. "Nobody ever runs in Little Silver, unless it's to my house."

The medical man was right, and Tommy announced that a labourer had fallen suddenly sick in the hayfield and appeared about to perish.

"Sunstroke for certain," declared the medical man. "If it's not asking too much, Miss Endicott, I would suggest that I borrowed your pony. It will take me up the hill a great deal faster than I can walk, and time may be precious."

Honor immediately dismounted, and Doctor Clack, with great entertainment to himself, sat side-saddle, and uttering a wild whoop sent the astounded pony at the hill in a manner both unfamiliar and undignified. He was soon out of sight; and Tommy, after winning back his breath, explained the nature of the disaster and gave the name of the sufferer.

An hour earlier in the day, those workers of Bear Down already seen, were assembled about their dinner beside the majestic bulk of the last rick. All was now gathered in and the evening would see conclusion of a most satisfactory hay-harvesting. With their bread and onions, cheese and cold puddings the labourers speculated upon the worth of the crop.

"I'm thinking 'twill go in part to fat the pocket of a lazy man," said Henry Collins, who knew of the recent scene between Christopher Yeoland and Mr. Cramphorn, and had his reasons for ingratiating the latter.

"Lazy an' worse. Look at my eye!" growled Jonah. "If it weren't for missis, I'd have laid him in clink afore now—vicious rip as he is! He'll never trouble Satan to find him a job. Born to the gallows like as not."

He dropped his voice and turned to Churdles Ash.

"I seen Cherry Grepe," he said. "She's took my money to be even with un. I didn't ax no questions, but 'twill go hard with un afore very long."

Mr. Ash pursed his lips, which were indeed always pursed from the fact of there being no teeth to mention behind them. He did not answer Jonah's dark news, but spoke upon the main question.

"Come to think of it, a honest scarecrow do more work in the world than him," he declared.

"No more gude than a bowldacious auld dog-fox," said Henry Collins.

"Worse," replied Jonah. "Such things as foxes an' other varmints be the creation of the Lard to keep the likes of Christopher Yeoland out o' mischief. But him—the man hisself—what can you say of wan as have got a sawl to save, an' behaves like a awver-fed beast?"

"A butivul soarin' sawl," assented Samuel Pinsent. "But wheer do it soar to? To kissin' honest gals on the highways by all accounts."

Mr. Cramphorn's dark visage wrinkled and twisted and contracted.

"Blast the viper! But I gived un a hard stroke here an' theer, I warn 'e. Might have killed un in my gert wrath, but for t'other. Walloped un to the truth of music I did—philandering beast! 'Tis pearls afore swine, missis to mate with him."

"Fegs! You'm right theer. I've said afore an' I'll say again that she should have bided longer an' tried for her cousin. He'm worth ten of t'other chitterin' magpie; an' ban't feared o' work neither," declared Mr. Ash.

"Wait!" murmured Jonah darkly and with mystery in his voice. Then he whispered behind his hand to the ancient. "Cherry Grepe had a gawlden half-sovereign! I knaw what's in that woman, if she's pleased to let it out. Bide an' see. An' her didn't burn the chap in a wax image stuffed with pins for nought! 'That'll do the trick presently,'[#] her said. So wait an' watch, Churdles, same as I be doin'."

[#] Presently = immediately.

Mr. Ash looked uneasy, but answered nothing. Then came a sudden interruption.

Sally was serving at the cider barrel and had just poured out a horn of sweet refreshment for a thirsty man. It was Mr. Libby, who, in working clothes to-day, had condescended to manual labour once more. Time being an object with the hay, Mr. Cramphorn offered the youth a week's employment, so, much to the secret satisfaction of one who loved him, Mr. Libby became enrolled. Now the supreme moment was at hand, and while Sally laughed, her heart throbbed in a mighty flutter and beat painfully against a little bottle in her bosom. It contained the philtre, now to be exhibited on the cold heart of Gregory. Danger indeed lurked in this act, but Sally felt steeled to it and well prepared to hazard any reasonable risk. Only the previous evening she had seen Mr. Libby and her sister very close together in the gloaming. Moreover, her father had babbled far and near of the incident on the moorland road, and certain men and women, to her furious indignation, had not hesitated to hint that only an unmaidenly and coming-on spirit could culminate in such tribulation.

Now she passed for one instant behind the rick, drew forth the phial, took out its cork with her teeth and poured the potion into Mr. Libby's horn of cider. Gregory, his holiday airs and graces set aside, thanked the girl, gave a grateful grunt of anticipation, and drained the beaker at a draught.

"That's better!" he said. Then he smacked his lips and spat. "Theer's a funny tang to it tu. 'Twas from the cask—eh?"

"Ess, of course; wheer should it be from?" said Sally. Then she fluttered away, scarcely seeing where she walked.

The boy, Tommy Bates, was sitting beside Libby, and a moment later he spoke.

"Lard, Greg! what's tuke 'e? You'm starin' like a sheep."

"Doan't knaw, ezacally. I'm—I'm——"

"You'm gone dough-colour, an' theer's perspiration come out 'pon 'e so big as peas!" cried candid Tommy.

"I'm bad—mortal bad—'struth, I be dyin' I b'lieve! 'Tis here it's took me."

He clapped his hands to his stomach, rolled over on the ground and groaned, while his companion hastened to cry the catastrophe.

"Greg Libby's struck down! He'm thrawin' his life up, an' wrigglin' an' twistin' like a gashly worm!"

"Ah, I seed un wi'out his hat," said Mr. Ash calmly.

"A bit naish an' soft, I reckon; comes o' not standin' to work," spoke Henry Collins contemptuously.

"Or might be tu much cider," suggested Pinsent.

Without undue haste they strolled over to the sufferer. His head was in Sally's lap, and she screamed that he was passing away before their eyes.

"Put the poll of un off your apern, will 'e!" snapped Mr. Cramphorn. "Give awver hollerin', an' get on your legs, an' run home to Mrs. Loveys for the brandy. The man's took a fit seemin'ly. An' you, Bates, slip it down the hill for Doctor Clack. Loose his shirt to the throat, Collins, and drag un in the shade."

Jonah's orders were complied with, and soon, brandy bottle in hand, Mrs. Loveys hastened to the hay field with Sally sobbing behind her. But meantime Nature had assisted Mr. Libby to evade the potion, and a little brandy soon revived his shattered system. He was sitting up with his back against the hayrick describing his sensations to an interested audience when Doctor Clack arrived. The physician, who loved well the sound of his own voice, lectured on the recumbent Libby as soon as he had learnt particulars.

"First let me assure you all that he's in no danger—none at all," he began. "Nature is more skilful, more quick-witted, more resourceful than the most learned amongst us. Even I, beside Nature, am as nothing. I should have ordered an emetic. Behold! Nature anticipates me and takes all the necessary steps. Really one might have suspected a case of *Colica Damnoniensis*—which doesn't mean a damned stomach-ache, as you might imagine, having no Latin, but merely 'Devonshire Colic'—an old-time complaint—old as cider in fact—but long since vanished. It was caused by the presence of deleterious substances, or, as you would describe it more simply, dirt, in the apple-juice; and those eminent men, Doctor John Huxham and Sir George Baker, arrived at the conclusion some hundred years ago that the ailment arose from presence of lead in the cider vats. Nowadays such things cannot happen; therefore, to return to our friend here, we must seek elsewhere for an explanation of his collapse. Whatever he was unfortunate or unwise enough to partake of has happily been rejected by that learned organ, the human stomach—so often wiser than the human head—and my presence ceases to be longer necessary. A little more brandy and water and our friend will be quite equal to walking home."

Myles and Honor had now reached the scene, and the mistress of Endicott's insisted that a cart should convey Gregory to his mother. The unconscious victim of love therefore departed making the most of his sufferings.

Sally also withdrew from the toil of the day, retired to her little bedroom in Mr. Cramphorn's cottage near Bear Down, and wept without intermission for a space of time not exceeding two hours. She then cheered up and speculated hopefully upon the future.

To explain these matters it need only be said that, like many a better botanist before her, the girl had mistaken one herb of the field for another, and, instead of gathering innocent wild chamomile, collected good store of mayweed—a plant so exactly like the first to outward seeming that only most skilled eyes detect the differences between them. Thus, instead of receiving the beneficent and innocuous *Matricaria chamomilla*, Mr. Libby's stomach had been stormed by baleful *Anthemis cotula*, with the results recorded.

CHAPTER VII.
A BADGER'S EARTH

While Myles Stapledon played a busy part at the farm and found ample outlet for his small capital, ample occupation for his energies, Honor roamed dreaming through the August days with Christopher. As for Myles, he was a practical farmer and soon discovered what Mark Endicott had anticipated, that no mean possibilities lurked in Bear Down. The place indeed cried out for spending of money and increase of stock, but it promised adequate return upon outlay—a return at least reasonable viewed from the present low estate and reduced capabilities of English land. Stapledon was not hungry for any immediate or amazing profit, but Endicott's seemed certain to produce a fair interest upon the two thousand pounds he embarked there; he liked the farm and he was satisfied. At his cousin's particular desire, Myles stayed to see the money spent according to his will. Some of it went in building; and bygone beauties of old ripe thatches and cob walls that crumbled their native red through many coats of mellow whitewash, now vanished, yielding place to bricks, blue slates, and staring iron. A new atmosphere moved over the stagnation of Endicott's and the blind man settled into a great content.

The mistress had other matters to fill her thoughts, and, as the autumn approached, private concerns wholly occupied her. For Honor was more frank with herself than is possible to a soul that lacks humour; and a problem now rose ahead of her beyond the solution of days and nights; a mystery that developed, deepened, heightened, until it became a distraction and a trouble. Yet there was laughter in it, but of a sub-acid sort, neither wholesome nor pleasant.

Once in position of proud possessor, Christopher Yeoland exhibited no further alarm and but little apparent eagerness in the matter of his united future with Honor. Marriage appeared to be the last thing in his thought, and the temperament of the man at this crisis became visible and offered matter of comment for the most cursory observers. The fact of delay suited Honor well enough in reality, for she had little intention or desire to marry immediately, but that Christopher should be of this mind piqued her. His perfect equanimity before the prospect of an indefinite engagement secretly made Honor somewhat indignant. It did not become her lover in her eyes. He was not indifferent, that she knew; he was not cold, that she hoped; but his temper in this perfect readiness to postpone matrimony showed him to Honor in a new sidelight. Naturally enough she did not understand the trait, though it was characteristic; and her discomfort existed in a vague sense that his attitude, so much the reverse of a compliment to her, must have been awakened by some deficiency in herself. That the imperfection lay in him she did not imagine; that his love was a little anæmic in a positive direction she could not be supposed to suspect. Intellectually at least Christopher always sufficed, and Honor's uneasiness usually evaporated when in his company, though it was prone to take shape and substance again when absent from him. He always spoke of marriage as a remote goal—wholly desirable indeed—but approached by such pleasant ways that most rambling and desultory progress thereto was best; and, though entirely of his mind, it is a fact that the girl felt fluctuations of absolute annoyance that this should be his mind.

From which cause sprang secret laughter, that was born of fretfulness, that died in a frown.

Other trouble, of a sort widely different, also appeared upon Honor's horizon. After a period of supreme command, to find another enjoying almost like share of obedience and service at Bear Down seemed strange. But with absolute unconsciousness Myles Stapledon soon blundered into a prominence at Endicott's second only to her own. Nor was his position even second in some directions. Labouring folk follow a strong will by instinct, and Myles was striking such a dominant note of energy, activity, despatch in affairs, that the little community came presently to regard him as the new controller of its fortunes. Stapledon's name was upon the lips of the people more often than Honor's; even Jonah Cramphorn, whose noblest qualities appeared in a doglike and devout fidelity to the mistress, found Myles filling his mind as often as the busy new-comer filled his eye. At such times, in common with Churdles Ash and any other who might have enough imagination to regret an impossibility, Jonah mourned that it was Yeoland rather than Stapledon who had won his mistress's heart.

But the latter, full of business and loving work as only those love it who have devoted life thereto, overlooked the delicacy of his position at various minor points; and with sole purpose to save his cousin trouble he took much upon himself. It was sufficient that she said nothing and Mark Endicott approved. Once he offered to pay the hands at the accustomed hour of noon on Saturday; whereupon Honor blushed, and, becoming aware that he had hurt her, Myles expressed contrition with the utmost humility and heaped blame upon his blunder.

"It was only to save you trouble," he concluded.

"I know it; you are always doing so," she answered without irony. "But pay-day—that's the farmer's work."

Her answer, though not intended to do anything of the sort, forcibly reminded Myles that he had but a limited interest in Bear Down.

"Be frank," he said. "I'm such a thick-skinned fool that I may have blundered before and hurt you and never known it. Do not suffer me to do so again, Honor. I'm only very jealous for you and all that is yours."

"You are a great deal too kind to me, Myles, and have done more than I can find words to thank you for. You are the good genius here. I don't like to think of the loneliness we shall feel when you go from us."

"I'm not going yet awhile, I promise you," he answered.

Honor indeed appreciated her cousin's goodness fully, and, after this incident, had no more occasion to deplore his tact. She only spoke truth when affirming regret at the possibility of his departure. Her earliest sensations of oppression in his society had passed upon their walk over the Moor. From that moment the woman began to understand him and appreciate the strenuous simplicity of him. Sometimes he looked almost pathetic in his negations and his lonely and forlorn attitude towards the things of Hope; at others he rose into a being impressive, by that loneliness—a rare spirit who, upon "inbred loyalty unto Virtue, could serve her without a livery," and without a wage. Thus seen he interested Honor's intellect, and she speculated upon the strength of his armour if Chance called upon him to prove it. Not seldom she found herself in moods when a walk and a talk with Myles invigorated her; and she told her heart that such conversations made her return to Christopher with the greater zest, as an olive will reveal the delicate shades of flavour in fine wine. She assured herself of this fact repeatedly, until the reiteration of the idea caused her conscience to suspect its truth. She wilfully shut her eyes to its absurdity for a month, then changed her simile. Now she fancied that Christopher and Myles must impart an intellectual complement to one another, in that their qualities differed so extremely.

The result of this attitude was inevitable upon a woman of Honor's temperament. Comparison being impossible, she began to contrast the two men. One could be nothing to her; the other she had promised to marry; and even in the midst of her critical analysis she blamed herself, not without reason, in that her love for Christopher had no power to blind her. She asked herself bitterly what an affection was worth that could thus dwell in cold blood upon a lover's weaknesses. She answered herself that it was Christopher's own fault. She felt glad that he was what he was. His defects looked lovable; and only in the rather chilly daylight thrown by Stapledon's characteristics did Christo's blemishes appear at all. Then Honor grew very angry with herself, but tried to believe that her anger was directed against Myles. She flew upon him savagely to tear him to pieces; she strove furiously, pitilessly to strip him to his soul; but she was just between the ebullitions of anger, and, after her hurricane onset, the lacerated figure of her cousin still stood a man. He was difficult to belittle or disparage by the nature of him. One may trample a flower-bed into unlovely ruin in a moment; to rob a lichen-clad rock of its particular beauty is a harder and a lengthier task. Granted that the man was ponderous and lacking in laughter, he could yet be kind and gentle to all; granted that he appeared oppressed with the necessity of setting a good example to the world, yet he was in earnest, of self-denying and simple habit, one who apparently practised nothing he did not preach. She turned impatiently away from the picture of such admirable qualities; she told herself that he was little better than a savage in some aspects, a prig in all the rest. Yet Honor Endicott had lived too close to Nature to make the mistake of any lengthened self-deception. Myles was living a life that would wear, as against an existence which even her green experience of the world whispered was irrational; and though the shrewdness of Stapledon appeared a drab and unlovely compound beside Christopher's sparkling philosophy, yet Honor knew which stood for the juster views of life and conduct. One represented a grey twilight, clear and calm if wholly lacking any splendid height of hue; the other promised wide contrasts, tropical sunshine, and probable tempests. Not a little in the sobriety of the first picture attracted her; but she was none the less well pleased to think that she had already decided for the second. Herein she followed instinct, for her nature was of the sort that needed variable weather if intellectual health was to be her portion.

Yet these dissimilar men, as chance willed it, proved excellent friends, and, from the incident of their first meeting, grew into a sufficiently warm comradeship. Myles found himself gasping a dozen times a day before the audacities of Christopher. Sometimes indeed he suspected Yeoland's jewels of being paste; sometimes he marvelled how a professed Christian could propound certain theories; sometimes also he suspected that the Squire of Godleigh spoke truer than he knew. Christopher, for his part, welcomed the farmer, as he had welcomed any man whose destiny it was to lighten Honor's anxiety. That the new-comer was putting a couple of thousand pounds into Endicott's proved passport sufficient to Yeoland's esteem. Moreover, he liked Myles for other reasons. They met often in the fields and high places at dawn, and from standpoints widely different they both approached Nature with love. Christopher took a telescopic survey, delighted in wide harmonies, great shadows, upheavals of cloud, storms, sunsets, rivers overflowing and the magic of the mist. He knew the name of nothing and shrank from scientific approach to natural objects—to bird or bud or berry; but he affected all the wild animate and inanimate life of his woods and rivers; he was reluctant to interfere with anything; he hated the mournful echo of a woodman's axe in spring, though each dull reverberation promised a guinea for his empty purse. Stapledon, on the contrary, while not dead to spacious manifestations of force, was also microscopic. He missed much that the other was quick to glean, but gained an intimate knowledge of matters radical, and, being introspective, dug deeper lessons out of Devon hedgerows and the economy of Dartmoor bogs than Yeoland gathered from the procession of all the seasons as displayed in pomp and glory under the banner of the sun.

On a day when as yet no shadow had risen between them; when as yet Myles contemplated his cousin's engagement without uneasiness, and Christopher enjoyed the other's ingenuous commentary upon Honor's rare beauty of mind and body, they walked together at sunset on the high lands of Godleigh. Above the pine trees that encircled Yeoland's home and rose behind it, an offshoot from the Moor extended. Deep slopes of fern and grass, mountain ash and blackthorn, draped the sides of this elevation, and upon the crown of a little hill, sharing the same with wild ridges and boulders of stone, spread ruins and lay foundations of a building that had almost vanished. A single turret still stood, ceiled with the sky, carpeted with grass; and all round about a glory of purple heather fledged the granite, the evening scent of the bracken rose, flames of sunset fire touched stones and tree-tops, and burnt into the huge side of distant Cosdon Beacon, until that mountain was turned into a mist of gold.

"There would be a grand sky if we were on the Moor to-night," said Christopher; "not one of the clear, cloudless sort—as clean and uneventful as a saint's record—but what I call a human sunset—full of smudged splendour and gorgeous blots and tottering ruins, with live fire streaming out of the black abysses and an awful scarlet pall flung out to cover the great red-hot heart of the sun as he dips and dips."

"A sunset always means to-morrow to me."

"You're a farmer. Nothing ever means to-morrow to me."

"I can't believe that, Yeoland—not now that you've won Honor."

Christopher did not answer, but walked on where many an acre of fern spread over the southern face of the slope.

"Here you are," he said presently, indicating a burrow and a pile of mould. "Tommy Bates found it when he was here picking sloes and told me about it. I won't be sure it isn't a fox myself; though he declares the earth to be a badger's."

"Yes, I think that dead white grass means a badger. He brought it up from the valley."

"Then Tommy was right and I'm glad, for any distinguished stranger is welcome on my ground. What does the brute eat?"

"Roots and beech mast for choice. But he's carnivorous to the extent of an occasional frog or beetle; and I'm afraid he wouldn't pass a partridge's nest if there were eggs in it."

"That's a black mark against the beggar, but I'll pretend I don't know it."

They strolled forward and Myles kept his eyes upon the ground, while Christopher watched the sunset.

"It's a singular puzzle, the things that make a man melancholy," said the latter suddenly. "Once I had a theory that any perfect thing, no matter what, must produce sadness in the human mind, simply out of its perfection."

"A country life would be a pretty miserable business if that was so—with the perfect at the door of our eyes and ears all day long."

"Then I discovered that it depended on other considerations. Love of life is concerned with it. Youth saddens nobody; but age must. Our love of life wakes our sorrow for the old who are going out of it. 'Tis the difference between a bud and a withered blossom. Sunrise makes no man sad. That's why you love it, and love to be in it, as I do. The blush of dawn is like the warm cheek of a waking child—lovely; but sunset is a dying thing. There's sadness in that, and the more beautiful, the more sad."

"I cannot see anything to call sad in one or other."

"No, I suppose you can't; you've got such a devilish well-balanced mind."

A faint shadow of annoyance if not absolute contempt lurked in the tones of the speech; but Stapledon failed to see it.

"I wish I had," he answered. "There are plenty of things in Nature that make a man sad—sounds, sights, glimpses of the eternal battle under the eternal beauty. But sadness is weakness, say what you will. There's nothing to be sentimental about really. It's because we apply our rule of thumb to her; it's because we try to measure her wide methods by our own opinions on right and justice that we find her unjust. I told Honor something of this; but she agrees with you that Nature's quite beyond apology, and won't be convinced."

"You've told her so many things lately—opened her eyes, I'm sure, in so many directions. She's as solemn as an owl sometimes when I'm with her. Certainly she doesn't laugh as often as she used to."

Myles was much startled.

"Don't say that; don't say that. She's not meant to take sober views—not yet—not yet. She's living sunlight—the embodiment of laughter, and all the world's a funny picture-book to her still. To think I should have paid for the pleasure she's brought me by lessening her own! I hope you're utterly wrong, Yeoland. This is a very unquieting thought."

The man spoke much faster than usual, and with such evident concern that Christopher endeavoured to diminish the force of his speech.

"Perhaps I'm mistaken, as you say; perhaps the reason is that we are now definitely engaged. That may have induced gravity. Of course it is a solemn thing for an intelligent girl to cast in her lot with a pauper."

But Myles would not be distracted from the main issue.

"Her laughter is characteristic—marvellously musical—part of herself, like bells are part of a fair church. Think of making a belfry dumb by a deliberate act! Honor should always be smiling. A little sister of the spring she seems to me, and her laughter goes to my heart like a lark's song, for there's unconscious praise of God in it."

Yeoland glanced at the other.

"You can be sentimental too, then?"

"Not that, but I can be sad, and I am now. A man may well be so to think he has bated by one smile the happiness of Honor."

"Sorry I mentioned it."

"I'm glad. It was a great fault in me. I will try desperately to amend. I'm a dull dog, but I'll——"

"Don't, my dear chap. Don't do anything whatever. Be yourself, or you won't keep her respect. She hates shams. I would change too if I could. But she'd be down on me in a second if I attempted any reformation. The truth is we're both bursting with different good and brilliant qualities—you and I—and poor Honor is dazzled."

Stapledon did not laugh; he only experienced a great desire to be alone.

"Are you going to wait for the badger?" he asked, as they turned and retraced their way.

"Good Lord, no! Are you?"

"Certainly. It's only a matter of hours at most. I can sit silent in the fern with my eyes on the earth. I thought you wanted to see him."

"Not an atom. It's enough for me that he's here in snug quarters. My lord badger will show at moonrise, I expect. You'd better come down to the house and have a drink after the manifestation."

He tramped away; his footfall faded to a whisper in the fern; and Myles, reaching a place from which the aperture below was visible, settled himself and took a pipe from his pocket from habit, but did not load or light it. He had an oriental capacity for waiting, and his patience it was that had won much of his curious knowledge. A few hours more or less under the stars on a fine summer night were nothing but a pleasure to him. Rather did he welcome the pending vigil, for he desired to think, and he knew that a man may do so to best purpose in the air.

Once out of sight Christopher also stopped awhile and sat down upon a rock with his face uplifted. The rosy sky was paling, and already a little galaxy of lights afar off marked the village of Chagford, where it stood upon its own proper elevation under the Moor. Thus placed, in opposition to the vanished sun, detail appeared most clearly along the eastern hills and valleys. Cot, hamlet, white winding road stood forth upon the expanse, and while Christopher Yeoland watched the dwindling definition on earth there ascended a vast and misty shield of pearl into the fading sky. Through parallel bands of grey, like a faint ghost, it stole upwards into a rosy after-glow. Then the clouds faded, and died, and wakened again at the touch of the moon, as she arose with heightened glory and diminished girth, to wield a sceptre of silver over sleep. There descended then the great silence of such places, the silence that only country dwellers understand, the silence that can fret urban nerves into absolute suffering. Bedewed fern-fronds gathered light, and flung it like rain across the gloom, and brought far-reaching peace and contentment to the mind of Christopher. He dreamed dreams; he rose in spirit through the moony mist—a dimensionless, imponderable, spirit thing, ready to lose himself in one drop of diamond dew, hungry to fill high heaven and hug the round moon to his heart. For a little season he rejoiced in the trance of that hushed hour; then the moment of intoxication vanished, and he rose slowly and went his way.

The other man, after long waiting, was also rewarded. From beneath him, where he sat, there came at last a sound and a snuffling. The badger appeared, and the moonlight touched his little eyes and gleamed along his amber side-streaks as he put up his nose, sniffed the air with suspicion, stretched himself, scratched himself, then paddled silently away upon his nightly business through the aisles of the fern.

CHAPTER VIII.
OUT OF THE MIST

The calm awakened of moonlight, as quickly died, and Christopher Yeoland found himself in some uneasiness when he thought of his love. Whereon he based this irritation would have been difficult to determine, but a variety of small annoyances conspired to build it. These trifles, separately, laughter could blow away at a breath, but combined they grew into a shadow not easily dispelled. Already the name of Myles had oftener sounded upon Honor's lips than seemed necessary, even when Stapledon's position and importance at Bear Down were allowed; and now her name similarly echoed and re-echoed in the utterances of her cousin. Still Christopher smiled in thought.

"It's the novelty of him after me. I'm a mere rollicking, irresponsible brook—only good to drink from or fish in—for ideas; he's a useful, dreary canal—a most valuable contrivance—smooth, placid, not to say flat. Well, well, I must shake Honor up; I must——"

He reflected and debated upon various courses though immediate marriage was not included amongst them. But a fortnight later the situation had developed.

Honor and Christopher were riding together over the Moor; and, albeit the physical conditions promised fair enough until sunset-time, when both man and woman turned homewards very happy, yet each had grown miserable before the end, and they parted in anger upon the heathery wastes where northern Teign and Wallabrook wind underneath Scor Hill. For the weather of the high land and the weather of their minds simultaneously changed, and across both there passed a cloud. Over against the sunset, creeping magically as she is wont to creep, from the bosom of the Moor and the dark ways of unseen water, arose the Mist Mother. She appeared suddenly against the blue above, spread forth diaphanous draperies, twined her pearly arms among the stocks and stones and old, wind-bent bushes of the waste. Catching a radiance from the westering sun, she draped the grey heads of granite tors in cowls of gold; she rose and fell; she appeared and vanished; she stole forward suddenly; she wreathed curly tendrils of vapour over sedge and stone, green, quaking bog, still waters, and the peat cuttings that burnt red-hot under the level rays of the sun. Great solitary flakes of the mist, shining with ineffable lustre of light, lessened the sobriety of the heath; and upon their dazzling hearts, where they suddenly merged and spread in opposition to the sun on the slope of western-facing hills, there trembled out a spectral misty circle—a huge halo of colourless light drawn upon the glimmering moisture. Within it, a whitethorn stood bathed in a fiery glow without candescence; and from beneath the tree some wild creature—hare or fox—moved away silently and vanished under the curtain, while a curlew cried overhead invisible. The riders reined up and watched the luminous frolics of the Mist, where she played thus naked, like an innocent savage thing, before them.

"These are the moments when I seem to glimpse antique life through the grey—wolf-skins and dark human skins, coarse faces, black hair, bead-bright eyes, strange speech, the glimmer of tents or rush thatches through the mist. These, and the bark of dogs, laughter of women, tinkle of stone on stone, where some Damnonian hunter fabricates his flints and grunts of the wood-bears and the way to kill them."

"Always dreaming, dearest. I wonder what you would have done in those days? Did the Damnonians have Christos too?"

"Undoubtedly. I should have been a bard, or a tribal prophet, or something important and easy. I should have dreamed dreams, and told fortunes, and imparted a certain cultured flavour to the lodge. I should have been their oracle very likely—nice easy work being an oracle. In it you'll find the first dawn of the future art of criticism."

"Creation is better than criticism."

"That's your cousin, I'll swear! The very ring of him. No doubt he thinks so. Yet what can be more futile than unskilful creation? For that matter the awful amount of time that's wasted in all sorts of futile work."

"You're certainly sincere. You practise the virtues of laziness as well as preach them," said Honor without amusement.

"I do; but there's not that old note of admiration at my theories in your voice of late, my angel girl."

"No, Christo; I'm beginning to doubt, in a fleeting sort of way, if your gospel is quite the inspired thing you fancy it."

"Treason! You live too much in the atmosphere of honest toil, sweetheart. And there's hardly a butterfly left now to correct your impressions."

"No; they are all starving under leaves, poor things."

"Exactly—dying game; and the self-righteous ant is counting his stores—or is it the squirrel, or the dormouse? I know something or other hoards all the summer through to prolong his useless existence."

Honor did not answer. Then her lover suddenly remembered Myles, and his forehead wrinkled for a moment.

"Of course I'm not blind, Honor," he proceeded, in an altered tone. "I've seen the change these many days, and levelled a guess at the reason. Sobersides makes me look a weakling. Unfortunately he's such a real good chap I cannot be cross with him."

"Why should you be cross with anybody?"

"That's the question. You're the answer. I'm—I'm not exactly all I was to you. Don't clamour. It's true, and you know it's true. You're so exacting, so unrestful, so grave by fits lately. And he—he's always on your tongue too. You didn't know that, but it's the case. Natural perhaps—a strong personality, and so forth—yet—yet——"

"What nonsense this is, Christopher!"

"Of course it is. But you don't laugh. You never do laugh now. My own sober conviction is this; Stapledon's in love with you and doesn't know it. Don't fall off your pony."

"Christopher! You've no right, or reason, or shadow of a shade for saying such a ridiculous thing."

"There's that in your voice convinces me at this moment."

"Doesn't he know we're engaged? Would such a man allow himself for an instant——?"

"Of course he wouldn't. That's just what I argue, isn't it? He stops on here because he doesn't know what's happened to him yet, poor devil. When he finds out, he'll probably fly."

"You judge others by yourself, my dearest. Love! Why, he works too hard to waste his thoughts on any woman whatsoever. Never was a mind so seldom in the clouds."

"In the clouds—no; but on the earth—on the earth, and at your elbow."

"He's nothing of the kind."

"Well, then, you're always at his. Such a busy, bustling couple! I'm sure you're enough to make the very singing birds ashamed. When is he going?"

"When his money is laid out to his liking, I suppose. Not yet awhile, I hope."

"You don't want him to go?"

"Certainly I don't; why should I?"

"You admire him in a way?"

"In a great many ways. He's a restful man. There's a beautiful simplicity about his thoughts; and——"

"And he works?"

"You're trying to make me cross, Christo; but I don't think you will again."

"Ah! I have to thank him for that too! He's making you see how small it is to be cross with me. He's enlarging your mind, lifting it to the stars, burying it in the bogs, teaching you all about rainbows and tadpoles. He'll soak the sunshine out of your life if you're not careful; and then you'll grow as self-contained and sensible and perfect as he is."

"After which you won't want me any more, I suppose?"

"No—then you'd only be fit for—well, for him."

"I don't love you in these sneering moods, Christo. Why cannot you speak plainly? You've got some imaginary grievance. What is it?"

"I never said so. But—well, I have. I honestly believe I'm jealous—jealous of this superior man."

"You child!"

"There it is! It's come to that. I wasn't a child in your eyes a month ago. But I shall be called an infant in arms at this rate in another month."

"He can't help being a sensible, far-seeing man, any more than you can help being a——"

"Fool—say it; don't hesitate. Well, what then?"

Honor, despite her recent assertion, could still be angry with Christopher, because she loved him better than anything in the world. Her face flushed; she gathered her reins sharply.

"Then," she answered, "there's nothing more to be said—excepting that I'm a little tired of you to-day. We've seen too much of one another lately."

"Or too much of somebody else."

She wheeled away abruptly and galloped off, leaving him with the last word. One of her dogs, a big collie, stood irresolute, his left forepaw up, his eyes all doubt. Then he bent his great back like a bow, and bounded after his mistress; but Yeoland did not attempt to follow. He watched his lady awhile, and, when she was a quarter of a mile ahead, proceeded homewards.

She had chosen a winding way back to Bear Down, and he must pass the farm before she could return to it.

The man was perfectly calm to outward seeming, but he shook his head once or twice—shook it at his own folly.

"Poor little lass!" he said to himself. "Impatient—impatient—why? Because I was impatient, no doubt. Let me see—our first real quarrel since we were engaged."

As he went down the hill past Honor's home, a sudden fancy held him, and, acting upon it, he dismounted, hitched up his horse, and strolled round to the back of the house in hope that he might win a private word or two with Mark Endicott. Chance favoured him. Tea drinking was done, and the still, lonely hour following on that meal prevailed in the great kitchen. Without, spangled fowls clucked their last remarks for the day, and fluttered, with clumsy effort, to their perches in a great holly tree, where they roosted. At the open door a block, a bill-hook, and a leathern gauntlet lay beside a pile of split wood where Sally Cramphorn had been working; and upon the block a robin sat and sang.

Christopher lifted the latch and walked through a short passage to find Honor's uncle alone in the kitchen and talking to himself by snatches.

"Forgive me, Mr. Endicott," he said, breaking in upon the monologue; "I've no right to upset your reveries in this fashion, but I was passing and wanted a dozen words."

"And welcome, Yeoland. We've missed you at the Sunday supper of late weeks. How is it with you?"

"Oh, all right. Only just now I want to exchange ideas—impressions. You love my Honor better than anybody else in the world but myself. And love makes one jolly quick—sensitive—foolishly so perhaps. I didn't think it was in me to be sensitive; yet I find I am."

"Speak your mind, and I'll go on with my knitting—never blind man's holiday if you are a blind man, you know."

"You're like all the rest in this hive, always busy. I wonder if the drones blush when they're caught stealing honey?"

"Haven't much time for blushing. Yet 'tis certain that never drone stole sweeter honey than you have—if you are a drone."

"I'm coming to that. But the honey first. Frankly now, have you noticed any change in Honor of late days—since—well, within the last month or two."

Mr. Endicott reflected before making any answer, and tapped his needles slowly.

"There is a change," he said at length.

"She's restless," continued Christopher; "won't have her laugh out—stops in the middle, as if she suddenly remembered she was in church or somewhere. How d'you account for it?"

"She's grown a bit more strenuous since her engagement—more alive to the working-day side of things."

"Not lasting, I hope?"

"Please God, yes. She won't be any less happy."

"Of course Myles Stapledon's responsible. Yet how has he done it? You say you're glad to see Honor more serious-minded. Well, that means you would have made her so before now, if you could. You failed to change her in all these years; he has succeeded in clouding her life somehow within the space of two months. How can you explain that?"

"You're asking pithy questions, my son. And, by the voice of you, I'm inclined to reckon you're as likely to know the answers to them as I am. Maybe more likely. You're a man in love, and that quickens the wits of even the dullest clod who ever sat sighing on a gate, eating his turnip and finding it tasteless. I loved a maid once, too; but 'tis so far off."

"Well, there's something not wholly right in this. And they ought to know it."

"Certainly they don't—don't guess it or dream it. But leave that. Now you. You must tackle yourself. The remedy lies with you. This thing has made you think, at any rate."

"Well, yes. Honor isn't so satisfied with me as of old, somehow. Of course that's natural, but——"

"She loves you a thousand times better than you love yourself."

"And still isn't exactly happy in me."

"Are you happy in yourself? She's very well satisfied with you—worships the ground you walk on, as the saying is—but that's not to say she's satisfied with your life. And more am I, or anybody that cares about you. And more are you."

"Well, well; but Myles Stapledon—this dear, good chap. He's a—what? Why, a magnifying glass for people to see me in—upside down."

"He thinks very little about you, I fancy."

"He's succeeded in making me feel a fool, anyhow; and that's unpleasant. Tell me what to do, Mr. Endicott. Where shall I begin?"

"Begin to be a man, Yeoland. That's what a woman wants in her husband—wants it unconsciously before everything. A man—self-contained, resolute—a figure strong enough to lean upon in storm and stress."

"Stapledon is a man."

"He is, emphatically. He knows where he is going, and the road. He gets unity into his life, method into his to-morrows."

"To-morrow's always all right. It's to-day that bothers me so infernally."

"Ah! and yesterday must make you feel sick every time you think of it, if you've any conscience."

"I know there isn't much to show. Yet it seems such a poor compliment to the wonderful world to waste your time in grubbing meanly with your back to her. At best we can only get a few jewelled glimpses through these clay gates that we live behind. Then down comes the night, when no man may work or play. And we shall be an awfully long time dead. And what's the sum of a life's labour after all?"

"Get work," said Mark, "and drop that twaddle. Healthy work's the first law of Nature, no matter what wise men may say or poets sing. Liberty! It's a Jack-o'-lantern. There's no created thing can be free. Doing His will—all, all. Root and branch, berry and bud, feathered and furred creatures—all working to live complete. The lily does toil; and if you could see the double fringe of her roots above the bulb and under it—as I can well mind when I had eyes and loved the garden—you'd know it was so. There's no good thing in all the world got without labour at the back of it. Think what goes to build a flash of lightning—you that love storms. But the lightning's not free neither. And the Almighty's self works harder than all His worlds put together."

"Well, I'll do something definite. I think I'll write a book about birds. Tell me, does Honor speak much of her cousin?"

"She does."

"Yet if she knew—if she only knew. Why, God's light! she'd wither and lose her sap and grow old in two years with Stapledon. I know it, in the very heart of me, and I'd stake my life on it against all the prophets. There's that in close contact with him would freeze and kill such as Honor. Yes, kill her, for it's a vital part of her would suffer. Some fascination has sprung up from the contrast between us; and it has charmed her. She's bewitched.

And yet—be frank, Mr. Endicott—do you believe that Stapledon is the husband for Honor? You've thought about it, naturally, because, before she and I were engaged, you told me that you hoped they might make a match for their own sakes and the farm's. Now what do you say? Would you, knowing her only less well than I do, wish that she could change?"

The other was silent.

"You would, then?"

"If I would," answered old Endicott, "I shouldn't have hesitated to say so. It's because I wouldn't that I was dumb."

"You wouldn't? That's a great weight off my mind, then."

"I mean no praise for you. I should like to chop you and Stapledon small, mix you, and mould you again. Yet what folly! Then she'd look at neither, for certain."

"Such a salad wouldn't be delectable. But thank you for heartening me. I'm the husband for your niece. I know it—sure as I'm a Christian. And she knew it a month ago; and she'll know it again a month hence, I pray, even if she's forgotten it for the moment. Now I'll clear out, and leave you with your thoughts."

"So you've quarrelled with her?"

"No, no, no; she quarrelled with me, very properly, very justly; then she left me in disgrace, and I came to you, hoping for a grain of comfort. I'm a poor prattler, you know—one who cannot hide my little dish of misery out of sight, but must always parade it if I suspect a sympathetic nature in man or woman. Good-bye again."

So Christopher departed, mounted his horse, and trotted home in most amiable mood.

CHAPTER IX.
THE WARNING

There was a custom of ancient standing at Bear Down Farm. On working days the family supped together in a small chamber lying off the kitchen, and left the latter apartment to the hands; but upon Sunday night all the household partook at the same table, and it was rumoured and believed that, during a period of two hundred years, the reigning head of Endicott's had never failed to preside at this repast, when in residence. Moreover, the very dishes changed not. A cold sirloin of beef, a potato salad, and a rabbit pie were the foundations of the feast; and after them followed fruit tarts, excepting in the spring, with bread and cheese, cider and small beer.

Two days after Honor's quarrel with Christopher, while yet they continued unreconciled, there fell a Sunday supper at which the little band then playing its part in the history of Endicott's was assembled about a laden board. But matters of moment were astir; a wave of excitement passed over the work folk, and Myles, who sat near the head of the table on Honor's left, observed a simultaneous movement, a whispering and a nodding. There were present Mr. Cramphorn and his daughters, who dwelt in a cottage hard by the farm; Churdles Ash, Henry Collins, the red-haired humorist Pinsent, and the boy Tommy Bates. Mrs. Loveys took the bottom of the table; Mark Endicott sat beside his niece, at her right hand.

A hush fell upon the company before the shadow of some great pending event. The clatter of crockery, the tinkle of knives and forks ceased. Then Myles whispered to Honor that a speech was about to be delivered, and she, setting down her hands, smiled with bright inquiry upon Mr. Cramphorn, who had risen to his feet, and was darting uncomfortable glances about him from beneath black brows.

"D'you want to tell me anything, Cramphorn?" she inquired.

"Ma'am, I do," he answered. "By rights 'tis the dooty of Churdles Ash, but he'm an ancient piece wi'out gert store o' words best o' times, an' none for a moment such as this; so he've axed me to speak instead, 'cause it do bring him a wambliness of the innards to do or say ought as may draw the public eye upon un. 'Tis like this, mistress, we of Endicott's, here assembled to supper, do desire to give 'e joy of your marriage contract when it comes to be; an' us hopes to a man as it may fall out for the best. Idden for us to say no more'n that; an' what we think an' what we doan't think ban't no business but our awn. Though your gude pleasure be ours, I do assure 'e; an' the lot of us would do all man or woman can do to lighten your heart in this vale o' weariness. An' I'm sure we wants for you to be a happy woman, wife, mother, an' widow—all in due an' proper season, 'cordin' to the laws o' Nature an' the will o' God. An' so sez Churdles Ash, an' me, an' Mrs. Loveys, an' my darters, an' t'others. An' us have ordained to give e' a li'l momentum of the happy day, awnly theer's no search in' hurry by the look of it, so as to that—it being Henery Collins his thought—us have resolved to bide till the banns be axed out. 'Cause theer's many a slip 'twixt the cup an' the lip, 'cordin' to a wise sayin' of old. An' so I'll sit down wishin' gude fortune to all at Endicott's—fields, an' things,[#] an' folk."

[#] Things = stock.

Mr. Cramphorn and his friends had been aware of Honor's engagement for three months; but the bucolic mind is before all things deliberate. It required that space of time and many long-winded, wearisome arguments to decide when and how an official cognisance of the great fact might best be taken.

The mistress of Bear Down briefly thanked everybody, with a smile on her lip and a tear in her eye; while the men and women gazed stolidly upon her as she expressed her gratitude for their kindly wishes. When she had spoken, Mr. Cramphorn, Collins, and Churdles Ash hit the table with their knife-handles once or twice, and the subject was instantly dismissed. Save in the mistress and her uncle, this incident struck not one visible spark of emotion upon anybody present. All ate heartily, then Honor Endicott withdrew to her parlour; Mrs. Loveys and Cramphorn's daughters cleared the table.

The men then lighted their pipes; Mark Endicott returned to his chair behind the leathern screen; the deep settle absorbed Churdles Ash and another; Jonah took a seat beside the peat fire, which he mended with a huge "scad" or two from the corner; and the customary Sunday night convention, with the blind man as president or arbiter, according to the tone of the discussion, was entered upon. Sometimes matters progressed harmoniously and sleepily enough; on other occasions, and always at the instance of Mr. Cramphorn, whose many opinions and scanty information not seldom awoke an active and polemical spirit, the argument was conducted with extreme acerbity—a circumstance inevitable when opposing minds endeavour to express ideas or shades of thought beyond the reach of their limited vocabularies.

To-night the wind blew hard from the west and growled in the chimney, while the peat beneath glowed to its fiery heart under a dancing aurora of blue flame, and half a dozen pipes sent forth crooked columns of smoke to the ceiling. Mr. Cramphorn, by virtue of the public part he had already taken in the evening's ceremonial, was minded to rate himself and his accomplishments with more than usual generosity. For once his suspicious forehead had lifted somewhat off his eyebrows, and the consciousness of great deeds performed with credit cast him into a spirit of complaisance. He lightly rallied Churdles Ash upon the old man's modesty; then, thrusting his mouth into the necessary figure, blew a perfect ring of smoke, and spat through it into the fire with great comfort and contentment.

Gaffer Ash replied in a tone of resignation.

"As to that," he said, "some's got words and some hasn't. For my paart, I ban't sorry as I can't use 'em, for I've always thanked God as I was born so humble that I could live through my days without never being called 'pon to say what I think o' things in general an' the men an' women round about."

"Least said soonest mended," commented Pinsent.

"Ess fay! 'Tis the chaps as have got to talk I be sorry for—the public warriors and Parliament men an' such like. They sweat o' nights, I reckon; for they be 'feared to talk now an' again, I'll wager, an' be still worse 'feared to hold theer peace."

"You're pretty right, Ash," said Mr. Endicott. "It takes a brave man to keep his mouth shut and not care whether he's misunderstood or no. But 'tis a bleating age—a drum-beating age o' clash and clatter. Why, the very members of Parliament get too jaded to follow their great business with sober minds. If a man don't pepper his speeches with mountebank fun, they call him a dull dog, and won't listen to him. All the world's dropping into play-acting—that's the truth of it."

"I didn't make no jokes howsoever when I turned my speech 'fore supper," declared Mr. Cramphorn; "an' I'm sure I'd never do no such ondacent thing in a set speech. Ban't respectful. Not but what I was surprised to find how pat the right word comed to me at the right moment wi'out any digging for un."

"'Tis a gert gift for a humble man," said Mr. Ash.

"A gift to be used wi' caution," confessed Jonah. "When you say 'tis a gift, last word's spoken," he added, "but a man's wise to keep close guard awver his tongue when it chances to be sharper'n common. Not as I ever go back on the spoken word, for 'tis a sign of weakness."

Myles Stapledon laughed and Mr. Cramphorn grew hot.

"Why for should I?" he asked.

"If you never had call to eat your words after fifty years o' talkin', Jonah, you're either uncommon fortunate or uncommon wise," declared the blind man. "Wise you are not particular, not to my knowledge, so we must say you're lucky."

The others laughed, and Jonah, despite his brag of a tongue more ready than most, found nothing to say at this rebuke. He made an inarticulate growl at the back of his throat and puffed vigorously, while Henry Collins came to the rescue.

"Can 'e tell us when the weddin's like to be, sir?" he inquired of Stapledon, and Myles waited for somebody else to reply; but none did so.

"I cannot tell," he answered at length. "I fancy nothing is settled. But we shall hear soon enough, no doubt."

"I suppose 'tis tu inquirin' to ax if you'll bide to Endicott's when missis do leave it?" said Samuel Pinsent.

"Well—yes, I think it is. Lord knows what I'm going to do. My home's here for the present—until—well, I really cannot tell myself. It depends on various things."

There was a silence. Even the most slow-witted perceived a new revelation of Stapledon in this speech. Presently Churdles Ash spoke.

"Best to bide here till the time-work chaps be through wi' theer job. Them time-work men! The holy text sez, 'Blessed be they as have not seed an' yet have believed'; but fegs! 'tis straining scripture to put that on time-work. I'd never believe no time-work man what I hadn't seed."

"Anybody's a fool to believe where he doesn't trust," said Mark Endicott. "You open a great question, Ash. I believed no more or less than any other chap of five-an'-twenty in my young days; but, come blindness, there was no more taking on trust for me. I had to find a reason for all I believed from that day forward."

"Was faith a flower that grew well in the dark with you, uncle?" inquired Myles, and there was a wave of sudden interest in his voice.

"Why, yes. Darkness is the time for making roots and 'stablishing plants, whether of the soil or of the mind. Faith grew but slowly. And the flower of it comes to no more than this: do your duty, and be gentle with your neighbour. Don't wax weak because you catch yourself all wrong so often. Don't let any man pity you but yourself; and don't let no other set of brains than your own settle the rights and wrongs of life for you. That's my road—a blind man's. But there's one thing more, my sons: to believe in the goodness of God through thick and thin."

"The hardest thing of all," said Stapledon.

Mr. Cramphorn here thought proper to join issue. He also had his own views, reached single-handed, and was by no means ashamed of them.

"As to the A'mighty," he said, "my rule's to treat Un same as He treats me—same as we'm taught to treat any other neighbour. That's fair, if you ax me."

"A blasphemous word to say it, whether or no," declared Ash uneasily. "We ban't teached to treat folks same as they treat us, but same as we wish they'd treat us. That's a very differ'nt thing. Gormed if I ban't mazed a bolt doan't strike 'e, Jonah."

"'Tis my way, an' who's gwaine to shaw me wheer it fails o' right an' justice?"

"A truculent attitude to the Everlasting, surely," ventured Myles, looking at the restless little man with his hang-dog forehead and big chin.

"Who's afeared, so long as he'm on the windy side o' justice? I ban't. If God sends gude things, I'm fust to thank Un 'pon my bended knees, an' hope respectful for long continuance; if He sends bad—then I cool off an' wait for better times. Ban't my way to return thanks for nought. I've thanked Un for the hay for missus's gude sake a score o' times; but thank Un for the turmits I won't, till I sees if we'm gwaine to have rain 'fore 'tis tu late. 'No song, no supper,' as the saying is. Ban't my way to turn left cheek to Jehovah Jireh after He's smote me 'pon the right. 'Tis contrary to human nature; an' Christ's self can't alter that."

"'Tis tu changeable in you, Cramphorn, if I may say it without angering you," murmured Collins.

"Not so, Henery; ban't me that changes, but Him. I'm a steadfast man, an' always was so, as Mr. Endicott will bear witness. When the Lard's hand's light on me, I go dancin' an' frolickin' afore Him, like to David afore the ark, an' pray long prayers week-days so well as Sundays; but when He'm contrary with me, an' minded to blaw hot an' cold, from no fault o' mine—why, dammy, I get cranky tu. Caan't help it. Built so. 'Pears to me as 'tis awnly a brute dog as'll lick the hands that welts un."

"What do 'e say to this here popish discoorse, sir?" inquired Churdles Ash; and Mark answered him.

"Why, Jonah only confesses the secret of most of us. We've got too much wit or too little pluck to tell—that's all the difference. He's blurted it out."

"The 'state of most of us'?" gasped Mr. Collins.

"Surely, even though we don't own it to our innermost souls. Who should know, if not me? It makes a mighty difference whether 'tis by pleasant paths or bitter that we come to the throne of grace. Fair weather saints most of us, I reckon. I felt the same when my eyes were put out. God knows how I kept my hands off my life. I never shall. Before that change I'd prayed regular as need be, morn and night, just because my dear mother had taught me so to do, and habit's the half of life. And after my eyes went the habit stuck, though my soul was up in arms and my brain poisoned against a hard Providence. And what did I do? Why, regular as the clock, at the hour when I was used to bless God, I went on my knees and lifted my empty eyes to Him and cursed Him. 'Twas as the psalmist prayed in his awful song of rage: my prayer was turned into sin. I did that—for a month. And what was the price He paid me for my wickedness? Why, He sent peace—peace fell upon me and the wish to live; and He that had took my sight away brought tears to my eyes instead. So I reached a blind man's seeing at the last. I've lived to know that man's misty talk and thought upon justice is no more than a wind in the trees. Therefore Jonah is in the wrong to steer his life by his own human notion of justice. There's no justice in this world, and what fashion of stuff will be the justice in the next, we'll know when we come to get it measured out, not sooner. One thing's sure: it's not over likely to be planned on earthly models; so there's no sight under heaven more pitiful to me than all mankind so busy planning pleasure parties in the next world to make up for their little, thorny, wayside job in this."

"The question is, Do we matter to the God of a starry night?" asked Stapledon, forgetting the presence of any beyond the last speaker. "We matter a great deal to ourselves and ought to—I know that, of course," he added. "We must take ourselves seriously."

Mark laughed and made instant answer.

"We take ourselves too seriously, our neighbours not seriously enough. It's the fault of all humans—philosophers included."

"An' I be sure theer's immortal angels hid in our bones, however," summed up Mr. Ash.

"If so, good," answered Stapledon with profound seriousness. "But thought won't alter what is by the will of God; nor yet what's going to be. The Future's His workshop only. No man can meddle there. But the present is ours; and if half the brain-sweat wasted on the next world was spent in tidying the dirty corners in this one—why, we might bring the other nearer—if other there be."

"You'll know there's another long before your time comes to go to it, my son," said the blind man in a calm voice. Then the tall clock between the warming-pans struck ten with the sonorous cadence and ring of old metal.

At this signal pipes were knocked out and windows and doors thrown open; whereupon the west wind, like the voice of a superior intellect, stilled their chatter with sweet breath, soon swept away the reek of tobacco, and brought a blast of pure air through the smoke. All those present, save only Myles and Endicott, then departed to their rest; but these two sat on awhile, for the old man had a hard thing to say, and knew that the moment to speak was come.

"How long are you going to stop here?" he asked suddenly.

"I can't guess. I suppose there's no hurry. I've really not much interest anywhere else. Why do you ask?"

"Because it's important, lad. Blind folks hear such a deal. And they often know more than what belongs to the mere spoken word. There's an inner and an outer meaning to most speech of man, and we sightless ones often gather both. It surprises people at times. You see we win nothing from sight of a speaking mouth or the eyes above it. All our brain sits behind our ear; there's no windows for it to look out at."

"You've surprised me by what you have gleaned out of a voice, uncle."

"And I'm like to again. Not pleasantly neither. I've thought how I'd found something on your tongue long ago; but I've kept dumb, hoping I was mistaken. To-night, my son, there's no more room for doubt."

"This is a mystery—quite uncanny."

"I don't know. 'Tis very unfortunate—very, but a fact; and you've got to face it."

"Read the riddle to me," said Stapledon slowly. His voice sounded anxious under an assumption of amusement.

"Do you remember after supper how Pinsent asked you whether you would stop on here when his mistress was married? You answered that the Lord knew what you were going to do. Now it was clean out of your character to answer so."

"I hope it was; I hope so indeed. I was sorry the moment afterwards."

"You couldn't help yourself. You were not thinking of your answer to the question, but the much more important thing suggested by the question. That's what made you so short: the thought of Honor's marriage."

"I own it," confessed the other. A silence fell; then Mark spoke again more gravely.

"Myles, you must clear out of here. I'm blind and even I know it. How much more such as can see—you yourself, for instance—and Honor—and Christopher Yeoland."

Stapledon's brow flushed and his jaw set hard. He looked at the sightless face before him, and spoke hurriedly.

"For God's sake, what do you mean?"

"It's news to you? I do think it is! And it has come the same way to many when it falls the first time. The deeper it strikes, the less they can put a name to it. But now you know. Glance back along the road you've walked beside Honor of late days. Then see how the way ahead looks to you with her figure gone. I knew this a week ago, and I sorrowed for you. There was an unconscious tribute in your voice when you spoke to her—a hush in it, as if you were praying. Man, I'm sorry—but your heart will tell you that I'm right."

A lengthy silence followed upon this speech; then the other whispered out a question, and there was awe rather than terror in his tone.

"You mean I'm coming to love her?"

"I do—if only that. Remember what you said the first day you came here about the false step at the threshold."

"But she is another man's. That has been familiar knowledge to me."

"And you think that fact can prevent a man of honour from loving a woman?"

"Surely."

"Not so at all. Love of woman's a thing apart—beyond all rule and scale, or dogma, or the Bible's self. The passions are pagans to the end—no more to be trusted than tame tigers, if a man is a man. But passions are bred out nowadays. I don't believe the next generation will be shook to the heart with the same gusts and storms as the last. We think smaller thoughts and feel smaller sentiments; we're too careful of our skins to trust the giant passions; our hearts don't pump the same great flood of hot blood. But you—you belong to the older sort. And you love her—you who never heard the rustle of a petticoat with quickened breath before, I reckon. You're too honest to deny it after you've thought a little. You know there's something seething down at the bottom of your soul—and now you hear the name of it. Go to bed and sleep upon that."

Stapledon remained mute. His face was passive, but his forehead was wrinkled a little. He folded his arms and stared at the fire.

"God knows I wish this was otherwise," continued Mark Endicott. "'Twould have been a comely and a fitting thing for you to mate her and carry on all here. So at least I thought before I knew you."

"But have changed your opinion of me since?"

"Well, yes; I did not think so highly of you until we met and got to understand each other. But I doubt if you'd be a fit husband for Honor. There's a difference of—I don't know the word—but it's a difference in essentials anyway—in views and in standpoint. Honor's a clever woman to some extent, yet she takes abundant delight in occasional foolishness, as clever women often do. 'Tisn't your fashion of mind to fool—not even on holidays. You couldn't if you tried."

"But she is as sober-minded as I am at heart. Under her humorous survey of things and her laughter there is——"

"I know; I know all about her."

"We had thought we possessed much in common on a comparison of notes now and again."

"If you did, 'tis just what you wouldn't have found out so pat at first sight. There's a great gulf fixed between you, and I'm not sorry it is so, seeing she's another man's. Yeoland looks to be a light thing; I grant that; but I do believe that he understands her better than you or I ever could. I've found out so much from hearing them together. Moreover, he's growing sober; there's a sort of cranky sense in him, I hope, after all."

"A feather-brain, but well-meaning."

"The last leaf on an old tree—even as Honor is."

"At least there must be deep friendship always—deep friendship. So much can't be denied to me. Don't talk of a great gulf between us, uncle. Not at least a mental one."

"Truly I believe so, Myles."

"We could bridge that."

"With bridges of passing passion—like silver spider-threads between flowers. But they wouldn't stand the awful strain of lifelong companionship. You've never thought what that strain means in our class of life, when husband and wife have got to bide within close touch most times till the grave parts them. But that's all wind and nothing. She's tokened to Yeoland. So no more need be spoken on that head. You've got to think of your peace of mind, Stapledon, and—well, I'd best say it—hers too. Now, good-night. Not another word, if you're a wise man."

Mark Endicott was usually abroad betimes, though not such an early riser as Myles, and on the following morning, according to his custom, he walked in the garden before breakfast. His pathway extended before the more ancient front of Bear Down, and in summer, at each step, he might stretch forth his hand over the flower border and know what blossom would meet it. Now there fell a heavy footfall that approached from the farmyard.

"Good morning," said Stapledon, as he shook Mark by the hand.

"Good morning, my lad."

"I'm going on Saturday."

Mr. Endicott nodded, as one acknowledging information already familiar.

"Your loss will fall heavily on me," he said, "for it's not twice in a month of Sundays that I get such a companion spirit to chop words with."

CHAPTER X.
THREE ANGRY MAIDS

Upon the day that Myles Stapledon determined with himself to leave Little Silver, Christopher's patience broke down, and he wrote to Honor concerning their protracted quarrel. This communication it pleased him to begin in a tone of most unusual severity. He struck the note in jest at first, then proceeded with it in earnest. He bid his lady establish her mind more firmly and affirm her desires. He returned her liberty, hinted that, if he so willed, he might let Godleigh Park to a wealthy Plymouth tradesman, who much desired to secure it, and himself go abroad for an indefinite period of years. Then, weary of these heroics, Christopher became himself on the third page of the note, expressed unbounded contrition for his sins, begged his sweetheart's forgiveness, and prayed her to name a meeting-place that he might make atonement in person. With joke and jest the letter wound to its close; and he despatched it to Bear Down upon the following morning.

Mr. Gregory Libby happened to be the messenger, and of this worthy it may be said that, while now a person well-to-do in the judgment of Little Silver, yet he displayed more sense than had been prophesied for him, kept his money in his purse, and returned to his humble but necessary occupation of hedge-trimming. He was working about Godleigh at present, and being the first available fellow-creature who met Yeoland's eye as he entered the air, letter in hand, his temporary master bid Gregory drop gauntlet and pruning-hook that he might play postman instead for a while.

The youth departed then to Endicott's under a personal and private excitement, for his own romance lay there, as it pleased him to think, and he was conducting it with deliberate and calculating method. Libby found himself divided between the daughters of Mr. Cramphorn, and, as those young women knew this fact, the tension between them increased with his delay. Upon the whole he preferred Sally, as the more splendid animal; but the man was far too cunning to commit himself rashly. His desires by no means blinded him, and he looked far ahead and wondered with some low shrewdness which of the maids enjoyed larger part of her father's regard, and which might hope for a lion's share of Jonah's possessions when the head-man at Bear Down should pass away. In this direction Mr. Libby was prosecuting his inquiries; and the operation proved difficult and delicate, for Cramphorn disliked him. Margery met the messenger, and gave a little purr of pleasure as she opened the kitchen door.

"Come in, come in the kitchen," she said; "I'm all alone for the minute if you ban't feared o' me, Mr. Libby."

"Very glad to see you again," said Gregory, shaking her hand and holding it a moment afterwards.

"So be I you. I heard your butivul singing to church Sunday, but me, bein' in the choir, I couldn't look about to catch your eye."

"Wheer's Sally to?" he asked suddenly, after they had talked a few moments on general subjects.

The girl's face fell and her voice hardened.

"How should I knaw? To work, I suppose."

"I awften wonder as her hands doan't suffer by it," mused Libby.

"They do," she answered with cruel eagerness. "Feel mine."

She pressed her palms into his, considering that the opportunity permitted her so to do without any lack of propriety. And he held them and found them soft and cool, but a thought thin to his taste. She dropped her eyelids, and he looked at her long lashes and the thick rolls of dark hair on her head. Then his eyes ranged on. Her face was pretty, with a prim prettiness, but for the rest Margery wholly lacked her sister's physical splendours. No grand curves of bosom met Mr. Libby's little shifty eyes. The girl, indeed, was slight and thin.

He dropped her hand, and she, knowing by intuition the very matter of his mind, spoke. Her voice was the sweetest thing about her, though people often forgot that fact in the word it uttered. Margery had a bad temper and a shrewish tongue. Now the bells jangled, and she fell sharply upon her absent sister. She declared that she feared for her; that Sally was growing unmaidenly as a result of her outdoor duties. Then came a subtle cut—and Margery looked away from her listener's face as she uttered it.

"Her could put you in her pocket and not knaw you was theer. I've heard her say so."

Mr. Libby grew very red.

"Ban't the way for a woman to talk about any chap," he said.

"Coourse it ban't. That's it with she. So much working beside the men, an' killin' fowls, an' such like makes her rough an' rough-tongued. Though a very gude sister to me, I'm sure, an'———"

She had seen Sally approaching; hence this lame conclusion. The women's eyes met as the elder spoke.

"Wheer's faither to, Margery? Ah! Mr. Libby—didn't see you. You'm up here airly—helpin' her to waste time by the look of it."

"Theer's some doan't want no help," retorted the other. "What be you doin' indoors? Your plaace is 'pon the land with the men."

"Wheer you'd like to be, if they'd let 'e," stung the other; "but you'm no gude to 'em—a poor pin-tailed wench like you."

"Ess fay! Us must have a brazen faace an' awver-blawn shape like yourn to make the men come about us! Ban't sense—awnly fat they look for in a female of coourse!" snapped back Margery; and in the meantime the cause of this explosion—proud of his power, but uneasy before the wrath of women—prepared to depart. Fortune favoured his exit, for Honor appeared suddenly at the other end of the farmyard with some kittens in her hands and a mother cat, tail in air, marching beside her and lifting misty green eyes, full of joy.

Libby turned therefore, delivered his letter, and was gone; while behind him voices clashed in anger, one sweet, one shrill. Then a door slammed as Margery hastened away upon a Parthian shot, and her sister stamped furiously, having no word to answer but a man's. Sally immediately left the house and proceeded after the messenger; but a possibility of this he had foreseen, and was now well upon his way back to Godleigh. Sally therefore found herself disappointed anew, and marked her emotions by ill-treating a pig that had the misfortune to cross her stormy path.

Another woman's soul was also in arms; and while Margery wept invisible and her sister used the ugliest words that she knew, under her breath, their mistress walked up and down the grass plot where it extended between the farm and the fields, separated from the latter by a dip in the land and a strange fence of granite posts and old steel rope.

Honor had now come from seeing Myles Stapledon. Together, after breakfast, they had inspected a new cow-byre on outlying land, and, upon the way back, he told her that he designed to return to Tavistock at the end of that week. Only by a sudden alteration of pace and change of foot did she show her first surprise. Then she lifted a questioning gaze to his impassive face.

"Why?" she asked.

"Well, why not? I've been here three months and there is nothing more for me to do—at any rate nothing that need keep me on the spot."

"There's still less for you to do at Tavistock. You told me a month ago that there was nothing to take you back. You've sold the old house and let the mill."

"It is so; but I must—I have plans—I may invest some money at Plymouth. And I must work, you know."

"Are you not working here?"

"Why, not what I call work. Only strolling about watching other people."

Honor changed the subject after a short silence.

"Did you see Christopher on Sunday? I thought you were to do so?"

"Yes; the linen-draper from Plymouth has been at him again. He's mad about Godleigh; he makes a splendid offer to rent it for three years. And he'll spend good money upon improvements annually in addition to quite a fancy rent."

"Did you advise Christopher to accept it?"

"Most certainly I did. It would help to lessen his monetary bothers; but he was in one of his wildly humorous moods and made fun of all things in heaven and earth."

Honor tightened her lips. Their first great quarrel, it appeared, was not weighing very heavily on her lover.

"He refused, of course."

"He said that he would let you decide. But he vows he can't live out of sight of Godleigh and can't imagine himself a trespasser on his own land. He was sentimental. But he has such an artist's mind. 'Tis a pity he's not got some gift of expression as an outlet—pictures or verses or something."

"That can have nothing to do with your idea of going away, however, Myles?" asked Honor, swinging back to the matter in her mind.

"Nothing whatever; why should it?"

"I don't want you to go away," she said; and some passion trembled in her voice. "You won't give me any reason why you should do so, because there can be none."

"We need not discuss it, cousin."

"Then you'll stop, since I ask you to?"

"No, I cannot, Honor. I must go. I have very sufficient reasons. Do not press me upon that point, but take my word for it."

"You refuse me a reason? Then, I repeat, I wish you to stay. Everything cries out that you should. My future prosperity cries out. It is your duty to stay. Apart from Bear Down and me, you may do Christopher much good and help him to take life more seriously. Will you stay because I ask you to?"

"Why do you wish it?" he said.

"Because—I like you very much indeed; there—that's straightforward and a good reason, though you're so chary with yours."

She looked frankly at him, but with annoyance rather than regard in her eyes.

"It is folly and senseless folly to go," she continued calmly, while he gasped within and felt a mist crowding down on the world. "You like me too, a little—and you're enlarging my mind beyond the limits of this wilderness of eternal grass and hay. Why, when Providence throws a little sunshine upon me, should I rush indoors out of it and draw down the blinds?"

He was going to mention Christopher again, but felt such an act would be unfair to the man in Honor's present mood. For a moment he opened his mouth to argue the point she raised, then realised the danger and futility. Only by an assumption of carelessness amounting to the brutal could he keep his secret out of his voice. And in the light of what she had confessed so plainly, to be less frank himself was most difficult. Her words had set his heart beating like a hammer. His mind was overwhelmed with his first love, and to such a man it was an awful emotion. It shook him and unsteadied his voice as he looked at her, for she had never seemed more necessary to him than then.

"Don't be so serious," he said. "Your horizon will soon begin to enlarge with the coming interests. I've enjoyed my long visit more than I can tell you—much more than I can tell you; but go I must indeed."

"Stop just one fortnight more, Myles?"

"Don't ask it, Honor. It's hard to say 'No' to you."

"A week—a little week—to please me? Why shouldn't you please me? Is it a crime to do that? I suppose it is, for nobody ever thinks of trying to."

"I cannot alter my plans now. I must go on Saturday."

"Go, then," she said. "I'm rewarded for being so rude as to ask so often. I'm not nearly proud enough. That's a distinction you've not taught me to achieve with all your lessons."

She left him, but he overtook her in two strides, and walked at her right hand.

"Honor, please listen to me."

"My dear cousin, don't put on that haggard, not to say tragic, expression. It really is a matter of no moment. I only worried you because I'm spoiled and hate being crossed even in trifles. It was the disappointment of not getting my way that vexed me, not the actual point at question. If you can leave all your interests here without anxiety and trust me so far—why, I'm flattered."

"Hear me, I say."

"So will the whole world, if you speak so loud. What more is there to hear? You're going on Saturday, and Tommy Bates shall drive you to Okehampton to catch the train."

"You're right—and wise," he said more quietly. "No, I've nothing to say."

Then he made a ghastly effort to be entertaining.

"And mind, Honor, I shall be very sharp if my cheque does not come each quarter on the right day. A hard taskmaster I shall be, I promise you."

"Don't, Myles," she answered instantly, growing grave at his simulated merriment.

A few minutes afterwards she left him, sought out the squeaking kittens to calm her emotions, presently deposited them in a sunny corner with their parent, and, taking Christopher's letter, walked out again upon the grass.

A storm played over her face which she made no attempt to hide. Tear-stained Margery, peeping from the kitchen window, noticed it, and Samuel Pinsent, as he passed from the vegetable garden, observed that his salute received no recognition.

Honor Endicott knew very well what she now confronted, and she swept from irritation to anger, from anger to passion before the survey. Ignoring the great salient tragedy that underlaid the position, she took refuge in details, and selecting one—the determination of Myles to depart—chose to connect Christopher Yeoland directly with it, decided to believe that it was at Yeoland's desire her cousin now withdrew. The rectitude of the act added the last straw to her temper. The truth perhaps was not wholly hidden from her; she had been quick to read Myles by light thrown from her own heart. And here, at a point beyond which her thought could not well pass, she turned impatiently to the letter from her lover, tore it open, and scanned the familiar caligraphy.

Half a page sufficed, for her mood just then was ill-tuned to bear any sort of reproof. Anger had dimmed both her sense of proportion and her knowledge of Christopher; round-eyed she read a few lines of stern rebuke and censure, a threat, an offer of liberty, and no more. The real

Christopher, who only began upon a later folio, she never reached. There was a quick suspiration of breath, a sound suspiciously like the gritting of small teeth, and her letter—torn, and torn, and torn again—was flung into the hand of the rough wind, caught, hurried aloft, swept every way, scattered afar, sown over an acre of autumn grass.

"This is more than I can bear!" she said aloud; and after the sentiment—so seldom uttered by man or woman save under conditions perfectly capable of endurance—she entered the house, tore off her gloves, and wrote, with heaving bosom, an answer to the letter she had not read.

CHAPTER XI.
PARTINGS

When Christopher Yeoland received his sweetheart's letter at the hand of Tommy Bates, he read it thrice, then whistled a Dead March to himself for the space of half an hour.

He retired early with his tribulation, and spent a night absolutely devoid of sleep; but Nature yielded about daybreak, when usually he rose, and from that hour the man slumbered heavily until noon. Then, having regarded the ceiling for a considerable time, he found that Honor had receded to the background of his mind, while Myles Stapledon bulked large in the forefront of it. To escape in their acuteness the painful impressions awakened by his letter, he destroyed it without further perusal; he then wandered out of doors, and climbed above his pine woods to reflect and mature some course of action. He retraced the recent past, and arrived at erroneous conclusions, misled by Honor's letter, as she had been deceived from the introductory passages in his. He told himself that she had yielded to his importunities through sheer weariness; that in reality she did not love him and now knew it, in presence of this pagan cousin, sprung up out of the heather. From finding herself in two minds, before all the positive virtues of Stapledon, she was doubtless now in one again, and he— Christopher—had grown very dim, had quite lost his old outline in her eyes, in fact had suffered total eclipse from the shadow of a better man.

To these convictions he came, and while still of opinion—even after the catastrophe of her letter—that no more fitting husband could have been found for Honor than himself, yet was he equally sure, since her indignation, that he would never ask her to marry him more. Thus he argued very calmly, with his body cast down under the edge of the pine woods, his eyes upon the dying gold of oak forests spread over an adjacent hill. Against Honor he felt no particular resentment, but with Stapledon he grew into very steadfast enmity.

Under his careless, laughter-loving, and invertebrate existence Yeoland hid a heart; and though none, perhaps not Honor herself, had guessed all that his engagement meant to him, the fact remained: it began to establish the man in essential particulars, and had already awakened wide distaste with his present uncalculated existence. Thus Honor's promise modified his outlook upon life, nerved him, roused him to responsibility. He was not a fool, and perfectly realised what is due from any man to the woman who suffers him henceforth to become first factor in her destiny. Yet his deeply rooted laziness and love of procrastination had stood between him and action up to the present. All things were surely conspiring to a definite step; but events had not waited his pleasure; another man now entered the theatre, and his own part was thrust into obscurity even at the moment when he meditated how to make it great. But the fact did not change his present purpose. Ideas, destined to produce actions during the coming year, were still with him, and recent events only precipitated his misty projects. He resolved upon immediate and heroic performance. He began by forgiving Honor. He marvelled at her unexpected impatience, and wondered what barbed arrow in his own letter had been sharp enough to draw such serious wrath from her. There was no laughter in her reply—all thunder, and the fine forked lightning of a clever woman in a passion on paper. He felt glad that he had destroyed the letter. Yet the main point was clear enough, though only implicitly indicated; she loved him no more, for had she done so, no transient circumstance of irritation or even active anger had been strong enough to win such concentrated bitterness from her. He did not know what had gone to build Honor's letter; he was ignorant of Stapledon's decision, of the fret and fume in his sweetheart's spirit when she heard it, of the mood from which she suffered when she received his note, and of the crowning fact that she had not read all.

So Christopher made up his mind to go away without more words, to let Godleigh to the enamoured linen-draper for a term of years, and join his sole surviving relative—an ancient squatter in New South Wales—who wrote to his kinsman twice a year and accompanied each missive with the information that Australia was going to the dingoes and must soon cease to be habitable by anything but a "sun-downer" or a kangaroo. Hither, then, Christopher determined to depart; and, viewed from beneath his whispering pines, the idea had an aspect so poetical that he found tears in his eyes, which set all the distant woods swimming. But when he remembered Myles, his sorrow dried, scorched up by an inner fire; and, as he looked into the future that this stranger had snatched away from him, he began to count the cost and measure the length of his life without Honor Endicott. Such calculations offered no standpoint for a delicate emotion. They were the difference between visions of billowing and many-breasted Devon, here unrolled before him, glorious under red autumn light, and that other in his mind's eye—a sad-coloured apparition of Australian spinifex and sand.

His anger whirled up against the supplanter, and he forgot his former charitable and just contentions uttered before this blow had fallen. Then he had honestly affirmed to Honor that in his judgment Stapledon was in love with her and scarcely realised his position. That utterance was as nearly true as possible; but in the recollection of the woman's anger he forgot it. How the thing had come about mattered nothing now. To inquire was vain; but the knowledge that he had done no deed to bring this storm upon himself proved little comfort. His patience and humour and philosophy went down the wind together. He was, at least to that extent, a man.

To Honor's letter he returned no answer; neither did he seek her, but avoided her rather and pursued an active search for Myles Stapledon. Accident prevented a meeting until the morning of the latter's departure, and, wholly ignorant that his rival was at that moment leaving Bear Down for good and all, Christopher met him in a dog-cart on the road to Okehampton, not far from the spot where had fallen out their first introduction.

The pedestrian raised his hand, and Myles bid Bates, who drove him, pull up.

"Well met," he said.

"Would you mind giving me a few minutes of your time, Stapledon?" inquired Christopher coldly; whereupon Myles looked at his watch, and then climbed to earth.

"Trot on," he said to his driver, "and wait for me at the corner where Throwley road runs into ours. And now," he continued, as the vehicle drew out from ear-shot, "perhaps you won't mind turning for half a mile or so. I must keep moving towards Okehampton, or I shall miss my train."

They walked in step together; then Yeoland spoke.

"You'll probably guess what I've got to say."

"Not exactly, though I may suspect the subject. Hear me first. It'll save you trouble. You know me well enough to grant that I'd injure no man willingly. We must be frank. Only last Sunday did I find what had overtaken me. I swear it. I didn't imagine such things could happen."

"Don't maunder on like that! What do I care what's overtaken you? You say you suspect the thing I want to speak about. Then come to it, or else let me do so. When first we met you heard that I was the man your cousin had promised to marry. You won't deny that?"

"You told me."

"Then why, in the name of the living God, did a man with all your oppressive good qualities come between us? That's a plain question anyway."

A flush spread over Stapledon's cold face and as quickly died out. He did not answer immediately, and the younger spoke again.

"Well? You're the strong man, the powerful, self-contained, admirable lesson to his weak brethren. Can't you answer, or won't you?"

"Don't pour these bitter words upon me. I have done no deliberate wrong at all; I have merely moved unconsciously into a private difficulty from which I am now about to extricate myself."

"That's too hard a saying for me."

"It is true. I have wakened from an error. I have committed a terrible action in ignorance. A blind man, but not so blind as I was, showed me my stupidity."

"Say it in so many words. You love Honor."

"I do. I have grown to love her—the thing farthest from my thoughts or dreams. I cannot help it. I do not excuse it or defend myself. I am doing all in my power."

"Which is——?"

"Going—going not to come back."

"It is too late."

"Do not say so, Yeoland. What could I be to her—such a man——?"

"Spare me and yourself all that. And answer this one question—on your oath. Did she tell you of the letter she wrote to me?"

"She did not."

"Or of my letter?"

"Not a word."

"One question more. What did she say when you told her you were going?"

"She deemed it unnecessary at the time."

"She asked you to stop?"

Stapledon did not answer immediately; then his manner changed and his voice grew hard. He stood still, and turned on his companion and towered above him. Their positions were suddenly reversed.

"I will suffer no more of this. I have done you no conscious wrong, and am not called upon to stand and deliver at your order. Leave a man, who is sufficiently tormented, to go his way alone. I am moving out of your life as fast as my legs will carry me. I mourn that I came into it. I acknowledge full measure of blame—all that it pleases you to heap upon me; so leave me in peace, for more I cannot do."

"'Peace!' She did ask you not to go?"

"I have gone. That is enough. She is waiting for you to make her your wife. Don't let her wait for ever."

"You do well to advise—you who have wrecked two lives with your—'private difficulty'!"

Yeoland stood still, but the other moved hastily on. Thus they parted without further words, and Christopher, at length weary of standing to watch Stapledon's retreating shape, turned and resumed his way.

He had determined, despite his sneer, to take Stapledon's advice and go back to Honor. The bonds woven of long years were not broken after all. How should events of a few short weeks shatter his lifelong understanding with this woman? Recent determinations vanished as soon as his rival had done so, and Yeoland turned and bent his steps to Bear Down, resolved that the present hour should end all and place him again in the old position or dethrone him for ever. His mind beat like a bird against the bars of a cage, and he asked himself of what, in the name of all malevolent magic, was this man made, who had such power to unsettle Honor in her love and worship, to thrust him headlong from his high estate. He could not answer the question, or refused to answer it. He swept on over the sere fern, with the soft song of the dead heather bells in his ear; but the message of stone and heath was one: She had asked the other man not to go.

Before that consummation his new-kindled hope faded, his renewed determinations died. The roads of surrender and of flight were all that stretched before him. To Honor he could be nothing any more; and worse than nothing if he stopped. Complete self-sacrifice and self-effacement seemed demanded of him if his love was indeed the great, grand passion that he had imagined it to be. Impressed with this conviction he passed from the Moor and sought his nearest way to Godleigh; and then the mood of him suffered another change, and hope spoke in the splendours of sunset. Myles Stapledon had certainly gone; and he had departed never to return. That was his own assurance. Honor at least might be asked, and reasonably asked, to tell her mind at this crisis in affairs.

And so he changed the road again and set his face for Bear Down. A dark speck met his gaze while yet he was far distant; and he knew it for the mistress and hastened to her, where she walked alone on the little lawn.

Coming quietly over the grass Yeoland surprised her; she lifted a startled face to his, and he found her moist of eye while in her voice was a tremor that told of tears past.

"Why d'you steal on me like this?" she asked suddenly, and her face flushed, and her hands went up to her breast. "You frighten me. I do not want you. Please, Christopher, go away."

"I know you do not want me, and I am going away," he answered gloomily, his expectations stricken before her words. "I'm going, and I've come to tell you so."

"How much more am I to suffer to-day?"

"You can ask me that, Honor? My little girl, d'you suppose life's a bed of roses for me since your letter?"

"A bed of roses is the sum of your ambitions."

"Why, that's like old times when you can be merely rude to me! But is the old time gone? Is the new time different? Listen, Honor, and tell me the truth."

"I don't know the truth. Please go away and leave me alone; I can tell you nothing. Don't you see I don't want you? Be a man, if you know how, and go out of my sight."

The voice was not so harsh as the words, and he thought he saw the ghost of a hope behind it.

"Curious!" he said. "You're the third person this week who has told me to be a man. Well, I'll try. Only hear this, and answer it. I've just left Myles Stapledon on his way to Okehampton—gone for good."

"What is that to me?"

"Your looking-glass will tell you. Now, Honor, before God—yes, before God, answer me the truth. Do you love him?"

"You've no right to stay here prattling when I bid you go."

"None; and I'm not going to stay and prattle. But answer that you shall. I've a right at least to ask that question."

The girl almost wrung her hands, and half turned from him without speaking; but he approached and imprisoned both her arms.

"You must tell me. I can do nothing until I know, Your very own lips must tell me."

"You don't ask me if I love you?"

"Answer the other question and I shall know."

"Blind—blind—selfish egotists—all of you," she cried. Then her voice changed. "Is it my fault if I do love him?" she asked.

"I'm no judge. To part right and wrong was a task beyond me always—excepting on general, crude principles. Answer my question."

"Then, I do."

He bent his head.

"I love him, I love him, I love him."

Neither spoke for some seconds; then the man lifted up his head, shook it as though he had risen from a plunge, and laughed.

"So be it. Now here's news for you, that I can relate since you've been so frank. D'you remember what I whispered to you when I was a little boy, of the cracks on my ceiling and the chance patterns I found on my window-blind when I used to lie awake in the grey of summer mornings, waiting for the first gold? You forget. So had I forgotten until a few days since. Then, being lazy, I lay abed and thought, and thought, and fell to tracing the old stories told by the lines on blind and ceiling. Chance patterns of bays and estuaries, continents and rivers, all mapped out there—all more real to me than those in my atlas. I remember a land of blackamoors, a sea of sharks, an island of cannibals, a desert of lions, in which the little flies figured as monsters of the wilderness. Such dreams of deeds by field and flood I weaved in those grey, gone mornings to the song of the thrush and the murmur of the old governor snoring in the next room! And now—now I'm smitten with the boy's yearning to speed forth over the sea of sharks—not after lions, but after gold. I'm going to justify my existence—in Australia."

"You couldn't go further off if you tried."

"Not well—without slipping over the edge altogether."

"You mustn't do this, Christopher."

"It's done, dearest. This is only a ghost—an adumbration that's talking to you. I ask for my freedom, Honor—sweetheart Honor. Thank God we are humorists both—too sensible to knock our knuckles raw against iron doors. You'll be happy to-morrow, and I the day after. We mustn't miss more laughter than we can help in this tearful world. And friends we must always be. That can't be altered."

"I quite understand. You shall not do this, Christopher. I love you for suggesting it. You may go—as far as London, or where the steamer starts from. Then you must come back to me. You've promised to marry me."

"Forget it. I'm in earnest for once. At least you must credit that. There's Mrs. Loveys at the window calling you to tea. We'll meet again in a day or two very likely."

"Don't go; don't go, Christo; I'm so lonely, and wretched, and——"

But the necessary iron in him cropped up at this hour of trial. He hardened his heart and was gone before she had finished speaking.

Two days later Honor, who had heard nothing of Christopher since their last meeting, sent a message to him. He returned an evasive answer, which annoyed her for the space of three days more. Then, still finding that he kept at home, she went to seek him there. Between ten and eleven o'clock one morning she started, but breaking her bootlace near the outset, returned home again. The total delay occupied less than fifteen minutes, and presently she reached Godleigh to find Mrs. Brimblecombe, wife of Noah Brimblecombe, the sexton of Little Silver, on her knees, scrubbing in the porch. The charwoman readily desisted from work and answered Honor's question.

"He kept it that 'mazin' quiet from us all, Miss. An' you never told nobody neither. Gone—gone to foreign lands, they tell me; an' the place in a jakes of a mess; an' the new folks comin' in afore Christmas."

As she spoke a dog-cart wound up the steep hill to Chagford, and a man, turning in it, stopped and looked long at the grey house in the pines. Had anybody walked on to the terrace and waved a handkerchief, he must have seen the signal; but as Honor spoke to Mrs. Brimblecombe the trap passed from sight.

"When did he go?" she asked unguardedly.

"Lard! Doan't 'e knaw 'bout it—you of all folks?"

"Of course; of course; but not the exact hour."

"Ten minutes agone or less—no more certainly; an' his heavy boxes was took in a cart last night, I hear."

Honor hurried on to the terrace and looked at the road on the hill. But it was empty. Mrs. Brimblecombe came also.

"Sails from Plymouth this evenin', somebody telled us, though others said he'm gwaine to Lunnon fust; an' it seems that Doctor Clack knawed, though how a gen'leman so fond of the moosic of his awn tongue could hold such a tremenjous secret wi'out bustin' I can't fathom."

Honor Endicott walked slowly back to Bear Down. The significance of her own position, as a woman apparently jilted, did not weigh with her in the least. She reflected, with a dull ache and deadness, that her accident, with a delay of ten little minutes resulting from it, had altered the whole scope and sweep of her life and another's. That Christopher Yeoland had taken his great step with very real difficulty the fact of his continued absence before it made sufficiently clear. He had not trusted himself to see her again; and now Honor's conviction grew: that her presence even at the last moment, must surely have broken down his determination and kept him at home had she so willed.

She asked herself what she might have done in the event of that ordeal, and believed that she would have tried hard to keep him.

CHAPTER XII.
THE DEFINITE DEED

Life, thus robbed of love for Honor Endicott, was reduced to a dreary round of mere duties. Within one fortnight of time these two men, severally responsible for the music and sunshine of her life, had departed out of it in a manner perfectly natural, conventional, and inevitable. Given the problems that had arisen, this was the solution to have been predicted. Mark Endicott, indeed, put it very bluntly to her; but Honor viewed the tragedy with more tender pity for her own feelings. She marvelled in secret at the great eternal mystery of human affections, at the evolution of the love instinct, which now, ennobled and sublimated through the generations of men, had achieved its present purity and perfection in the civilisation of monogamous nations; while her uncle told her, in fewer words and homelier, that between two stools she had fallen to the ground.

She was supremely miserable through dwindling days, and each of them to her seemed longer than those of the summer that was past. The shadows of two men often accompanied her lonely rides, and circumstances or places would remind her of each in turn, would suddenly stab her into acute suffering as they wakened the image of Christopher or of Myles in very life-colours.

There came a laugh once, when she overheard Pinsent and Collins congratulating each other that Bear Down had not been too precipitate in the purchase of the wedding "momentum"; but the salt was gone out of humour for a little while; and with her uncle, at least, she never laughed at all. His boundless sympathy was strained before her wayward unhappiness. She flew to paradoxes, contradictions, and whimsical conceits, all vain, and worse than vain in his judgment. She sometimes talked at random with no particular apparent object save to waken opposition. But the knitting-needles ticked placidly through long evenings beside the glowing peat: and it asked an utterance beyond measure flagrant to set them tapping, as an indication that the blind man's patience was exhausted.

About mid-December they sat together in the little parlour of the kitchen, and Honor, who lolled beside the fire, employed her pretty fingers upon no more useful task than playing with a piece of string from a grocer's parcel.

"What are you doing?" asked Mark suddenly.

"Making cats' cradles," she answered, and won from him the reproof that such a confession invited.

"How is it you've given up reading of late days?"

"I've sunk into a lazy way. The lazier you are the less time there is for anything."

"You ought to read; you've ample leisure to improve your mind; and ample need to."

"That's just it—the ample leisure. When I had Christo to look after, though every precious moment of the day was full, I could find time for all. And that shows a busy man or woman's more likely to see well after affairs than a leisurely one. Some men can actually *make* time, I believe—Myles could. But now—through these black, hateful, sunless days—I feel I'm always wanting to creep off to bed, and sleep, and forget."

"That's never my brave girl spoke that?"

"I'm not brave; and I'm tired of the awful stores of things worth knowing collected by people who are dead. How the men who wrote books must look back from the other world and shiver at the stuff they've left behind them in this—knowing all they know there! But Myles was right in that. He used to say he'd learned more from leaning over gates than from any books. And I believe he had."

"He was grounded in solid knowledge by lessons from wise books to start with. They taught him to learn."

"Such a way as he had of twisting everything into a precept or example!"

"You'd have held that prosy talk presently."

"Speak of sermons in stones! He found whole gospels in a dead leaf."

"But you would have grown mighty impatient of all that after a while."

"Very likely indeed. And yet I doubt it; for never being in earnest myself, I admire it in others," she said.

"Never in earnest and never of one mind! 'Tis a poor character, and I'd not like to hear anybody give it to you but yourself, Honor."

"With two minds you get light and shade into life—shade at any rate. If I hadn't been—but you'll grow as weary of that as I am. Yet a woman's days are so drab if she never changes her mind—all cut and dried and dead. Why, every morning I open my eyes and hope I shall get a new idea. I love my ideas to jostle about and fight and shift and change and dance, like colours in a cloud. I like to find myself helpless, shaken, bewildered, clutching at straws. You don't understand that, Uncle Mark. Ideas are the beautiful, budding flowers of one's thoughts."

"And fixed opinions the roots—or should be. What's the value of poor blossoms 'pon the top of a tree when the storm comes an' puny petals are sent flying down wind? You talk foolishness, and you know 'tis foolishness. Done to vex me, I could almost think. 'Tis your ideas that make you miserable now. A feather in a gale is a stable thing beside you, Honor. You must turn to books if only to please me."

She promised to do so presently, but did not keep her promise; and thus, to little purpose, oftentimes they talked. Then a circumstance quite unexpected made Honor think less of her ill fate and start into new and lively touch with her existence. After long intervals it chanced that some intelligence both of Yeoland and Stapledon reached Bear Down on the same morning; and Doctor Clack it was who brought news of his friend; while information concerning Myles came more directly from himself.

Doctor Clack dismounted with some parade, and made his announcement before Honor and her uncle. That he might perchance move the girl to emotion troubled him but little, for the physician was a staunch partisan, and held that Christopher had been very badly treated.

"A communication from the wanderer," said he. "Yeoland was leaving Sydney for his kinsman's up-country place when he wrote six weeks ago. All is well with him—at least so he declares, and—what do you think? He desires me to join him. Such a romantic notion!"

"Well?"

"Well, Mr. Endicott, positively I don't see why I should not. Little Silver without Christopher is, frankly, a howling wilderness from my point of view—a mere solitary tomb. And nobody ever ill—nobody ailing—no opportunities. When folk do succumb it means the end of them and the inevitable dose of churchyard mould—that final prescription none can escape."

"The health of the place is your highest tribute surely."

"Not at all—far from it. I've nothing to do with the matter. Drugs decaying in their vases; steel rusting in its velvet. Besides, the loneliness. A fishing-rod is but a vain thing to save a man—especially when it's close time as now; and the new people at Godleigh haven't asked me to a single shoot. In fact there's to be no shooting this year at all. So my case is desperate."

"Come and see us oftener," said Mark.

"I will; I positively must; but I think I'll go abroad. There's a saying that a man who can live quite happily alone must be one of two things: an angel, or a demon. Now I'm neither to my knowledge, and since Christo has vanished I've lived alone, and it's telling on me. I shall drift into one of those extremes, and I leave you to guess which."

"But you're always welcome everywhere, my dear Clack."

"I know it—at least I think so; but there's such fear of wearing out a welcome in a small place. Hereditary modesty, you'll say. If so, it's on the mother's side, not the father's. But, in all seriousness, why should not I join him?"

"You know your own business best. Is there money to be made there?"

"Plenty for a professional man. They are to have a qualification of their own, I believe; but at present a practitioner with English degrees gets the pull—very right and proper of course. Thus the old country drives her sons away; but not before she's arranged ample accommodation for them elsewhere—God bless her! So I'm wise to go—eh?"

"Nothing like seeing the ends of the earth and enlarging the mind," said Mark.

"Well, don't any of you develop anything in the nature of an interesting indisposition to tempt me to stop."

Margery brought in a letter at this moment as the postman had just penetrated to Bear Down—a feat he rarely accomplished much before midday. Doctor Clack wondered in secret whether her old lover had also communicated with Honor, but seeing that his own missive was charged with a general message of goodwill to all at Endicott's, he suspected the letter came from elsewhere.

Soon he was gone; then, without comment, Mark's niece read aloud a brief note from Myles Stapledon. It did no more than set forth his determination to return in a fortnight's time. Reason for the step was not given, as the writer disdained any excuse. His words were bald. "I will arrive on such a date, if convenient," he concluded; and Mark Endicott, reading ahead and reading backwards also, was saddened, even amazed, as one standing before the sudden discovery of an unsuspected weakness or obvious flaw in a work he had rejoiced to believe near perfection.

The stages by which Myles had arrived at the determination now astonishing Mark Endicott had extended over three months, and the curtain rose upon his battle exactly a week after he left the farm, for at that date he learned how the engagement between Honor and Christopher was definitely at an end, and how the latter would be on the sea before his words were read. The announcement came from Yeoland himself, and was written in London on the eve of his departure. Then began the fight that ended with a determination to return, and caused such genuine disappointment in Mr. Endicott. Mark, however, forgot the force of the passion his niece had awakened in this man; and certain it is that neither he nor any other could have guessed at the storm which swept Stapledon's soul when he learned how Honor had regained her freedom. Soaked as he was in love, to remain away from Endicott's with this knowledge for three months had proved no mean task to Myles. The battle fought and won with his passion while it had no right to exist proved but a prelude to encounters far more tremendous upon Christopher Yeoland's departure.

There grew within him a web of sophistry spun through sleepless nights. This at first, with the oncoming of morning, he swept away; but, spider-like, and with a spider's patience, the love in him renewed each mesh, and asked his conscience a question that his conscience seemed powerless to answer. He fought, yet knew not the name of the foe. To-day he marvelled at his own hesitation, and asked himself what still held him back; to-morrow a shadow of Yeoland shamed his troubled longings, and the word of Mark Endicott, "between you is a great gulf fixed," reverberated drearily upon his thoughts. Then the cloud castles fell to earth, and the sanguine glow upon their pinnacles vanished away. Yet against that saying of the blind man's every pulse in his body often throbbed furiously. He knew better, and Honor knew better also. It was not for nothing that they had walked over the Moor together; not for nothing they had stood silently, each by the other's side, on moonlight nights.

Out of darkness Christopher Yeoland sometimes took shape, but only as an abstraction that grew more misty with passage of days. He had gone for all time; and Honor was left alone. Myles burnt to know something of her mind; how much or how little she had forgotten; how much or how little she wondered at his attitude; in what she blamed him; whether such blame grew daily greater or was already fading away—perhaps along with his own image—in her recollection.

The great apparition of Duty rose. In the recent past he had made others supremely unhappy and tormented himself. That was over; and now—the slave of duty from his youth up—he stood in doubt. For the first time the man discerned no clear sign-post pointing to his road. Wherein lay duty now? He wearied his brain with dialectics. Sometimes duty looked a question of pure love; sometimes it hardened into a problem of pure logic. He would have risked all that he had for one glimpse of Honor's attitude towards the position; and finally he decided that his duty lay in ascertaining that attitude. This much might very easily be done without a word upon the vital theme. He told himself that a few hours under the same roof with her—the sound of her voice, the light in her eyes—would tell him all he needed to know. He dinned this assurance upon his own mind; but his heart remained dead, even before such a determination, and the cloud by no means lifted itself from off him. He presented the somewhat uncommon spectacle of a man trying to deceive himself and failing. His natural instincts of justice and probity thrust Christopher Yeoland again and again into his thoughts. He began three letters to the traveller on three separate occasions, but these efforts ended in fire, and the letter that was written and posted went to Bear Down.

Through turmoil, tribulation, and deepening of frontal furrows he reached this step, and the deed done, his night thickened around him instead of lifting as he had hoped and trusted. Perhaps the blackest hour of all was that wherein he rode through familiar hamlets under the Moor upon his way to Honor. Then came the real sting of the certainty that he had lapsed from his own lofty rule; and love itself forsook him for a space beneath Cosdon's huge shadow at sunset time. He hastened, even galloped forward to the sight of the woman; he told himself that in her presence alone would be found balm to soothe this hurt; and the very feebleness of the thought fretted him the more.

So he came back, and Chance, building as her custom is on foundations of the trivial, wrought from his return the subsequent fabric of all his days. For out of the deliberate action, whether begun in laughter or prayer, whether prompted by desire or inspired by high ambition, springs issue, and no deed yet was ever barren of consequence, hidden or revealed. Never, since conscious intelligence awakened here, has that invention of the dunces justified itself—never once has any god from any chariot of fire descended to cut one sole knot in a tangle of earthly affairs. The seeds of human actions are sown to certain fruition but uncertain crop, and Fate and Chance, juggling with their growth, afford images of the highest tragedy this world has wept at; conjure from the irony of natural operations all that pertains to sweet and bitter laughter; embrace and environ the whole apparition of humanity's progress through time. Life's pictures, indeed, depend upon play of ridiculous and tragic chance for their rainbow light, for their huge spaces of formless and unfathomable shadow, for their ironic architecture, their statuary of mingled mice and mountains—flung together, fantastic and awful. In Titan visions these things are seen by lightning or by glow-worm glimmer; or sunned by laughter; or rained upon with tears; or taking such substance and colour as wings above the reach of either.

Thus, his deed done, through chaos of painful thoughts, came Myles Stapledon; and then, standing amid the naked beds of Bear Down garden, he found Honor Endicott's little hand in his at last. Whereupon he whispered to his soul that he had acted wisely, and was now about to pass from storm into a haven of great peace.

CHAPTER XIII.
SNOW ON SCOR HILL

There came a day when Honor and Myles rode out upon a dry and frozen Moor under the north wind. The man, who had brought his own great horse to Endicott's, now galloped beside Honor's pony, and the pace warmed them despite the extreme coldness of the weather. Presently, upon their homeward way from Watern's granite castles, they stopped to breathe their horses, where a ring of horrent stones sprouted abrupt, uneven, irregular, out of the waste, and lay there, the mark of remote human activity. All the valley presented a stern spectacle unsoftened by any haze, untouched by any genial note of colour. The Moor's great, iron-grey bosom panted for coming snow; and Teign, crying among her manifold stairways, streaked the gorges with ghostly foam light, where naked sallows and silver birches tossed lean arms along the river. Only the water offered action and sound in the rocky channels; all else, to the horizon of ashy hills under a snow-laden sky, waited and watched the north.

Two horses stood steaming in Scor Hill Circle—that ancient hypæthral high place of the Damnonians—while their riders surveyed the scene and one another. Both long remembered the incident, and for them, from that day forward, the spot was lighted with a personal significance, was rendered an active and vital arena, was hallowed by interest more profound than its mere intrinsic attributes of age and mystery had formerly imparted to it.

Myles Stapledon did not reach the speedy conclusion he anticipated upon return to Bear Down. A month had now lapsed since his arrival, and, while very thoroughly assured of his own sentiments, while gulfed and absorbed, heart and soul, in a transcendent love of Honor that swept all before it and left him a man of one hope, one daily prayer, he had yet to learn her explicit attitude. His own humility helped to blind him a little at first, but she made no attempt to disguise her pleasure in his society, and by her unconventional companionship and intercourse wakened strong hopes within him. For he attached an obvious meaning to many actions, that had perhaps been conclusive of intention in any other woman, but were not in Honor. She went everywhere with him alone—to Chagford on horseback, to Exeter by train. Moreover, she let her cousin do as he would with the farm, and when he suggested embarking further capital and acquiring a half interest of all—she made no personal objection, but consulted Mr. Endicott. The inevitable sequel now stared Bear Down in the face, yet, when his niece put the question to him in private, Mark refused to give advice.

"That's a point none can well decide but yourself," he said. "The future's your own, as far as a human being can claim such control. As you act now, so the man will assume you mean to do afterwards."

"I mean nothing at all but the welfare of the farm and—you won't advise, then?"

"No. It looks all cut and dried to me."

Honor stamped her foot like a child.

"Everything's always cut and dried in my hateful life—try as I will," she said. Then she swept away, and he knitted on without visible emotion, though not lacking an inner sympathy. For he understood her desire to escape from the monotonous, and foresaw how this imminent incident would not bring about that end. Personally Stapledon had served to brighten his sightless life not a little, had set new currents running in his mind, had sweetened back waters grown stagnant by disuse; for Myles, as Endicott believed, was fine metal—wise, self-contained even in his love, a sober and discreet man—super-excellent save in the matter of his return to Bear Down. Even there, however, on second thoughts, Mark did not judge him. He only felt the lover to be human, and it was viewed in the character of a husband for Honor that the old man regarded his nephew without enthusiasm. Stapledon's very goodness, simplicity, and content with rural interests would suffice to weary the wife he wanted soon or late. And Christopher Yeoland must probably return to his home some day.

Thus he argued, but, meantime, full of hope, and arriving at a right logical conclusion on a wrong hypothesis of logical intention in Honor, Stapledon resolved to speak. And now, before the beauty of her, kissed into a sparkle by her gallop, her bosom rising and falling, a tiny cloud around her lips, caught and carried away by the wind at each expiration—before this winter vision his heart found a tongue; and, as they walked their horses in the grey circle, he spoke.

"It's a strange place this to tell you, yet these things are out of one's keeping. I must say it I must. Honor, do you care for me at all?"

"Of course I care for you."

"Do you love me?"

"Now, dear Myles, please don't say anything to make me cry in this wind. Think of the freezing misery of it! Please—Please."

"To make you cry! I hope not—indeed. I hope not that. Yet it's solemn enough—the most solemn thing a man can say to a woman."

"That's all right, then," she said cheerfully. "Nothing solemn ever makes me cry."

He looked bewildered, wistful, and her heart smote her; but the inopportune fiend would speak. She remembered how that Christopher had proposed marriage in a flippant spirit, while she craved for something so different. Here was no frivolous boy in a sunny wood, but a strong, earnest man under skies full of snow. His great voice and his eyes aflame made her heart beat, but they had no power to alter her mood.

"I love you!" he said simply. "I loved you long before I knew it, if you can believe so strange a thing. I loved you, and, finding it out, I left you and poured all the bitter blame on myself that I could. Then I heard how you had agreed to part. He was going. He went. And now I stand before you all yours. You are unlinked by any tie. He said so—he——"

"Oh you wretches of one idea!" she burst out, interrupting him. "You self-absorbed, self-seeking, selfish men! How can I explain? How can I lay bare my weaknesses before such superiority? He was the same—poor Christo—just the same. I suppose nearly all of you must be; and women are frightened to speak for fear of shocking you. So we pretend, and win from you a character for huge constancy that we often deserve no more than you do. Why attribute so many virtues to us that you don't possess yourselves? Why demand a single, whole-hearted, utter, ineffable love from us that not one in a thousand of you can give?"

"All this is nothing to the purpose," he said in a puzzled voice. "What can you answer, Honor?

"Well, I'll speak for myself, not for the hosts of single-hearted women. I won't tar them with my black brush. You want me to marry you, Myles?"

"God knows how dearly."

"And because I love you, you think I ought to marry you. Yet if I love somebody else too? I wish I had fine words, though perhaps plain ones are better to describe such an unheroic muddle. When I told Christo I loved you—yes, I told him that—he bowed his head as though he had heard his death knell. Yet I did not tell him I loved him less than before."

"You still love him?"

"Of course I do. Can a quarrel kill a live love? He was made for somebody to love him. And I love you—love you dearly too. And I'm not ashamed of it, however much you may think I should be."

"The end of that?" he said drearily.

"Clear enough. I've spoilt two lives—no, not all, I hope, but a part of two lives."

"It is I that have done so," he answered bitterly and slowly; then he stopped his horse and looked aloft where scattered flakes and patches of snow began to float heavily downward from the upper grey.

"No, no, no," said Honor. "It's just a snappy, snarling, unkind fate that wills it so. Two's company, and three's none, of course."

"Your knowledge is imperfect," he said, "and so your argument is vain. If you were a type, the foundation of civilisation would fail. Surely no woman worth thinking of twice can love in two places at once?"

"Then think of me no more," she answered, "for I do—if I know love at all. Is not the moon constant to earth and sun? A woman can love two men—as easily as a man can love two women. You couldn't—I know that; but you're not everybody. Most men can. Christianity has made a noble, exalted thing of love, and I was born into the Christian view. Yet I'm unfortunately a barbarian by instinct. Just an accidental primitive heathen who has cropped up in a respectable family. You can't alter any particular cranky nature by pruning. Oh, dear Myles, if I could marry you both! You for the working weeks and Christo for Sundays and holidays!"

He merely gasped.

"Yet I love to think you love me. But you know what naughty children say when they're crossed? I can't have you both, so I won't have either."

"This you say for love of him?"

"Don't trouble to find reasons. At any rate I'm speaking the truth. Should I have confessed to such a depraved and disgraceful frame of mind to a man I love if I had not been deadly serious despite laughter? Hate me, if you must, but I don't deserve it. I would marry you and be a good wife too; but there's a sort of sense of justice hid in me. Christo noticed it. So don't drive me into marriage, Myles dear."

"You love him better than me at any rate?"

"Arithmetic can't be brought to bear upon the question. I love you both."

There was a pause; then she added suddenly—

"And if there were a hundred more men like you and Christopher, I should love them all. But there are no more."

"You've got a big heart, Honor."

"Don't be unkind to me. It's a very unhappy heart."

"It should not be."

"That fact makes it so much the more unhappy."

"Do you know your own mind in this matter?"

"Of course I don't. Haven't you found that out?"

"It's going to snow," he said. "We'd better hurry."

"No, walk to the top of the hill; I like it."

"You must be made happy somehow," he continued. "It's everybody's duty who loves you to make you that, if it can be done."

"You great, generous thing! How I wish I could do what you ask me to; but I should be haunted if I did. You don't want a haunted wife, Myles?"

"Leave that. I have spoken and you have answered. I shall not speak again, for I pay you the respect and honour to believe your 'No' means no."

"Yes," she said; "you would." Then she turned away from him, for her tears were near at last. "Every flake lies on the frozen ground. D'you see how black the spotless snowflakes look against the sky? Isn't there some moral or other to be got out of that, Myles?"

"Why did you let me buy half Endicott's?" he asked, not hearing her last speech.

"Because you wanted to. And I wanted some money."

"Money!"

"Yes—I can tell you just at this moment. It will help to show you what I am. I sent a thousand pounds to Christo."

"He'll never take it!"

"Of course not. Yet, somehow, it comforted me for quite two days to send it."

"How we fool ourselves—we who think we stand firm! I fancied I was getting to understand you, Honor, and I knew nothing."

"You'd know everything, and find that everything was nothing if you weren't in love. There's nothing to know beyond the fact that I'm a very foolish woman. Uncle Mark understands me best. He must do so, for he can always make me angry, sometimes even ashamed."

Snow began to fall in earnest, and fluttered, tumbled, sidled, scurried over the Moor. The wind caught it and swept it horizontally in tattered curtains;

the desolation grew from grey into white, from a spotted aspect, still lined and seamed with darkness, into prevailing pallor. The tors vanished; the distance was huddled from sight; Honor's astrakhan hat caught the snow, and her habit also. She shook her head, and shining drops fell from her veil. Then Myles went round to ride between her and the weather, and they hastily trotted down the hill homeward.

Already a mask of snow had played magic pranks with the world, reduced known distances, distorted familiar outlines, brought remote objects close, dwarfed the scene, and much diminished its true spaciousness. The old familiar face of things was swallowed by a new white wilderness, like in unlikeness to the earth it hid.

Early darkness closed down upon the land before tremendous snow. Within the farm candles guttered, carpets billowed, cold draughts thrust chill fingers down stone passages, and intermittent gusts of wind struck upon the casement, like reverberations of a distant gun.

CHAPTER XIV.
THE WISDOM OF DR. CLACK

That night, despite the heavy snow, and not averse from a struggle with the weather, Myles set out, after supper, for Little Silver, three-quarters of a mile distant, in the valley beneath Bear Down. Progress was difficult, but though snow already stood above Stapledon's knees in the drifts, he found strength more than sufficient for the battle, and presently brought a blast of cold air and a snow wreath into the small dwelling of Doctor Clack, as he entered without formal announcement. Courteney Clack—deeply immersed in packing for his departure—marvelled at the advent of any visitor on such a night and abandoned his labours.

"Get out of that coat and come to the fire," he said. "I'm afraid this means something serious, or you wouldn't have turned out in such a tempest. Who's ill, and what's amiss?"

"Nobody—nothing. I wanted this wild weather against my face to give me a buffet. I also want a talk with you—if I can trespass on your time."

The physician was much relieved to learn that it would not be necessary for him to go out of doors.

"I sail on Thursday," he said, "but, until that date, I am, as usual, at the beck and call of all the world. Sit down and I'll get the necessary ingredients. Need I say that I refer to a glass of punch?"

"In six weeks," began Myles abruptly, "you'll be seeing Christopher Yeoland."

"God willing, that pleasure is in store for me."

Stapledon took out his pipe, and began to fill it mechanically.

"I want you to do a very delicate thing," he said. "The task will need even all your tact and skill, doctor. Yet it happens that if I had to pick a man out of England, I should have chosen you."

"Now that must be flattery—a mere country apothecary."

"No, it's true—for particular reasons. You are Yeoland's best friend."

"A proud privilege. I have his word for it."

"And, therefore, the man of all others to tackle him. Yet it's not to your personal interest either. I'll be frank. That is only fair to you. In the first place, what was the position between Miss Endicott and your friend when he finally left here?"

"Well, Stapledon, I suppose you've the right to ask, if anybody has; and not being blind, I can't speak the truth, perhaps, without hurting you. The rupture was pretty complete, I fancy—final in fact. I didn't know whether to be glad or sorry. Miss Honor is a girl who wants a tight hand over her. I say it quite respectfully, for her good—and yours."

"Don't drag me in, Clack. The point is that she still loves Yeoland. That's what I came here to explain to you. It is right that he should know it, and you are the man to tell him. The information must come from yourself, remember—from nobody else. The point is, how are you to be furnished with proofs?"

"Are you sure there exist proofs? Is it true?"

"She told me so herself."

Doctor Clack had little difficulty in guessing at the nature of the conversation wherein such a confession had made a part. He was impulsive, and now did a thing that a moment's reflection had left undone. He stretched out his hand and gripped Stapledon's.

"I'm sorry," he said. "You have my sincere sympathy. Forgive me if I offend."

Myles flushed, and as the other had been surprised into sudden speech, so now was he. Indeed he answered most unexpectedly, on the spur of the moment, stung thereto by this assault on self-esteem.

"You mistake!" he answered. "She loves me also."

Doctor Clack whistled.

"How spacious! These times are really too cramped for such a girl. This is the sort of knot that could be cut so easily in mediæval days; but now the problem is most difficult. You want to drop out of the running in favour of Christo? Carlyle says that the heroic slumbers in every heart. It woke in Yeoland's when he turned his back on Little Silver and everything that made life worth living for him. Now it wakes in you."

"I do not want her life to be made a lonely, wretched thing by any act of mine."

"Of course not."

"We must save her from herself."

"Ah, that means that she has announced a determination not to marry at all."

"Yes. We are both so much to her that she cannot marry either."

The doctor smothered a smile—not at Stapledon's speech, but before the monumental sternness with which he uttered it.

"How characteristic!"

"Against that, however, I have the assurance that she does not know her own mind. Women, I think, if I may say so without disrespect and upon slight experience, are very contradictory. Miss Endicott has not been in the habit of analysing her emotions. Not that she is not lucidity itself. But—well, if he were here and I—if I were out of the way—I only want her happiness. It seems to lie there. He must come back to her. I can't say all I feel about this, but you understand."

"You're set on her happiness. Very altruistic and all the rest; but I'm afraid she's not built for it. To get happiness into her life will be difficult. Too humorous to be happy, don't you think? Omar al Khattab remarks, very wisely, that four things come not back to man or woman. They are the spoken word, the sped arrow, the past life, and the neglected opportunity. She sent Yeoland about his business. Now there is a sort of love that won't brook cruelty of that pattern."

"Cruelty's too big a word for it. She called it a lover's quarrel herself. Eliminate me, and judge whether the spoken word might not be retrieved and forgotten if he came back to her again."

"Of course improbability's the only certainty with a woman. Don't fancy I'm letting my own interest stand in the way. I, too, in common with all human clay, contain the germ of the heroical. I'll tell Christo everything; that he still has half—is it half or a lesser or greater fraction?—of Miss Honor Endicott's heart. Here we are—three able-bodied men: you, Christo, and myself. Well, surely with a little expenditure of brain tissue we can—eh? Of course. One of you chaps is the obstacle to the other. You pull her heart different ways. She is suspended between your negative and positive attractions like a celestial body, or a donkey between two bundles of hay. So you both go free. Now, if one of you heroes could only find comfort in another woman such a circumstance might determine—you follow me?"

"Her happiness?"

"Not so much her happiness as her destination. Well, I'll urge upon Yeoland the advisability of coming home; I'll tell him how things stand, and of course keep you out of it."

"She would be happier with him than with me: that's the point."

"Say rather: that's the question. He may not think so. I don't want to flatter you, but I don't think so myself. There is that in Christo not usually associated with the domestic virtues. He and I are bachelors by instinct—natural, unsophisticated beasts, in no sense educated up to the desirable and blessed, but extremely artificial, state of matrimony. You, on the contrary, are a highly trained creature with all your emotions under your own control, and capable of a consistent unselfishness in the affairs of life which is extremely rare in the male animal. No; merely considered as a husband, Christo would not have a look in with you—could hardly expect to get a vote—certainly not mine."

"He might make a better husband for Honor."

"Not for any woman."

"Don't tell him so, if you think it."

"Leave me to do what I deem wise. Like you, I'm solely actuated with a desire to brighten Miss Endicott's life. But you must not dictate my line of action. My judgment is not wont to be at fault."

"I know that very well. This great cause is safe in your hands. Put it first. Put it first, before everything. You can't feel as I do, and as Yeoland must; but you're a man of very wide sympathy—that's to say a man of genius more or less. And you're his first friend—Yeoland's, I mean; so for his sake—and hers——"

"And yours—yes. I shall glory in bringing this matter to an issue—happy for choice, but definite at any rate—if only to prove all your compliments are not vain. Light your pipe and drink, and fill your glass again."

"No more—perfect punch—perfect and very warming to the blood."

"Your punch-maker, like your poet, is born. The hereditary theory of crime, you know."

"Now I must get up the hill. And thank you, Clack. You've lightened my anxiety, I think. We shall meet again before you go?"

"Certainly—unless you are all snowed up at Bear Down. Good-night! Gad! I hope nobody will want me! Not my weather at all."

The storm screamed out of the darkness. Beyond a narrow halo of light from Courteney Clack's open door all was whirling snow and gloom; and through it, his head down, Stapledon struggled slowly back to the farm.

The significance of his own position, the bitterness of his defeat, the nature of his loss, and the gnawing sting of suffering had yet to come. This effort to ameliorate the lonely life of Honor by bringing Yeoland back into it was indeed laudable; but mere consciousness of right has no power to diminish the force of great blows or obliterate the awful meaning of a reverse in love. His future stretched desolate as the weather before Myles Stapledon, and these physical exercises under the storm, together with his attempts on behalf of others, might serve to postpone, but could not diminish by one pang, the personal misery in store for him.

CHAPTER XV.
SUN DANCE

On the morning of Easter Sunday, some three months after the departure of Doctor Clack from Little Silver, certain labouring men in their best broadcloth ascended Scor Hill at dawn. Jonah Cramphorn, Churdles Ash, Henry Collins, and the lad Tommy Bates comprised this company, and their purpose was to behold a spectacle familiar and famous in ancient days but unheeded and little remembered at the period of these events. Ash had attracted the younger men to see the sun dance on Easter morn, and of those who accompanied him, Mr. Cramphorn was always willing to honour a superstition, no matter of what colour; Collins came to gain private ends; while the boy followed because he was promised a new experience.

"T'others may go to the Lard's Table for their bite an' sup, an' a holy act to theer betterment no doubt," declared Churdles; "but, for my paart, 'tis a finer deed to see the gert sun a-dancin' for sheer joy 'pon Resurrection Marnin', come it happen to be fine. A butivul day, sure enough, an' the elements all red an' blue, like the Saviour's clothes in the window-glasses to church."

Mr. Ash's dim eyes scanned the sweetness of an April sky, and the party moved onward to the crown of the hill. Through pearly dews they went, and passed forward where the soft, green mantle of on-coming spring hung like a veil on hedgerows and over wild waste places. A world stretched before them lighted by the cold purity of spotless dawn, and the day-spring, begemmed with primrose stars, was heralded by thrushes in many a dingle, by the lark on high. As yet earth lay in the light that is neither sunshine nor shadow, but out of the waxing blue above, from whence, like a shower, fell his tinkling rhapsody, one singing bird could see the sun, and himself shone like a little star.

To the upland heath and granite plodded these repositories of obsolescent folk-lore; and they talked as they went, the better to instil Collins and the boy with a proper understanding in the matter of those superstitions a scoffing generation agreed to disregard. Henry, on his part, felt more than uneasy, for he much doubted the sanctity of this present step. But love was responsible; Collins pined for Sally in secret, and his great desire to conciliate Mr. Cramphorn was such that, when Jonah invited him to the present observation, he undertook at once to be of the party. Now he recollected that he had also promised the vicar to go to the Sacrament that morning.

"You must knaw," said Churdles Ash to Tommy, "that this holy season be a gert time for signs an' wonders up-along an' down-along. I tell 'e these things, 'cause you'm a young youth, an' may profit an' hand 'em on to your childern in fulness of time. Theer be Gude Friday—a day of much vartue, I assure 'e. Not awnly the event o' the Lard's undoing by they bowldacious Jews, but the properest for plantin' vegetables in the whole of the year."

"An' the best for weanin' of childern," said Mr. Cramphorn. "Sally was weaned 'pon that day, an' went straight to cow's milk so natural an' easy as a born calf; an' look at her now!"

Mr. Collins sighed deeply.

"Butivulest gal in Debbensheer, I reckon," he said.

Jonah grunted assent, and Henry, feeling the moment for a certain vital question had arrived, mopped his wet brow and tremulously approached the matter.

"Fall back a pace or two, will 'e, maister? Your darter—I daresay you might have seed as I was a bit hit in that quarter?"

"I've seed it, I grant you. I'm all eyes wheer my gals be consarned."

"These things caan't be helped. I mean no disrespect, I'm sure. 'Tis the voice of nature in a man."

"I'm sorry for 'e, Henery."

"For that matter I couldn't wish myself out o' the evil, though 'tis perplexin' an' very onrestful to my head. I be mazed when I consider how a man of my modest way could think twice 'bout a rare piece like Sally. Never seed such a wonnerful strong arm 'pon any woman in all my born days."

Jonah frowned and shook his head.

"Never mind her paarts. Don't become you or any man to name a limb of her separate from the rest. Baan't respectful!"

"Then I'm sorry I said it. An' as for respectfulness, I'd go on my bended knees to her to-morrow."

"Have you?" inquired the parent. "That's the question. Have 'e axed her an' got a answer?"

"Not for the world," stammered Henry. "Not for the world afore gettin' your leave. I knaw my plaace better."

Mr. Cramphorn's nose wrinkled as though it had caught an evil odour.

"Bah! You say that! You'm so chicken-hearted that you come to me 'fore you go to she! Then I sez 'No.' I forbids you to speak a word of the matter, for I reckon your way be more tame an' soft than the likes of her or any other high-spirited female would suffer."

"You'm tu violent—I swear you be," protested Mr. Collins. "You'd have been the fust to blame me if I'd spoke wi'out axin' you. Besides, caan't a man talk apart from usin' his tongue in this matter? I've a looked at her time an' again wi' all the power of the eye. Theer's a language in that, an' she knawed what I meant, or I'm a fule."

"Theer be such a language for sartain," admitted Jonah; "but not for you. No more power o' speech in your gert eyes than a bullock's—I don't mean as it's to be counted any fault in you, but just the will of Nature. An' so enough's said."

"Quick! Run, the pair of 'e!" cried Tommy's voice. "Her's risin' nigh the edge o' Kes Tor Rock all copper-red!"

Cramphorn quickened his pace, and Collins, now merged in blank despair, strode alter him. Together they approached Mr. Ash, and joined the aged man upon a little granite elevation at the south-eastern extremity of Scor Hill. Below them, a watercourse, now touched to fire, wound about the shoulder of the elevation; and beneath, much misty, new-born verdure of silver birch and sallow, brightened the fringe of fir woods where Teign tumbled singing to the morning.

Over against the watchers, lifted above a grey glimmer of ruined Damnonian hut villages and primæval pounds, there towered the granite mass of Kes Tor, and from the distant horizon arose the sun. He bulked enormous, through the violet hazes of nightly mist that now dwindled and sank along the crowns of the hills; then the effulgent circle of him, ascending, flashed forth clean fire that flamed along unnumbered crests and pinnacles of far-flung granite, that reddened to the peaty heart each marsh and mire, each ridge and plane of the many-tinted garment that endued the Moor.

Silently the labourers watched sunrise; then was manifested that heliacal phenomenon they had come to see. A play of light, proper to the sun at ascension, ran and raced twinkling round his disc; and, like an empyreal wheel, the blazing star appeared to revolve and spin upon its upward way.

"He be dancin'! He be dancin', now!" declared Mr. Ash.

"For sure, if I could awnly keep the watter out o' my eyes," added Jonah; while Collins, by his comment, reflected personal tribulations and exhibited an impatient spirit in presence of this solemn display.

"I've seed un shimmer same as that scores o' times on working-days," he said sourly.

"Granted—in a lesser fashion; but not like he be doin' now. He knaws as the Lard o' Hosts leapt forth from the tomb to the biddin' of cherub angels 'pon this glad marnin'—nobody knaws it better than him. An', for all his size, he'm as giddy an' gay an' frolicsome by reason of it, as the high hills what hop in the Psalms o' David."

Thus speaking, Gaffer Ash regarded the source of light with a benignant and indulgent smile.

"An' us all did ought to feel the same, I'm sure," moralised Jonah Cramphorn, wiping the tears from his eyes and blinking at a huge red spot now stamped upon his retina and reproduced in varying size against everything which he regarded. "For my part I hold that not a heathen in the land but ought to rise into a gude Christian man afore that gert act."

They waited and watched until the growing glory defied their vision; then all started to return homewards, and both the elder men declared themselves much refreshed, invigorated, and gladdened by what they had seen. Each, inspired by the incident, occupied himself with time past and matters now grown musty. They related stories of witches and of ghosts; they handled omens, and callings, and messages from dead voices heard upon dark nights; they explained the cryptic mysteries hidden in hares and toads, in stars, in 'thunder-planets,' and the grasses of the field. They treated of turning stones against an enemy; of amulets to protect humanity from the evil eye; of ill-wishing and other magical misfortunes; of oil of man; and of the good or sinister forces hidden in wayside herbs.

"'Tis the fashion 'mongst our young school-gwaine fules to laugh at auld saws an' dark sayings because theer teachers laugh at 'em; but facts doan't change, though manners may," said Mr. Cramphorn. "Theer's witches descended from Bible witches, same as theer be saints an' 'postles comed from laying on of hands. An' Cherry Grepe's of 'em; she doan't want for power yet, or my brain be no better'n tallow. I seed Chowne's oxen charmed into gude health again, an' gerter wonders than that onder my awn eyes. Ten shillin' she had of mine—" he added, lowering his voice for the ear of Mr. Ash alone—"ten shillin' to bring harm 'pon Christopher Yeoland. An' she drawd a circle against un before my faace an' done a charm wi' wax an' fire. ''Twill all act presently,' she said; and act it did, as you knaw, for he'm crossed in love, an' a wanderer 'pon the faace of the airth, like Cain at this minute; an' worse to come, worse to come."

Mr. Ash looked very uneasy.

"I could wish as you hadn't told me that," he answered. "You'm allus lickin' your lips on it, an' I'd rather not knaw no more. Ban't a pleasant side o' your carater."

Shouts from Tommy interrupted Churdles, and all looked where the boy pointed—to see some white object vanish under a gate before their eyes. As for himself, heedless of Cramphorn's loud warning, Tommy Bates picked up a stone and ran after the object.

"'Ful to me!" cried Cramphorn, "did 'e see it—a rabbit as I'm a sinful man!"

"The white coney o' Scor Hill! An' that's death wi'in the year to some wan us knaws! Fegs! A bad business for sartain."

"Death inside the week," corrected Jonah solemnly. "It may have awvertook some poor neighbour a'ready."

"Or it may be ordained for wan of ourselves," murmured Mr. Ash gloomily.

"I wish to Christ I'd gone to church then!" burst out Collins. "For it's been a cruel hard marnin' for me from time I rose, sun dance or no sun dance; an' now to cap it wi' this gert, hidden calamity, an' death in the wind."

"Sure as night follows day," declared Churdles Ash.

The love-sick Collins tramped on his way without further speech; Tommy did not return from pursuit of the apparition, and Ash argued with Cramphorn as to who might now be numbered with the majority. Upon this delicate point they could by no means agree; and they were still wrangling as to the identity of their ill-starred acquaintance when a man met them hard by the main entrance of Bear Down, and they saw that it was Myles Stapledon.

After Doctor Clack's departure and within a few days of the scene in gathering snow upon Scor Hill, Myles had left Endicott's and taken him rooms at Little Silver, in the dwelling of Noah Brimblecombe, sexton to the parish. This man owned a pleasant abode somewhat greater than a cottage—an establishment the bulk of which its possessor annually under-let to advantage in the summer months. Hither came the rejected, his plans for the future still unformed. And here he dwelt for three long months and laboured like a giant to crush the agony of his spirit, the black misery of every waking hour. Bear Down once thoroughly invigorated by his capital and improved by his knowledge, he determined to leave; but while work still remained to do he stopped at the gates of the farm and exercised a painful self-control. Honor he saw not seldom, but the former friendship, while still quite possible for her, was beyond the power of the man. She pitied him, without wholly understanding; and very sincerely pitied herself in that circumstances now deprived her not a little of his cherished society. The difficulty lay in her attitude towards him. To behave as one who loved him was impossible under the constraint that now hedged him in; so she attempted to imitate his manner, and failed. A great awkwardness and unreality characterised present relations, and Honor found in these circumstances ample matter for mental distraction, if only of a painful nature; while Stapledon waited for the season of spring to finish his labours, and counted that each post might bring some message from Christopher.

To-day he had news definite and tremendous enough The last of the Yeolands was coming back to his fathers—that he might sleep amongst them; for he was dead.

With a face darkened, Myles asked Cramphorn where he might find Mr. Endicott, and Jonah, seeing that something was amiss, himself made an inquiry.

"Maister Mark be in the garden most likely. An' what ill's walkin' now, sir, if a man may ax? Theer's a black story in your faace as you caan't hide."

"Black enough," said Stapledon shortly. "You'll know in good time."

He passed by and left them staring.

"That dratted white rabbit!" murmured Mr. Ash; while the messenger of sorrow approached Mark, where he walked up and down under the walls of the farm, beside uprising spikes of the orange-lilies and early growth of other things that stood along his way.

"You, Stapledon? Good morning. There's the feel of fine weather on my cheek."

Above them a window, set in cherry-buds, stood open, and within Honor, who had just returned with her uncle from a celebration of the Lord's Supper, was taking off her hat at her looking-glass.

"Good morning, uncle. I've brought some awfully sad and awfully sudden news. Here's a letter from Clack. I rode early to Chagford about another letter I expected, and found this waiting, so saved the postman. Christopher Yeoland—he has gone—he is dead."

"Dead! So young—so full of life! What killed him?"

"Died of a snake-bite near Paramatta. It's an orange-growing district near Sydney, so the doctor says. He was there with his cousin—an old settler—a survivor from a cadet branch of the family, I fancy. And it seems that it was Yeoland's wish to lie at home—his last wish."

"Then no doubt Clack will look to it. Gone! Hard to credit, very hard to credit."

"I'm thinking of Honor. It will be your task to tell her, I fear. My God! I can't believe this. I had hoped for something so different. She loved him— she loved him still."

"Is there any reason why she should not read the letter?" asked Mr. Endicott.

"None—not a line she need not see. It is very short—cynically short for Clack. He was probably dazed when he wrote; as I am now."

"Give it to me, then. I will go up to her at once. Yes, I must tell her—the sooner the better."

But Honor Endicott knew already. She had heard through her casement, and stood like a stone woman staring up into the blue sky when Mark knocked at her door.

"Come in, uncle," she said; and then continued, as he entered groping, "I have heard what you want to say. So you are spared that. Give me the letter and I will read it to you."

"You know!"

"My window was open. I could not choose but hear, for the first word chained me. Christo is dead."

He held out the letter and left her with it; while she, as yet too shocked to see or feel beyond the actual stroke, read tearlessly.

And, gazing with the eye of the mind through those great spaces that separated her from this tragedy, she saw her old lover again, remembered his joy of life, heard his laughter, and told herself that she had killed him.

Below, in the kitchen, all Bear Down assembled about breakfast. Then Mark Endicott told the company this news, and unutterable glances passed between Ash, Cramphorn, and Collins.

"You'd best to keep dumb 'bout your share, Jonah," muttered Churdles under his breath, with round eyes that indicated aversion. "I wouldn't say the law mightn't overget 'e, if it knawed."

"As to that, I fear nothin', an' the tears I shed won't drown a midge," answered the other in a defiant whisper. "I've forgived his wrong; forget it I never shall."

Collins was busy telling Sally and Margery of the spectral rabbit.

"An' 'tis plain the ill-convenient beast didn't run for nought. Who shall laugh at such deeds now? Not the vainest man amongst us," he concluded.

"Him of all to go!" sighed Mrs. Loveys; "an' when us thinks of what might have been an' how one short word will make or mar a life——"

Then a question from Margery as to where Tom Bates might be was answered by the sudden appearance of that youth, and Mrs. Loveys, with a mind somewhat overwrought, found outlet for emotion in an attack upon him.

"Doan't 'e knaw the hour for eatin', you ugly li'l twoad?" she demanded sharply. "An' to come to the table in such a jakes of a mess tu! You ought to be shamed."

But the boy paid no heed. He returned breathless with a comforting discovery, and now cried it aloud to his companions of the morning.

"'Tis all right," he said; "no call for no upstore nor trouble at all. That theer white bastey I mean. I followed un half a mile to the furze meadows down-long to make sartain, then I lost un, an' presently if I didn't see un again—wi' a young rabbit he'd catched! Nought but that baggerin' auld ram cat as they've got to Creber Farm!"

"Quiet! you young fule!" said Mr. Cramphorn roughly; "shut your mouth, will 'e? or I'll scat 'e awver the ear-hole! You to pit your green brains against our ripe wans! A man be dead, an' so 'tis sartain us seed what us seed."

"Sartain as doom us seed what us seed," echoed Gaffer Ash, "for a man be dead."

CHAPTER XVI.
A SHELF OF SLATE

A blackbird, with sleepy notes and sad, warbled in a green larch at dawn; and the pathos proper to his immemorial song was well suited to the scene. For the larch raised her lovely foliage, begemmed with rubies, above many graves in the burying-place of Little Silver; and a streamlet also murmured there, uttering a sort of purring harmony that mingled with the contralto of the bird. From an ivy-tod, at hand in the grave-yard hedge, bright eyes peeped and the mother, with head and tail alone visible and sooty-brown body pressed close upon four eggs, listened to her lord. Elsewhere a man also heard the music, but heeded it not. He stood at his house door, yawned and sniffed the morning; while his whitewashed walls that faced the east were warmed into a glowing melon colour, and sunshine wove golden threads along the ancient straw of the thatch above.

Noah Brimblecombe, the sexton, was a man of middle age, with grey whiskers, clean-shaved lips and chin, a strong mouth, and a reflective forehead. His back had grown rounded by digging of graves from early manhood, and the nature of his life's labours appeared in a tinge of gloom that marked his views. He passed through the world with an almost morbid severity in his disparagement of all mundane concerns, triumphs or possessions. The man now stood and fixed his small grey eyes upon the church, but little more than a hundred yards distant. Then, bearing great keys in one hand, an inch or two of candle in the other, he proceeded to the burying-ground upon an errand connected with his calling.

Little Silver is a hamlet of almost beggarly simplicity. In the midst stands a trinity of three great buildings beneath the bosom of a hill; certain ruined barns, with a few thatched cots and a pound, embrace the remainder of the village; while a duck-pond outside the churchyard gate, orchard lands sloping to the valleys beneath, a little winding road and a stone wall, beside which grow yellow bullace plums, complete the picture. Variety in form and wide divergence in point of age characterise the central features of this spot. Paramount, by virtue of years and pristine significance, stand the ruins of Little Silver Castle; the church comes next—an erection of the customary moorland pattern, with a ring of small, sweet-toned bells, and a crocketted tower, something too tall for its breadth; while, between these two, there stands an old-time manor-house—empty as the ruined castle at the date of this narrative; but more recently repaired for habitation. Here spread the familiar theatre of Mr. Brimblecombe's life. Every stone of the old fourteenth-century castle was familiar to him, and he delighted to take chance visitors of antiquarian taste upward by a winding stair into the time-fretted, ivy-mantled abode of the lords of Little Silver. Now the sky was its covering; the lancet windows, through which once frowned war-like faces behind crossbow, matchlock, or petronel, were the dwelling of a thousand soft green things and framed the innocent eyes of wild flowers; in the upper chamber rowans stood rooted upon old hearthstones; briar and many grasses, pellitory of the wall and blue speedwells superseded bygone mural tapestries; and where antlers of the red deer hung and brazen sconces for the torch aforetime sprang, there now rose the fronds of hart's-tongue and shield ferns, with tangle of woodbine and ivy and networks of rootlets that hid the mossy homes of wrens. Beneath the ruin there still existed a dungeon-vault, gloomy and granite-groined; yet, save for broken wall and stairway, perfect as when poor wretches mouldered there at the mercy of their feudal masters. Now not so much as one spectre of a vanished sufferer haunted the place; only the bats passed their sleeping hours among the arches of the roof, and hung from five-clawed hands, with sinister, wrapped wings—like little dusky cherubim that worship with veiled faces at some mystery-seat of evil.

Mr. Brimblecombe was not concerned with castle or with church at the present time. His eye roamed forward to a ponderous mausoleum that lay amid lush grasses and rank, sappy, umbelliferous plants in a corner of the churchyard. A conical yew tree flanked each angle, and the larch, whereon a blackbird sang, extended high overhead. Here stood the vault of the Yeolands, and the last six generations of them slept within, for no further accommodation existed under the church flags, where earlier members of the race lay jowl to jowl with their historic enemies, the Prouzes. The family tomb was of granite, with white marble tablets upon three sides and a heavy metal door in the fourth or eastern face. Above grinned decoration of a sort, and the architect, following sepulture fashions at that date, had achieved a chaplet of marble skulls, which Time was toying with from year to year. Now their foreheads, their crowns, and occiputs were green and grimy; their eyes and jaws were stuffed with moss; trailing toad-flax crept out of their noses; and stray seeds, bird-planted, hung bright blossoms above them in summer-time.

Hither came Brimblecombe, and his feet stamped over the graves of many more dead than the mounds of the churchyard indicated. A young man, the sexton's assistant, sat and smoked among the marble skulls, waiting for his master there; and now he rose, put out his pipe, and gave Noah "Good morning." A moment later the blackbird had fled with a string of sharp ejaculations, for a harsh note grated upon the air as the sexton turned his key in the Yeoland vault door. A flood of light from the risen sun streamed in where, "sealed from the moth and the owl and the flitter-mouse," lay the dead. A few giant woodlice rushed to concealment before this shattering incursion of sunshine, and other curling, crawling things made like haste to disappear. Then Brimblecombe's blinking eyes accommodated themselves to the inner gloom. Two ledges of slate lay on each side of the mortuary, and coffins, whose nails had long turned green, poked head and feet from rotting palls upon three of these. The place struck very cold, with a fungus smell. A few puny fragments of asplenium found life amid the interspaces of the stone-work and lived dismally in the dark where damp oozed and granite sweated. The fourth ledge bore a coffin that held Christopher Yeoland's father, and its pall had as yet resisted the decaying influences of this gloomy spot, for only a few round circles of mould dimmed the lustre of the velvet.

It was the custom of the family that the last four of their dead should lie here upon these shelves; but now another needed his place and the most ancient of the four—a matron who had flourished in the first George's days—was to be deposed and lowered into the charnel below. Brimblecombe moved an iron grating in the floor; then, with his assistant's help, carried a slight and much tarnished shell to its place in the ultimate desolation beneath.

"'Tis awful how the watter gains down here," declared Noah. "Small wonder them ducks of Mother Libby's do graw to be so heavy. They gets the very cream an' fatness of the churchyard into 'em, an' 'tis a'most a cannibal act to eat 'em."

"'Tis lucky this here gen'leman's last of his race seemin'ly," said the younger man, raising a candle above his head and spitting among the coffins; "for theer ban't no more room to bury a beetle. Full up above an' below by the look of it."

"Last of his line—'tis so—an' comed of gude havage[#] as ever a man need to boast on. A poor end to such a high family. Just a worm stinged un an' he'm falled into lifeless dust, no better than the founder of the race. To think this heap o' rags an' bones be all that's left of a mighty folk as was."

[#] Havage = ancestry.

"An' not a Yeoland left to carry on the name, they tell me."

"Not wan, Sam Reed; not a single bud left to bloom. Auld tree be dead of sheer age, I reckon, for 'tis with families as with nations, as parson said 'pon the Sunday after auld Jarvis died. They rise up gradual an' slow to theer high-watter mark; then, gradual or fast, they tumble back into the dust wheer they started. All dust—nations an' men like you an' me—all draws our life an' power from dust—airth, or gold, or grass, or what not. An' awnly lookin' 'pon the whole story of a man or a family when 'tis told to the end, can you say wheer 'twas it reached the high-watter mark an' measure the sum weight of the gude or bad to be set against its name. Do you take me?"

Young Reed nodded.

"In paart I do," he said.

"Very well, then. Now I be gwaine to my meal."

Having made all ready for a new-comer, as yet upon the sea, Mr. Brimblecombe locked up the Yeoland vault again. He then walked to a rubbish heap at the back of the church behind the tower, there deposited the rags of a pall taken from the coffin that he had just deposed, and so returned home.

At his door stood Stapledon, smoking a pipe before breakfast; indeed of late Myles had fallen much upon tobacco and the company of his horse and dogs. But neither narcotic nor the trustful eyes of the dumb animals he loved possessed power to lighten loads that now weighed upon his heart. They lay beyond the alleviation of drug or the affectionate regard of beasts. This sudden death had shocked him immeasurably, and in process of time he began to accuse himself of it and saddle his conscience with the self-same deed that Honor had instantly committed to her own account on hearing the ill tidings. Stapledon felt that he was sole cause of the disastrous catastrophe; that by blundering blindly into the united lives of this woman and man he had destroyed the one and blackened all the future days of the other. Before this spectacle, very real, very bitter contrition and self-accusation overwhelmed him. And that the lash fell vainly rendered its sting the greater. But he could not punish himself adequately, and at length even remorse fainted before the sure knowledge that Yeoland was beyond all reach of prayer or petition. Stapledon's was not a nature that could grieve for long over an evil beyond possibility of cure. In any sort of future he disbelieved; yet, if such existed, then there might be time in it for Christopher Yeoland to settle with him. Meanwhile, a living, suffering woman remained. He thought without ceasing of Honor, he asked himself by how much this event altered his duty with regard to her, and finally determined, through turmoil of sleepless nights and much torture of the mind, to do as he had already determined before this sad news came, and leave Bear Down when certain buildings were completed and the new stock purchased.

For some weeks he had seen nothing of Honor, and purposely abstained from seeking her. Concerning her, however, he had learnt from Sally Cramphorn, who described how the mistress kept her room for two days from Easter Sunday, how she had then reappeared, dressed in mourning, and how that ever since she had spent most of her time with Mr. Endicott, and preserved an unusual silence. For nearly three weeks Honor did not pass beyond her garden; and this fact confirmed Stapledon in a suspicion that she had so acted and avoided the land to escape from sight of him. He felt such a desire natural in her, and only wondered that she had not known him well enough to rest assured he would not seek her or cross her path.

Then he learned that the girl was going from home for a while to visit an aunt at Exeter; and, once assured of her departure, he hastened to Bear Down and won a lengthy conversation with Mark Endicott. Women were at work in the kitchen; so, setting down his needles and worsted, Mark walked out of doors, took the arm Myles offered, and moved with him slowly along the hillside. They spoke first of Christopher Yeoland.

"I can't believe it yet somehow. A man so full of life and possibilities, with all the world before him to do some good in. A sad death; a cruel death."

"As to that, I don't know," answered the elder. "He's out of earshot of our opinions now, poor fellow; but I'm not ashamed to say behind his back what I told him to his face more than once. Never a man played a poorer game with his time. 'Tis the life of him looks sad and cruel to me—not the death."

"So young as he was."

"What's that? Only a woman would be soft enough to mourn there. 'Tisn't the years of a man's life that matter, but the manner of living 'em. The length of the thread's no part of our labour—only the spinning of it. He went—poor soul—but left no ball of yarn behind him—nought but a tangle of broken ends and aimless beginnings. 'Tis the moral sticking out of this I speak for—not to blame the man. God knows I don't judge him unkindly. My youth was no better spent—maybe not so well."

Stapledon's mind continued to be occupied by the former figure.

"The spinning—yes, the spinning," he said. "That's a true saying; for, if you look at it, all life's much like a ropewalk, where we toil—walking backwards—with our faces turned away from fate."

"Some are blind for choice—such as you," answered Mr. Endicott; "some judge they've got the light; some hope they have; some know they have. That last sort denies it to all but themselves, an' won't even let another soul carry a different pattern candlestick to their own. But a man may envy such high faith, for it's alive; it rounds the rough edges of life; sets folk at peace with the prospect of their own eternity; smooths the crumples in their deathbeds at the finish."

"I don't know. I've never heard that your thorough-paced believers make a better end than other folks," Myles answered. "My small experience is that they regard death with far more concern and dread than the rudderless ones who believe the grave is the end."

"That's only to say a fear of death's nature-planted and goes down deeper than dogma. Most makes of mind will always shrink from it, so long as life's good to live. Faith is a priceless treasure, say what you may, if a body has really got it. I'll maintain that so long as I can talk and think. The man who pretends he has it, and has not, carries his own punishment for that daily lie with him. For the Lord of the Blessings never could abide pretence. Take Him or leave Him; but don't play at being sheep of His fold for private ends. That's a game deserves worse damnation than most human baseness."

"Yes, yes. Take Him as He is; and take what He brought, and be thankful. Lord of the Blessings! Isn't that a title high enough? But here's my thought and sure belief, uncle. The discovery called Christianity depended on no man, no single advent of a prophet, or poet, or saviour. It was a part of human nature always, a gold bred in the very heart's core of humanity. And Christ's part was to find the gold and bring it into the light. Burn your book; let the beautiful story go. It is ruined, worm-eaten, riddled by the centuries and follies and lies heaped upon it. Sweep your institutions all clean away and Christianity remains, a sublime discovery, the glorious, highest known possibility of man's mind towards goodness. Lord of the Blessings! What dogma intrudes amongst them to blind and blight and make our hearts ache? They are alive and eternal—as all that is true must be eternal. They were waiting—hidden in human hearts—left for a man to discover, not for a God to invent. Who cares for the old dead theories that explained rainbows and precious stones, and the colour of a summer-clad heath and the strength of the solid earth? We have the things themselves. And so with the message of Christ."

"Wild man's talk," said Mark. "And quite out of your usual solid way of thought. There's more hid in the Rock of Ages than a vein of gold opened by a chance good man; but you and me won't argue on that, because we're not built to convince each other. With years may come light; Potter Time may mould a bit of faith into the fabric of even you presently; who can tell? But spin slow and sure, as you mostly do—look to the thread and see you leave no knot or kink behind as won't stand the strain that life may call it to bear any moment."

"There's another thought rises from what you said; and I'll tell you why I'm on that morbid tack in a moment. You declare the length of the thread is out of our keeping, and that a mind will shrink naturally from death so long as life is good. But how many a poor fool does determine the length and cut the thread when life ceases to be good?"

"Determine the length they don't. They are the puppets, and when the string is pulled they make their bow and go off the scene—by their own hand, if it is to be."

"Humanity holds suicide a crime now. Once, I learn, it was not so. Great heathen men destroyed themselves, yet do not lack marble statues for it. Only yesterday, as one might say, a man was cut off and buried at crossroads with a stake through his belly if he dared to die by his own hand. The Church recognises no shades of meaning in this matter, and so to-day, as often as not, a coroner's jury bleats out a solemn and deliberate lie—so that a man shall be buried with the blessing of the Church and rest in God's acre against the trump. But there's no greater piece of solemn humbug than that eternal verdict."

"I thought much of these things when my eyes were put out. I have been on the brink myself, but 'twas ordained my thread should run. A man must be mad to destroy himself—mad or else a coward."

"Most times cowardly perhaps," answered Myles. "But to be a coward is not to be a lunatic. Suicide is one of those matters we shut our eyes about—one of the things we won't face and thresh out, because the Church is so determined on the point. Not but a man may picture circumstances when a self-death would be a great deed. You may lay down your life for your friend in more ways than one. Such a thing can rise to greatness or sink to contempt according to the mainspring of the action. Some at least might think so, and that's why I'm on this subject. I feel a shadowy fear sometimes that Christopher Yeoland might have had some such fancy—would even have done such a crack-brained deed for love of Honor. I bid his friend be very plain with him and explain the gap that his going left in her life. I made it as clear as I had power to. Honor distinctly told me that she still loved him too well to marry any other man. That was all he had need to know, and I asked Clack to make Yeoland return to her on the strength of her confession."

"And now he does."

"How might he have argued when you consider his great love for her? Is it not possible that he thought so? Is it not possible that he said, 'I am the obstacle. Let me go beyond reach, and Honor—who still feels that nothing can wipe out our old understanding—will be in reality free?' Might he not reason in that way?"

The old man shook his head.

"Not to the extent of blotting himself out by death. Had the cases been reversed, I could almost picture you destroying yourself, since your views are what they are. You might do it, worse luck—Yeoland never. Besides, what necessity? Such a course would be merely like a stage play under these circumstances."

"But there was an inclination towards just that in him; towards a theatrical sort of way—unreal."

"You read him like that. But he wasn't so superficial as he seemed to a man of your build of mind. You don't find Honor superficial? No—he wouldn't kill himself, because the necessity wouldn't appear from his point of view. As I say, you'd blunder into the act much sooner than Yeoland."

"Not so at all. You misunderstand me."

"Well, at least you can't see what would be easier and pleasanter, and answer the purpose just as well under our present civilisation. Consider. How stands the problem if Yeoland married somebody else? You'll find that meets the case at every point. I'm not belittling Yeoland. Who knows what chances of greatness there may have been hidden and lost in him? Life only calls into play a thousandth part of any man's powers during his brief tale of days, and most of us die full of possibilities unguessed even by ourselves, because the hazard never rose; but Yeoland's greatness, if greatness he had, would not have led him off the stage by that road. He didn't die willingly, I promise you. Come back he might have upon your message, if he had lived; or married he might have, even out of consideration for Honor's future. We'll allow him all the credit belonging to possibilities. Meantime, the only thing that we know beyond his death is a last wish expressed to Clack—a wish quite in keeping with his character."

"To be brought home again."

"Yes, the desire to rest his bones in Little Silver. Struck for death, the thought in his mind was not death, nor Honor, nor you. His love for the grass and the trees and the earth of his mother-land woke in him; dying, his heart turned to Godleigh and his own old roof-tree. The picture of the place was the last on his brain when all things were fading away."

The other bowed his head; then he asked concerning Honor.

"It's hit her hard," answered Mark Endicott. "This sudden end of him has been a burnish on the glass of memory—polished it very bright. She has lived through the summer weather with him and talked fitfully of woodland walks by him, and chatter of birds, and shining of Teign, and cutting of letters on tree trunks. The glow and glory of love slowly growing in them— sad enough to look back on for those that love her."

"Sad enough. And my share of the pain's all too light."

"Who knows how much or how little you deserve? You were sent to play your part in her life. Just a bit of the machine. Change—change—change—that's the eternal law that twists the wheel and opens the womb; digs the grave and frets the name off the tombstone; gnaws away the stars; cools the sun in heaven and the first love of a young maid's heart. You brought something new into her life—for better or for worse. Something new and something true, as I think; but maybe truth's not always the right medicine at all hours. Anyhow change will work its own way with time and space and the things that belong to them. She was torn in half between you, and brave enough to make naked confession of it. That proclaimed her either a greater character than we thought once, or a poorer thing every way—according to the mind that views the case."

"I didn't know such a tangle could happen."

"Every sort of tangle can happen where men and women are concerned. Not that she's not a puzzle to me, too, every hour. She has gone now for a while to Exeter. I advised that she should bide there until after the funeral, but she scorned the thought. 'I'm chief mourner in truth, if not in name,' she said; and so she will be. Time must do the rest."

"The last resource of the wretched."

"And the best to be relied on."

"I can only hope to God she's not to be unhappy for ever."

"She gets her happiness, like a bee gets honey—here, there, everywhere, by fits and snatches. Too quick to see the inner comedy of human affairs to be unhappy for ever, or happy for long. And what are you going to do, Myles?"

"I thought to go for good—yes, for good this time."

"Couldn't do better. She will read you into these chapters of her life. Can't help it. But Time's on your side too, though you slight him. And this, at least, you'll remember: if she wants you to come back, she won't hesitate to let you know it."

CHAPTER XVII.
SPRING ON SCOR HILL

Often it happens that small matters demand lengthy spaces in time for their development, while affairs of import and interests involving high changes are carried through at comet speed upon the crest of some few splendid or terrible moments. Thus did concerns of note to those playing a part of their history under our eyes tumble unexpectedly to the top, and an event take place wholly unforeseen by Myles Stapledon, though predicted and prophesied for a more or less remote future by Uncle Endicott. For this surprise one woman was responsible.

Honor returned from Exeter in time to be present at Christopher Yeoland's funeral; and with her she bore a fair wreath of Eucharis lilies, which Mr. Brimblecombe consigned to a rubbish heap behind the church tower as soon as her back was turned, because he held flowers out of place on the coffin of quality. Those now occupying Godleigh for a term of years gladly allowed the recent possessor to pass his last night among men beneath that roof, and not a few folk representative of the district attended the obsequies in person or by proxy. So Christopher Yeoland was laid upon his shelf of slate, and Doctor Courteney Clack, for the benefit of such as cared to listen, told how a whip snake, falling from a tree, had fastened upon the dead man's neck, and how, with few words and one wish to be buried at home, he had quickly passed away under the poison.

So that chapter closed at the mausoleum, whose guardian cherubs were moss-grown skulls; and day followed day, month succeeded upon month, into the time of early summer; of misty silver nights and shining noons; of warm rain and steaming fields; of the music of life from birds' throats; of the scent of life in the chalices of bluebells; of the very heart-beat and pulse of life under the glades of green woods and beside the banks of Teign.

Then, in a June day's shape, Time, of many disguises, began his work with Honor Endicott. A revulsion followed the gloom that had passed and pressed upon her; she mourned still, but for choice in the sunshine; and, growing suddenly athirst for the river and the manifold life that dwelt upon the brink of it, she took her rod as an excuse, passed upward alone, descended Scor Hill, and pursued her way eastward to a lonely glen where Teign winds into the woods of Godleigh. Many fair things broke bud about her, and in secret places the splendour of summer made ready. Soon the heather would illuminate these wastes and the foxgloves carry like colour aloft on countless steeples of purple bells; soon woodbine and briar would wreathe the granite, and little pearly clusters of blossom spring aloft from the red sundews in the marsh; while the king fern already spread his wide fronds above the home of the trout, and the brake fern slowly wove his particular green into the coombs and hills.

Despite a sure conviction that melancholy must henceforth encompass her every waking hour, Honor Endicott was not armed against the magic of this blue and golden day. She could fish with a fly, and that skilfully; and now, before the fact that a brisk rise dimpled and dappled the river, passing temptations to kill a trout wakened and were not repulsed. She set up her rod, and by chance mused as she did so upon Myles Stapledon. Him she had not seen for many days, but her regard had not diminished before his abstention. Indeed she appreciated it up to a point, though now it began to irk her. She did not know that he was about to depart definitely; for Mark Endicott had deemed it unnecessary to mention the fact.

At her third cast Honor got a good rise, and hooked a fish which began its battle for life with two rushes that had done honour to a heavier trout. Then it leapt out of the water, showed itself to be a half-pounder or thereabout, and headed up stream with a dozen frantic devices to foul the line in snag or weed. But Honor was mistress of the situation, turned the fish with the current, and, keeping on the deadly strain, soon wearied it. Then she wound in the line steadily, steered her victim to a little shelving backwater, and so, having no net, lifted the trout very gently out of its element on to the grass. Flushed with excitement, and feeling, almost against her will, that she was young, Honor gazed down upon gasping fario, admired the clean bulk of him, his fierce eye, dark olive back spotted with ebony and ruby, the lemon light along his plump sides, his silver belly, perfect proportions, and sweet smell. He heaved, opened his gills, sucked deep at the empty air, and protested at this slow drowning with a leap and quiver of suffering; whereupon, suddenly moved at thought of what this trout had done for her, Honor picked him up and put him back into the water, laughing to herself and at herself the while. After a gulp or two, strength returned to the fish, and like an arrow, leaving a long ripple over the shallow, he vanished back to the deep sweet water and his own sweet life.

Other trout were not so fortunate, however, and by noon, at which time all rise ceased, the angler had slain above half a dozen and was weary of slaughter. She fished up stream, and had now reached the tolmen—a great perforated stone that lies in the bed of Teign near Wallabrook's confluence with it. And resting here awhile, she saw the figure of Myles Stapledon as he approached the river from a farm on the other side. The homestead of Batworthy, where it nestles upon the confines of the central waste, and peeps, with fair silver thatches, above its proper grove, shall be seen surrounded by heather and granite. The river babbles at its feet, and on every side extends Dartmoor to the high tors—north, south, and west. From hence came Myles Stapledon, after gathering certain information from a kindly colleague; and now he strode across the stream and on to within ten yards of Honor, yet failed to see her, where she sat motionless half hidden by ferns and grasses. He moved along, deep plunged in his own thoughts, and she determined to let him pass, until something in the weary, haggard look of him tempted her to change her mind. He was lonely— lonelier than she; he had nobody to care about him, and all his life to be lived. Perhaps, despite these sentimental thoughts, she had suffered him to go, but one circumstance decided her: on the arm of his workaday coat appeared a band of black. And, guessing something of his recent tribulations, she lifted her voice and called him.

"Myles! Why do you avoid me?"

He started and slipped a foot, but recovered instantly, turned, and approached her. His face betokened surprise and other emotion.

"How good of you to call me—how kind. I did not know that you were out on the Moor, or within a mile of this place. Else I would have gone back another way."

"That's not very friendly, I think. I don't bite."

"I thought—but like all thoughts of mine, though I've wasted hours on it, nothing was bred from it. At least I may accompany you back. It was most kind to call me. And most strange and culpable of me not to see you."

She noticed his gratitude, and it touched her a little.

"I've killed eight trout," she said; "one nearly three-quarters of a pound."

"A grand fish. I will carry them for you. Fine weather to-day and the summer really at the door."

"It was thoughtful of you to keep away, Myles. I appreciated that."

"I should have gone clean and haunted the land no further; but there was much to do. Now all is done, and I'm glad of this chance to tell you so. I can really depart now. You'll think it a cry of 'Wolf!' and doubt my strength to turn my back on Bear Down again; but go I must at last."

She was reflecting with lightning rapidity. That he meant what he said she did not doubt. The news, indeed, was hardly unexpected; yet it came too suddenly for her peace of mind. There existed a side to this action in which she had an interest. Indeed with her might lie the entire future of him, if she willed it so. Decisions now cried to be made, and while even that morning they had looked afar off, vague, nebulous as need be, now they rushed up from the horizon of the future to the very zenith of the present. Yet she could not decide thus instantly, so temporised and asked idle questions to gain time.

"Of what were you thinking when I saw you cross the river with your head so low?" she asked, and hoped that his answer might help her. But nothing was further from his mind than the matter in hers. He answered baldly—

"My head was bent that I might see my way on the stepping-stones. As to my thoughts, I only had a muddled idea about the season and the green things—friends and foes—all growing together at the beginning of the race—all full of youth and sap and trust—so to speak; and none seeing any danger in the embrace of his companion. Look at that pest, the beautiful bindweed. It breaks out of the earth with slender fingers, weak as a baby's, yet it grows into a cruel, soft, choking thing of a thousand hands—more dangerous to its neighbour than tiger to man—a garotter, a Thug, a traitor that hangs out lovely bells and twines its death into fair festoons that it may hide the corpse of its own strangling."

"And then?"

"That was all my thought. Yet I seemed to feel akin to the plant myself."

"Something has changed you since we dropped out of one another's lives. Fancy a practical farmer mooning over such nonsense! Bindweed can be pulled up and burnt—even if it's growing in your heart."

"How like you to say that! It is good to me to hear your voice again, Honor."

"Take down my rod then, and tell me why you are going. Half of Endicott's is your own."

"I thought—I believed that you would be happier if I did so. And I still suspect that is the case. I owe you deeper reparation than ever a man owed a woman."

"You are too good, but your goodness becomes morbid."

"I'm only a clumsy fool, and never knew how clumsy or how much a fool until I met you."

"No, I say you are really good. Goodness is a matter of temperament, not morals. Some of the most God-fearing, church-going people I know can't be good; some of the worst people I ever heard about—even frank heathens like yourself—can't be bad. There's a paradox for you to preach about!"

But he shook his head.

"Your mind's too quick for me. Yet I think I know what you mean. By 'goodness' and 'badness' you signify a nature sympathetic or otherwise. It's all a question of selfishness at bottom."

"But the day looks too beautiful for such talk," answered Honor.

"So it is; I don't desire to talk of anything. You can't guess what it is to me to hear your voice again—just the music of it. It intoxicates me, like drink."

"You're dreaming; and, besides, you're going away."

The light died out of his face, and they walked together in silence a few paces. Then the girl's mind established itself, and her love was a large factor in that decision, though not the only one. She determined upon a course of action beyond measure unconventional, but that aspect of the deed weighed most lightly with her.

They were passing over the face of Scor Hill when she turned to the left, where stood that ancient monument of the past named Scor Hill Circle.

"I'm going down to the old ring," she said; "I've a fancy to visit it."

He followed without speech, his mind occupied by a frosty picture of their last visit to the same spot. Now it basked under sunlight, and spring had touched both the splinters of granite and the lonely theatre in which they stood. Upon the weathered planes of the stones were chased quaint patterns and beads of moss, together with those mystic creatures of ochre and ebony, grey and gold, that suck life from air and adamant and clothe the dry bones of Earth with old Time's livery.

Upon a fallen stone in the midst, where young heather sprouted in tufts and cushions, Honor sat down awhile; and seeing that she remained silent, Myles uttered some platitudes concerning the spot and the ceremonies of heathen ritual, state, or sacrifice that had aforetime marked it. The upright stones surrounded them where they sat beside a sort of central altar of fading furze. The giant block of the circle stood on the north of its circumference, and upon more than one of the unshaped masses were spots rubbed clean by beasts and holding amid their incrustations red hairs of cattle, or flecks of wool from the fleeces of the flocks. Even now a heifer grazed upon the grass within the circle; its herd roamed below; round about the valley rose old familiar tors; while sleepy summer haze stole hither and thither upon the crowns of Watern and Steeperton, and dimmed the huge bulk of Cosdon Beacon where it swelled towards the north.

"When did we last come here?" began Honor suddenly.

"On the day of the snowstorm."

"Ah, yes. We were riding, and stopped a moment here. Why?"

Stapledon looked at her, then turned his head away.

"If you have forgotten, it is good," he said.

"What did I say to that great question, Myles?"

"Spare me that, Honor. I have been punished enough."

"Don't generalise. What did I say?"

"That you could marry neither of us—neither Yeoland nor me—out of consideration for the other."

"And you gasped when you heard it; and I kept my word. Now the pity is that you must keep yours."

"Mine?"

"Never to ask again what I would not give then."

"Honor!"

"Hush. Don't break your word for such a trifle as a wife. I'm accustomed to doing unmaidenly, horrible things, so this doesn't hurt me as much as it would a proper-thinking, proper-feeling woman. I love you; I always have loved you since I knew you. And I suppose you love me still—more or less. He who has gone—has gone. There will never be another Christo for me, Myles. You cannot take his place; and if you were dead and he was alive, he could never have taken yours. That's my peculiarly deranged attitude. But here I sit, and I should like to be your wife, because life is short and a woman's a fool to throw away good love and starve herself when plenty is offered."

Stapledon's dog looked up from his seat on the heather, barked and wagged his tail, knowing that his master was happy; and the heifer, startled by these canine expressions of delight and sudden ejaculations uttered aloud in a man's deep voice, flung up her hind legs wildly and cutting cumbrous capers, to indicate that she too appreciated the romance of the moment, shambled away from the grey circle to join her companions in the valley below.

CHAPTER XVIII.
ROSES AND ROSETTES

"Us'll go down-long awver the plough-path; then us'll be in full time to see the butivul bride arrive," said Tommy Bates. He stood in Sunday attire among his betters, and the sobriety of much black broadcloth was brightened by unusual adornment, for Cramphorn, Ash, Collins, Pinsent, and the rest were decorated with large rosettes of satin ribbon. Many also wore roses in their buttonholes, for one of Stapledon's few friends was a big rose-grower at Torquay, who, from the abundance of his scented acres, had despatched countless blooms—crimson and cream, snow-white, ivory and orange-yellow, pink and regal purple—to brighten a glorious day.

But in the judgment of Ash and the elders no flower of cultivation could compare in significance or beauty with the sham sprigs of orange-blossom at the centre of the rosettes. Churdles himself also carried a bulky parcel in the tail of his coat, which added another protuberance to his gnarled form. It was not a prayer-book, as he gave Collins to understand with many nods and winks.

The party stood upon the grass plot before Bear Down—a space separated from the main great grass lands of the farm. These latter subtended the level ground and swelled and billowed under waves of colourless light that raced free as the wind over another year's hay harvest. Far beneath, just visible above a green hedge between elms, four small peaks arose and a White Ensign fluttered from a flagstaff in the midst, where stood the village church.

Mr. Cramphorn and his friends set forth and improved the occasion with reflections upon what would follow the wedding, rather than in much consideration of the ceremony itself.

"They be gwaine straight off from the church door," said Mr. Ash, "an' so they'll miss the fun of the fair up long, though 'tis theer money as'll furnish the junketings. A braave rally of neighbours comin' to eat an' drink an' be merry by all accounts; an' not a stroke more'n milkin' cows an' feedin' things to be done to-day by man or woman."

"They ought to bide to the eating whether or no," said Mr. Cramphorn. "An' I be gwaine to tell a speech, though they'll be half ways to Exeter before I does. I hold it my duty. She'm the best mistress an' kindest woman in the world to my knawledge, an' my gift o' words shan't be denied at her solemn weddin' feast, whether she be theer or whether she han't."

Mr. Collins applauded these sentiments, for his private ambitions were strong at heart under the rosy atmosphere of the hour.

"I lay you'll tell some gude talk come bimebye," he said. "'Tis a gert power—same as the gift of tongues in the Bible seemin'ly."

"Theer'll be some plum drinkin' by all accounts," said Mr. Ash, pouting up his little wrinkled mouth in cheerful anticipation. "Brown sherry wine for us, an' fizzy yellow champagne an' auld black port for the quality. An' it's a secret hope of mine, if I ban't tu bowldacious in thinkin' such a thing, as I may get a thimbleful of the auld wine—port—so dark as porter but butivul clear wi' it, an' a sure finder of a man's heart-strings. I be awful set upon a sup of that. I've longed for fifty years to taste it, if so be I might wi'out offence. It have been my gert hope for generations; an' if it awnly comes 'pon my death-bed I'll thank the giver, though 'twould be a pleasanter thing to drink it in health."

"I seed larder essterday," said Tommy Bates. "My stars! The auld worm-eaten shelves of un be fairly bent."

"Purty eating, no doubt," assented Cramphorn, though as one superior to such things.

"Ess fay! Fantastic pastry, more like to cloam ornaments for the mantelshelf than belly-timber. God knaws how they'll scat 'em apart."

"Each has its proper way of bein' broke up," said Mr. Cramphorn. "Theer's manners an' customs in all this. Some you takes a knife to, some a fork, some a spoon. The bettermost takes a knife even to a apple or pear."

"Things a lookin' out o' jellies, an' smothered in sugar an' transparent stuff! I'd so easy tell the stars as give a name to half of 'em. But theer was a pineapple—I knawed un by seein' his picksher in the auld Bible, where Joseph was givin' his brothers a spread. But they didn't have no such pies an' red lobsters as be waitin' up-long. Such a huge gert cake 'tis! All snow-white, an' crawled awver wi' silver paper, an' a li'l naked doll 'pon top wi' blue eyes an' gawld wings to un. A pixy doll you might say."

"Her ought to bide an' cut that cake herself, not dash away from church as though she'd done murder 'stead of praiseworthy matrimony," grumbled Mr. Cramphorn. "'Tis defying the laws of marryin' and givin' in marriage. Theer may be trouble to it presently."

"If they'm both of a mind, they'll do what they please," said Collins.

"Ay, an' 'twon't hurt none of us, nor make the vittles an' drinks less sweet," declared Samuel Pinsent.

"That's truth," assented Gaffer Ash; "an' when you come to be my ripe years, Jonah, you'll go limpin' to meet the li'l pleasures that be left to 'e half-way, 'stead of fearin' evil. As for the pains—fegs! they meets you half-way!"

"'Twill be a happy marriage, I should reckon," ventured Pinsent.

"We'll pray it will be, though he'm a thought tu deep in love for my money," declared Cramphorn.

"Can a man love his maiden more'n enough?" asked Henry Collins in amazement; and the other answered that it might be so.

"Love be well knawn for a mole-blind state, Henery—a trick of Nature to gain her awn ends; an' the sooner new-fledged man an' wife see straight again better for their awn peace of mind. Maister Myles be a shade silly here and theer, though Lard knaws if ever a man's to be forgiven for gettin' his head turned 'tis him. A marvellous faace an' shape to her. But ban't the wise way to dote. She'm a human woman, without disrespect; and her sawl's to save like poorer folk. In plain English, he'll spoil her."

"Couldn't—no man could," said Mr. Ash stoutly. "To think of a sovereign to each of us, an' two to me by reason of my ancient sarvice!"

"You've toiled 'pon the land for a fearsome number of years, I s'pose, Maister Ash?" asked Tommy respectfully.

"Me? I was doin' man's work in the reign of the Fourth Gearge. I've ate many an' many a loaf o' barley bread, I have; an' seed folks ride pillion; an' had a woman behind me, on the auld-fashion saddles, myself, for that matter. An', as for marriage, though I never used it, I've seed scores o' dozens o' marriages—sweet an' sour. Marriages be like bwoys playin' leapfrog, wheer each lad have got to rucksey down in turn; an' so man an' wife have got to rucksey down wan to t'other at proper times an' seasons. Each must knaw theer awn plaace in the house; an' Mrs. Loveys was right, when us gived 'em the cannel-sticks for a gift. You call home how she said, 'I wish 'e patience wan wi' t'other, my dearies, 'cause theer ban't nothin' more useful or more like to be wanted 'bout the house o' newly married folk than that!'"

The party now mingled with those already assembled in Little Silver. A crowd drawn from Throwley, Chagford, and elsewhere stood and admired flags that waved between green-garlanded poles at the churchyard gate. Many passed from the hot sunshine into the shadow of the holy building; many had already entered it.

"Us'll bide here till our brows be cool an' she've a-come. Then us'll go in an' sit usual plaace, left side o' the alley," said Mr. Cramphorn.

Presently Myles Stapledon appeared, and a hum of friendship rose for him. He looked somewhat anxious, was clad in a grey suit, white waistcoat, and a white tie with his solitary jewel in it—an old carbuncle set in gold that had belonged to his father and adorned that gentleman's throat or finger on the occasion of his marriage. In the bridegroom's buttonhole was a red rosebud, and now and again his hand went nervously across to an inner pocket, where reposed the money for the honeymoon. He walked to the vestry, made certain entries in the book spread open for him, and presented Mr. Scobell with two guineas. He then entered a choir stall and sat down there, facing the eyes of the increasing company without visible emotion.

Outside came stroke of horse-hoofs and grinding of wheels. Then entered an ancient aunt of the bridegroom's with her two elderly daughters. A second carriage held Honor's relatives from Exeter, and a third contained Mrs. Loveys and Sally and Margaret Cramphorn; for it was Honor's wish that her serving-maids should be her bridesmaids also, and she knew none of her sex who loved her better. Each had a bouquet of roses; each wore a new dress and now waited at the entrance for their mistress, with many a turn and twist, perk of head, and soft rustle from the new gowns. The eyes of Mr. Collins watered as he beheld Sally, and his huge breast rose, heaved up by mountainous sighs. Meantime, she had secretly handed a rosette to Mr. Greg Libby, who, in company of his old mother, adorned the gathering; and Margery too, at the first opportunity, presented the young man with a rosette. Thus it came about that Gregory gloried in dual favours and attached both to his marriage garment; whereupon two maiden hearts under dove-coloured raiment were filled with emotions most unsisterly, and all men, save one, laughed at the luck of the gilded hedge-tacker.

The glory of Little Silver church centres in an ancient screen of many colours. Upon it shall be found elaborate interlacing of blue and gold, pale blue and dark crimson; while through the arches of it may be seen the Lord's Table under a granite reredos. Pulpit and lectern are also of the good grey stone, and to-day a riot of roses that made the little place of worship very sweet climbed the old pillars and clustered in the deep embrasures of the windows. The walls, painted with red distemper, ascended to a waggon roof; and upon pews, where the humble living stood or knelt above dust of noble dead, frank daylight entered through plain glass windows.

Along the base of the ornate screen stood figures of the saints mechanically rendered, and about one, standing upon the right hand of the choir entrance, there twined a text that indicated this figure stood for John the Baptist. "The voice of one crying in the wilderness" were those graven words; and now by chance they caught a pair of downcast eyes, as Honor

Endicott bent her young head and passed onward from independence into the keeping of a man.

She came with her uncle, and those in church rose amid mighty rustlings and clink of iron-shod boots, and those outside crowded into their places. A little harmonium groaned gallantly, and Mr. Scobell billowed up the aisle from the vestry. Honor walked to meet Myles with her hand holding Mark Endicott's. At the steps, under the screen, she stopped for him to feel the step, and as she did so caught sight of the text. Then a big, florid face, with the plainest admiration exhibited upon it, met her gaze, and she also became dimly conscious of a tall, grey man at her right elbow. The florid face belonged to Mr. Scobell, who, recollecting himself and chastening his features, frowned at the back of the church, and began the ceremony. But the grey man was waiting for her, longing for her, "to have and to hold from this day forward, for better for worse, for richer for poorer, in sickness and in health, to love and to cherish," until death should part them.

Yet the text—that voice in the wilderness—haunted her mind all the while, as it is the way with irrelevant ideas to intrude upon high moments. Presently Honor put her hand into her husband's, felt the gold slip over her finger, and marvelled to feel how much heavier this ring was than the little toy of diamond and pearl she had been wearing of late. Then all was accomplished, and Mr. Ash and his friends quite drowned the squeak and gasp of a Wedding March, with which the vicar's daughter wrestled upon the harmonium; for they all clattered out of church and drew up in a double line outside along the pathway. Churdles then produced his mysterious packet and exhibited a bag of rice. This was opened, and old, tremulous hands, knotted and veined like ivy-vines upon an oak, flung the grain as lustily as young plump ones, while man and wife came forth to face the benignant shower.

At the gate two stout greys and an old postillion—relic of days flown—were waiting to take Myles and his lady to Okehampton for the London train. Mark Endicott, led by Tommy Bates, stood at the carriage door; and now he felt warm lips on his blind face and a tear there.

"Be a good uncle," whispered Honor; "and don't weary your dear hands too much for those Brixham fishermen. Home we shall come again in a month; and how I'm going to do without you for so long, or you without me, I can't guess."

He squeezed her hands, and for once the old Spartan was dumb.

"God bless 'e!"

"Long life an' happiness to 'e!"

"Good luck to the both of 'e!"

Then a jumble and buzz of many speaking together; lifting of voices into a cheer; a gap in the road, where the carriage had stood; a puff of dust at the corner by the old pound; and courageous fowls, clucking and fluttering and risking their lives for scattered rice, among crushed roses and the legs of the people.

The bells rang out; the dust died down; personages drove slowly up the hill to the banquet; certain persons walked up. Mr. Cramphorn, fearful of a love contagion in the air, convoyed his daughters home himself, and Libby, growing faint-hearted before the expression on Jonah's face, abandoned his design of walking by Sally's side for half the distance and with Margery for the rest. Henry Collins was also deprived of the society he craved, and by ill-fortune it chanced that Ash, Pinsent, and the two rivals found themselves in company on the journey home. Collins thereupon relieved his wounded soul by being extremely rude, and he began with a personal remark at the expense of Gregory's best coat and emerald tie.

"All black an' green, I see—mourning for the devil that is," he said, in a tone not friendly.

"Aw! Be he dead then?" inquired Mr. Libby with great show of interest.

"Not while the likes of you's stirrin'. An' what for do 'e want to make a doomshaw of yourself—wearin' two rosettes, like a Merry Andrew, when other men have but wan?"

"Grapes are sour with you, I reckon, Henery. You see I puts this here left bow just awver my 'eart, 'cause Sally Cramphorn gived it to me."

Collins blazed into a fiery red, and a fist of huge proportions clenched until the knuckles grew white.

"Have a care," he said, "or I'll hit 'e awver the jaw! Such a poor penn'orth as you to set two such gals as them by the ears!"

"Who be you to threaten your betters? You forget as I'm a man wi' money in the bank, an' you ban't."

"Ah, so I did then," confessed Collins frankly. "I did forget; but they didn't. Keep your rosettes. 'Tis your gert store o' money winned 'em—same as bullock, not farmer, gets the ribbons at Christmas fair. So, every way, it's dam little as you've got to be proud of!"

Mr. Libby became inarticulate before this insult. He rolled and rumbled horrible threats in his cleft palate, but they were not intelligible, and Collins, striding forward, left him in the rear and joined Gaffer Ash and Pinsent, who dwelt peaceably on the joys to come.

"A talk of moosicians there was," said Samuel.

"Right. The Yeomany band to play 'pon the lawn. An' gude pleasure, tu, for them as likes brass moosic."

"How Maister Stapledon girned like a cat when the rice went down onderneath his clean collar!"

"Ess, he did; 'twas a happy thought of mine."

"What's the value or sense in it I doan't see all the same," objected Collins, whose day had now suffered eclipse. "'Pears to me 'tis a silly act whether or no."

"That shaws how ill you'm learned in affairs," answered Mr. Ash calmly. "The meanin' of rice at a weddin's very well knawn by onderstandin' men. 'Tis thrawed to ensure fruitfulness an' a long family. A dark branch of larnin', I grant 'e; but for all that I've awnly knawed it fail wance; an' then 'twern't no fault of the magic."

But Henry had been taught to regard a full quiver as no blessing.

"If that's what you done it for, 'twas a cruel unfriendly act," he declared, "an' I stands up an' sez so, auld as you be. Devil's awn wicked self caan't wish no worse harm to a innocent young pair than endless childer. I knaw—who better?—being wan o' thirteen myself; an' if I heard that was the use of it, not a grain would I have thrawed at 'em for money."

Churdles blinked, but was quite unmoved.

"You speak as a bachelor, my son, not to say as a fule. Black dog's got 'pon your shoulder this marnin'. A pity tu, for 'tis a perspiring day wi'out temper. No rough language to-day. All peace an' plencheousness; an' a glass o' black port, please God. Us'll feast wi' thankful hearts; an' then go forth an' sit 'pon the spine-grass in the garden an' smoke our pipes an' listen to the moosickers in the butivul sunshine."

"'Pears to me," said Gregory Libby, who had now rejoined them, "that you chaps o' Endicott's did ought to give some return for all this guzzling an' holiday making."

"Theer you'm wrong, as you mostly be, Greg," answered old Ash with a serene smile, "for 'tis awnly a small mind caan't take a favour wi'out worrittin' how to return it."

BOOK II.

CHAPTER I.
THE SEEDS

In late summer a strong breeze swept the Moor, hummed over the heather, and sang in the chinks and crannies of the tors; while at earth-level thin rags and tatters of mist, soaked with sunshine, raced beneath the blue. Now they swallowed a hill in one transitory sweep of light; now they dislimned in pearly tentacles and vanished magically, swept away by the riotous breezes; now moisture again became visible, and grew and gathered and laughed, and made a silver-grey home for rainbows. Beneath was hot sunshine, the light of the ling, the wild pant and gasp of great fitful zephyr, as he raced and roared along the lower planes of earth and sky; above, free of the fret and tumult, there sailed, in the upper chambers of the air, golden billows of cloud, rounded, massed and gleaming, with their aerial foundations levelled into long true lines by the rush of the western wind beneath them. Other air currents they knew and obeyed, and as they travelled upon their proper way, like a moving world, their peaks and promontories swelled and waned, spread and arose, billowed into new continents, craned and tottered into new golden pinnacles that drew their glory from the gates of the sun. To the sun, indeed, and above him—to the very zenith where he had climbed at noon—the scattered cloud armies swept and ascended; and their progress, viewed from earth, was majestic as the journey of remote stars, compared with the rapid frolics of the Mother o' Mist beneath.

A man and a woman appeared together on the high ground above Bear Down, and surveyed the tremendous valleys where Teign's course swept to distant Whiddon and vanished in the gorges of Fingle. There, gleaming across that land of ragged deer park and wild heathery precipices crowned with fir, a rainbow spanned the river's channels, and the transparent splendour of it bathed the distance with liquid colour, softened by many a mile of moist air to the melting and misty delicacy of opal.

"How flat the bow looks from this height," said the man.

"Fancy noting the shape with your eyes full of the colour!" answered the woman.

He started and laughed.

"How curiously like poor Christopher Yeoland you said that, Honor. And how like him to say it."

Myles and his wife were just returning from payment of a visit. They had now been married a few months, and, with the recent past, there had lifted off the head of the husband a load of anxiety. He looked younger and his forehead seemed more open; he felt younger by a decade of years, and his face only clouded at secret moments with one daily care. Despite his whole-hearted and unconcealed joy he went in fear, for there were vague suspicions in his head that the happiness of his heart was too great. He believed that never, within human experience, had any man approached so perilously near to absolute contentment as he did then. Thus in his very happiness lay his alarm. As a reasonable being, he knew that human life never makes enduring progress upon such fairy lines, and he searched his horizon for the inevitable clouds. But none appeared to his sight. Every letter he opened, every day that he awakened, he expected, and even vaguely hoped for reverses to balance his life, for minor troubles to order his existence more nearly with his experience. He had been quite content to meet those usual slings and arrows ranged against every man along the highway side of his pilgrimage; and tribulation of a sort had made him feel safer in the citadel of his good fortune. Indeed, he could conceive of no shaft capable of serious penetration in his case, so that it spared the lives of himself and his wife. Now the balance was set one way, and Providence blessed the pair with full measure, pressed down and running over. All succeeded on their land; all prospered in their homestead; all went well with their hearts. On sleepless nights Stapledon fancied he heard a kind, ghostly watchman cry out as much under the stars; and hearing, he would turn and thank the God he did not know and sleep again.

"Gone!" said Honor, looking out where the rainbow died and the gleam of it was swept out of being by the sturdy wind.

"So quickly; yet it spoke a true word before the wind scattered it; told us so many things that only a rainbow can. It is everlasting, because it is true. There's a beauty in absolute stark truth, Honor."

"Is there? Then the multiplication table's beautiful, dear love. If a rainbow teaches me anything, it is what a short-lived matter beauty must be— beauty and happiness and all that makes life worth living."

"But our rainbow is not built upon the mist."

"Don't think about the roots of it. So you are satisfied, leave them alone. To analyse happiness is worse and more foolish, I should think, than hunting for rainbow gold itself."

"I don't know. What is the happiness worth that won't stand analysis? All the same, I understand you very well. I believe there is nothing like prosperity and such a love of life as I feel now to make a man a coward. Anybody can be brave when he's got everything to win and nothing to lose; but it takes a big man to look ahead without a quickened pulse when he's at the top of his desire, when he knows in the heart of him that he's living through the happiest, best, most perfect days the earth can offer. Remember that to me this earth is all. I know of nothing whatever in me or anybody else that merits or justifies an eternity. So I cling to every moment of my life, and of yours. I'm a miser of minutes; I let the hours go with regret; I grudge the night-time spent in unconsciousness; I delight to wake early and look at you asleep and know you are mine, and that you love to be mine."

"It's a great deal of happiness for two people, Myles."

"So much that I fear, and, fearing, dim my happiness, and then blame myself for such folly."

"The rainy day will come. You are like poor, dear Cramphorn, who scents mystery in the open faces of flowers, suspects a tragedy at crossing of knives or spilling of salt; sees Fate busy breeding trouble if a foot but slips on a threshold. How he can have one happy moment I don't know. He told me yesterday that circumstances led him to suspect the end of the world by a thunder-planet before very long. And he said it would be just Endicott luck if the crash came before the crops were gathered, for our roots were a record this year."

"His daughters bother him a good deal."

"Yes; I do hope I may never have a daughter, Myles. It sounds unkind, but I don't like girls. My personal experience of the only girl I ever knew intimately, inclines me against them—Honor Endicott, I mean."

"Then we disagree," he said, and his eyes softened.

"Fancy, we actually differ, and differ by as much as the difference between a boy and a girl! I would like a girl for head of the family. I've known it work best so."

Honor did not answer.

While her husband had renewed his youth under the conditions of & happy marriage, the same could hardly be said for her. She was well and content, but more thoughtful. Her eyes twinkled into laughing stars less often than of old. She made others laugh, but seldom laughed with them as she had laughed with Christopher Yeoland. In the note of her voice a sadder music, that had wakened at her first love's death, remained.

Yet she was peacefully happy and quietly alive to the blessing of such a husband. Her temperament found him a daily meal of bread and butter—nourishing, pleasant to a healthy appetite, easy to digest. But, while he had feared for his happiness, she had already asked herself if his consistent stability would ever pall. She knew him so thoroughly, and wished that it was not so. It exasperated her in secret to realise that she could foretell to a nicety his speech and action under all possible circumstances. There were no unsuspected crannies and surprises in him. Surprises had ever been the jewels of Honor's life, and she believed that she might dig into the very heart's core of this man and never find one.

"He seems to be gold all through," she thought once. "Yet I wish he was patchy for the sake of the excitement."

But Myles by no means wearied his wife in these halcyon hours. She was very proud of him and his strength, sobriety, common sense. She enjoyed testing these qualities, and did so every day of the week, for she was a creature of surprises herself, and appreciated juxtaposition of moods as an epicure desires contrary flavours. She never found him wanting. He was as patient as the high Moor; and she believed that she might as easily anger Cosdon Beacon as her husband. He ambled by her side along the pathway of life like a happy elephant. If ever they differed, it was only upon the question of Honor's own share in the conduct of the farm. Formerly she had been energetic enough, and even resented the man's kindly, though clumsy attempts to relieve her; since marriage, however, she appeared well content to let him do all; and this had not mattered, in the opinion of Myles, while Honor found fresh interests and occupations to fill those hours formerly devoted to her affairs. But she did not do so; she spent much time to poor purpose; she developed a passing whim for finer feathers than had fledged her pretty body as a maiden; she began buying dresses that cost a ten-pound note apiece. These rags and tags Myles cared nothing for, but dutifully accompanied to church and upon such little visits of ceremony as the present. Then he grew uncomfortable and mentioned the trifle to Mark Endicott, only to hear the old man laugh.

"'Tis a whim," he said; "just one blind alley on the road towards happiness that every woman likes to probe if she can; and some live in it, and, to their dying day, get no forwarder than frocks. But she won't. Praise the new frill-de-dills when she dons them. Please God there's a time coming when she'll spend money to a better end, and fill her empty time with thoughts of a small thing sprung from her own flesh. No latest fashions in a baby's first gear, I believe. They don't change; no more do grave clothes."

Man and wife walked homeward beside tall, tangled hedges, full of ripeness and the manifold delicate workmanship and wrought filigrane of seed-vessels that follow upon the flowers. Honor was in worldly vein, for she had now come from calling upon folks whose purse was deeper than her own; but Myles found the immediate medley of the hedgerow a familiar feast, and prattled from his simple heart about what he saw there.

"You hear so often that it's a cheerless hour which sees the summer flowers dying, but I don't think so, do you, sweetheart? Look at the harvest of the hedges in its little capsules and goblets and a thousand quaint things! But you've noticed all this. You notice everything. Take the dainty cups, with turned rims, of the campions; and the broadswords or horse-shoes of the peas-blossomed things; and the cones of the foxgloves and the shining balls of starry stitchworts; and the daggers of herb Robert; and the bluebell's triple treasure-house; and the violet's; and the wood-sorrel, that shoots its grain into space; and the flying seeds of dandelions and clematis. And the scarlet fruits—the adder's meat, iris, the hips and aglets, bryony and nightshade; and the dark berries of privets and madders and wayfaring-tree and dogwood; and then the mast of oak and beech and chestnut—it is endless; and all such fine finished work!"

She listened or half listened; then spoke, when he stopped to draw breath.

"Poor Christo used to say that he saw Autumn as a dear, soft, plump-breasted, brown woman sitting on a throne of sunset colours—sitting there smiling and counting all the little cones and purses and pods with her soft hazel eyes, until falling leaves hid her from his sight in a rain of scarlet and gold and amber, under crystalline blue hazes. And sometimes he saw her in the corn, with the round moon shining on her face, while she lingered lovingly in the silver, and the ripe grain bent to kiss her feet and stay her progress. And sometimes"—she broke off suddenly. "You have an eye like a lynx for detail, Myles. Nothing escapes you. It is very wonderful to me."

He was pleased.

"I love detail, I think—detail in work and play. Yet Yeoland taught me more than he learned from me. The seeds are symbols of everlasting things, of life being renewed—deathless."

Honor yawned, but bent her head so that he should not see the involuntary expression of weariness. Believing that he had her attention, he prosed on.

"For my part I often think of the first sowing, and picture the Everlasting, like a husbandman, setting forth to scatter the new-born, mother-naked earth with immortal grain."

"And I suppose the slugs came as a natural consequence; or d'you think Providence only had the happy thought to torment poor Adam with prickles and thorns and green flies and caterpillars and clothes after he'd made that unfortunate effort to enlarge his mind?"

Myles started.

"Don't, Honor love! You should not take these things so. But I'm sorry; I thought I was interesting you."

"So you were; and those heavy, brick-red curtains of Mrs. Maybridge were interesting me still more. I don't know whether I liked them or hated them."

"Well, decide, and I'll write to Exeter for a pair if they please you. Where you'll put them I don't know."

"More do I, dearest. That's why I think I must have a pair—to puzzle me. Nothing ever puzzles me now. I've read all the riddles in my world."

"How wise! Yet I know what you mean. I often feel life's got nothing left that is better than what it has brought. We want a hard winter to brace us—with anxiety, too, and perhaps a loss here and there. So much honey is demoralising."

She looked at him with curiosity.

"Are you really as happy as all that? I didn't know any human being could be; I didn't think it possible to conscious intelligence. That's why I never quite grasped the perfect happiness of the angels—unless they're all grown-up children. Nobody who has trodden this poor, sad old world will ever be quite happy again even in heaven. To have been a man or woman once is to know the shadow of sorrow for all eternity."

But he was thinking of her question, and heard no more. It came like a seed—like some air-borne, invisible, flying spore of the wild fern—touched his heart, found food there, and promised to rise by alternative generation to an unrest of like pattern with the mother-plant in Honor's own heart.

"You're not as happy as I am then?" he asked, with a sudden concern in his voice. "D'you mean that? You must mean it, for you wonder at the height of my happiness, as though it was beyond your dreams."

"I'm very, very happy indeed, dear one—happier than I thought I could be, Myles—happier by far than I deserve to be."

But the seed was sown, and he grew silent. In his egotism the possibility of any ill at the root of his new world, of a worm in the bud of his opening rose, had never struck him. His eyes had roamed around the horizons of life; now there fell a little shadow upon him from a cloud clean overhead. He banished it resolutely and laughed at himself. Yet from that time forward it occasionally reappeared. Henceforth unconsciously he forgot somewhat his own prosperity of mind in attempting to perfect Honor's. He laboured like a giant to bring her measure of full peace. Her days of light and laughter were his also; while when transitory emotions brought a chill to her manner, a cloud to her eyes, he similarly suffered. The wide distinctions in their nature he neither allowed for nor appreciated. Concerning women he knew nothing save this one, and all the obvious, radical differences of essence and nature, he explained to himself as necessary differences of sex.

Man and wife proceeded together homeward, and Honor, acutely conscious of having raised a ripple upon the smooth sea of his content, entered with vigour into her husband's conversation, chimed with his enthusiasm, and plucked seeds and berries that he might name them. Without after-showing of the bitter she had set to his lips, Myles serenely returned to the hedgerow harvests; and so they passed downward together towards the farm, while the sky darkened and pavilions of the coming rain loomed large and larger.

"Just in time," said the man. "I heard Teign's cry this morning; but bad weather is not going to last, I think."

Yet the day closed in drearily, after set of sun. The wind fell at that hour and backed south of west; the mist increased and merged into the density of rain; the rain smothered up the gloaming with a steady, persistent downpour.

CHAPTER II.
CHERRY GREPE'S SINS

Where Honor's head lay upon her pillow by night, a distance of scarcely one yard separated it from the famous cherry tree of Endicott's. This year, owing to a prevalence of cold wind, the crop, though excellent, had been unusually late, and it happened that the thrushes and blackbirds paid exceptional attention to the fruit. Once, in a moment of annoyance at sight of her shining berries mutilated by sharp bills, and pecked to the purple-stained stones, Honor had issued an impatient mandate to the first servant who chanced to meet her after discovery of the birds' theft. Henry Collins it was, and his round eyes grew into dark moons as she bid him shoot a few of the robbers and hang their corpses Haman-high as a dreadful lesson to the rest.

For a fortnight after this stern decree Collins, full of private anxieties, paid no heed to his mistress's command, and Honor herself dismissed the matter and forgot her order as completely as she forgot those moments of irritation that were responsible for it; but anon Henry recollected the circumstance, borrowed Jonah Cramphorn's gun, rose betimes, and marched into the garden on a morning soon after the rainstorm. A flutter of wings in the cherry tree attracted him, and firing against the side of the house he brought down a fine cock blackbird in a huddled heap of ebony feathers now streaked with crimson, his orange bill all stained with juice from the last cherry that he would spoil. The shot echoed and re-echoed through the grey stillness of dawn, and Myles, already rising, hastened to the window, while Honor opened her eyes, for the report had roused her.

"It's Collins!" exclaimed her husband, staring into the dusk of day; "and the brute has shot a blackbird! Is he mad? How did he dare to come into the private garden with his gun? And now you'll most probably have a headache—being startled out of sleep like that. Besides, the cruelty of it."

"What a storm in a teacup, my dear! The man is only doing as I ordered him. The birds are a nuisance. They've eaten all my cherries again this year. I bid Collins thin them a little."

"*You* told him to shoot them? Honor!"

"Oh, don't put on that Sunday-school-story look, my dearest and best. There are plenty of blackbirds and thrushes. The garden is still my province, at any rate."

"The birds do more good than harm, and, really, a handful of sour cherries——"

"They're *not* sour!" she cried passionately, flaming over a trifle and glad of any excuse to enjoy an emotion almost forgotten. "My father loved them; my great-grandfather set the tree there. It's a sacred thing to me, and I'll have every bird that settles in it shot, if I please."

"Honor!"

"And hung up afterwards to frighten the rest."

"I'm surprised."

"I don't care if you are. You'll be more surprised yet. 'Sour'! They're better cherries than ever you tasted at Tavistock, I know."

"Collins——"

"Collins must do what I tell him. You're master—but I'm mistress. If the house is going to be divided against itself——"

"God forbid! What in heaven's name are you dreaming of? This is terrible!"

"Then let Collins kill the thrushes and blackbirds. I wish it. I hate them. If you say a word I'll turn the man off."

But two go to a quarrel. Myles, much alarmed and mystified by this ebullition, vowed that Collins might shoot every bird in the county for him; then he departed; and his lady, only regretful that the paltry little quarrel had endured so short a time, arose much refreshed by it. The sluggish monotony of well-balanced reciprocal relations made her spirits stagnant, while pulses of opposition, like sweet breezes, seemed always a necessity of health to invigorate and brighten it. Stapledon appeared at breakfast with anxious eye and a wrinkle between his brows; his attitude towards Honor was almost servile, and his demeanour to the household more reserved than common; but the mistress had obviously leapt from her couch into sunshine. She chatted cheerfully to all, granted Sally a morning away from work, when that maiden begged for some leisure; and herself, after breakfast, announced a determination to go afield and see whether the recent rain had improved the fishing. Myles offered to make holiday also, but, with the old ripple in her voice and between two kisses, she refused him.

"No, dear heart. 'Tis my whim to go alone. I'm feeling a good girl to-day, and that's so rare that I don't want to spoil the sensation. So I mean catching some trout for your supper and Uncle Mark's. Don't come. A day alone on the Moor will blow away some cobwebs and make me better company for my dear, good husband."

Presently she tramped off to northern Teign, where it tumbles by slides and rocky falls through steep valley under Watern's shoulder; and as she left the men at the garden, Mr. Endicott turned his blind eyes upon Myles with a sort of inquiry in them.

"What's come over her to-day? Fresh as a daisy seemingly, and happy as a lark. Got a new ring or bracelet out of you? The old note, that I've missed of late and sorrowed to miss. But I can name it now, because it's come back. What's the reason?"

"I can't tell you. You hurt me a good deal when you say you've missed any indication of happiness in her. As a matter of fact we had a brief passage of words this morning. Nothing serious of course. That wasn't it at any rate."

Mr. Endicott chuckled.

"But it was though, for certain! You set a current flowing. You've done her a power of good by crossing her. I don't want any details, but a word to the wise is enough. Labour keeps your life sweet; she wants something else. Some women must have a little healthy opposition. I wager she loves you better for denying some wish or issuing some order."

"Not at all. Since we're on this incident I may mention that I gave way completely. But 'twas a paltry thing."

"Then if a breeze that ends tamely, by her getting her will, can shake her into such brave spirits, think how it would be if you'd forbid her and had your way! Learn from it—that's all. Some natures can't stand eternal adoration. They sicken on it. There's no good thing, but common-sense, you can't have too much of. So don't be—what's the word?"

"Uxorious," said Myles Stapledon drearily.

"Yes. Don't pamper her with love. You're all the world to her and she to you; but take a lesson from her and hide more than you show. Man and woman's built for stormy weather, and as calm seas and snug harbours breed grass and barnacles on a ship's bottom, so you can reckon it with sheltered souls. I've seen whole families rot away and vanish from this sort of self-indulgence. It saps strength and sucks the iron out of a man. There's metal in you both. Don't try and stand between her and the weather of life."

"I understand you, uncle. I'm only waiting for trouble to come. I know all this happiness isn't entirely healthy. But it's natural I should wish to shield her."

"Right, my son. Only remember she's a hardy plant and won't stand greenhouse coddling. How would you like it yourself?"

They parted, the younger impressed with a new idea; yet, as the day wore on, he began to think of Honor, and presently strolled up the hill to meet her. Once he laughed to himself as he tramped to the heights; but it was a gloomy laugh. This idea of quarrelling as a counter-irritant, of coming nearer to her by going further off, he little appreciated.

Myles wandered to the circle of Scor Hill and mused there. Here she had denied him in snow, offered herself to him in springtime. Honor he did not see, but another woman met his gaze. She was aged and bent, and she passed painfully along under a weight of sticks gathered in the valley. He spoke from his seat on a stone.

"I should not carry so much at one load, Cherry; you'll hurt yourself."

Gammer Grepe, thus accosted, flung her sticks to the ground and turned to Myles eagerly.

"'Tis a gude chance I find 'e alone," she said, "for I'm very much wantin' to have a tell with 'e if I may make so bold."

"Sit down and rest," he answered.

Then the gammer began with tearful eagerness.

"'Tis this way. For years an' years the folks have been used to look sideways 'pon me an' spit awver theer shoulders arter I'd passed by. An' I won't say the dark things my mother knawed be hid from me. But I never could abear the deeds I've been forced into, an' was allus better pleased doin' gude than harm. God's my judge of that. But I've so fair a right to live as my neighbours, an' I've done many an' many a ugly thing for money, an' I shall again, onless them as can will come forrard and help me. Eighty-four I be—I'll take my oath of it; an' that's a age when a lone woman did ought be thinkin' of the next world—not doin' dark deeds in this."

Myles had seen his wife far off and caught the flutter of her dress in the valley a mile distant. She was still fishing as her tardy progress testified, but where she stood the river was hidden under a tumble of rocky ledges. He turned in some surprise to the old woman.

"D'you mean that here, now, in the year eighteen hundred and seventy-one, folks still ask you for your help to do right or wrong and seriously think you can serve them?"

"Ess fay; an' I do serve them; an' 'tis that I'm weary of. But, seein' theer's nought betwixt me an' the Union Workhouse but theer custom, I go on. Theer's cures come fust—cures for childern's hurts an' the plagues of beasts."

"That's not doing harm, though it's not doin' good either."

"Listen, caan't 'e? Ban't all. I killed a man last year for ten shillin'! An' it do lie heavy upon me yet. An' the mischief is, that my heart be so hard that I'd do the same to-morrow for the same money. I must live, an' if I caan't get honest dole at my time of life, I must make wicked money."

Stapledon inwardly decided that the sooner this old-time survival was within the sheltering arm of the poor-house the better. He suspected that she was growing anile.

"You mustn't talk this nonsense, mother. Surely you know it is out of your power to do any such thing as 'ill-wish,' or 'overlook,' let alone destroy anybody?"

"That's all you knaw! Us o' the dark side o' life be so auld as Scripture. The things we'm taught was never in no books, so they'm livin' still. Print a thing and it dies. We'm like the woman as drawed up Samuel against Saul. We can do more'n we think we can here an' theer. I killed a man other end of the world so sure's if I'd shot un through the heart; for them as seed my deed, which I offered up for ten shillin' o' money, has ears so long as from here to hell-fire; an' they sent a snake. I drawed a circle against Christopher Yeoland, an' picked him, like a bullace, afore he was ripe. An', along o' poverty, I'd do the same against anybody in the land—'cepting awnly the Lard's anointed Queen—so theer! That's the black state o' wickedness I be in; an' 'tis for you at Bear Down to give me gude money an' a regular bit weekly, else theer'll be more mischief. Yet 'tis a horrible thing as I should have to say it—me so auld as I be, wi' wan foot in the graave."

"So it is horrible," said Myles sternly, "and if you were not so old I should say the ancient remedy of a ducking in a horse-pond would be the best way to treat you. To wish evil to that harmless man! Surely you are not such a malignant old fool as to think you destroyed him?"

"Me! Gude Lard A'mighty, I wouldn't hurt a long-cripple or a crawling eft. 'Twas awnly to earn bread. Who paid me I caan't tell 'e, for we has our pride; but I was awnly the servant. Us larns a deal 'bout the inner wickedness of unforgiving sawls in my calling."

"It must have been a strange sort of brute who would wish to hurt Christopher Yeoland; but you needn't be concerned, old woman. Be sure your tomfoolery didn't send death to him."

Cherry reddened under her wrinkles.

"'Tis you'm the fule!" she cried. "I knaw what I knaw; an' I knaw what power be in me very well, same as my mother afore me. An' best give heed or you might be sorry you spoke so scornful. I'm a wise woman; an' wise I was years an' years afore your faither ever got you. I doan't ax for no opinions on that. I ax for money, so I shall give up these things an' die inside the fold of Jesus—not outside it. Because my manner of life be like to end in an oncomfortable plaace, an' I'd give it up to-morrow if I could live without it."

"You're a very wicked woman, Charity Grepe!" flamed Stapledon, "and a disgrace to the countryside and all who allow themselves to have any dealings with you. I thought you only charmed warts and such nonsense. But, here at the end of your life, you deal in these disgusting superstitions and apparently gull intelligent human beings with your tricks. Be sure a stop shall be put to that if I can bring it about. The hands at Endicott's at least won't patronise you any more. You might be locked up if half this was known."

"Then you won't help me to a higher way of living an' regular wages?"

"You must reform first. I can promise nothing."

Cherry, in doubt whether to bless or curse, but disposed towards the latter expression of her emotions, rose and eyed Stapledon suspiciously. He too rose, helped her with her bundle, and again assured her that she must promise reformation before he could undertake any practical assistance. So she hobbled away, uneasy and angered. Actual wounded feeling was at the bottom of her resentment. Whatever her real age, she was human, and therefore not too old to be vain. Since the death of Christopher Yeoland, Gammer Grepe had taken herself very seriously and been much impressed with the nature of her own powers.

Ten minutes later husband and wife met, and Stapledon spoke of his recent experience.

"Scor Hill Circle seems destined to be the theatre of all my strangest accidents."

"And most terrible, perhaps?"

"And most precious. But this last is grim enough. Just now that old hag Cherry Grepe was here begging and threatening in a breath. Think of it: she says she killed Christopher Yeoland!"

Time is like a Moor mist and weaves curtains of a density very uncertain, very apt to part and vanish in those moments when they look most impenetrable. Moods will often roll away the years until memory reveals past days again, and temperaments there are that possess such unhappy power in this sort that they can rend the curtain, defy time, and stand face to face at will with the full proportions of a bygone grief, though kindly years stretch out between to dim vision and soften the edges of remembrance.

Honor often thought of her old lover, and during this day, alone with her mind and the face of the Moor, she had occupied herself about him. She had a rare faculty for leaving the past alone, but, seeing that he was now dead, and that she believed in eternity, Honor pictured that state, and wondered if a friendship, impossible between two men and a woman, would be practicable for the three when all were ghosts. An existence purely spiritual was a pleasant image in her esteem, and to-day, while all unknowing she hovered on the brink of incidents inseparably entwined with flesh and womanhood, she bent her thoughts upon radiant pictures and dreamed strange dreams of an eternal conscious existence clothed only with light.

The crude announcement of Gammer Grepe's confession came inharmoniously upon her thoughts from one direction, yet chimed therewith at the standpoint of the supernatural. She shivered, yet laughed; she declared that Cherry and her cottage should be conveyed entirely to Exeter Museum as a fascinating relic of old times; yet recollected with a sort of discomfort the old woman's predictions concerning herself when, as a girl, and in jest, she had sought to hear her fortune.

CHAPTER III.
A SECRET

Mark Endicott showed not a little interest in the matter of Cherry Grepe. Such a survival astonished him, and being somewhat of a student in folk-lore, he held that, far from discouraging the wise woman, she should be treated with all respect, and an effort made to gather a little of her occult knowledge.

By a coincidence, soon after Stapledon's conversation with the wise woman, there came further corroboration of Cherry's powers from the mouth of one among her steadfast clients. After supper, at that hour when the hands were wont to utter their opinions or seek for counsel from those in authority over them, Mr. Cramphorn opened a great question vital to his own peace of mind and the welfare of his daughters. Jonah loved them both with a generous measure of paternal regard for one of his mental restrictions. Next to his mistress in his esteem came Sally and Margery; and now, with passage of days, there grew in him a great perplexity, for his daughters were old enough to take husbands and both apparently desired the same; while, as if that did not present complication sufficient, the man their ardent hearts were fixed upon by no means commended himself to Cramphorn's judgment.

As for Mr. Libby, with an impartiality very exasperating, he committed himself to no definite course. He made it plain that he desired an alliance with Jonah; yet, under pressure of such monkey brains as Providence had bestowed upon him, and secretly strong in two strings to his bow, he held the balance with great diplomacy between these maids and exercised a patience—easy to one who in reality possessed little love for either. His aim was to learn whether Sally or her sister had greatest measure of her father's regard, for he was far-seeing, knew that Mr. Cramphorn might be considered a snug man, and must in the course of nature presently pass and leave his cottage and his savings behind him. The cottage lease had half a hundred years to run, and an acre of ground went with it. So Gregory, while he leant rather to Sally Cramphorn by reason of her physical splendours, was in no foolish frenzy for her, and the possible possession of a house and land had quickly turned the scale in favour of her sister. Moreover, he was alive to the fact that the father of the girls held him in open dislike; another sufficient cause for procrastination.

With indifferent good grace Jonah recorded his anxieties to Myles and Mark Endicott.

"Both wife-auld, an' be gormed if I knaw what to do 'bout it. A gude few would have 'em, but not wan's for theer market seemin'ly except that fantastical chap, Greg Libby, who stands between 'em, like a donkey between two dachells. I may as well awn up as I seed Cherry Grepe on it, but for wance seems to me as I thrawed away my money. Two shillin' I gived her an' got nought."

"What did she say?" asked Mr. Endicott.

"Her took me by a trick like. Fust her said, 'Do 'e reckon your gals have brains in theer heads?' An' I said, 'Coourse they have, so gude as any other females in theer station o' life.' Then her said, 'You'm satisfied with theer intellects?' An' I said, 'Why for shouldn't I be?' Then said Cherry, 'Very well, Jonah; let 'em bide an' find men for theerselves. Ban't your business, an' you'll be a fule to make it so. 'Tis awnly royal princesses,' she said, 'an' duchesses an' such like as have to set other people husband-huntin' for 'em. But us humble folks of the airth—'tis the will of Providence we may wed wheer we love, like the birds. Let 'em bide, an' doan't keep such a hell-hard hold awver 'em,' said her to me, 'an' then they'll larn you in theer awn time what they be gwaine to do 'bout husbands,' she said."

"Don't see who can give you better advice, Jonah. I can't for one. Looks to me as if old Cherry's got more sense than I was led to believe. Let them find their own men—only see to it when found that they're sound in wind and limb. Libby's got a cleft palate, and, likely as not, his child will have one. 'Tisn't in reason that a lovesick girl should think for her unborn children; but for his grandchildren a man ought to think if chance offers. Anyway, never give a flaw any opportunity to repeat itself, when you can prevent such a thing. Not enough is done for love of the unborn in this world. 'Tis them we ought to make laws for."

By no means satisfied, Cramphorn presently went to bed, and Myles pursued the subject for a while. Then he too retired, taking the lamp with him, and the blind man knitted on for a space, while a choir of crickets chirruped and sped about upon the hearth.

But though Stapledon went to his chamber, the day was not yet done for him, the theme in his thoughts not yet to be extinguished. Since their trivial quarrel Honor and her husband had been as happy together as man and woman need pray to be, and that dim, dreary shadow which Myles had stared at, Honor shut her eyes upon, might be said to have retreated to a point of absolute disappearance. The ache in the man, that showed at his eyes, had passed like any other pain; the twinge in the woman, revealed not at all, though generally followed by a humorous speech, troubled her no more at this moment. She grew pensive and very self-absorbed; she stared absently through the faces of those who addressed her; she dwelt much with her own thoughts and discoveries.

This night she was not in bed when Myles entered her room, but sat beside the open window, her elbows upon the sill and her face between her hands.

"Myles," she said, "there's a man down in the meadow. I saw him distinctly pass between two of the sleeping cows. Then he drifted into the shadow of the hedge—a man or a ghost."

"A man, sweetheart, though I know you would rather think it something else and so get a new sensation. Pinsent probably, as a matter of prosy fact. I bid him get me some rabbits. Shut the window and come to bed. You'll catch cold."

"No; I'm cold-proof now—so the old wives say when—— Come here a minute, Myles, and sit here and look at the moon and listen to the dor beetles. There will not be many more such nights and such silvery mists this year."

"You can almost see the damp in the air," he said.

"Yes, and down below, with ear to grass, one might hear the soft whisper of the little mushrooms breaking out of Mother Earth, while the fairies dance round them and scatter the dew."

"You're not wise to sit there, dear love."

"I must be humoured—we must be."

He threw off his coat and stretched his great arms in pleasant anticipation of rest and sleep.

"Whatever do you mean, my pretty?"

"I mean that I have a long, tedious, tremendous enterprise in hand. A most troublesome enterprise. You're always at me not to waste time. Now I'm really going to be busy."

"You couldn't tell me anything I'd like to hear better."

"Couldn't I? Remember!"

He did remember.

"That—yes—all in good time."

"Not a moment more shall I waste. You'll guess I'm in earnest, for I'm going to work night and day."

"A fine resolve! But keep your work for working hours, sweetheart. And how many are to benefit by this great achievement?"

"Who can tell that? It may be for good or for harm. Yet we have a right to be hopeful."

"You make me most curious. How shall I view it, I wonder?"

"Well, you ought to be rather pleased, if you've told me the truth. And— look!"

A meteor gleamed across the misty moonlight. It seemed to streak the sky with radiance, was reflected for an instant in the pond among the rhododendrons, then vanished.

"D'you know what that means?" asked Honor.

"A wandering atom from some old, ruined world perhaps, now burnt up in our atmosphere."

"And do new-born souls come wandering from old, ruined worlds, I wonder? The German folk say that a shooting-star means a new life brought down from above, Myles. And—and how I do wish next May was come and gone; and if it's a girl, my dear one, I believe I shall go mad with disappointment."

So new fires were lighted in the man's deep heart, and blazed aloft like a signal of great joy and thanksgiving. His first impulse was to cuddle her to his breast; then he felt her to be a holy thing henceforth, separated from him by a veil impenetrable.

Long after his wife slept he lay in thought, and his spirit was much exalted, and his grey mind filled to bursting with sense of unutterable obligations. Nature was not enough to thank; she alarmed him rather, for, upon the approach of such experience, men fear the impassive Earth-Mother as well as love her. But that night he felt with unusual acuteness the sense of the vague power behind; and it pressed him on to his knees for a long, silent, wordless hour with his soul—an hour of petition and thanksgiving, of renewed thanksgiving and renewed petition.

CHAPTER IV.
THE WISDOM OF MANY

When the news spread to all ears at Endicott's and beyond it, Mr. Cramphorn, ever generous of his great gift, and always ready to speak in public if a high theme was forthcoming, proposed to make an official congratulation in the name of himself and his companions. His love of his mistress prompted him to the step; yet he designed a graceful allusion to Myles also.

It was with much difficulty that Churdles Ash prevailed upon Jonah to postpone this utterance.

"'Tis a seemly thought enough," admitted the ancient, "an' I, as knaws your power of speech, would be the fust man to hit 'pon the table an' say 'Hear, hear' arter; but ban't a likely thing for to do just now, 'cause fust theer's the bashfulness of her—an' a woman's that bashful wi' the fust—that shaame-faaced an' proud all to wance, like a young hen lookin' round to find a plaace gude enough to lay her fust egg in, an' not findin' it. Then theer's the laws of Nature, as caan't be foretold to a hair by the wisest; so, all in all, I'd bide till the baaby's born if I was you. You'm tu wise to count your awn chickens 'fore they'm hatched out; then why for should 'e count any other party's? But bide till arter—then you'll give us a braave discoourse no doubt."

So Jonah delayed his next important declaration as mouthpiece of Bear Down; but while he thus restrained the warmth of his heart and denied himself the pleasure of his own voice uplifted in a public capacity, neither he nor any other adult member of the little community saw reason to desist from general conversation upon so interesting a subject. During Sunday evenings, after supper, while the men smoked their pipes upon departure of Honor and her maids, the welfare of the little promised one grew to be a favourite theme; and Myles, proud but uneasy at first, in the frank atmosphere of conjecture, theory, and advice, now accepted the reiterated congratulations as a matter of course, and listened to the opinions and experiences of those who might be supposed to have deeper knowledge than his own in such delicate affairs.

There fell a Sunday evening hour towards Christmas, when Mr. Ash, full of an opinion awakened in him at church, began to utter advice concerning Honor; and the rest, chiming in, fell to recording scraps of sense and nonsense upon the great subject in all its relations.

"Seed missis down-along to worship's marnin'," said Mr. Ash; "an' fegs! but she was a deal tu peart an' spry 'pon her feet if you ax me. She did ought to keep her seat through the psalms an' hymns an' spiritual songs; an' theer's another thought, as rose up in sermon: Onless you want for your son—come a bwoy—to be a minister, 'tis time missis gived up church altogether till arter."

"Why for not a parson?" inquired Cramphorn. "'Tis a larned, necessary trade, though other folk, tu, may knaw a little 'bout principalities here an' there. Still, seein' all they do—why they'm so strong as Lard Bishops come to think of it, 'cept for laying on of hands—though why that calls for a bigger gun than a marryin' I never yet heard set out. You'd say a weddin' was the stiffest job—the worst or the best as man can do for his fellow-man. However, a larned trade 'twill be no doubt—not farmin', of course," he concluded.

"As to that, it depends," said Stapledon quite seriously, "if he showed a strong taste."

"We'll hope he'll be ambitious," declared Mark. "Yes, ambitious and eager to excel in a good direction. Then he'll be all right."

"But he might be blowed away from his ambition by the things as look gude to young gen'lemen, so I should keep un short of money if I was you," advised Mr. Ash.

"Blown away! Not he—not if his ambition is a live thing. If he lets pleasure—dangerous or harmless—come between him and his goal—then 'twill be mere vanity, only wind, nothing. But let me see a lad with a big, clean ambition. Nought keeps him so straight or makes his life a happier thing to himself and others."

"You never do see it," declared Myles. "A fine idea, but it hardly ever happens."

"Not lawyering," begged Jonah, drawing down his eyebrows. "Doan't 'e let un go for a lawyer, maister. 'Tis a damn dismal trade, full of obstructions and insurrections between man an' man, an' man an' woman."

"So it is then!" ejaculated Mr. Endicott heartily. "A damn dismal trade! You never said a truer word, Jonah. They live in a cobweb world of musty, dusty, buried troubles, and they rake justice out of stuff set down by dead men for dead men. 'Tis precedent they call it; and it strangles justice like dogma strangles religion. Myles understands me."

"They'm a solemn spectacle—the bettermost of 'em be—savin' your honor's pardon," ventured Pinsent. "The fur an' robes an' wigs of 'em do look terrible enough to a common man."

"Terrible tomfoolery! Terrible science of escaping through the trap-doors of precedent from common-sense!"

"But I seed a high judge to Exeter," persisted Pinsent. "An' 'twas at the 'Sizes; an' he told a man for hangin'; an' his eyes was like gimlets; an' his lean face was so grey as his wig; an' a black cap he had; an', what's worse, left no room for hope of any sort."

"Rogues, rogues," growled the blind man. "I'd sooner see son of mine fighting with the deep sea or building honest houses with moor-stone. A vile trade, I tell you; a trade to give any young mind a small, cunning twist from the outset!"

To hear and see Mr. Endicott show heat upon any subject, and now lapse from his own judicial attitude upon this judicial theme, provoked a moment of silence and surprise. Then Mr. Ash returned to his practical starting-point.

"Gospel truth and the case against law put in a parable," he declared; "but theer's a gude few things to fall out afore the cheel's future performances call for minding. Fegs! He've got to be born fust, come to think of it. 'Tis the mother as you must be busy for, not the cheel; an' I'd warn 'e to fill her mind with gude, salted sense; an' also let her bide in the sunshine so much as her can these dark days. An' doan't let her read no newspapers, for the world's a bloody business by all accounts, with battles an' murders an' sudden deaths every weekday, despite the Litany Sundays—as doan't make a ha'porth o' differ'nce seemin'ly. Keep her off of it; an' never talk 'bout churchyards, nor ghostes, nor butcher's meat, nor any such gory objects."

"I won't—in fact I never do," answered Myles, who was as childlike as the rest of the company upon this subject. "No doubt a calm and reposeful manner of living is the thing."

"Ess," concluded Mr. Ash; "just Bible subjects, an' airly hours, an' such food as she fancies in reason. 'Seek peace and ensue it,' in Scripture phrase. An' leave the rest to Providence. Though in a general way 'tis a gude rule to leave nought to Providence as you can look arter yourself."

"Shall 'e lift your hand to un, maister?" inquired Mr. Collins. "They tell me I was lathered proper by my faither afore I'd grawed two year auld. Do seem a gentle age to wallop a bwoy; yet here I be."

"'Tis a very needful thing indeed," declared Cramphorn—"male an' female for that matter. A bwoy's built to larn through his hide fust, his head arterwards. Hammer 'em! I sez. Better the cheel should holler than the man groan; better the li'l things should kick agin theer faither's shins than kick agin his heart, come they graw."

"If we could only be as wise as our words," said Myles. "I'm sure I gather good advice enough of nights for a king's son to begin life with. So many sensible men I never saw together before. You're likely to kill him with kindness, I think."

The boy Tommy Bates returned home from a walk to Chagford at this moment, with his mouth so full of news that he could not get it out with coherence.

"A poacher to Godleigh last night! Ess fay! An' keeper runned miles an' miles arter un, if he's tellin' truth; an' 'twas Sam Bonus—that anointed rascal from Chaggyford by all accounts. Not that keeper can swear to un, though he's very near positive. Catched un so near as damn it—slippery varmint! An' his pockets all plummed out wi' gert game birds! But theer 'tis—the law ban't strong enough to do nought till the chap's catched red-handed an' brought for trial."

Thus the advent of a precious new life at Endicott's was discussed most gravely and seriously. Mark Endicott indeed not seldom burst a shell of laughter upon so much wisdom, but Stapledon saw nothing to be amused at. To him the subject was more important and fascinating than any upon which thought could be employed, and he permitted no utterance or canon of old custom to escape unweighed. At first he repeated to his wife a little of all that eloquence set flowing when she retired; but Honor always met the subject with a silver-tongued torrent of irreverent laughter, and treated the ripest principles of Mr. Ash and his friends with such contemptuous criticisms that her husband soon held his peace.

Yet he erred in forgetting the blind man's warning under this added provocation of a little one in the bud; he spent all his leisure with his wife; he tried hard to catch her flitting humours, and even succeeded sometimes; but oftener he won a smile and a look of love for the frank failure of his transparent endeavours.

"Don't be entertaining, sweetheart," she said to him. "I cannot tell how it is, but if you are serious, I am happy; if you jest and try to make me laugh, my spirits cloud and come to zero in a moment. That's a confession of weakness, you see; for women so seldom have humour. Everybody says that. So be grave, if you want me to be gay. I love you so; and gravity is proper to you. It makes me feel how big and strong you are—how fortunate I am to have you to fight the battle of life for me."

"I wish I could," he said. "But you're right. I'm not much of a joker. It's not that you have a weak sense of humour that makes me miss fire; it's because you have a strong one."

Sometimes the veil between them seemed to thicken from his standpoint. Even a little formality crept into his love; and this Honor felt and honestly blamed herself for. Mark Endicott also perceived this in the voice of the man; and once he spoke concerning it, when the two walked together during a January noon.

It was a grey and amber day of moisture, gentle southern wind and watery sunlight—a day of heightened temperature, yet of no real promise that the earth was waking. Ephemera were hatched, and flew and warped in little companies, seen against dark backgrounds. Hazardous bud and bird put forth petal and music, and man's heart longed for spring; but his reason told him that the desire was vain.

"No lily's purple spike breaking ground as yet, I doubt?" said Mark Endicott, as he paced his favourite walk in the garden.

"Not yet. But the red japonica buds already make a gleam of colour against the house.

"What good things this coming springtime has hidden under her girdle for you, Myles! Leastways, one's a right to hope so. That reminds me. Is Honor happy with you alone? Not my business, and you'll say I'm an old cotquean; but I'm blind, and, having no affairs of my own, pry into other people's. Yet Honor—why, she's part of my life, and the best part. She seems more silent than formerly—more and more as the days pass. Natural, of course. I hear her thread, and the click of her needle, and her lips as she bites the cotton; but her work I can't follow with my ears now, for it's all soft wool, I suppose. She said yesterday that she much wished I could see her new garb—'morning gown' she called it. She's pleased with it, so I suppose you've praised it."

"Yes, uncle, and was sorry that I had. I don't know how it is, but I contradict myself in small things, and she never forgets, and reminds me, and makes me look foolish and feel so. This gown—a brown, soft, shiny thing, all lined with silky stuff the colour of peach-blossom, warm and comfortable—I admired it heartily, and said it was a fine thing, and suited her well."

"You could do no more."

"But somehow I was clumsy—I am clumsy, worse luck. And she said, 'Don't praise my clothes, sweetheart; that's the last straw.' 'Last straw' she certainly said, yet probably didn't guess how grave that made the sentence sound. Then she went on, 'You know my gowns don't match earth and sky one bit; and you love better the drabs and duns of the folk. You've told me so, and I quite understand. You'd rather have Sally's apron and sun-bonnet, and see her milking, with her apple cheeks pressed against a red cow, than all my most precious frippery. And, of course, you're right, and that makes it so much the more trying.' Now that was uncalled for. Don't you think so? I say this from no sorrow at it, God bless her! but because you may help read the puzzle. I don't understand her absolutely, yet. Very nearly, but not absolutely."

"No, you don't, that's certain. The mistake is to try to. You're wise in what you let alone, as a rule. But her nature you can't suffer to grow without fuss. There's a sound in your voice to her—afore the hands, too—like a servant to his mistress."

"I am her servant."

"Yes, I know; so am I also; but—well, no call to tramp the old ground. You might guess she'd look for gentleness and petting, yet——"

"She asks for it one moment, and grows impatient at it the next."

"Well, you'll learn a bit some day; but you've not got the build of mind to know much about women."

Myles sighed, and drummed his leg with a whip.

"It's all so small and petty and paltry—these shades and moods and niceties and subtleties."

"Women will have 'em."

"Well, I try."

"Go on trying. The world's full of these small things, speaking generally. You're built for big, heavy game. Yet it's your lot to catch gnats just now—for her. And she knows how hard you try. It'll come right when she's herself again. Life brims with such homespun, everyday fidgets. They meet a man at every turn."

"I long to be heart and heart with her; and I am; but not always."

"Well, don't addle your brains about it. Your large kindness with dogs and beasts, and love of them, and discipline would please her best. If you could only treat her as you treat them."

"Treat her so! She's my wife."

"I know; and lucky for her. But remember she can't change any more than you can. The only difference is that she doesn't try to, and you do. All this brooding and morbidness and chewing over her light words is not worthy of a man. Be satisfied. You'll wear—you can take that to your comfort. You'll wear all through, and the pattern of you is like to be brighter in her eyes ten years hence than now. No call to go in such a fog of your own breeding. Wood and iron are different enough in their fashion as any two creatures in the world; but that doesn't prevent 'em from cleaving exceeding tight together. She knows all this well enough; she's a woman with rather more sense of justice than is common to them; and your future's sure, if you'll only be patient and content; for she loves you better far than she's ever told you, or is ever likely to."

CHAPTER V.
IN SPRING MOONLIGHT

Another springtime gladdened the heart of man and set the sap of trees, the blood of beasts, the ichor of the wild wood gods a-flowing. A green veil spread again, a harmony of new-born music, colour, scent, all won of sunshine, rose from feathered throats, from primroses, from censers of the fragrant furze; and there was whisper of vernal rains, ceaseless hurtle of wings, and murmur of bees; while upon new harps of golden green, soft west winds sang to the blue-eyed, busy young Earth-Mother, their immemorial song.

Honor Endicott moved amid the translucent verdure; and her eyes shadowed mystery, and her heart longed for her baby's coming, as a sick man longs for light of day. She found an awakening interest in her own sex—a thing strange to her, for few women had ever peeped within the portals of her life; but now she talked much with Mrs. Loveys and the matrons of Little Silver. She listened to their lore and observed how, when a woman's eyes do dwell upon her child, there comes a look into them that shall never be seen at any other time. She noticed the little children, and discovered with some surprise how many small, bright lives even one hamlet held. Black and brown-eyed, blue-eyed and grey; with white skins and red; with soft voices and shrill; rough and gentle; brave and fearful—she watched them all, and thought she loved them all, for the sake of one precious baby that would come with the first June roses. The little life quickened to the love-songs of the thrushes; it answered the throbbing music of river and wood; its sudden messages filled her eyes with tears; her heart with ineffable, solemn thrills of mother-joy. Great calm had spread its wings about Honor. She approached her ordeal in a high spirit, as of old-time mothers of heroes. She abstracted herself from all daily routine, but walked abroad with her husband in the long green twilights, or sat beside Mark Endicott and watched his wooden needles tapping as he talked. A recent pettiness of whim and fancy had almost vanished, though now and again she did express a desire and rested not until the fulfilment. Fear she had none, for the season of fear was passed, if it had ever clouded her thoughts. To Myles her attitude insensibly grew softer, and she found his wealth of affection not unpleasant as her time approached. She accepted his worship, received his gifts, even pretended to occasional fancies that he might have the pleasure of gratifying them.

There came an evening of most lustrous beauty. Mild rain had fallen during the day, but the sky cleared at nightfall, when the clouds gleamed and parted in flakes of pearl for the pageant of a full May moon. Silently she swam out from the rack of the rain; spread light into the heart of the spring leaves; woke light along the glimmering grass blades; meshed and sprinkled and kissed with light each raindrop of them all, until the whole soaking world was bediamonded and robed in silver-grey.

Honor turned from beholding her dim grass lands, the time then being nine.

"I must go out," she said. "The night is alive and beckoning with its lovely fingers. The peace of it! Think of this night in the woods! I must go out, and you must take me, Myles."

"Not now, dearest one. It is much too late, and everything soaking wet after the rain."

"I can wrap up. I feel something that tells me this is the very last time I shall go out till—afterwards. Just an hour—a little hour; and you can drive me. I've got to go whether you will or not."

"Let us wait for the sun to-morrow."

"No, no—to-night. I want to go and feel the peace of the valley. I want to hear the Teign sisters kissing and cuddling each other under the moon. I'll put on those tremendous furs you got me at Christmas, and do anything you like if you'll only take me."

"Doctor Mathers would be extremely angry!" murmured her husband.

"He need know nothing about it. Don't frown. Please, please! It would hearten me and cheer me; and I promise to drink a full dose of the red wine when I come in. You shall pour it out. There—who could do more?"

She was gone to make ready before he answered, and Mark spoke.

"She cannot take hurt in this weather if she's wrapped up in the furs. The air feels like milk after the rain."

Stapledon therefore made no ado about it, but marched meekly forth, and himself harnessed a pony to the little low carriage purchased specially for his wife's pleasure.

Soon they set off through the new-born and moon-lit green, under shadows that lacked that opacity proper to high summer, under trees which still showed their frameworks through the foliage. Inflorescence of great oaks hung in tassels of chastened gold, and a million translucent leaves diffused rather than shut off the ambient light. Unutterable peace marked their progress; no shard-borne things made organ music; no night-bird cried; only the rivers called under the moon, the mist wound upon the water-meadows, and the silver of remote streamlets twinkled here and there from the hazes of the low-lying grass land or the shadows of the woods—twinkled and vanished, twinkled and vanished again beyond the confines of the night-hidden valley.

"A fairy hour," said Honor; "and all things awake and alive with a strange, strange moon-life that they hide by day."

"The rabbits are awake at any rate. Too many for my peace of mind if this was my land."

"Don't call them rabbits. I'm pretending that their little white scuts are the pixy people. And there's Godleigh under the fir trees—peeping out with huge yellow eyes—like the dragon of an old legend."

"Yes, that's Godleigh."

"Drive me now to Lee Bridge. It was very good of you to come. I appreciate your love and self-denial so much—so much more than I can find words to tell you, Myles."

"God be good to you, my heart! I wish I deserved half your love. You make me young again to hear you speak so kindly—young and happy too—happy as I can be until afterwards."

"It won't be many more weeks. The days that seemed so long in winter time are quite short now, though it is May. That is how a woman's heart defies the seasons and reverses the order of Nature on no greater pretext than a paltry personal one."

"Not paltry!"

"Why, everything that's personal is paltry, I suppose, even to the bearing of your first baby."

"I should be sorry if you thought so, Honor."

"Of course, I don't really. Hush now; let me watch all these dear, soft, moony things and be happy, and suffer them to work their will on my mind. I'm very near my reformation, remember. I'm going to be so different afterwards. Just a staid, self-possessed, sensible matron—and as conservative as a cow. Won't there be a peace about the home?"

"Honor!"

"Honour bright. Look at Forde's new thatch! I hate new thatch under the sun, but in the moonlight it is different. His cot looks like some golden-haired, goblin thing that's seen a ghost. How pale the whitewash glares; and the windows throw up the whites of their eyes!"

"Don't talk so much. I'm sure you'll catch cold or something. Now we're going down to valley-level. Lean against me—that's it. This hill grows steeper every time I drive down it, I think."

They crossed Chagford Bridge, where a giant ash fretted the moonlight with tardy foliage still unexpanded; then Myles drove beyond a ruined wool factory, turned to the right, passed Holy Street and the cross in the wall, and finally reached the neighbourhood of Lee Bridge. Here the air above them was dark with many trees and the silence broken by fitful patter of raindrops still falling from young foliage. The green dingles and open spaces glittered with moisture, where the light fell and wove upon them a fabric of frosted radiance touched with jewels, to the crest of the uncurling fern-fronds, and the wide shimmer of the bluebell folk—moon-kissed, as Endymion of old. Pale and wan their purple stretched and floated away and faded dimly, rippling into the darkness; but their scent hung upon the air, like the very breath of sleeping spring.

"Stop here, my love," said Honor. "What a bed for the great light to lie upon! What a silence for the tiny patter of the raindrops to make music in! And thoughts that hide by day—sad-eyed thoughts—peep out now upon all this perfection—hurry from their hiding-places in one's heart and look through one's eyes into these aisles of silver and ebony; and so go back again a little comforted. The glory of it! And if you gaze and listen closer, surely you will see Diana's own white self stealing over the mist of the bluebells, and hear perhaps her unearthly music. Nay, I must talk, Myles, or I shall cry."

"I'm only thinking of all this ice-cold damp dropping upon you out of the trees," he said.

They proceeded, then stopped once again at Honor's urgent desire. The great beech of the proposal stood before her, and she remembered the resting-place between its roots, the words carved upon its trunk. Its arms were fledged with trembling and shining foliage; its upper peaks and crown were full of diaphanous light; its huge bole gleamed like a silver pillar; and spread under the sweep of the lower branches there glimmered a pale sheen of amber where myriads of little leaf-sheafs had fallen and covered the earth as with spun silk.

Great longing to be for one moment alone with the old tree seized upon Honor. Suddenly she yearned to gaze at the throne of her promise to Christopher, to see again those letters his hand had graven upon the bark above. The desire descended in a storm upon her, and shook her so strongly that her voice came, tremulously as bells upon a wind, to utter the quick plan of her imagination.

"I wish you'd go to the bridge yonder and get me some water to drink. Your tobacco pouch will do if you rinse it well, as you often have upon the Moor. I'm frantically thirsty."

"My dear child—wait until we get home. Then you've promised me to drink some wine."

"No, I can't wait; I'm parched and I want the river water. To please me, Myles. It won't take you a moment—straight between the trees there, to that old bridge of ash poles. That's the nearest way. I must drink—really I must. It's unkind to refuse."

He grumbled a little and declared what with the dropping trees, she might have enough water; but then he saw her face in the moonlight, and she kissed him, and he departed to do her bidding.

The rustic bridge, crossed by Honor at the outset of this record, was a structure but seldom used save by gamekeepers. It spanned Teign some seventy yards away from the great tree; but Myles, who did not know the spot well, found that he must now cross a tangled underwood to reach the river. The place was difficult by night, and he proceeded with caution, emptying the tobacco out of his pouch into his pocket as he did so. One fall, got from a treacherous briar, he had; then he arrived beside the bridge and noted where faint indication of a woodland path led from it. By following this his return journey promised to be the easier. Myles knelt and scrambled to the brink, sweetened the rubber pouch and filled it as well as he could with water. He had, however, scarcely regained his feet when a shrill scream of fear twice repeated frightened the dreaming forests from their sleep, rang and reverberated to the depths of the woods, and revealed a sudden echo close at hand that threw back upon its starting-point the deep horror of the cry. For a second Stapledon made no movement, then he charged into the woods and tore his way back to the road. There he arrived a minute later, torn and bleeding. The pony stood unmoved, but Honor had disappeared. As Myles looked wildly about him, it seemed that in her fearful expression of sudden terror his wife had vanished away. Then, amid the dark spaces of shadow and the silver interspaces of light he found her, lying with the moon upon her white face and one small hand still clutching a few bluebells. She had fallen midway between the carriage and the great beech; she had been stricken senseless by some physical catastrophe or mental shock.

The man groaned aloud before what he saw, dropped down on his knees beside her, gathered her up gently, and uttered a thousand endearing words; but her head fell forward without life towards him, and setting her down, he gathered the wet, shining moss and pressed it about her forehead and neck and unfastened the buttons at her throat. Great terror came upon him as she still remained unconscious, and he picked her up to carry her back to the carriage. Then she moved and opened her eyes and stretched her hands to him; whereupon, in his turn, he cried aloud and thanked God.

As she began to apprehend, to order the broken tangles of thought and take up again the threads so suddenly let fall, he feared that she would faint once more, for with return of memory there came a great wave of terror over her eyes; but she only clung to him and breathed with long, deep gasps of fear, yet said no word. Then it seemed that a physical pang distracted her mind from the immediate past; a strange, bewildered look crossed her upturned face, and she bowed herself and pressed her hand into her side and moaned.

"Oh, I was a mad fool to do this!" he cried. "I am to blame for it all. Let me drive—back through Godleigh. That's nearest. We've the right, though we never use it. Say you're better now."

But she could not answer yet, and he made the pony gallop forward until it crossed the bridge over Teign, then turned into the private park-lands beyond.

Presently Honor spoke.

"I'm so sorry I screamed out. I frightened you and made you hurry from the river and tear your face. It's bleeding very badly still. Take my handkerchief—poor Myles!"

"What happened? What were you doing?"

"I had a sudden longing to gather some of the bluebells with the moonlight and dew on them. Nothing happened—at least———"

"Something must have nearly frightened you to death from your terrible shriek."

"I don't know. I can't remember. A tree moved, I think—moved and seemed alive—it was some dream or trick of the light."

"All my fault. Why am I thus weak with you?"

"Oh, it was so grey, Myles. You saw nothing?"

"Nothing but you. I had eyes for nothing else."

She shivered and nestled close to him.

"But I'm so sorry I cried out like that."

"Don't think more about it. Half the terror was in your mind, and half in the pranks of the moonlight among the trees. They look enough like ghosts. I only hope to heaven no harm will come of this. The fall has not hurt you, has it?"

"No, no, no; I shall be all right. I was only——"

Then suffering overtook her again, and she shrank into herself and said no more. But as they left the gates of Godleigh and prepared to mount the hill homewards, Honor spoke in a small, faint voice.

"While we are here in Little Silver, dearest, perhaps—Doctor Mathers—I don't know whether it's anything, but I'm not very well, dear Myles. I'm— indeed I think baby's going to be born to-night. Perhaps we had better call and tell him before going home."

Her husband was overcome with concern. He ran to the physician's little dwelling, distant two hundred yards off in the village, delivered his message, and then, returning, put the astounded pony at the hill in a manner that caused it to snort viciously and utter a sort of surprised vocal remonstrance almost human. The sound made Honor laugh even at her present crisis; but the laugh proved short, and in three minutes Myles was carrying her to her room and bawling loudly for women.

Soon the household knew what had happened; Doctor Mathers arrived; and Tommy Bates, hurled out of sleep, was despatched at high pressure for Mrs. Brimblecombe, the sexton's wife—a woman of significance at such times.

Very faintly through the silence a noise of voices came to the ear of Collins where he slept in a spacious attic chamber with Churdles Ash. Thereupon Henry left his bed and wakened the elder man.

"Theer's the douce of a upstore down house 'bout somethin'. Please God we ban't afire!"

Mr. Ash grunted, but the last word reached his understanding; so he awoke, and bid the other see what was amiss. Collins thereupon tumbled into his trousers and proceeded to make inquiries. In three minutes he returned.

"'Tis missus took bad," he said. "A proper tantara, I can tell 'e, an' doctor in the house tu. Ought us to rise up? Might be more respectful in such a rare event."

"Rise up be damned!" said Mr. Ash bluntly. "Not that I wouldn't rise up to the moon if I could take the leastest twinge off of her; but 'tis woman's work to-night. The sacred dooty of child-bearin' be now gwaine on, an' at such times even the faither hisself awnly looks a fule. Go to sleep."

"The dear lady be afore her date seemin'ly," remarked Collins, returning to his bed.

"'Tis allus so wi' the fustborn. The twoads be mostly tu forrard or tu back'ard. An' they do say as them born late be late ever after, an' do take a humble back plaace all theer days; while them born airly gets ahead of or'nary folks, an' may even graw up to be gert men. I've seed the thing fall out so for that matter."

"An' how might it have been wi' you, I wonder, if theer's no offence? How was you with regards to the reckoning?"

"'Tis a gude bit back-along when I was rather a small bwoy," answered Churdles, laughing sleepily at his own humour; "but, so far as I knaw, I comed 'pon the appointed day to a hour."

"Just what us might have counted upon in such a orderly man as you," mused Collins.

"'Tis my boast, if I've got wan, that I never made my faither swear, nor my mother shed a tear, from the day that I was tucked-up.[#] No fegs! Never. Now you best go to sleep, or you might hear what would hurt your tender 'eart."

[#] Short-coated.

CHAPTER VI.
SORROW'S FACE

Throughout that short summer night the young successor of Doctor Courteney Clack was torn in two between a birth-bed and a death-bed. For the old mother of Gregory Libby was now to depart, and it chanced that the hour of her final journey fell upon a moment of great peace before the dawn. Then, when she had passed, while her son yet stared in fear from the foot of the bed, Doctor Mathers dragged his weary limbs up the hill again to Bear Down. Now he rendered the household happy by his announcement that he had come to stop until all was concluded.

He sat and smoked cigarettes and soothed Myles, who tramped the parlour like a caged animal. He spoke cheerily, noted the other's mangled face, and congratulated him upon a narrow escape, for his left cheek was torn by a briar to the lid of the eye. Presently he yawned behind his hand, gladly partook of a cup of tea, and prayed that the expected summons from the dame above might not be long delayed. And when the sun was flaming over the hills and the air one chant of birds, there came a woman with a kind face, full of history, and spoke to Doctor Mathers.

"Now, sir, us would like to see you."

Myles turned at the voice, but his companion was already gone. Then the terrific significance of these next few moments surged into the husband's mind, and he asked himself where he should go, what he should do. To go anywhere or do anything was impossible; so he hardened his heart and tramped the carpet steadily. There was a vague joy in him that his child should be born at the dawn hour.

A moment later Mark Endicott entered. He, too, had not slept but he had spent the night in his own chamber and none knew of his vigil. Now he came forward and put out his hand.

"Be of good heart, lad! She's going on very well with great store of strength and spirit, Mrs. Loveys tells me."

"If I could only—"

"Yes, every man talks that nonsense. You can't; so just walk out upon the hill along with me an' look at the first sun ever your child's eyes will blink at. A fitting time for his advent. A son of the morning you are; and so will he or she be."

"Last night it is that makes me so fearful for Honor."

"A shock—but time enough to fret if there's any harm done. Wait for the news quiet and sensible."

They walked a little way from the house, Myles scarcely daring to look upward towards a window where the cherry-blossom reigned again; but when they stood two hundred yards distant, a cry reached them and Tommy Bates approached hurriedly.

"Maister! Maister Stapledon, sir! You'm wanted to wance!"

"Go!" said Mark, "and tell Tom to come and lead me back."

So, for the second time in twenty-four hours, Myles Stapledon ran with heavy and laborious stride. In a few moments he reached the house, and finding nobody visible, entered the kitchen and made the china ring again with his loud summons. Then Mrs. Loveys entered, and her apron was held up to her eyes. Behind her moved Cramphorn and his daughter Margery, with faces of deep-set gloom.

"What's this? In God's name speak, somebody. Why are you crying, woman?"

"She's doin' cleverly—missis. Be easy, sir. No call to fret for her. All went butivul—but—but—the dear li'l tiny bwoy—he'm dead—born dead— axin' pardon for such black news."

"Honor knows?"

"Ess—'pears she knawed it 'fore us did. The dark whisper o' God—as broke it to her in a way no human could. 'Twas last night's fright an' fall as killed un, doctor reckons."

The man stared, and sorrow set his face in a semblance more than common stonelike.

"Bear up, dear sir," ventured Jonah. "She'm doin' braave herself, an' that's more'n a barrel-load o' baabies to 'e, if you think of it aright. An' gude comes out o' evil even in such a case sometimes, for he might have been born a poor moonstruck gaby, as would have been a knife in his mother's heart for all time."

But Stapledon did not answer. He walked past them, returned to the parlour and resumed his slow tramp up and down. What of the great event waited for, hoped for, dreamed about through near nine months—each a century long? He felt that all the past was true, but this last half-hour a dream. He saw the chair that Doctor Mathers had occupied, observed his empty cup, his litter of cigarette-ends about the hearth. It seemed hard to believe that the climax was come and passed; and for one brief and bitter moment the man's own suffering dominated his heart. But then he swept all personal tribulation out of mind, and went upon his knees and thanked the Unknown for His blessings, in that it had pleased Him to bring Honor safely through her ordeal. He prayed for her sorrow to be softened, her pain forgotten, and that her husband might be inspired in this trial to lighten his wife's supreme grief. He begged also for wisdom and understanding to support her and lift her burden and bear it himself as far as that was possible.

He still knelt when Doctor Mathers suddenly entered, coughed, and plunged a hand into his pocket fiercely for more cigarettes. Then Myles rose, without visible emotion, to find the young physician red and angry. Indeed he now relieved his mingled feelings by swearing a little.

"Your wife's all right, and of course I'm infernally sorry about this. You know it's not my fault. The shock quite settled the matter, humanly speaking. A most unlucky chance. What in the name of God were you doing in the middle of the night in the woods? It's enough to make any doctor get savage. I'm heartily sorry for you both—heartily; but I'm mighty sorry for myself too. As a man with his way to make—but, of course, you don't know what all the fools on the countryside will say, though I well do. It's always the doctor's fault when this happens. However, I can't expect you to be sorry for me, I know."

"I am, Mathers. The blame of this sad thing is mine—all. I should have been firm, and not yielded to an unwise idea. And if you've no objection, I should like to see my wife and tell her how entirely I blame myself."

"It's no good talking like that, my dear sir; but, fault or no fault, let it be a lesson to you next time. Be firm. Mrs. Stapledon was frightened by the ghost of the devil apparently. Anyway, I can't learn what the nature of the shock was. 'Something grey—suddenly close to me,' is all she will say. That might be a wandering donkey. It's all very cruel and hard for you both—a jolly fine little boy he would have been. Better luck next time. I'll be back again in a few hours."

"I may see Honor?"

"Yes, certainly; but cut it short, and don't talk about fault or blame on anybody. Let her think you're glad—eh?"

"She wouldn't believe it."

"Well, well, don't make a fuss. Just say the right thing and then clear out. I want her to sleep before I come back. You know how sorry I am; but we must look ahead. Good morning."

A little later Stapledon, his heart beating hard and a sort of fear upon him, knocked at the door of his wife's room and was allowed to enter. In the half light he saw Mark sitting by Honor, and heard the old man speak in a voice so soft and womanly that Myles could scarce believe it was his uncle.

"Why, your good, brave heart will tide you over for all our sakes. 'Twas part of the great web of woman's sorrow spun in the beginning, dearie. It had to be. You thought how life was going to change for you; but it hasn't changed—not yet—that's all the matter. Take your life up again where you set it down; and just go on with it, like a brave girl. Here's Myles come. I hear his breathing. He'll say the same, in better words than mine. We must all live through the cloud, my Honor, and see it sink before the good sunshine that will follow. 'Twasn't Nature's will this should happen so, but God's own. There's comfort in that for you. And we'll have God and Nature both to fight on our side come next time."

He departed, and husband and wife were left alone. For a moment he could only hold her hand and press it and marvel to see how young she appeared again. Her eyes were very bright—like stars in the dim room. She looked at him and pressed back on his hand. Then a flicker of a whimsical smile woke at the corner of her lips and she spoke in a little voice.

"I'm so—so sorry, dear heart. I did my very best—I——"

"Don't," he said; and the old nurse in the next room frowned at his loud, hoarse tones.

"You'll say that I've been wasting my time again—I know you will."

"Please, please, Honor. For God's sake not at a minute like this—I——"

Then he stopped. Where was the answer to his prayer? Here he stood ranting and raving like a lunatic, while she, who had endured all, appeared calm and wholly self-possessed.

"The fault was all mine—every bit of it," he began again quietly. "If I had not let my headstrong little love go into the woods, the child——"

"Don't blame yourself. The past is past, and I'll never return to it in word or in thought, if I can help doing so. Only there are things we don't guess at, Myles—terrible things hidden and not believed in. Our little son had to die. It is cruel—cruel. I cannot explain—not now. Perhaps some day I will if I am ever brave enough."

"Don't talk wildly like this, my darling Honor. You are overwrought; you will be better very soon. Uncle Mark was right. Life has not changed for us."

"It never will. Things hidden—active things say 'No'! Oh, the grey horror of it there!"

She shivered and put her arms round Myles, but Mrs. Brimblecombe had heard her patient's voice lifted in terror, and this was more than any professional nurse could be expected to stand. As the medical man before her, she considered her own great reputation, and, entering now, bade Myles take his leave at once.

"Please to go, sir," she said aside to him. "You really mustn't bide no longer; an' 'tis very ill-convenient this loud talking; an' your voice, axin' your pardon, be lifted a deal tu high for a sick chamber."

"I'll go," he answered; "but don't leave her. The cursed accident of light or shade, or whatever it was that frightened her overnight, is in her mind still. She's wandering about it now. Soothe her all you can—all you can. And if she wants me, let me know."

In the passage red-eyed women of the farm met him, and Mrs. Loveys spoke.

"We'm all broken-hearted for 'e, I'm sure; an'—an' would 'e like just to see the dear, li'l perfect bwoy? Her wouldn't—missis. But p'raps you would, seein' 'tis your awn. An' the mother of un may be glad to knaw what he 'peared like later on, when she can bear to think on it."

Myles hesitated, then nodded without words and followed Mrs. Loveys into an empty room. There he looked down, among primroses and lilac that Sally had picked, upon what might have been his son; and he marvelled in dull pain at the dainty beauty of the work; and he stared with a sort of special blank wonder at the exquisite little hands and tiny nails. Presently he bent and kissed this marred mite, then departed, somehow the happier, to plan that it should lie within the churchyard for Honor's sake.

He broke his fast soon after midday, and, upon learning that his wife slept peacefully, sought for his own comfort the granite counsellors of the high hills. There was an emptiness in life before this stroke; it left him helpless, not knowing what to turn to. His great edifice of many plans and hopes was all a ruin.

Much to their own regret, Cramphorn and Churdles Ash met Stapledon as he climbed alone to the Moor. They were very sorry for him in their way, and they felt that to touch their hats and pass him by without words at such a moment would not be fitting.

"Sure, we'm grievous grieved, all the lot of us," said Jonah grimly—"more for her than you, because, bein' an Endicott, she'm more to me an' Ash than ever you can be. But 'tis a sad evil. Us had thought 'twould be osiers as you li'l wan would rock in—soft an' gentle by his mother's side; but 'tis elm instead—so all's ended, an' nought left but to bend afore the stroke."

Mr. Ash was also philosophical.

"'Tweern't death ezacally as comed 'pon the house, neither; nor yet life, you see. 'Cause you can't say as a babe be dead what never drawed breath, can 'e?"

"An' theer's another cheerful thought for 'e," added Cramphorn, "for though 'tis as painful for a woman to bear a wise man as a fool, no doubt, yet so it might have failed out, an' the pain ends in wan case and turns to joy; an' in t'other case it never ends. An' as 'twas odds he'd have been a poor antic, 'tis better as her should mourn a month for un dead than for all the days of his life, as Scripture sez somewheers."

"Well spoke," commented Churdles. "Never heard nothin' wiser from 'e, Jonah. An', beggin' your pardon, theer's a gert lesson to such a trouble, if a body ban't tu stiff-necked to see it. It do teach us worms o' the airth as even God A'mighty have got a pinch of somethin' human in the nature of Un—as I've allus said for that matter. This here shows how even He can alter His purpose arter a thing be well begun, an' ban't shamed to change His Everlasting Mind now an' again, more'n the wisest of us. Theer's gert comfort in that, if you please."

Stapledon thanked both old men for their consolation, and set his face to the Moor.

CHAPTER VII.
PLOTS AGAINST AN ORPHAN

The departure of Mrs. Libby and its probable effect upon her son became a matter of local interest, because she had toiled with her old bones for him to the end, and he had taken all her service as a matter of course, but would now feel the loss of his home comforts exceedingly.

"He'll have to get a wife," said the man Pinsent at Sunday supper. All were assembled save Honor, who had now been in her room for three weeks, and still kept it.

"If 'tis awnly for somebody to cook his victuals, the man must marry," declared Collins. Then with some craft he added, "And the question in Little Silver is who's to be the gal."

"He'm a comical tempered chap, to my thinking; an' they do say a man wi' a tie in his speech——" began Pinsent. But he found himself sharply taken to task from the quarter he had secretly aimed at.

"You'd best to mind your awn business, Samuel!" flamed out Sally, then blushed rose-red to the roots of her hair at the laughter her confession won. Her relations alone did not laugh. Margery bent over her plate and grew white rather than red; and Mr. Cramphorn roundly rated the speaker for such a lapse of manners.

"'Fore the whole world, would 'e? I blush for 'e—though you can for yourself still, it seems. An' him never so much as opened his lips on it! 'Tis a most unmaidenly thing, an' never to have been looked for in no darter o' mine."

"Sorry I drawed it from her, notwithstanding," said Pinsent. "I'm sure I'd rather have bit my tongue out than bring red to any gal's cheeks."

"Nobody would hurt her for gold," added Collins.

But Sally was now in tears. She left her supper, and withdrew weeping; her sister gave vent to a little hard laugh; while a moment later Cramphorn, in some discomfort, followed his elder daughter. Then, familiar with Jonah's estimate of Libby, and having no desire to breed further storm, Mark Endicott spoke to Ash.

"What's your opinion of the man, Churdles?"

"A poor creation, your honour," answered the patriarch promptly. "Not a penn'orth o' nature in un, else he'd have had some gal squeezed to his heart so soon as ever he comed by enough money to marry. He'm cold clay, an' awnly waitin' to see which of Jonah's maids be in highest favour—which is most like to have the cottage left to her. His faither was another most calculating chap. The woman what's just gone had awnly half a score short of a hunderd pound saved when he offered hisself. Married for money, in fact; an' that's a 'mazin' thing to happen except among respectable people."

"What d'you say to that, Margery?" asked Myles Stapledon bluntly. He did not like Margery, and her attitude at her sister's discomfiture had not escaped him.

"Ban't for me to speak against my elders," she answered slowly, with a malignant look at the placid veteran. "Mr. Ash—auld as he is—do find it so hard to mind his awn business as other people seemin'ly. He ban't paid for pokin' his ancient nose into Gregory Libby's consarns, I s'pose. But he'm past larnin' manners now, no doubt."

The boyish features of Mr. Ash flushed suddenly and his head shook a little.

"Theer's a sour speech—an' her so young! Worse'n any vinegar you'll be in the marriage cruet, woman, whoever 'tis that's daft enough to take 'e! Fegs! I pity un; an' I pity the Dowl when it's his turn—as it will be some day. To talk to a auld man so!"

Unwonted wrinkles appeared in Mr. Ash's apple-face, and he showed a great disinclination to let the matter drop, though Stapledon bid him be silent. He chattered and growled and demanded an apology, which Margery declined to offer. Then she instantly left the kitchen, so that no argument should rise upon her refusal. She glowered sullenly about her, restrained a strong desire to scream, and then withdrew.

Yet Churdles, though he knew it not, and must have much deplored the fact if it had come to his understanding, was responsible for a practical and valuable lesson to Margery. His words, though they angered her, had not fallen upon deaf ears. She sulked away now in the corner of an empty room and set her wits to work. Mr. Libby was in one respect like heaven; he had to be taken by storm, and Churdles Ash unwittingly indicated the direction of attack.

Margery indeed loved this shifty youth; she adored his cane-coloured hair cut straight across his low forehead, like a child's fringe, his uncertain eyes, his moustache—with a most "gentleman-like droop to it," as she had discovered. She loved him—not for his money but for himself, and her sister's infatuation was of a similar genuine quality. They were primitive maidens both and had seen little of the other sex, owing to their father's suspicions that every man on the eastern side of Dartmoor would run away with them, given the opportunity. Now passion worthy of a better cause burnt in their young hearts, and each raged against the other—inwardly for the most part. Their weapons were different, and whereas Margery's sarcasms proved wholly wasted on her sister, Sally's anger, when roused, generally took the shape of a swinging box on the ear—a retort contemptible enough, no doubt, yet not easy to be ignored. Margery's waspish tongue was no match for her sister's right arm, therefore open quarrels seldom happened; yet each daily strained every nerve, and since Gregory had come to be a mere womanless, desolate orphan, the efforts of both girls were redoubled. It had, however, been left to the sensation of that evening to quicken their wits; and now each, by ways remote, set about a new and more pressing investment of Mr. Libby's lonely heart.

Margery took the word of Mr. Ash to herself, and realised that if her loved one was really waiting to get a hint of Jonah Cramphorn's intentions, her own course must be modified. She knew that her father, despite his surly and overbearing disposition, might be influenced without difficulty; and she possessed the tact and discretion proper to such a task. She had never desired any influence over him until the present, and had indeed thought but little of the future, excepting with reference to herself and Gregory. Now, however, the danger of allowing Sally even an indirect ascendency was made manifest, and Margery determined that her sister must be put out of court at home, by fair means if possible, by foul if necessary.

In a most cold-blooded and calculating spirit she approached the problem of making herself so indispensable to her father that he should come to regard her as his better and more deserving child. That situation once established, no doubt Gregory Libby would be the first to perceive it. If he was backward in doing so, then might she delicately aid his perception; indeed she doubted not that this course would be necessary, for the control she now set herself to maintain over her parent must be more real than apparent at first. She hoped that within a month at the latest it would be safe to hint to Gregory that such supremacy existed.

And meanwhile, hanging over a gate out of doors, so that her tear-stained cheeks might cool, Sally also meditated some definite action whereby the halting regard of the desired object should grow established and affirmed. To a determination she also came, but it fell far short of her sister's in subtlety. She merely fell back upon the trite conceit of a *tertium quid*, and hoped how, once reminded of the fact that other men also found her pleasant in their eyes, Mr. Libby would awaken into jealousy and so take action. Her father she did not consider, because his opinions had long since ceased to weigh with her, when it was possible to disregard them. Sally approached the future in a sanguine spirit, for within the secret places of her heart there lurked an honest belief that Gregory loved her to desperation. Why he delayed to mention the fact, under these distracting circumstances, was not easy to explain; but now, upon his mother's death, there had come a climax in the young man's life; and Sally felt that in the present forlorn circumstances she ought to be, and probably was, his paramount object of reflection.

So she determined to precipitate the imminent declaration by parading another possible husband; and that point established it remained only to decide upon whom this thankless part should fall. Henry Collins naturally offered himself to her mind. His emotions were perfectly familiar to her, though in that he had scrupulously obeyed Jonah and never dared to offer marriage, Sally regarded him with some natural derision. But he loved her very well, and would come when she whistled, and frisk at her side with great content and joy. Whereupon, driven frantic before the spectacle of Collins lifted to this giddy fortune, she doubted not but that Gregory would declare himself and make a definite offer. His words once spoken, she felt no fear for the future. She held herself in some esteem, and was satisfied of her powers to keep Libby, or any other man, to a bargain.

Thus both maids, within the space of an hour, had braced their minds to a course of vital action; and it remained for time to show which, if either, was to succeed in the result.

CHAPTER VIII.
A NECKLACE OF BIRDS' EGGS

There came a Sunday, yet not so soon as Doctor Mathers hoped, when Honor declared herself able and desirous to take the air again. She chose the Moor as the scene of this return to life; and, as Stapledon had departed for the day to see an acquaintance at Okehampton before his wife decided to go forth, her uncle, and not her husband, accompanied her—to the deep chagrin of the latter when he returned home.

Through the long hours of a weary and empty convalescence, Honor said little concerning the incident responsible for wreck of hope; but her loss had grown into an abiding grief nevertheless; and while the man was stricken most sorely at first, but had now become resigned, devoting only leisure thought to his private sorrow, the woman took this trial to her heart with increasing bitterness through those lonely hours that followed upon it. There was, moreover, an added element of terror and a superstitious despair bred of her alarm in the woods. This died but slowly, for she would not share the experience with any other; yet, as physical health increased, all lesser emotion dwindled before the ever-present sense of loss. From Myles she hid the heavy misery of it, that his own sorrow might not be increased; but she liked to speak with her uncle of the little flower lost in the bud, and he was patient and never weary of comforting her to the best of his power.

It is to be noted, however, that Myles somewhat misunderstood Honor's extreme reticence, and her assumed air of brightness and good hope misled him perhaps more completely than Honor designed. He was secretly surprised that this matter had not left a deeper mark; he did not guess at a scar out of his sight; but he marvelled that his wife could still laugh and even jest upon occasion. Under her tranquillity and humour he failed to probe, but he bade the inner wonder in his mind be dumb. Not until long afterwards did he learn the truth and realise the depth of the sorrow she had masked for love of him.

The little open carriage crept up over Scor Hill, then proceeded by a steep way to Charity Grepe's cottage. There Honor left half-a-crown in person, for since certain rumours that poor Cherry must go to the work-house, the mistress of Bear Down had become her active champion. Then the pony was turned, climbed the hill again, and presently stood above Teign valley, at a point on the hillside where a little lakelet reflected the blue sky above it, and shone framed in rushes and verdant sphagnum, in rosy sundews all frosted and agleam, in small scattered flames of the bog asphodel, and in many lesser things that love a marsh.

Away on the wide front of Watern, great gloomy tracts, still dark from fire, spread forth over many an acre. There a "swaling" had freed the land of heath and furze, and provided light and air for grass; but the spot seen from this distance was naked as yet.

"There's a great scar over against us on the hill—black—black against the green and the grey and the blue overhead—all charred and desolate. That's how my heart feels, Uncle Mark—so dreary and forlorn—like an empty nest."

"Look again," he said; "look at what seems so black upon the hill, and think as you look, and you'll remember the ash and ruin are all full of young, sweet blades, sprouting strong, brimming with sap to hide the rack of dead char. 'Twill be so with you, my dear; for there's the bend and spring of youth in your heart still. Wait till the heather's out again, and the foxgloves are nodding along the low ridges over the Teign, and the whortle bells be turned to purple berries once more."

"How you remember!" she said, "despite all the long years of darkness."

"Yes; I remember, thank God. I smell the damp near where you've pulled up; and I see the marsh, down to the little bluebell flower that creeps in the grass, and the spotted leaves of orchis, and the white wisps of the cotton grass in summer, and all the rest, that I never thought upon when I had my eyes. But there's a quiet, unknown mercy that works through the morning hours of a man's life if he lives in the lap of Nature and is true to her. Keen sight stores the memory unbeknown to us; and none can tell how deep that unconscious, unguessed gathering-up may be but those who fall upon blindness. No credit to me at all; yet the pictures come as the seasons come—at bud-break; at the sound of the west wind and the call of the river; at the music of rain on the leaves; at the whirr of the cutter in the hay; at the touch of snow on my face and in my eyebrows. I know—I know it all, for my eyes reaped and my brain garnered at the merciful will of God. Without those mind picture-books I should be blind indeed."

"You're so brave. I wish that I had more of you in me. I'm not a true Endicott."

"As to that, 'tis only those who won't see are blind. Eyesight's the window of the house, but the ear is the door. A blow-fly on the window-pane is big enough to hide the evening star—if you're content to let it; but shut your eyes and you'll see the star in the blue, with nought between it and your thoughts."

"It's so hard to be wise; and words are not warm, live things you can cuddle. Oh, I want something smaller than myself to love! I had lighted such a great fire of love; and now it's all burnt out, and no green hope springing through the ashes."

"Be patient. Look forward, my Honor."

"There's nothing there—all blank."

"You're morbid; and that's the last foolishness I should ever have thought to tax you with. Myles——"

"No—no; you don't understand. How should you understand?"

"Moonshine!"

"It wasn't moonshine. I wish I could think it was. But you must be patient with me. It's so cold to open your eyes every morning with the dull feeling that something sad is waiting for you to remember it. I'm all winter, while the rest of the world is full of spring."

"And spring will touch you presently."

"I had built such castles in the air—painted such futures. First, my boy was to be a soldier; but I grew frightened of that when I began to fill in details of the picture; and then a farmer, but that did not satisfy me at all. Presently my heart went out to the thought of his being an artist—either in words or pictures, but an artist in deeds at any rate. You don't know what I mean by that. One who thought and felt like an artist—and walked so. He was to magnify the Lord and love the earth, and all green things, and birds especially, and the changeful sky. I did not think of him as loving men and women very much—excepting me. So my silly thoughts sped and I shut my eyes, that nobody should see my hope looking out of them. I was going to be the mother of a great man—and I am only the mother of a great sorrow, after all."

"A shared sorrow; don't forget that, my dear. There's three hearts to take each a part of the load. More than that, for, beyond Myles and me, every man's breast and woman's bosom is heavy for you here. A widespread, real regret, though 'tis not their way to make much ado."

"They are very good to me—better than I deserve. I shall have more thoughts for them now. Sorrow at least teaches sympathy. But my soul has quite lost heart of late days, and I feel so old."

At this moment from the valley there came two persons along the path where Honor's pony carriage stood. One appeared uneasy, the other in a very halcyon halo of delight; for Sally, true to her resolve, had indicated that a little attention from Mr. Collins would not be unwelcome; and now they moved side by side upon a stolen walk. Elsewhere Margery accompanied her parent to see a neighbour, and Sally was supposed to be at the farm.

The pair made awkward acknowledgments and were proceeding, when Honor noted an unusual decoration about her milkmaid's neck. In addition to a string of glass pearls, a little necklace of birds' eggs—alternate thrush and blackbird—adorned Sally's plump throat, and the spectacle, suggestive as it was of robbed nests, woke a wave of passing indignation in Honor's heart.

"What is that round your neck?" she asked with a sudden hardness in her voice; and Sally's hands went up gingerly to the frail adornment, while she looked at Collins, whose gift, snatched from screaming birds, she wore. Seeing explanation was expected from him, Henry stood forward, touched his Sunday hat, and spoke with many stumblings.

"Beggin' pardon, I'm sure, ma'am, I——"

"You robbed the birds, Collins?"

"Ess, I did, but if you call home last cherry-time, ma'am; if I may say so— you see I did as you bid an' shot a braave lot last autumn, as you wanted— them being so bowldacious as to eat your fruit; an' come autumn an' winter, I catched a gude few in traps what I teeled in the garden. Then, come spring, I had a bright thought that if I took the eggs of 'em 'twould mean gert thinning out o' the birds. An' no account neither, if I may say so; 'cause a egg's just life in the raw, waitin' for warmth an' time to quicken it. They never lived like, savin' your presence, so the airth ban't the poorer by a bird's note, 'cause us caan't lose what we never had. 'Tis no more'n a seed spoiled, or a leaf-bud nipped by frost, or a cheel still——"

He clapped his hand over his mouth and heard Sally say "Fule!" under her breath; but his mistress nodded and bid him go on his way.

"You may be right; but take no more eggs from the birds."

So Mr. Collins got himself out of sight to the tune of a reprimand from Sally that made his ears tingle.

"You gert, clumsy-mouthed gawk! To utter such a speech an' tellin' that stuff to her, an' go mumblin' on, like a bumble-bee in a foxglove; an' end up so! Not the sense of a sheep you ain't got!"

She tore off his gift and stamped on the blown shells, while he merely stood and rolled his great eyes wretchedly.

Elsewhere Endicott spoke to his niece.

"Strange how a chance word out of a fool's mouth will often come pat. These things—eggs—buds—babies are so little account in the great sum total. Nature's units don't trouble her. The crushed windflower will bud and blow again next year. What is a year to her? The robbed mother-bird screams for an hour, then goes on with the vital business of preserving her own life; and the robbed mother-woman—her heart aches to-day, but the pain soothes off presently as the months and years roll over first memories. We're built to forget; else the world would be a madhouse, or just one great welter of sorrow. 'Tis God's way, I judge, seldom to put upon us more than we can bear. If grief or pain's past bearing—why then the heart or something cracks and there's an end of us. But sorrow alone never killed a healthy being. I'd rather count it the torch that lights to the greatest deeds we're built to do. I hoped that a little child would draw you together—Myles and you—close, close as soil and seed; but 'tis a shared grief must do it—instead of a shared joy. Such a welding, as by fire, may last longest after all."

She sighed, touched her pony with the whip, in a sort of thoughtful caress, and turned him homewards.

"I don't know what Myles thinks about it. Either he hides all he feels to save me—or he is forgetting, as you say. It is natural that he should. No man that ever lived can know how long those nine months are to a woman. But I—I—there it is in the wind—in the rustle of the leaves. I hear it so often—the sound of a rocking cradle. I must wait until the wind sings a different song before I can be wise. Some day I shall wake up strong again—strong to acknowledge all your goodness and everybody's goodness and sympathy. I cannot yet."

The old man was moved for her. He put his hand on hers and patted it.

"I think I understand as much as an ancient bachelor may. But you must do your share and help the powers to help you. There's an effort called for. Hard to make, but you must make it. Take up your life again—the old life that you laid down; an' do it with a single heart."

"I cannot yet. I left it behind so gladly. I must go back for it. I do not care about any life just now. I cannot cry or laugh with my heart. It's all pretence—think what that means. I look at everything from the outside—like Christo used to. I'm a dead, withered bough still on the tree; and what is it to me that the next bough is busy about new leaves?"

"You do yourself a wrong to say so, and I'd not listen to anybody else who spoke so ill of you. You must come back to yourself—your own good self—and the sooner the better. That's a plain duty at least—not to be escaped from. That's a call, whether your heart's sad or merry. 'Tis the honest, everyday duty of a woman to be good, dear heart—same as it's the duty of a Mary lily to be white. Keep your proper colour, as God meant you, and as God taught you. Live as you have lived: with a sense of duty for the sake of those that love you, if no better reason."

She sighed again, aweary of the subject.

"Now we'll go home. We're wasting my first breath of sweet air in words. Better to draw it in silently and not turn it into talk."

Mark Endicott laughed.

"Why, yes, it does the heart more good that way, no doubt. You're a deal wiser than I am, niece, for all my grey hairs and jackdaw chatter."

Then slowly down the hill, without more speech, they drove together.

CHAPTER IX.
AN OLD-TIME PRESCRIPTION

From the occasion of her drive upon the Moor, Honor, instead of proceeding towards good health, fell away in that desired progress. What chance had conspired to an effect so unfortunate none knew, but the fact was apparent, and as days passed and summer returned, there stole gradually upon her a listless and inert attitude of spirit—a state of the mind that reflected upon her physical condition and appeared in a most despondent outlook upon life. From time to time some transient gleam of returning health and happiness gladdened those who loved her; but weeks passed and still Honor's temper was of a sort that kept Myles anxious and Doctor Mathers exasperated. For she proved not a good patient and none could prevail upon her to consider the foreign travel and sea voyage that her physician stood out for at every visit. She told them that she was well enough at home; that her health improved; and that they need be under no concern for her. Meanwhile, her life grew narrower and narrower, both in its bounds of thought and performance. Her reflections indeed she kept to herself for the most part, and certainly the event responsible in great measure for her sustained ill-health she imparted to no one; but her actions were obvious, and Myles began to grow care-worn as he watched a life so full of energy and various interest now sink into mere mechanical existence. Her walks dwindled to strolls; Nature brought Honor no particular delight; and the old haunts failed to cheer her. Until midday she rarely stirred from her own room, and sometimes she would keep her bed altogether from sheer indifference toward affairs.

This life of ashes, which neither love nor duty seemed capable of rousing into renewed activity and vigour, was beheld in its dreary unfolding by the little population of Bear Down; and that busy hive, both in season and out, discussed this grave crisis in the fortunes of its mistress and offered all manner of suggestions and advice upon it. Some opinions were undoubtedly sensible enough, as when Churdles Ash counselled forcible compliance with the doctor's orders.

"You'm her lawful lard an' master," he said to Stapledon; "so 'tis your dooty to hale your lady away to furrin paarts, whether her will or no. She'll be fust to thank 'e, dear sawl, come her gets whole again."

But Myles knew Honor well enough, or little enough, to believe that such a high-handed course must be futile. Long and anxious were the deliberations he held with his uncle, and there came a time when Mark suggested a visit from some great physician of expert knowledge.

"Have a London chap," he proposed. "Honor doesn't care a fig for Mathers. But maybe a keen pair of eyes, and a big forehead, and a big voice, and the knowledge it's cost perhaps a hundred pounds to fetch it all down to see her, might bring the woman to some sense."

"I proposed it. She wouldn't hear of it."

"Very well; don't let her hear of it—till the man is in the house. Get Mathers to tell you of some great wonder whose strong point is all these nerve twists and tangles that Honor's struggling under. For a woman to take to thinking, is as bad as for a man to take to drinking—sometimes. It breeds a wrong habit and interferes with Nature. There's a mystery under all this—ever since that sad mischance—and as she won't tell those that love her maybe a clever doctor, who understands the springs of healthy mental action, will find a way to bring back her peace."

"There's a secret, as you say; and I've known it on her tongue; I've felt that it was to be revealed at last. Then there has come a sigh, like the shutting of a door of the mind—a door not to be opened from the outside."

"That is so—and it may be a doctor's work to open that door, instead of a husband's. We'll hope I'm right. Fetch such a man along, if it costs the hay harvest. It's all drouthy nothings here with this fever eating the girl alive."

While Mark Endicott and his nephew thus debated the question of the hour and sought for one able to storm the dim domain of Honor's neurotic disorders, Mr. Ash, Mr. Cramphorn, and others of Endicott's took counsel among themselves how best the tribulation might be overcome.

Ash now regarded the illness as a moonstroke, and was of opinion that doses of lunar radiance alone would restore their mistress.

"Moon must undo what moon's done," he announced. But Cramphorn knew of no precedent, and therefore scoffed at the idea.

"Never was I lower in my spirits," the head-man declared; "an' the plague is that gen'lefolks be so exalted in their awn opinions that no word of ours will they heed, though we spoke wi' the tongues of fire. What do they care for organy tea an' such-like herbs of the field? Yet here I stand, a living sawl, as would be dust at this hour, but for that an' other such-like simples. Cherry Grepe's 'pon theer black books, or, if they'd had sense, they'd have thrawed awver that bwoy—that Mathers—an' gived her a chance to shaw her gert gifts. So like as not she've got a cunning remedy for this dark complaint—a mess of some sort as would put our lady right, mind an' body, in a week. Many a time have I seen a wise man or woman by mere force of words, wi'out so much as striking the sickness, charm it that sudden, as wan might a'most say he seed the evil fly from a party's mouth—like a leather-bird,[#] a-screechin' across the dimpsy light."

[#] A leather-bird = a bat.

"Ess; 'tis pity they doan't give Mother Grepe a chance," admitted Churdles Ash; "for wi' all her little ways an' secrets, she do worship the same Saviour in heaven as her betters do—onless she'm a liar."

"A white witch for sartain," declared Collins. "An' her charmed a wart for Tommy Bates but last week, an' done it in the name of Jesus Christ, an' awnly axed a threp'ny-bit."

So the men discussed Honor's evil case during a dinner interval on the land, then returned to work, regretful that those most involved thus persisted in overlooking a possible means of grace in their hour of tribulation.

But while Collins and the rest dismissed this matter before work and those personal interests of life uppermost in all minds, Mr. Cramphorn continued to dwell darkly upon the subject. This cross-grained, surly soul loved his mistress with an affection superior to that commanded by his own flesh and blood. Herein circumstances and even heredity were strong upon him. Sprung from a line that had laboured at Endicott's through many generations, the descendant of men who were born heirs of toil upon this land and looked to the reigning powers as their immediate lords under Providence, a traditionary regard dwelt in the blood of him, and the concerns of those who controlled his destiny became Cramphorn's own concerns. Such a spirit modern education and the spread of knowledge drives quickly forth, for the half-educated class of to-day scorns gratitude as a base survival; but Jonah dated from long before the Board Schools, and their frosty influence was no more in his heart than upon his tongue. Sour, conceited, a very rustic Malvolio, he might be; but the nobler qualities of Malvolio, he also possessed. It was not the least among his vague regrets that the name of Endicott must presently vanish from Bear Down, even as the name of Cramphorn was destined to.

And now Jonah thought upon the word of Churdles Ash concerning the wise woman. His own experience of her powers also inclined him in that direction, and finally he decided to visit her again. That Cherry had destroyed Christopher Yeoland he did not doubt; that she might, if she would, cure his mistress, he was assured. He determined that if the thing could be done for half a sovereign, done it must be. And should Cherry's charm prove powerful enough to work without the patient's connivance, so much the better.

That same evening he visited the cottage of the sorceress, where it lay behind the low wall, and the row of ox vertebræ, and the torch of the great mullein, that now towered aloft with its first blossoms shining in the gloaming above a woolly spire.

Gammer Grepe was at home and in her garden. She stood with her arms folded on the gate, and Cramphorn observed that she smoked a clay pipe with the manner of long experience. He asked civilly for a little conversation and followed the old woman into her cottage.

"Walk in an' welcome, if there's any money to it," she said bluntly. "'Tis 'bout them gals again, I s'pose. Tu gert a handful for 'e, eh? You'm a fule to fret, for they'll go theer ways wi'out axin' your leave. Be your peas a-come to the farm? Might let 'em knaw as I've got half a quart or so, if Mrs. Stapledon fancies 'em."

"Ess, our peas be come, an' it 'idden 'bout my darters I'm here; an' fule or no fule, it takes two to make a weddin'; an' if the proper chap ban't on-coming, us have got to sit down an' wait, like nesseltripe. I be here touching the mistress of Endicott's."

Cherry frowned.

"I've no word against her, as you knaw, but the rest of 'em—that auld blind piece an' her husband—specially him—I doan't set no store by. She'm what a Endicott should be. T'others I'd so soon ill-wish as not—just to larn 'em the things they doan't believe."

Her eyes glimmered with anger, and the candlelight played pranks with her aged but not venerable face.

"Well, 'tis peace rather than war so far as I'm consarned. I know what you can do—who better?"

"Ess; an' for all theer hard words I'd rather starve than hurt Endicott's. 'Tis his loss, not mine—this furriner she've married. Not but what I might to-morrow——"

"'Tis the very thing I be come upon," interrupted Jonah eagerly. "Her—the mistress. What do this green youth by name of Mathers knaw? If he'd got the wit of a louse he'd never have let the cheel slip through his fingers. But her—she'll slip through his fingers next."

"Ban't no doctor's job now," said Cherry. "The things that could cure her trouble doan't come out of shops. For tearings of heart, an' black night vapours, an' such-like deep ills the very herbs o' the fields are vain. You want sterner food."

"'Tis her sawl be sick by all the looks of it," explained Jonah. "An' it tells 'pon the butivul body of her, like a blight 'pon a rose. She've been ill, to an' from, ever since the bearin' of that dead baaby; an' from being a woman of ready spirit she've grawed that down-daunted as you'd a'most say she'd cry or run if a goose hissed at her. An' now, be gormed if she ban't comin' to be a regular bed-lier! Think of her, so peart an' spry as she was, keepin' her room these summer days! Caan't 'e offer for to cure her, Cherry? I lay theer'd be gude money to it an' plenty, whatever hard thoughts some have got against you."

"Theer's but wan cure as I knaws for her," said the old woman gloomily; "an ugly, savage cure, an' fallen out of use these many days now. But a sure balm and a thing as eats to the heart like a cancer, rubbed under a woman's left breast."

"God's truth, mum!"

"'Tis as I tell 'e. Like a cancer; but 'stead of being death to the livin', 'tis life to the dyin', or them like to die. A savage cure, an' such latter-day stuff as Myles Stapledon would awnly cock his nose at it; so it won't be done, however. An' her'll die—her'll die for need of oil of man. 'Tis that—a thing in no books—a secret as'll be a dead and buried secret in a few years' time, when me an' the likes of me be dead an' buried."

"Oil of man? I've heard Churdles Ash name it."

"Ess, he'd be sure to knaw at his age. 'Tis simple enough. Theer's a virtue in all bones—that everybody knaws who's drinked soup, I s'pose."

"Surely; an' the better the bone, the better the broth," assented Jonah.

"That's it! You've hit the point I was comin' to. So it happens that a Christian bone of a human be fuller far of virtue than any saved from a sheep or other beast."

Cramphorn felt a cold shiver slide up his spine like a speedy snail, and spread out upon his neck and shoulders.

"Christ A'mighty! What be tellin' 'bout? Would 'e have folks turn into black cannibals?"

"Didn't I say 'twas used outwardly, you gaby? Oil of man be rubbed 'pon the heart, or be burnt like a candle. In that shaape 'tis a torch held up for them wanderin' in the world to come home to others as yearns for 'em. Both ways be precious deeds. Theer ban't none wanderin' she wants; so us must rub it 'pon her heart against this fit she'm suffering from."

"Wheer's such a thing to be got?"

"You ax that! As for preparin' the bones, 'tis my work. Gettin' of 'em be a man's."

Mr. Cramphorn breathed hard.

"A sure cure?" he asked.

"Sure as Scripture. An' a thing knawed for centuries, so my mother used to tell me. She made it a score o' times a'most. Men was braver then."

"Just—churchyard—bones," murmured Jonah with an expression like a dog half frightened, half angry.

"The skull of a man—no more. Bones as have held human brains. I'll do my paart for ten shillin'—same as you gived me when——"

"Hush, for the Lard's sake! Doan't 'e go back to that."

She laughed.

"You knaw at any rate that I ban't a vain talker. I'll say no more. Awnly if you'm serious set on restorin' Honor Stapledon to her rightful health, 'tis in your power. Mrs. Loveys can rub the stuff in when she's asleep if she won't consent to no other way. An' her'll come to herself again in a fortnight."

"Be so mortal light of evenings now, an' never dark all night," said Cramphorn, his mind running ahead.

"That's your outlook. If you'm man enough to go an' dig——"

"I be in a maze," he confessed. "Never heard tell of such a fearful balm in my born days."

"Very likely. Theer's more hid than you'll ever knaw, in this world or the next."

"I must think upon it. 'Tis a onruly, wild, dangerous deed. Might lead to trouble."

"'Tis a rightful, high act if you ax me. God'll knaw why for you be theer. Theer's a reward for the salvation of our fellow-creatures in next world if not this; an' I'm sure theer did ought to be, for I've saved enough in my time."

"I'll think about it serious," said Cramphorn, who was now desperately anxious to be gone.

"Just a bone against a woman's life. You think about it as you say."

"So I will, then, wi' all my strength."

Before he had reached the gate Cherry Grepe called him back.

"An' look here, I'll do my share for three half-crowns, seein' it's for her. I'm allus awnly tu glad to do gude deeds so cheap as can be, though wi' evil actions 'tis differ'nt. They win high wages all the world awver."

Then Jonah retreated with his dreadful idea, yet found that as it became more familiar it began to look less terrible. For all his follies and superstitions, he lacked not physical courage, and once assured by Gammer Grepe that such a sacrilege would be judged by his Maker from the standpoint of its motive, he troubled no further as to the performance of the deed. Thenceforward his mind was busy with details as to how such an enterprise might be safely achieved, and through his head passed the spectacle of many green graves. Even before the familiar memories of those who slept beneath them the dogged Jonah winced not; but presently a new reflection glared in upon his mind—an idea so tremendous that the man stood still and gasped before it, as though petrified by the force of his own imagination. For a moment this aspect peopled the night with whispering phantoms; it even set Jonah running with his heart in his mouth; then the wave of personal fear passed and left him well over the shock his thought had brought with it. But the effect of so much excitement and such unwonted exercise took a longer time to depart; his nerves played him some tricks; he was more than usually taciturn at supper, and retired to rest soon after that meal.

Yet, once in bed, Jonah's thoughts kept him such active and unfamiliar company that sleep quite forsook his couch, and it wanted but a little time of the hour for rising when finally he lost consciousness—to do grim deeds in dreamland.

CHAPTER X.
OIL OF MAN

Concerning this weird medicament, it is only necessary to state that memory of the nostrum lingers yet in ancient and bucolic minds; while the tradition, now nearly extinct, is nevertheless founded upon matters of fact from a recent past. For your Oil of Man was counted precious medicine through bygone centuries, and in the archives it may be gleaned that Moses Charras, author of a Royal Pharmacopoeia, published two hundred years ago, indicates the nature of its preparation, and declares how that the skulls of healthy men, slain in full flush of their strength by lead or steel, best meet its requirements. One Salmon of London prepared and sold *Potestates cranii humani* at the sign of the "Blew Bull," in Shoe Lane, during the sixteenth century; *oleum humanum* has within man's memory been a source of advantage to the porters of our medical schools; and, at a date even later than that of which we treat, a physician practising hard by Dartmoor received applications for the magic antidote from one who found herself in private trouble beyond reach of common drugs. She believed that oil of man must still be a medicinal commodity general as rhubarb or syrup of squills.

It was not surprising, therefore, that Cherry Grepe remembered the potent force of this remedy, or that Jonah Cramphorn, once satisfied that the decoction alone stood between his mistress and her end, determined to procure it. A great thought kept him waking until the sun was ready to ascend above the remote gorges of Fingle; but when Jonah rose, cold water and daylight finally dwarfed the dim horrors of his project until they grew perfectly plain before him. That the plan was defensible his strenuous spirit had long since decided. But an accomplice seemed necessary to such a design, for the feat was of too great a magnitude and peril to be achieved single-handed. The common operation of two willing workers might, however, make all the difference, and while he regretted a need for assistance, Jonah felt it to be imperative. Upon the subject of punishment in event of detection, he did not waste thought. The prospect from that standpoint was undoubtedly dark—too dark to dwell upon. The power of the law he could only guess at, and in his mind was a tumultuous upheaval of old recollections touching the theme. He remembered Burke, Hare, and others of their trade; but they had killed men; he proposed no action more unlawful than taking of bones long dead.

To choose his assistant for a matter so delicate appeared difficult in one aspect, yet simple enough viewed practically. That he must broach such a subject to a sane man offered no embarrassment to Mr. Cramphorn; but to select a kindred soul, of stuff sufficiently stern to help with the actual details, promised a harder problem. Scarcity of choice, however, tended towards elucidation. The field was narrowed to an option between Pinsent and Collins; of whom Jonah quickly decided for the latter. By midday indeed he determined that Henry should participate both in the peril and the privilege of restoring Honor to health.

The men met soon after noon near the farmyard, and Cramphorn seized his opportunity.

"Come in here, an' put home the door behind 'e, Henery Collins," he said; "I've got somethin' mighty serious to say to you. For your ear awnly 'tis; an' you'll be very much dumbfounded to larn as you an' me be chosen by Providence for a gert, far-reachin' deed."

In the dim light of a stable Mr. Collins gazed with round, innocent eyes at the speaker; then he began to clean his boots on a spade.

"Whatever do 'e mean? Providence doan't chose the likes of me for its uses, I reckon."

"I stand for Providence in this thing; an' I mean missus. Theer's no nature left in her now, as you must see along wi' the rest. An' why for? 'Cause she'm fadin' away like a cloud. So wisht an' hag wi' her trouble—an' her not quarter of a century auld yet. Dyin'—dyin' afore our eyes; an' theer's awnly one creation as'll save her; an' that's for you an' me to get, my son. 'Tis ordained as we'm the parties."

"Sure, I'd go to world's end for her," declared Mr. Collins.

"No need. No call to go further'n Little Silver buryin' ground."

"Then, if 'tis any deed of darkness, you'd best to put it in other hands to wance."

"No fay—you an' me. An' a high an' desperate act—I won't deceive you theer—but a act righteous in the eye of God; though, if it got knawed by humans, theer'd be trouble."

"I'm tu peaceful in my ways for it then, an' I'll take it very kind if you'll say no more about it to me at all. Ban't in my line."

"Tu late; you'm in the plot; an' you ought to be a proud man if you do feel all for missus as I've heard 'e say scores o' times, in drink an' out. Ess, you must do what I ax you; theer ban't no gwaine back now."

Mr. Collins reflected. He believed, despite the eggshell necklace, that he still gained ground with Jonah's elder daughter in that she tolerated him at less than a yard's distance by fits and starts; but the necessity for not proposing marriage Henry felt to hamper his movements. That Sally might refuse—perhaps a dozen times—was nothing against the argument, for a rustic love-maker is as patient as Nature's self. But in the heart of Collins, obedience to anybody who ordered him with voice sufficiently loud, was a rooted instinct. He had abided by Jonah's clear utterance during time past; and now he remembered it, and, astonished at his own astuteness, sought to make a bargain.

"If I help 'e with this thing, will 'e let me offer marriage to your eldest darter?"

The other was much astonished, for his views upon the subject of Sally had changed somewhat under Margery's delicate manipulation.

"Offer! Powers! I thought as you'd axed her years agone. What's to hinder 'e? 'Tis a free country, an' you'm auld enough to knaw your awn minds, ban't 'e?"

The younger labourer was hurt, and showed as much.

"Your memory's grawin' short seemin'ly," he said. "No matter. If you say I may ax her—'tis all I want. Then I'll serve 'e to the best of my power."

In less than half an hour Henry Collins departed from the stable a haunted man. His eyes roamed like those of a frightened horse; he would have given the wide world to be a thousand miles from Bear Down; for the deed without a name made him tremble to the foundations of his being and threw him into an icy perspiration each time that its significance crossed his mind. Only the permission to propose to Sally sustained him; and even his love could hardly stand the ordeal of this test, for, to tell truth, he doubted more than once whether the game was worth the candle.

How he lived through those moments that separated him from the night Henry never afterwards remembered; but the suspense only endured through some few hours, for Mr. Cramphorn, after revealing his design, perceived that it must be put into immediate execution if the other's help was to be counted upon.

"Give the fule time and he'll draw back or bolt," reflected Jonah.

But the sombre minutes, deep laden each with its own horrid burden of terror and presentment, flapped their bat-wings away into the limbo of time past, and a moment arrived—midnight between two days of late July—when Collins and his leader met by appointment at a spot in the great hayfield of Endicott's, and together proceeded down the hill to Little Silver.

Henry carried an unlighted bull's-eye lantern; Cramphorn's pocket bulged, and in his hand he bore a small bag of battered leather. Under their breath they discussed the matter. The night was moonless, and a haze of heat stole abroad upon the land. Pale green light shuddered along the north-eastern horizon, and the faces of umbel-bearing flowers caught it and spoke of it dimly out of the darkness. A dewy peace held the world—a peace only broken by the throb of the field-crickets that pulsed upon the ear infinitely loud in contrast with the alternate silences. Mist enveloped all things in the valleys, and as the men sank towards the churchyard, Collins shivered before cold moisture that brushed his face like a dead hand.

"'Tis a thing beyond all belief," he said; "an' I be very glad as you didn't give me more'n a day to think, else I should have runned away rather than faace it."

"'Tis a ugly thing done for a butivul purpose. 'Tis the best work as ever that brain-pan will have to its credit in this here world."

"'Struth! I cream all awver to hear 'e! Such courage as you've got. Did 'e get the keys?"

"Ess; when Noah Brimblecombe was up to the rectory. I seed un go; then went in the cottage an' waited, an' when his missus had her back turned at the door, I pulled the curtain in the corner, under the cloam images wheer the church keys all hang to. And them I wanted I found. To put 'em back wi'out him knawin' will be a harder job."

"An' arter the—the screws, theer'll be a lead case, I s'pose—have 'e thought 'pon that? But I lay you have."

"I've got a mall an' cold chisel in my bag. Ban't no harder than openin' a chest of tea," answered the old man grimly.

Mr. Collins whined and shivered.

"To think of it! The mystery of it! If she knawed—the very man she promised to wed. 'Tis tu gashly; I been ever since this marnin' broodin' awver the business."

"A gert thought—that's what it was, an' I be proud of it; an' if 'tis ever knawed an' telled about after I'm dead and gone, folks'll say 'tweern't no common man as carried out such a projec'. A fule would have digged in the airth an' be catched so easy as want-catcher kills moles; but theer's brains goes to this item. I minded Christopher Yeoland—him as was taken off in full power an' pride of life by a snake-sting; an' I minded how nought but the twist of a key an' the touch of a turnscrew still lay between him an' the quick."

"Twas 'cause you hated un so mortal bad livin' as your thoughts ran upon him dead," ventured Collins uneasily.

"Not so 'tall. As to hatin' un, I did; but that's neither here nor theer. I'm just a tool in this matter, an' the dead dust of Christopher Yeoland ban't no more to me than the ridge of airth a plough turns. 'Tis a fact this same dust an' me comed to blows in time agone; but all these frettings an' failings be forgotten now, though we weern't no ways jonic—a empty, lecherous man. Still, he've answered for his sins, an' I hates un no more. I awnly wants a bit of the 'natomy of un for a precious balm; then 'tis screws again, an' locks again; an' none wiser 'cept you an' me an' the spiders."

"Theer's God A'mighty."

"I doan't forget that. The Lard's on our side, or I shouldn't be here. No puzzle for Him. No doubt Judgment Day will find the man all of a piece again to take his deserts."

"You'm a wonder—to talk of such a fatal deed as if 'twas no more'n pullin' a turnip."

"An' that's how us should look 'pon it. An' if 'twas a turnip axed for, a turnip I'd have got."

They now entered the churchyard from its south-western side by a hole in the hedge. Mr. Collins lighted his lantern and passed over the graves like a drunken Will-o'-the-wisp with many a trip and stagger. Then he stood under the skulls of the Yeoland mausoleum, and glanced fearfully up where they grinned, and his light seemed to set red eyeballs rolling in their mossy sockets.

Soon both men had entered the sepulchre, and Henry happily burned himself with the lantern as he did so—an accident that served to steady his nerves and shut his mouth upon chattering teeth. Jonah, too, felt the tragedy of the situation, but in a higher spirit, and the peacock part of the man played him true, though only coffins were his audience. He thought how ages unborn might ring with this desperate deed; he even determined that, if the matter leaked out no sooner, he would himself confess it upon his death-bed, when ignoble retaliation would be impossible, and little time left for much save admiration and applause.

This he resolved as he lifted the pall of Christopher's coffin and observed how that damp had already begun to paint the brass inscription green.

He opened his bag, bade Henry keep the lantern steady and shut his mouth, then calmly removed his coat, turned up his sleeves, and began his work. But the task proved harder than he had anticipated, and his assistant, after one bungling effort to aid, was forced to abandon any second attempt. To hold the lantern proved the limit of his power; and even that bobbed every way, now throwing light among the dim shadows upon the shelves, now blazing into Jonah's eyes, now revolving helplessly over the ceiling of the vault. Presently Cramphorn grew annoyed as well as warm, and, aware that precious time was passing, swore so loudly that a new, material terror overtook his companion.

"For God's grace, doan't 'e bawl so loud!" he implored. "If p'liceman was ridin' past and catched us!"

Though he felt no flicker of fear, Jonah realised the value of this counsel. He looked to see that the door was shut fast, then proceeded with his work in silence. The reluctant screws came out quicker as he acquired increased skill, and from their raw holes issued a faint smell of eucalyptus, for the coffin was built of that wood.

At last the men together lifted the lid, and set it in a corner. Then a sterner task awaited them where the lead shell lay bare. Noise of mallet on chisel was now inevitable, and Collins heard himself directed to stand sentry at the churchyard gate, so that if the nightly patrol should pass that way on his uncertain round, silence might fall until he had departed beyond earshot. Probability of any other human visitor there was none, unless the doctor chanced to be abroad.

Henry therefore got out into the fresh air very willingly, and before long sat him down at the churchyard gate and listened to muffled activity from Jonah's mallet in the distance. One other sound disturbed the night. Already grey dawn stole along the eastern woods, but the deep, tranced hour before bird-waking was upon all things, and in its loneliness Collins found the lap and chuckle of a stream under the churchyard wall welcome as a companion. It knew action at least, and broke the horrible stillness. Once he heard slow footfall of hoofs, and was about to give an alarm, when, from the shadows, came forth an old white horse that wandered alone through the night. Like a ghost it dragged itself slowly past— perchance waking from pain, perchance wondering, as such aged brutes may wonder, why grass and water are no longer sweet. It hobbled painfully away, and the echo of its passing was swallowed up in the silence, and the apparition of its body vanished under the mist. There only remained the wakeful streamlet, leaping from its dim journey among coffins into the watercress bed, and a hollow reverberation of blows from the mortuary.

Presently, however, Mr. Cramphorn's mallet ceased to strike, and finding that the supreme moment had now come, Collins nerved himself to return. From the dawn-grey into gloom he stole to see the picture of Jonah in a round ring of lantern light sharply painted upon darkness. A coffin, with its inner leaden shell torn back, lay at Cramphorn's feet, and Henry instantly observed that some tremendous and unforeseen circumstance had fallen out during his vigil at the churchyard gate. The other man was glaring before him like a lunatic; his short hair bristled; his face dripped. Terrified he was not, yet clearly had become the victim of amazed bewilderment and even horror.

"For Christ's sake, doan't 'e glaze at me like that!" implored Henry. "What have 'e done? What's happened to 'e? Doan't tell me you'm struck into that shaape for this high-handed job!"

The other's mouth was open and his under-jaw hung limp. Apparently he lacked force to speak, for he merely pointed to his work; upon which Collins looked sideways into the coffin with stealthy dread. Instantly his face also became transformed into a display of liveliest astonishment and dismay; but in his case frank terror crowded over him like a storm. And thus three men—two living and one a corpse—each confronted the others, while the marble serenity of this death offered a contrast to the frenzied emotion on the faces of those that lived.

"God's gudeness! You've brawked into the wrong wan!" gasped Collins.

Jonah shook his head, for still he could not answer; yet the suspicion of his companion seemed natural, because not Christopher Yeoland but another lay at their feet.

Within the coffin, placid and little disfigured save where the eyes had fallen in and the skin tightened over his high, bald brow, appeared a venerable face—a face almost patriarchal. The dead man's beard gleamed nobly white upon his breast, and his features presented the solemn, peaceful countenance of one indifferent to this rude assault from busy souls still in life.

"'Tis magic—black, wicked magic—that's what it is. Else he've been took out an' another party put in unbeknawnst," stuttered Collins.

Then Cramphorn found his voice, and it came weak and thin with all the vigour strained out of it by shock.

"Not him at all—an' like as not he never was in. A far-reachin', historic action—that's what we've comed on. Our dark deed's brought to light a darker."

"Which us'll have to keep damn quiet about," gasped Henry.

"'Tis a gert question how our duty do lie. My brains be dancin' out of my eyes in water. Maybe we've found a murder. An' I caan't get the thread of action all in a minute."

"'Tis daylight outside, anyway."

"Then for God's sake do your share, if you'm a man. Hammer that lead back an' shut up this here ancient person—Methuselah he might be, from the look of un. I be gone that weak in the sinews that a cheel could thraw me. I must get a bite of air, then I'll help."

"You ban't gwaine!" cried Henry in terror; but Jonah remained in sight and soon returned. Then, to the younger's great satisfaction, he heard that his partner had quite abandoned the original enterprise and was only desirous to make good their desecration and depart.

"It caan't surely be as a dead man graws auld quick after he's put away?" asked Collins.

"A fule's question. 'Tis all a trick an' a strammin' gert lie worked for some person's private ends. An' the bite comes to knaw how we'm gwaine to let it out."

"Ess; we'm done for ourselves if we tell."

"Doan't talk; work. I must think bimebye when I'm out of this smell o' death."

Henry obeyed, and showed considerable energy and despatch.

"He may be a livin' man still!"

"Young Yeoland? I'd guess it was so, if I didn't knaw 'bout Cherry Grepe. Please God, mine be the intellects to smooth out this dark deed anyways, so that generations yet to come shall call me blessed. Awnly you keep your mouth shut—that's what you've got to do. Guy Fawkes an' angels, to be faaced wi' such a coil!"

"It'll want a powerful strong brain to come out of it with any credit to yourself," said Mr. Collins.

"As to that, such things be sent to those best able to support 'em."

"Well, no call to tell me to keep quiet. I'll not make or meddle, I swear to 'e. If theer's any credit due an' any callin' of anybody blessed, you may have the lot. I shall pray to God for my paart to let me forget everythin' 'bout this night. An' seein' the things I do forget, I awnly hope this will go like a breath o' air. Same time 'tis more likely to haunt me to my dyin' day than not."

"Doan't drink, that's all. Forget it you won't; but doan't drink 'pon it, else you'll let it out in the wrong ears for sartain. You ban't built to keep in beer an' secrets to wance. An' take care of Ash, as sleeps along wi' you. Have a lie ready if he's wakin' when you go back."

In twenty minutes the matter was at an end, an old man's coffin once more in its appointed place, and the family vault of the Yeolands locked and double-locked. Collins and Cramphorn then left the churchyard, but Jonah found himself without physical strength to start uphill immediately; so the men retired to rest awhile within the crumbling walls of Little Silver Castle, close at hand. There they sat, under the great groined arches of the dungeon chamber, and whispered, while the bats squeaked and clustered in their dark nooks and crannies at return of day.

Then Cramphorn and his assistant proceeded homewards as they had come—knee-deep through the grass lands—and before three o'clock both were back in their beds again. Yet neither slept, for each, in proportion to his intelligence, was oppressed by the thought of his discovery and by the memory of an ancient face, autumn brown, yet having a great white beard, that rippled over his breast and so passed out of sight beneath the engirding lead.

CHAPTER XI.
A CLEAN BREAST OF IT

As discoveries of moment hidden for long years or through all past time will suddenly and simultaneously burst, like Neptune, upon students widely separated, yet pursuing one goal by divers roads, so now this extraordinary circumstance stumbled upon by Jonah Cramphorn and his companion during their secret enterprise was noised abroad within a fortnight, yet without any action or intervention from them.

It is true that, despite his solemn promises, Henry Collins soon found himself constitutionally unequal to preserving the secret, and he confessed the same within a week of the incidents relating to it; but those before whom he published his experience took no step upon it until they heard the story in full detail at a later date. Then the whole curious truth was blazed abroad.

Mr. Cramphorn, as soon as Noah Brimblecombe's keys were back on their nail without awakening of suspicion, shut up his adventure stoutly enough, while he pondered how best to reveal the discovery; but his accomplice found the position far less endurable. Henry existed henceforth like a man struggling under some grim incubus by day as well as night. Sleep deserted him; his head ached; he found himself bungling his work, and, upon this development, the man grew alarmed for his brains and believed that he must be going mad. Even poor Henry's love-star dwindled somewhat while yet this cloud of horror hung over him, and though he had won permission from Sally's father to propose marriage, such was the tremendous nature of the price paid and its appendage of mental chaos that he found himself unequal to thoughts on any other theme. He could not profit by his new powers for the present; indeed, he felt that, until this knowledge was shifted on to other shoulders, life would hold no happy moment. Five days he spent with his secret; then, being strung to a pitch when his promise to Jonah ceased to weigh with him, he determined to make a clean breast of the whole matter. Everything should be divulged excepting only the name of his partner. First rose the question of an ear for this confession, and, hesitating only a moment between Mark Endicott and Myles, Mr. Collins decided that he would tell them both. He thought also of the vicar, but held, doubtless correctly, that his personal offence would bulk larger in the eyes of Mr. Scobell than upon the view of those at Bear Down.

Chance to make his revelation offered within two nights of Henry's decision, for then it happened that Cramphorn, his daughters, Churdles

Ash, and other of the hands tramped off to Chagford, where a travelling circus was attracting the countryside. Henry, though he angered Sally not a little by refusing to accompany her, found an opportunity excellent for his purpose, and seized upon it. Left alone with the blind man and Stapledon, Collins began tremulously to tell his story; and his eyes rolled as he proceeded; and his voice often failed him or rose into high squeaks between gulps of emotion; but he made his meaning clear, and so lifted a weight from off his soul.

"Please, your honours, I've got a thing in my head as be burstin' it, an' I'll thank you to let me have a tell now I be alone with you. A devilish secret 'tis, an' I caan't keep my lips shut 'pon it no more, or I shall go daft."

"Out with it then," said Stapledon. "Your brains weren't built for devilish secrets, Henry."

"No, they wasn't," admitted Collins, "an' I'm glad to hear you allow it. I do best I can wi' the gifts I've got—an' who could do more? An' 'twas last week as I promised to go along wi' another man whose name theer ban't no call to mention. He'll answer for hisself 'pon the Judgment Day; but I can't wait so long. I wants to get it awver now."

"Begin at the beginning, lad; talk quietly, and light your pipe. We're friends and shan't let out your secret where it can hurt you," said Mark.

"I'm sure I pray God to bless you for them words," answered Collins earnestly; "but I can't smoke—the very taste of tobacco be changed since. 'Tis like this—us wanted oil of man, which you might knaw 'bout, bein' so wise as you are."

"An old wife's remedy—well?"

"Whether or no, it was told to my mate that awnly oil of man stood between missus here an' her death. So we ordained to fetch what was needed in the faace of all men."

"For that old witch on the hill, I suppose?" asked Myles.

"I doan't name no names, axin' your humble pardon," answered Collins uneasily. "This is my awn sacred confession—awnly my business an' yours, if I may say it without rudeness. Anyway, we went for what was wanted; an' that was a man's head bones—a chap cut off in fulness of life for choice. An' my mate—a deep man, I allow that much—thought fust of Bill Cousins—him took off by sunstroke two years ago; an' then he reckoned 'twas beyond our power these short nights to dig for what we wanted between dimpsy-light of evening an' morn. An' when he comed to me he minded me how theer was quality buried above ground so well as poor folks under; an' a young man slain in his strength by mischance. Squire

Christopher Yeoland he meant. A gashly auld thought, sure enough; yet us steeled ourselves to it."

"You dared that sacrilege!" burst out Stapledon; but Collins merely stared at him. Time had taken the labourer so far beyond this point in the tragedy that not only did he forget its dramatic significance upon a new listener, but also how he himself had felt when Jonah first broke it to him.

"Ess; us set about the job. That ban't nothin'. 'Twas for love of missus us done it. An' I watched while t'other worked; an' when he stopped hammerin' an' I went back, he was starin' an' bristlin', 'cause afore him laid—not the gen'leman us counted 'pon—but a very auld, aged man, berry-brown from keepin', yet so sweet as a rose, wi' a gert white beard to un."

"You broke into the wrong coffin!"

"No fay, us didn't. 'Tis the carpse what comed from furrin paarts—anyways the box as did. Christopher Yeoland, beggin' his pardon, was the name 'pon the brass. An' my mate was mazed; an' us hammered back the lead all suent and tidy, an' screwed on the lid, an' put un 'pon his shelf wance more an' slipped it home. That's the tale, an' I'll take my oath of it afore God A'mighty's angel."

There followed a lengthy silence upon his story; then Mr. Collins made an end.

"'Tis the awful hardness of sharin' such a dreadful secret wi' wan other man as I caan't endure no more. An' I swear, by any deep word you choose, that I never meant no findin' of anybody's secrets—awnly gude to missus—as might have been saved by what we went for, but won't never be better without it."

"That's as may be, Henry," said Mr. Endicott. "For the rest, this thing is somebody's secret, as you say. Anyway you're not weighed down with it now. You may hold yourself free of it, and if you take my advice, having eased your mind, you'll go off to rest with a quiet conscience. No great harm can fall on you at any rate. Perhaps none at all, for I'll wager it was Cramphorn, not you, who hatched this piece of folly."

"Please, please, doan't name nobody, your honours!" implored Henry. "I promised the man to bide still as a worm 'bout it. In fact I swore I would. An' I did try to keep him off my tongue at any rate, an' thought as I had."

"We shall not take any steps against him or you. Now go to bed and sleep. You've done the right thing in telling us; but don't tell anybody else."

Mr. Collins, not sorry to depart, did so, and for some minutes Stapledon and the blind man continued to sit in silence, each busy with his own thoughts. Then Mark spoke.

"A stunning, dislocating, play-acting piece of foolery, if it's true. Yet somehow I know it is. There's a deal of light shed on darkness for me, and for you too I reckon, by such an upheaval."

"Not so. I see no light—unless you believe this means that Christopher Yeoland may still be alive."

"Yes, I think it means that; and such a return must be an earthquake more or less in all the lives that were once connected with him. Men can't die and live again without upsetting the world. A mad imagining. Perhaps no mother's son but him would have dreamed of it. But the motive——"

"That," said Myles quickly, "is all I can see. Knowing as much of the man as I do, so much looks clear. When Clack joined him, I sent a message. It was as urgent as need be, and to the effect that Honor loved him still. That she loved me too Clack probably added to my message. While one of us lived, Honor would never have married the other. So this thing he did to make her road easy."

"If you're right, the puzzle comes together piece by piece."

"Excepting the old man in the coffin—supposing that it was a man."

Endicott reflected; then was struck with an idea.

"It may be that the death of this old man put the cranky thought into Yeoland's head. If it was his kinsman that lies there instead of himself, all's smoothed out. What simpler way to clear Honor's road? This parade of evidence is made that there may be no doubt in any mind. A Yeoland dies and is buried in the tomb of his forefathers. But after all it wasn't our Yeoland."

"Did he mean to let this farce go on for ever?"

"No farce for him; yet, maybe, he got some solid joy out of it. A quick mind for all his vagabond, empty life. He saw the position, and reckoned that in fulness of time she might come to be a happy wife along with you. Then this old relative dies at the right moment and sets a spark to his imagination. No, I suppose we should never have known. His idea would be to keep his secret close hid for ever from those it concerned most— unless——"

He broke off and pursued his reflections in silence. Myles waited for him to speak again, but the blind man only resumed his knitting.

"He blotted himself clean out of life for love of Honor," Stapledon at length declared.

"That I believe. A strange, unlawful deed, yet 'tis a question whether the law has any punishment. To think of the immense confusion of human life if many graves yielded up their dead again!"

"And what is our course? Who can benefit or suffer if we state these things? There's such huge folly about it when you think of details that I feel as if it must all be a nightmare of Henry's."

"No, no; it's true enough."

"Then he may be married himself by this time, and in a new home, with England a mere dream behind him?"

"I wish I thought he was, Myles—for—for general peace of mind; but I don't. If he had a live, guiding, absorbing passion, after Honor, it was Godleigh—the woods and hills and songs of Teign. These things were in his blood. If I know him, they might have drawn him back with bands of steel."

"Why didn't they do so then?"

"How can we say that they didn't?"

"What! He may have been here—at our elbows?"

"I see the likelihood of that clearer than you, being blind. Yes, I can very easily think of him under shadow of night, with the true feel of a ghost, rambling beneath his own trees—his and not his—or listening to the river, or creeping to his own door when all men slept; or in the dawn—such a lover of cock-light as he was—he would steal through the dew with the birds to watch sunrise, then vanish and hide himself, or get above to some wild ridge of the moor and lie there till darkness gathered again. Such freaks would be meat and drink to him; and also to remember that he was only a live man in Australia, but a dead one in his own land. Just for argument suppose that was so; then look back a little way and think it out."

But Myles could by no means divine his uncle's drift. Practical even before this surprise, he was looking to the future, not backward, for study of the past appeared vain, and doubly vain to him in this crisis.

"Not much use turning back," he said. "I want to know about the time to come. These two—Collins and Cramphorn—through their fool's errand have certainly unearthed an extraordinary fact: Christopher Yeoland's secret, so to call it. And it is for us to determine whether our duty is to proclaim the thing or not. There's Godleigh—it falls empty again next autumn, for the people don't renew their lease."

"Well, Godleigh reverts to the man in Australia. The lawyers believe that man is an ancient settler; we know, or think we know, that the place has not really changed hands. Yeoland may reappear after giving Little Silver due warning."

"Or, being a rolling stone, and probably no better off now than when he left England, he may stop in Australia. Still, there's the chance of his returning."

"Be sure he will, even if he has not done so," said Mark Endicott firmly. "If 'tis only to the old life and old ways, he'll come back. He'll say, as likely as not, that the thing he meant to do is done. Honor is married and a happy wife. Who would deny him his own again after that sacrifice?"

"I only think of Honor and the awful shock to her. It might kill her."

"Don't fret yourself there, or torture over that point. Now I'll say what will astound you: I think Honor may very possibly be less amazed and staggered at this news than ever you were, or I either."

"Not amazed! What do you—what in God's name do you mean by that? That she knew? Knew it and hid it from me? That she suffers now because——"

He broke off and sprang to his feet, while the other maintained silence and let the stricken man stride away his passion and regain his self-control. Soon enough Myles grew cool and contained. Then he walked to Mark and put his hand on the old man's shoulder.

"Forgive me; but this is the utter, blasting wreck and ruin of my whole life that you are hinting at," he said calmly.

"I hint at nothing," answered the other with unusual roughness. "Had I thought any such impossible thing I should have been as big a fool as you are. You ought to know your wife better than to believe she'd act a lie of that sort."

"I don't believe it—I never said that I believed it Your words seemed to imply that you must believe it. Else why do you suggest that Honor would be less astonished to hear of this resurrection than you and I are?"

"If you had taken a look back as I bid you, Myles, instead of rushing forward without looking, you need not have asked me that question. Glance back, even now, and what has been dark as the pit may lighten and lift somewhat. Just call to mind the sorrow that has hung so heavily over us of late days—the little chick that we counted so precious—too soon."

But Stapledon was in no mental mood for retrospective or other thought. A wide turmoil tossed the sea of his soul into storm; the terrible weakness of the strong got hold upon him, and he rocked in one of those moments when capacity to think deserts the mind, when intellect seems overwhelmed.

"I cannot see what you see," he said. "I admit that I am blind and a fool, but for God's sake don't ask me any more questions beyond my power to answer. Tell me what you think, or know, or believe you know. Consider what this means to me—the fact that Christopher Yeoland may be alive— may have stood behind a hedge yesterday, and watched me pass, and laughed. Don't you see? I've got Honor by falsehood—a false pretence—a fraud."

"Not of your own breeding, if it is so. Your true and loving wife she is for all time now, whether the man be dead or alive—though of that there's a certain proof in my mind. I'd be the last to tear you with questions at this minute. I only wanted you to see what has rushed in upon me so sudden and fierce. Light in it every way—light in it for you and for Honor, I pray God. If what I make out of this puzzle is true, and Christopher Yeoland alive, then there may be matter for rejoicing in the fact rather than gloom. Not darkness anyway. Now call home to your mind that night in the woods, when at her silly whim, which I was fool enough to support, you took your wife for a drive to Lee Bridge."

"I remember it well enough."

"You left her to fetch water from the river, and while you were away she got out of the pony carriage, light-footed and silent as a moonbeam, to pick bluebells. Then suddenly there! Out of the mist and night—out of the dim woods—the man! Wandering alone no doubt They met, and she, being in no trim for such a fearful shock as the sight of one long dead walking the earth again, went down before it. Think of her suddenly eye to eye and face to face with him in the midst of night and sleep! It froze her blood, and froze the poor little one's blood too—that thawed no more. For she thought him a spectral thing, an' thinks so still—*thinks so still!* That's the dark secret she's dumb about and won't whisper to you or me, though she's been near telling us once or twice. That's what has been eating her heart out; that's what neither your prayers nor mine could get from her. She must be made to understand in careful words that will ask your best skill to choose aright She must learn that you have discovered what she's hiding, and that it was flesh and blood, not phantom, she saw. 'Tis a pity, if what I say is fact, that the fool ran away when he saw you coming to succour her. The harm was done by that time; and if we had known, how many of these ghost-haunted hours might we have saved her! I may be spinning thin air, yet I think what I tell is true."

But Stapledon was glaring at the impassive face before him with a gaze that seemed to burrow through Mark's sightless eyes and reach his brain. Now Myles spoke in a voice unfamiliar to his listener, for it was loud-pitched and turbulent with sudden passion.

"That man killed my child!"

A glass vessel 90 the dresser echoed the deep, dominant note of this cry and reverberated it; one moment of silence followed; and then came shuffle of feet on the flagged way, with laughter and echo of time-worn jests, as Churdles Ash, Pinsent, and the others returned from their pleasure. Mark Endicott, however, had opportunity for a final word.

"It may be as you say—a dark accident, and worse ten thousand times for him than even you. Be just—be very just to the madman, if he has really done this wayward deed and is coming back into your life again. Be just, and don't swerve an inch out of your even-handed course, for your road is like to get difficult if you do."

"Us have viewed a gert pomp of braave horsemanship," announced Mr. Ash. "Never seed no better riders nor merry-men nowheer, though the hosses was poor."

"An' Tommy Bates here be all for joinin' of 'em," laughed Samuel Pinsent; "but I tell un as he turns out his toes tu far to do any credit to hisself in such a wild course of life."

CHAPTER XII.
LIGHT

Beside his sleeping wife did Stapledon recline, and endeavoured, through the hours of a weary night, to gather the significance of those great things that he had gleaned. Sometimes he surprised his own thought—as a man's conscience will often burst in roughly upon his mind—and found himself hoping that this news was untrue and that Christopher Yeoland filled a coffin, if not at Little Silver. But the edifice of probability so carefully reared by Mark Endicott showed no flaw, and even amid the mazes of his present doubt Myles found time to marvel at the ratiocination of the old man. Before this explanation it seemed difficult to believe that another clue to the puzzle existed. A note of inner unrest, a question within a question, finally brought Myles out of bed at dawn. He rose, soon stood in the air, and, through the familiar early freshness of day, walked upwards to the Moor for comfort. What was it to him if this harebrained soul had thus played at death? He, at least, was no dreamer, and moved upon solid ground. He passed beside the kingdom of the blue jasione and navel-wort on the old wall, while above him wind-worn beeches whispered in the dawn wind. From force of habit he stood at a gate and rested his arms upon the topmost bar, while his great dog roved for a rabbit. Now the man's eyes were lighted to the depths of their disquiet from the east, and at sight of the distant woods his thoughts turned back to that meeting responsible for his child's death. He had yet to learn from Honor whether his uncle's suspicion was correct concerning the incident, but little doubt existed within his mind, and he breathed heavily, and his emotions almost bordered upon malignity. Better such a futile soul under the earth in sober earnest. So ill-regulated a human machine looked worse than useless, for his erratic course impeded the progress of others more potent, and was itself a menace and a danger. This man had killed his little son—that child of many petitions and wide hopes; had crushed him, like a sweet wild flower under the heel of a fool. So bitterly he brooded; then pondered as to how his wife would receive this tremendous message.

Upon the first heather ridges the cold breath of the Moor touched the man to patience and brought him nearer himself. He looked out into the dayspring; noted where one little flame-coloured forerunner of dawn already shone upon lofty granite afar off; and saw the Mist Mother rise from the ruddy seeding rushes of her sleeping-place. He beheld the ancient heron's grey pinion brighten to rose beside the river; heard cry of curlew and all the manifold music of the world waking again. Above him the sky flushed to the colours of the woodbine, while upon earth arose an incense and a savour of nightly dews sun-kissed. From marsh and moss, from the rush beds and the peat beds; from glimmering ridges cast upward by workers long gone by; from the bracken and the heather, and the cairns of the old stone men; from the gold eyes of the little tormentils, the blue eyes of the milkworts, the white stars of the galiums woven and interwoven through the texture of the budding heath—from each and all, to the horizon-line of peak and pinnacle, a risen sun won worship. Then did Stapledon's eyes soften somewhat and his brow clear in the great light, for there came songs from the Sons of the Morning—they who in time past had welcomed him as a brother; and their music, floating from the high places, soothed his troubled heart. Under that seraphic melody the life of man, his joys and his sorrows, peaked and dwindled to their just proportions; gradually he forgot his kind, and so thought only of the solemn world-order outspread, and the round earth rolling like an opal about the lamp of the sun, through God's own estate and seigniory of space.

That hour and the steadfast nature of him presently retrieved his patience; then Myles shone forth unclouded as the morning. Recollection of his recent fret and passion surprised him. Who was he to exhibit such emotion? The Moor was his exemplar, and had been so since his boyish eyes first swept it understandingly. For him this huge, untamed delight was the only picture of the God he did not know, yet yearned to know; and now, as oftentimes of old, it cooled his blood, exalted his reflections, adjusted the distortions of life's wry focus, and sent him home in peace.

Duty was the highest form of praise that he knew, and he prepared to fall back upon that. Let others order their brief journeys on lines fantastical or futile, he at least was wiser and knew better. He reflected that the folly of the world can injure no soul's vital spots. Only a man's self can wound himself mortally. He would live on agreeably to Nature—obedient as the granite to the soft, tireless touch of wind and rain; prompt as the bursting bud and uncurling tendril; patient as the cave spirits that build up pillars of stalagmite through unnumbered ages; faithful as the merle, whose music varies not from generation to generation. Life so lived would be life well guarded and beyond the power of outer evil to penetrate.

So he believed very earnestly, and knew not that his noble theory asked a noble nature to practise it. Only a great man can use perfectly a great tool; and this obtains with higher rules of conduct than Stapledon's; for of all who profess and call themselves Christians, not one in a thousand is mentally equipped to be the thing he pretends, or even to understand the sweep and scope of what he professes. It is not roguery that makes three parts of Christendom loom hypocrite in a thinker's eyes, but mental and constitutional inability to grasp a gospel at once the most spiritual and material ever preached and misunderstood. Centuries of craft stretch between man and the Founder's meaning; confusion bred of passion has divided the House against itself; politics and the lust of power have turned religion into a piece of state machinery; and the rot at the root of the cumbrous fabric will, within half a century, bring all down in far-flung conflagration and ruin. Then may arise the immortal part out of the holocaust of the Letter, and Christianity, purged of churchcraft as from a pestilence, fly back to brood upon the human heart once more in the primal, rainbow glory of the Sermon on the Mount, preached under heaven by a Man to men.

That day Myles Stapledon, with all caution and such choice of words as he had at command, broke the story to Honor, and his tactful language, born of love, was so skilful that the shock brought no immediate collapse with it. The narrative asked for some art, yet he developed it gradually, and found his reward where Mark had predicted. First Honor learnt what she herself had seen upon that fateful night; and when, in a very extremity of amazement, she confessed to the secret of a fancied spectre, Myles went further and led her to understand that what she had witnessed was flesh and blood, that a confusion, probably not intentional, had been created, and that Christopher Yeoland might be suspected still to live. Stapledon spared himself nothing in this narrative. Asked by his wife as to the reason that could have prompted her former lover to a step so extravagant, he reminded her of her own determination to marry neither of them; he explained how he had begged Christopher to come back, that her life might be as it had been; and added that doubtless the wanderer on his side, and for love of her alone, had put this trick upon them in the belief that such a course would contribute to her final happiness. Having set out this much with extreme impartiality, a human question burst from the heart of the man.

"For you he did this thing, love; he only thought of you and not of the thousand preposterous tangles and troubles likely to spring from such an action. Your happiness—that was all he saw or cared to see. And did he see it? Tell me, dear Honor—here on the threshold of his return perhaps—tell me; was it for your happiness? Thank God, I think I know; yet I should like to hear from your own lips the truth and that I am right."

The truth, as she believed it before this most startling fact, came instantly to Honor's lips. She was enfeebled and unstrung by weeks of wayward living consequent upon great fret of mind. She had nursed this dreadful belief in an apparition until it had grown into a sort of real presence, and the conviction, fabricated through weeks of brooding, would not be dispelled at a word. Deep was the impress left upon her mind, and time must pass before a shape so clear could fade. As a result, the man now thought to be returned from the dead frightened her for a season, scarcely less than his fancied ghost had done. She was timid before the amazing whisper that he still lived. In this fear she forgot for the moment what had prompted Yeoland to his typical folly; she dreaded him in the body as she had dreaded him in the spirit; she turned to the solid being at her side, clung to Myles in her weakness, and held his great arm tightly round her waist.

"For my happiness indeed, dearest one. You have loved me better than I deserved, and forgiven so many faults. This makes me shiver and grow cold and fear to be alone; yet how different to the thing I thought!"

"And he may come home."

"He will never be real to me again—not if I see him and hear him. Never so real as there—grey-clad with the moon on his face—a shadowy part of the great web of the night, yet distinct—all very ghost. I'm frightened still. You can forgive a little of what I made you endure, now that you know what I have suffered."

He hugged her up to his heart at these words, believed her as thoroughly as she believed herself, and thanked Heaven that blind Mark Endicott had been led to such a true prophecy.

A week passed, yet no step was taken, though the new position came to be accepted gradually by those acquainted with the secret. For Honor the knowledge was actually health-giving by virtue of the morbid cloud that it dispelled. Such tidings liberated her soul from a strange fear and offered her mind a subject of boundless interest. Many plans were proposed, yet scarcely a desirable course of action presented itself. Mark advocated no step, and Honor added her plea to his, for she openly expressed a hope that Christopher, if still he lived, would not return to Godleigh. And this she said upon no suspicion of herself, but rather from a continued dread of the man. It seemed impossible to her that she could ever think of him as among the living. Stapledon, on the contrary, desired an explanation, and his wish was gratified most speedily by an unexpected herald from Yeoland himself. An authentic representative arrived at Endicott's—a somewhat shame-faced and apologetic messenger laden with the facts.

For, upon a morning in August, Doctor Courteney Clack appeared, desired to see Mr. Endicott alone, and not only told the blind man that his theory was in the main correct, but begged that from the stores of his common sense and wisdom he would indicate the most seemly and least sensational means by which this news might be broken to those concerned. The doctor did not pretend to excuse himself or his part in the play. There was, indeed, no necessity for recrimination or censure. The future lay at the door, and Christopher Yeoland, who had, in truth, haunted his own domain by night, designed to return to it in earnest during the autumn. The temporary lease would then terminate, and circumstances now enabled the owner to free his land of every encumbrance and henceforth administer Godleigh in a manner worthy of its traditions.

The interview was an old man's triumph, for Mark Endicott, too frank to pretend otherwise, gloried in the relation of the story long afterwards, loved to dwell upon his own reasoned synthesis and explain how closely it fitted the revealed facts, despite their rare singularity. As for Courteney Clack, that gentleman's amazement, when he found his intelligence more than a fortnight old, may be guessed, but can hardly be stated. Mr. Endicott sent for Myles to substantiate him, and finally the astounded physician unfolded his own narrative, now shrunk to a tame and trivial thing—an echo for the most part of Mark's deductions.

On reaching Australia with Stapledon's messages the physician's first professional duty had been at the bedside of Christopher's ancient kinsman, with whom the young man was dwelling. For only two days after Doctor Clack's arrival, the old wool dealer was bitten by a whip-snake at his country seat on the Hawkesbury River, and there passed speedily out of life. This fact combined with Clack's news from home to determine Christopher Yeoland in the action he had taken, and the scheme, once adumbrated upon young Yeoland's mind, grew apace. The dead man, who was also named Christopher, proved to be very wealthy, and his money, willed to assist the establishment of technical schools in Sydney, had been withdrawn from that purpose after two months' intercourse with the youthful head of the race. Thus, in ignorance of his own near exit, the elder left it within Christopher's power to redeem the ancestral forests and roof tree in fulness of time. Apart from the imposition, built on the fact of his relative's sudden death, the traveller had already determined that he should lie in the family grave at home. It was the right place for one who had saved Yeoland credit at the last gasp and given the head of that family wherewithal to lift honour from the dust. Then came Stapledon's message and Clack's fearless gloss; so that, with wits quickened and a mind enlarged by his own unexpected good fortune, Christopher made final sacrifice of all love hope—a renunciation worthy of honest praise in sight of his own altered circumstances—and, with Clack's aid, practised his theatrical imposition that Honor's road might stretch before her straight and certain. Nothing less than his death would decide her, and so he let the implicit lie be told, and determined with himself at all cost to keep out of his own country until expiration of the period for which he had let Godleigh.

Clack indicated a circumstance in itself satisfactory at this stage in his story. Christopher's resurrection would not practically prove so far-reaching as Mark Endicott and Stapledon had imagined, for none existed with any right to question the facts. On the supposed death of the owner, Godleigh had reverted to a man of the same name in Australia—that was all the lawyers knew—and the legal difficulty of reclaiming his own and re-establishing his rights promised to be but trifling. Neither had the law very serious penalties in pickle for him, because it could not be showed where Christopher had wronged any man.

Time passed, and even the limits of patience that he had set himself were too great for Yeoland of Godleigh. Now he was rich, and hated Australia with a deep hatred. He returned home therefore, and those events related had fallen almost act for act as Endicott declared. In the flesh had the man haunted Godleigh. Once a keeper nearly captured him upon his own preserves; once, during the past spring, he had crept to the great beech tree, impelled thither at the same hour and moment as his old sweetheart. Her collapse had frightened him out of his senses, and, on seeing Stapledon approaching, he had retreated, concealed himself, and, upon their departure, returned to his hidden horse. Deeply perturbed, but ignorant of all that the incident really signified, he had ridden back that night to Exeter, and so departed to the Continent, there to dwell unrecognised a while longer, and wait, half in hope, half in fear, that Honor might proclaim him.

But no sound reached his ear, and of Little Silver news neither he nor Courteney Clack had learnt anything of note for many weeks. Now, however, with only two months between himself and his return to Godleigh, Christopher Yeoland felt the grand imposture must be blown away. It had at least served his purpose.

Thus spoke Clack; then his own curiosity was satisfied, and he learned how, by the lawless operation of obscure men, that secret hidden in the churchyard had become known, and how, upon the confession of one conspirator, three others beside the two discoverers had come to hear of it.

"And as for that terrible thing—the child killed by him accidentally—my child—" said Stapledon without emotion, "little use tearing a tender-hearted creature with that to no purpose. I do not want him to know it."

"I won't tell him, you may be sure," answered the doctor, still in a dream before this unexpected discounting of his great intelligence. "He will not hear of it from me. But know he must sooner or later. That can't be spared him. Only a question of time and some blurted speech."

"I'll tell him, then," declared Myles. "There's nobody more fitting. I don't forget."

The question next arose as to how Little Silver should be informed, and Mr. Endicott declared that the vicar must make a formal announcement after morning service on the following Sunday. Then, with further conversation upon minor points, Doctor Clack's great confession ended; while as for the matter of the desecration, he held with Mr. Endicott that no notice need be taken beyond, perhaps, warning Mr. Cramphorn that his egregious enterprise was known, and that his own safety rested in silence.

The doctor stopped a few days at Endicott's; saw Honor, who heard him with deep interest and decreasing fear; then wrote at length to Christopher in London; but, not caring to face the publication of Yeoland's existence and pending return, Clack finally took himself off until the sensation was on the wane. Before he set out, Myles had a private conversation with him in nature comforting enough, for, concerning Honor, the medical man gave it as his professional opinion that this counter-shock would serve adequately to combat her former hopeless, nerveless condition. The truth, despite its startling nature, must bring wide relief from spiritual terrors, and so probably participate in and hasten the business of recovery.

Then came the thunder-clap, whose echoes reverberated in journals even to the great metropolitan heart of things, and Christopher Yeoland achieved a notoriety that was painful to him beyond power of words to express. Only one gleam of satisfaction shone through all the notes and comments and unnumbered reasons for his conduct: not one came nearer the truth than the utterance of a West Country journalist, who knew the history of the Yeoland family, and opined that a touch of hereditary eccentricity was responsible for all.

Of Little Silver, its comments, theories, bewilderment, and general suspicion that there must be something rotten at the roots of the world while such deeds could be, there appears no need to discourse. How Ash and his kind reviewed the matter, or with what picturesque force it appealed to Noah Brimblecombe, janitor of the mausoleum, may easily be imagined; while for the rest it would be specially interesting, if pertinent, to describe the emotions of Jonah Cramphorn. Relief and disappointment mingled in his mind; he had made no history after all; he was not the mainspring of this commotion, and when he nodded darkly and showed no surprise, folks merely held him too conceited to display honest amazement like everybody else, and laughed at his assumption of secret knowledge. There came a night, however, when Mr. Endicott spoke with him in private, after which Jonah desired nothing more than silence for himself, and poured his pent-up chagrin and annoyance upon Charity Grepe, who—poor soul—derived little lustre from this resurrection.

BOOK III.

CHAPTER I.
VANESSA IO

Between Bear Down and the valley was fern and the breath of fern and great gleam and drone of summer flies under the living sun. Here Teign tumbled through deep gorges, and from the wind-swept granite of Godleigh hill, beneath unclouded noonday splendour, acres of bracken panted silver-green in the glare, dipped to the fringes of the woods below, and shone like a shield of light upon the bosom of the acclivity. At river-level spread a forest, where oak and alder, larch and pinnacles of pine shimmered in the haze. Dark shadows broke the manifold planes of them, and the song of the river beneath, with lull and rise on the lazy summer breeze, murmured from mossy granite stairways twining through the woods. Here shone masses of king fern, twinkled jewels of honeysuckle, and the deep, pink blossoms of eglantine. The atmosphere was very dry; the leaves on a little white poplar clapped their hands to the river melody; hirundines wheeled and cried in the upper blue, and there lacked not other signs, all dearer than rainbows to a farmer whose corn is ripe, of fine weather and its continuance.

In the shadow of a great stone upon the hillside, where, beneath the fairy forest of the fern, sad grasses robbed of sunlight seeded feebly, and wood strawberries gemmed the under-green, sat Honor Stapledon alone. Upon one hand sloped bare descents, already blistered somewhat by a hot July, patched with rusty colour where the heather had been roasted under the eye of the sun, painted with tawny, thirsty foliage, brightened by the blue spires of viper's bugloss, starred with pink of centauries. A great bramble bore red fruit and pale blossom together; and here butterflies made dancing, glancing gleam and tangle of colour as they came and went, flashed hither and thither, or settled to sun themselves on the flowers and rocks. One—*Vanessa Io*—feared nothing, and pursued his business and pleasure upon the bramble within a few inches of Honor's cheek.

As yet Christopher Yeoland had not plucked courage to return publicly, but that morning came rumours from Little Silver that he was upon a visit to Godleigh, as guest of the departing tenant. Noah Brimblecombe had actually seen him and mentioned the fact to Mr. Cramphorn. Honor, therefore, expecting an early visit, and feeling quite unequal to such an experience now that it had come so near—desiring moreover that Myles and not herself should first welcome the wanderer—had stolen away to the adjacent hillside, there to pass some hours with a book. But her thoughts proved of a nature more interesting than verses. Indeed they lacked not poetry and even images to be described as startling, for the matter was dramatic and sufficiently sensational to fire a less imaginative mind. So her book remained unopened, and she watched *Vanessa Io*, though her thoughts were not with him.

While Stapledon had grasped the fact of Christopher's continued existence and pending return somewhat sooner than his wife, the positions a month later seemed reversed. He faced the upheaval on the first proclamation, and she shrank from it with emotion bred from her recent terror; but now it was Honor who discussed affairs in the calmer spirit, and Myles who changed the subject, not always without impatience. The woman's frank interest daily grew, and she saw no cause to hide it; while the man, whose mind had been jolted from the rut of accepted things, now felt a desire to return into it and found himself come near resentment of this wonder. Such a tremendous circumstance hung over his days like a cloud, for it meant more to him than anybody, so at least he believed at that season. Stapledon's intellect was of a sort likely to be impatient at such monkey tricks. He found all the solid building of the past, all the logical sequences of events and movements leading to possession of Honor, tumbled into ruins around him. To his order-loving nature the skein of life grew in some measure tangled before such sleight and jugglery. Though he strove hard to keep in sight the sure knowledge that Yeoland had played his part for love of Honor, yet indignation would now and then awake to burn in him; and that first spark of passion, lighted when he thought of his child, after the earliest confession from Henry Collins, was not as yet wholly extinguished. Now, while the return of the wanderer came nearer, Myles shook himself into a resolute attitude and told himself that the uncertain depths and shallows of his own emotions must be discovered and his future line of conduct determined, as Mark Endicott had forewarned him. But while he stood thus, in unfamiliar moods of doubt, Honor, contrariwise, from a standpoint almost approaching superstitious fear, was come to accept the truth and accept it thankfully. The tremendous mental excitement, the shock and clash of thoughts afforded by this event, possessed some tonic faculty for her, and, as Doctor Clack had predicted, wrought more good than harm within her nature. For a little while she had wept after the first wave of fear was passed; she had wept and wondered in secret at the snarling cruelty of chance that willed this man, of all men, to rob her of her baby treasure; but the thought of his sorrow when the truth should reach him lessened her own.

The reason for Christopher's conduct Honor had of course learned. That much Myles set out for her with the most luminous words at his command; and he smarted even while he told of the other's renunciation and self-sacrifice. He explained many times how for love of her Yeoland departed and let it be imagined that he was no more; how, from conviction that her happiness was wound up with her present husband, he had done this thing. Myles strove to live in an atmosphere of naked truth at this season, for his instinct told him that the way was strange and that salvation only lay in stripping off it every cloud or tissue of unreality.

As for Mark Endicott, from mere human interest at an event beyond experience, he passed to estimate and appraisement of Christopher's deeds. Averse from every sort of deception, he yet found himself unable to judge hardly before the motives and the character of the first puppet in this tragi-comedy. Yeoland had meant well in the past, and the only question for the future was his own sentiments toward Honor. That these justified him in his return to Godleigh Mr. Endicott nothing doubted. He recollected the somewhat peculiar emotional characteristics of the man and felt no cause for fear, save in the matter of Myles.

As for Little Silver, intelligence that their squire, resuscitated in life and pocket, was returning to his own filled most hearts with lively satisfaction after the first amazement had sobered. Recollection of his generosity awakened; whereon the fathers of the village met in conclave and determined to mark their great man's home-coming with some sort of celebration, if only a bonfire upon the hill-top and some special broaching of beer-barrels.

Honor moved her parasol a little, mused on time to come, and wished the ordeal of meeting with Christopher behind her. The chapter of their personal romance was sealed and buried in the past, and her feelings were not fluttered as she looked back. The interest lay ahead. She thought of the life he had lived since last they met, and wondered what women had come into it—whether one above all others now filled it for him. She hoped with her whole heart that it might be so, and sat so quiet, with her mind full of pictures and possibilities for him, that *Vanessa Io* settled within a foot of her and opened and shut his wings and thanked the sun, as a flower thanks him for his warmth, by display of beauty. His livery caught the thinker and brought her mind back behind her eyes so that she noted the insect's attire, the irregular outline of his pinions, their dull brick-red and ebony, brown margins, and staring eyes all touched and lighted with lilac, crimson, yellow, and white. Within this splendid motley the little body of him was wrapped in velvet, and as he turned about upon a bramble flower his trunk, like a tiny trembling watch-spring, passed to the honeyed heart of the blossom. Then he arose and joined the colour-dance of small blue butterflies from the heath, of sober fritillaries, and other of his own Vanessa folk—tortoise-shells, great and small, and a gorgeous red admiral in black and scarlet.

Far beneath a horn suddenly sounded, and the music of otter-hounds arose melodious from the hidden valley. Flight of blue wood-pigeons and cackle of a startled woodpecker marked the progress of the hunt. Here and there, with shouts and cries, came glint of a throng through the trees that concealed them. Then Honor heard the grander utterance of an elderly foxhound who was assisting the pack. He had suddenly lighted on the scent of his proper prey, and a moment later she saw him away on his own account, climbing the opposite hill at speed. His music died, and the clamour beneath soon dwindled and sank until a last note of the horn, mellowed by distance, slowly faded away. But Honor was uninterested, for the modern fashion of otter-hunting at noon instead of grey dawn, though it may promise the presence of fair maidens at a meet, holds forth small likelihood of otters, who are but seldom slain upon these lazy runs.

Then the sound of a step sprang out of the silence, and the woman turned and drew breath at sight of Christopher Yeoland, standing knee-deep in the fern behind her. He was clad as when she saw him last, in grey country wear; and to her first startled glance he seemed unchanged.

"Never pass a parasol without looking under it, if I can," he said; and then, before she could rise, he had flung himself beside her and taken her left hand and squeezed it gently between his. Her other hand went unconsciously towards her breast, but now she lowered it into his and suffered the greeting she had no power to speak, be uttered by that pressure of palm on palm.

"What tremendous, tragic things we ought to whisper at this moment," he said; "yet, for the life of me, I can only think of a single question: Have you forgiven me for my far-reaching fool's trick? If you haven't, I can't live at Godleigh under the shadow of Endicott's frown. And I certainly can't live anywhere else, so, should you refuse to pardon, I must die in real earnest."

"If anybody can forgive you, it is I, Christopher. Oh dear—I am glad we are over this meeting. It has made me feel so strange, so curious. It seems only yesterday that I saw you last; and I could laugh, now that you are alive once more, to think your spirit had power to frighten me—or anybody. Yet I do not quite believe I shall ever feel that you are flesh and blood again."

"It will take time. I began to doubt myself when I came home and stole about in the old haunts, and felt how ghosts feel. Once a keeper chased me out of Godleigh, and I only escaped by the skin of my teeth! Thrice I saw you—at your window in moonlight, and driving with your husband, and—the last time."

His voice faltered; she saw tears in his eyes and knew that he had learned of the misfortune in the wood. The fact pleased her, in that this sorrow was bound to come to him and now it would not be necessary for Myles to speak about the past. A moment of silence passed between them, and she looked at Christopher softly and saw him unchanged. Every feature and expression, every trick of voice and gesture was even as it used to be. She knew his careless tie, his jerk of head, his habit of twisting up the corner of his moustache and then biting it.

"How wonderful this is!" she said, not heeding his broken sentence. "How mysterious to think I sit here talking to a man I have believed for two years to be dead! And yet each moment my heart grows calmer and my pulse beats more quietly."

"Things are always commonplace when you expect them to be theatrical and rise to fine, giddy heights. That's the difference between plays and real life. Chance works up to her great situations and then often shirks them in the most undramatic and disappointing way. But when she does want a situation, she just pitches people headlong into it—like our meeting at the old tryst by the beech. Memory took me there; what took you? God forgive me, I——"

"Leave that," she said quickly. "It can't be talked about. Have you seen Myles or Uncle Mark yet?"

"No; a proper attraction brought me here, and somehow I knew that I should find you. But I long to meet him too—your husband. It's a blessing to know that among the many who blame me he won't be counted. Please Heaven, I shall see a great deal of you both in the future. I always loved the west wind best, because it blew over Bear Down before it came to me. Sunshine ahead, I hope, and some for me. I've come home to be happy."

"Have you found a wife?"

"Honor!—No, I haven't looked for one. Godleigh's my wife. And I must set about spending some money on her, now I've got plenty. So strange— that lonely old cadet of our family. He was, I thought, as poor as a church mouse. Three parts of a miser, and lived hard and laughed at luxuries, as so many do who have had to make their own fortunes. Money-grubbing carries that curse along with it, that it often turns the grubber blind and deaf to all save the sight and clink of the hateful, necessary stuff. But the dear old boy somehow warmed to me; and I drew pictures of home for him; and he promised to come home and see me some day when he grew old. He was seventy-three then, but utterly refused to accept the fact. Then death suddenly rushed him, in the shape of a whip-snake, and dying, his thoughts turned home, and it was his wish, not my whim, that he should lie there. That put my plot into my head, for he was of the same name. Not until after his death did I know he had altered his will; and I can tell you, seeing the style he lived in and the size of his ideas, that I was staggered when I found he had left me a real fortune. That's my adventure—a mere bit of a story-book, yet a very pleasant bit to the hero of it."

Vanessa Io returned, and so still sat Honor that he settled boldly upon the sun-kissed folds of her skirt.

"Do you remember how I used to say you were all butterfly, though in grave moments you rather claimed for yourself the qualities of staid and sober twilight things—solemn beetles, whose weight of wing-case reminds them that life is real and earnest?"

"You were right upon the whole. I've got the same spirit in me as that little, gaudy, self-complacent atom there, opening and shutting his wings, like a fairy's picture-book upon your knee. Our rule of life is the same. I only hope he's having more luck with his existence than I have had with mine."

She reflected a moment. This was the first hint of his own sorrows in the past, of the price he had paid.

"But I'm not changed, for all the world of experiences that separates us," he continued quickly. "I'm only a thought older. Time is beginning to do a little gradual work in grey just above my ears. So delicate and apologetic and gentle he is that I can't grumble. Is Mr. Endicott well?"

"Very well."

"And Myles and the farm?"

"Both flourishing abundantly, I believe."

"And to think the sadness on your face is solely of my bringing—yet you can welcome me after what I have done!"

She marvelled a little that he could speak of it

"Pray, Christo, do not harp upon that. None accuses you. How could such a thing be thrown as blame upon anybody? Fate so often uses the kindest of us to do her cruel deeds. 'Tis the height of her cynic fun to plan parts in her plots and make the wrong actor play them."

"I ought to have used common sense and kept away altogether."

"Common sense!"

"I know; but I found it in Australia. There was no excuse for me. Can he forgive me?"

"I have not heard him breathe so much as one hasty word since he has known. You do not understand him to ask such a question. He is above admiration. No woman ever had such a good husband. And the better I love him, Christo, the better shall I love you, for giving him to me."

"Good God! you mustn't talk like that, must you?" he asked with some flutter; but she regarded him calmly as she answered.

"Why should not I? He knows that I loved you, and, therefore, love you. I am a most logical woman, and unchanging. It has all been very smooth and clear between Myles and me from the first, because we both hated any shadow of misunderstanding. That's the strength of our married life."

"My only fear centred in the recollection of his great straightness. He hates a trick, even though he may win by it."

"He loves me with all his heart."

"Yes—there it is. I didn't feel very anxious about the thing I did first; only about what I have done since I sometimes get a doubt. The question is whether, once dead, I was justified in coming to life again. Man's only built to be heroic in snatches—at least the average man—and when I found myself rich, instead of keeping it up and going through to the bitter end, as a bigger chap would have done, I thought of Godleigh. If you had lived a year and more among gum trees I think you might find it in you to forgive me for coming back. Those eternally lost gum trees! And springtime calling, calling from home! And here I am in God's good green again—His always, mine for a little while."

"Who can wonder that you came? The wonder would have been if you had stopped away. The thing you desired to bring about is done—happily and for ever."

"But Myles? He's so thorough. What does he think? Half-measures wouldn't win his respect."

"Half-measures you call them; but even a saint's life is only patchwork—all wrought in the drab colours of human nature, with a few bright stars marking the notable deeds. Yes, and lesser existences are a mere patchwork of good intentions, mostly barren."

"Not barren for certain. We sow decent grain and dragon's teeth mixed; and the poor sowers so often don't know which is which—till the crop's past praying for."

"That's your philosophy, then. I was wrong; you have changed."

"It's true. These things are in copybooks, but we never heed them when we are young. So that is why sometimes I have my doubts about Myles. Then I think along another line and the cloud vanishes."

"There can be no cloud, and he will soon rejoice that such a friend is in the land of the living."

But suspicion had already wakened in Yeoland.

"You say 'he will rejoice'; you don't say 'he does.'"

"Of course he does. How can you doubt it?"

"Tell him you have seen me, and that I am a perceptible shade wiser than when I left England. Tell him that incident in the wood has come near breaking my heart. I can feel great griefs if I don't show them. I do not expect him to slip into the old relations as you have. You and I were a couple of wild wood children together for years, until our elders trapped us and attempted to tame and educate and spoil us. Yet between him and me now there are close bonds enough—bonds as deep to me, as binding, as eternal as the dawn-light we both adore. But he's a fire-worshipper, or something, and I'm a Christian; so, when all's said, we shall never get straight to one another's hearts like Honor and Christo. It isn't possible. I thought to meet him with a handshake to bridge the years, and a silent understanding too deep for words; I pictured him all the way home as my friend of friends, and now—now I ought to go upon my knees to him and ask him to put his foot on my neck and forgive me for that moonlight madness."

"Now I know that it is you, not I, who fail to understand my husband," said Honor. "He is a greater man by far than you think or I know. Never utter or dream these things any more, for they are wrong. Forget them and look forward to happiness."

They talked a while longer on divers themes; then the woman rose to return home, and Christopher, declaring an intention to visit Endicott's that evening, went back to Godleigh.

Each now marvelled much from a personal point of view at this, their first meeting—at its familiarity of texture and lack of distinction. Both indeed felt dumbly astonished that, after such a gap, converse could be renewed thus easily; yet they joyed in the meeting; and while Yeoland ingenuously gloried in the sight and voice of the woman he had loved, Honor's pleasure was of a colour more sober, a quality more intricate.

CHAPTER II.
THE MEETING OF THE MEN

Christopher Yeoland visited Bear Down on the evening after his meeting with its mistress; but the hour was late when he arrived, and Honor had retired with a headache ere he entered the farm. Even as he reached the front door and lifted his hand to the bell Yeoland changed his mind and strolled round to the kitchen entrance. There he stood for an instant before marching boldly in according to his old custom. A voice fell upon his ear, and for a moment he thought that it must be Mark speaking to himself alone, as was the blind man's wont; but other speech broke in upon the first, and, catching his own name on Cramphorn's tongue, Christopher stood still, laughed silently, and listened.

An utterance from Churdles Ash was the first that came distinctly to him.

"Us o' Little Silver be like the twelve apostles, I reckon—all mazed wi' gert wonder to hear tell of a resurrection."

"Awnly theer's a world-wide differ'nce 'tween Lard o' Hosts an' this gormed Jack-o'-lantern," answered Cramphorn. "For my part I'd so soon—maybe sooner—he was wheer us thought him. Born he was to make trouble, an' trouble he'll make while he walks airth. No fay, I can't fox myself into counting this a pleasing thing. He'm takin' up gude room, if you ax me."

Christopher, having heard quite enough, himself answered as he came among them—

"That's honest, at any rate, Jonah. But I hope you're wrong. I've come back a reformed character—on my solemn word I have. Wait and see."

He shook hands with Stapledon first, afterwards with Mark Endicott and the assembled labourers. There fell a moment of awkward silence; then Jonah, who felt some word from him seemed due, knocked out his pipe and spoke before retiring. He contented himself with an expression of regret, but hesitated not to qualify it so extensively that little doubt arose concerning his real opinions.

"I didn't knaw as you was behind the door, Squire Yeoland, else I might have guarded my lips closer. An' bein' a living sawl—to save or damn accordin' to God's gudeness—'tweern't seemly for me to speak so sharp. Not that offence was meant, an' a man's opinions be his awn; though I trust as you'll order your ways to shaw I'm a liar; an' nobody better pleased than me, though not hopeful, 'cause what's bred in the bone comes out in the flesh. An' I may say you've proved wan thing—if awnly wan: that a sartain party by name of Charity Grepe be a auld, double-dealin' rascal, an' no more a wise woman than my awn darters. So gude-night all."

Pinsent and Collins retreated with Mr. Cramphorn, but old Churdles Ash remained to shake hands once again with the wanderer.

"I be a flat Thomas wheer theer's any left-handed dealings like this here," he said. "Most onbelievin' party as ever was, as well a man may be when the world's so full of evil. But by the hand of you and the speech of you, you'm flesh and blood same as the rest of us. I'm sure I hope, your honour, if you'll take an old man's respectful advice, as you'll bide above ground henceforrard an' do no more o' these dark, churchyard deeds 'mongst Christian folks. It may be very convenient an' common down-long in furrin paarts, but 'tidn' seemly to Little Silver, wheer theer's such a lot o' the risin' generation as looks to 'e for a example."

"I'll act as becomes me ever afterwards, gaffer," declared Christopher, whereon, gratified by this promise, Mr. Ash touched his forehead, praised God and the company, and so withdrew.

Then Yeoland began his story, and Mark put an occasional question, while Stapledon kept silence until he should have opportunity to speak with the other alone. A necessity for some recognition and utterance of personal gratitude weighed heavy on him. That Christopher desired no such thing he felt assured, but he told himself that a word at least was due, and must be paid, like any other debt. Myles had judged as the wanderer suspected: Yeoland's initial act seemed great to him; this return to life he accounted paltry and an anticlimax beside it. Putting personal bias out of the question, or believing that he did so, Stapledon endeavoured to estimate the achievement from an impartial spectator's standpoint, and so seen this homecoming disappointed him. He did not deny the man his right to return; he only marvelled that he had exercised it. Yet as Christopher, with many an excursus, chattered through his story, and spoke of his native land with manifest emotion, Stapledon wondered no more, but understood, and felt disinterested sympathy. Then he blamed himself for previous harsh criticism, and discovered that the leaven of a personal interest had distorted his point of view. Morbidly he began to think of Honor, and the dominant weakness of his character awoke again. He told himself that Yeoland would find out how perfect was the unanimity between husband and wife; then he gave himself the lie and wondered, with his cold eyes upon Christopher, if the returned wanderer would ever discover that the inner harmony of Honor's married life was not complete at all times.

When Yeoland had made an end, Mark asked him concerning his plans for the future, and listened to many projects, both happy and impracticable, for the glorification of Godleigh and the improvement of Little Silver.

"Clack's going to be my agent. After he practically perjured his immortal soul for me, I cannot do less for him than give him that appointment. And he's a good sportsman, which is so much nowadays."

With some element of restraint they discoursed for an hour or more, then Yeoland rose and Myles walked part of the way home with him. Under a night of stars the farmer spoke and said what he accounted necessary in the briefest phrases capable of rendering his sentiments.

"I want you to know that I understand and I thank you. My gratitude is measured by the worth of what you—you gave me. I can say no more than that."

"No need to have said as much. Your voice tells me you don't like saying it, Stapledon, and truly I had no desire to hear it. You see, we could only win her full happiness that way. I knew her character better than you could——"

"Impossible!"

"Now, no doubt, but not then, when these things happened. I pictured her with you, and with me. I appreciated your message, but I didn't agree with you. Honestly you have nothing to thank me for. We're on this now and will leave the bones of the thing clean-picked. It was love of the woman— desire to see her happy for all time—that made me act so. You asked her to marry you before you sent your message by Clack. So that showed me you believed that you could achieve her happiness if she let you try. But she would never have married you until she knew that I was out of it. The right thing happened. All's well that ends well. With a past so distinct and defined, it seems to me that the future could hardly look happier. We understand each other so well—we three, thank God. I threshed it all out through many a long, sleepless night, I can tell you. I'm no *tertium quid* come back into lives that have done with me; I'm not here to ruffle up a tangle already smoothed out by time. You understand that?"

Myles agreed with the younger man, and tried to believe him.

"Of course I understand. Friends we shall always be, and each welcome to the other when our devious ways may cross. Honor is not likely to be sentimental under such curious conditions. She will view this, your return, with the calm self-possession she displays in all affairs of life. It has done her good already, and lifted a cloud. I tell you so frankly. She was haunted. I hear you know all about that. There is no need for you to say what you feel about it. I will take your words as spoken. So here we stand—we three—and our lives must go forward and unfold to the ripening here on this hillside. What then? There is room enough?"

"Ample, I should imagine. That you should ask the question is a little astonishing. But I understand you better than you think. You can't help the defiance in your tone, Stapledon; you can't wholly hide the hardness in your voice. D'you think I don't know what's cutting you so deep when you look at me and remember that night? Forgive me. I have paid for it with grey hairs."

"You mistake. I should be a fool to blame you seriously for that. Merely evil fortune. Evil fortune was overdue in my life. I had been waiting long for reverses. You were the unconscious instrument."

"Your old, sombre creed, whose god is the law of chance. Anyhow, you and your wife shall find no truer friend than Christopher Yeoland in the years to come."

They shook hands and separated, the one perfectly happy and contented that this ordeal was over; the other already in a cloud of cares with his face lifted to meet troubles still invisible. The one saw a smooth and sunlit road ahead of him—a road of buds and flowers and singing birds; the other stood among pitfalls past numbering, and the way was dreary as well as dangerous.

As he returned home, Myles stopped and looked over a gate to set his thoughts in order. Whereupon he made discoveries little calculated to soothe or sustain him in this hour. First he found that lack of knowledge alone was responsible for his commotion—lack of knowledge of his wife; and secondly, reviewing his recent conversation with Christopher, he very readily observed a note in it unfamiliar to himself. This man's advent aroused an emotion that Myles had read of and heard about, but never felt. Upon the threshold of renewed intercourse, and despite so many friendly words, Stapledon recognised the thing in his heart and named it. He was jealous of Yeoland's return, and his discovery staggered him. The fact felt bad enough; the position it indicated overwhelmed him, for it shone like an evil light on the old fear; it showed that the understanding he boasted between himself and Honor by no means obtained. Herein lay his trial and his terror. No cloudless marital life could receive this miasma into its atmosphere for an instant, for jealousy's germ has no power to exist where a man and a woman dwell heart to heart.

Great forces shook Stapledon; then he roused himself, fell back upon years of self-discipline, shut the floodgates of his mind, and told his heart that he was a fool.

"The man shall be my friend—such a friend as I have never had yet," he said aloud to the night. "I will weary him with my friendship. He is honest, and has sacrificed his life for me. It is the vileness of human nature, that hates benefits received, which works in me against him. And if it pleases Fate to send me another child, this man, who believes in God, shall be its godfather."

His determination comforted Stapledon, and he passed slowly homeward conscious of a battle won, strong in the belief that he had slain a peril at its birth. He told himself that the word "jealousy" rang unreal and theatrical, in presence of his wife's slumber.

CHAPTER III.
FLAGS IN THE WIND

Godleigh forest was paying its debt to the Mother in good gold, and a myriad leaves flew and whirled aloft, tumbled and sailed downwards, rustled and hustled over the green grass, dropped amongst the forest boughs, floated away on Teign's bosom, eddied in sudden whirlwinds at gates and wind-swept gaps of the woodlands. The summer glory was extinguished once again, the tree-top life was ended for another generation of foliage; and now, final livery of russet or crimson won, the leaves fell and flew at the will of a wild wind, or waited in some last resting-place for latter rains, for alchemy of frost and for the sexton worm. Their dust is the food of the whole earth, and to the blind and patient roots, twisting gigantically at the hidden heart of things, they return obedient. For to them they owe every aerial happiness in gleaming dawns, every joy of the moonlight and starlight and deep nocturnal dews, song of birds and whisper of vernal rain, cool purple from shadows of clouds and all the glorious life of a leaf—of each small leaf that joins its particular jewel to the green coronet of summer.

Little Silver took a holiday from the affairs of working-day life on the occasion of the Squire's official return to Godleigh Park, and the day was set aside for rejoicing and marked with a white stone. A great banquet under canvas formed the staple attraction; the grounds were thrown open, and Christopher invited his small world to lunch with him in a noble marquee tricked out with flags and streamers. But the season and the day proved out of harmony with campestral merry-making. Nature's October russets, pale gold and red gold, killed the crude bunting colours; a high wind rollicked and raved through the woods and over the waste places; the great tents and the lesser creaked and groaned, billowed and bent; yet those driven from them by fear were sent back by heavy squalls of rain. The autumnal equinox welcomed Yeoland roughly to his home; but happily he drove under the triumphal arch of laurel and oak before an envious gust sent it sprawling; happily also the increasing wind blew the sky clean towards nightfall, though the rockets that then shrieked aloft chose perilous, unexpected places for their descent, and the bonfire was abandoned, for its conflagration must have threatened every rick of hay within half a mile east of it. Upon the whole, however, this celebration was counted successful, though one uncanny incident marred the day. At earliest dawn Mr. Brimblecombe discovered that some genius unknown had decorated the Yeoland mausoleum with heavy wreaths of autumn flowers and evergreens; but even the least imaginative recognised that such accentuation of the tomb at this moment showed a triumph of wrong-headedness.

Upon that great occasion did Henry Collins, whose patience, even in affairs of the heart, was almost reptilian, avail himself of the general holiday. And when Sally Cramphorn, who still philandered with him, though fitfully, promised that she would take a walk by his side after the feasting, Henry believed that the moment for speech was come at last. He had debated the form of his proposition for several months, and the girl's attitude now naturally led him to suspect an agreeable termination to his protracted sufferings. The time was that of eating and drinking, and Sally, who perceived that Mr. Gregory Libby, from his standpoint as carver at the head of one of the tables in the banqueting tent, viewed her position beside Collins with concern, hastened her meal and shortened it. Then, as soon as possible upon the speech-making, she took Henry by the arm and led him forth very lovingly under the nose of the other man. Together they proceeded through the woods, and the graciousness which she exhibited while Gregory's eye was yet upon her, diminished a little. Still the woman felt amiably disposed to her innocent tool, and even found it in her heart to pity him somewhat, for she guessed what now awaited her. Mr. Collins walked slowly along, with some strain and creaking of mental machinery as he shook his thoughts and ideas into order. He passed with Sally under pine trees, and at length found a snug spot sheltered from the wind.

"Us might sit here 'pon the fir-needles," suggested Henry.

"'Tis damp, I doubt," answered his companion, thinking of her best gown.

"Then I'll spread my coat for 'e. I want to have a tell along with you, an' I caan't talk travellin'. 'Tis tu distractin', an' what I've got to say'll take me all my power, whether or no."

He spread his black broadcloth without hesitation, and Sally, appreciating this compliment, felt she could not do less than accept it. So she plumped down on Henry's Sunday coat, and he appeared to win much pleasure from contemplation of her in that position. He smiled to himself, sighed rather loudly, and then sat beside her. Whereupon his tongue refused its office and, for the space of two full minutes, he made no remark whatever, though his breathing continued very audible.

"What be thinking 'bout?" asked Sally suddenly.

"Well, to tell plain truth, I was just taking pleasure in the idea as you'd ordained to sit 'pon my jacket. 'Twill be very comfortin' to me to call home as you've sat on un every time I put un on or off."

"If 'twas awnly another party!" thought the girl. "Doan't be such a fule," she said.

"That's what everybody have been advisin' me of late," he answered calmly, without the least annoyance or shame. "'Tis the state of my mind. Things come between me an' my work—a very ill-convenient matter. But, whether or no, I'll be proud of that coat now."

She sat comfortably beside him, and presently, after further silence, Henry lolled over towards her, and, taking a straw, sought with clumsy pleasantry to stick it into her hand under the white cotton glove which she was wearing.

"What be about?" she asked sharply. "Go along with 'e! Doan't 'e knaw me better than to think I be so giddy?"

Thus repulsed, Mr. Collins apologised, explained that in reality he did know Sally better, that his action was one of pure inadvertence, and that he admired her character by special reason of its sobriety. Silence again overtook them, and, while Sally fidgeted impatiently, the man's owl eyes roamed from off her face to the woods, from the woodland back again to her. He stuffed his pipe slowly, then returned it to his pocket; he sighed once or twice, tied up his boot-lace, and cleared his throat. After a painful pause the woman spoke again.

"Be us at a funeral or a junketing? You look for all the world as if you'd catched something hurtful. Wheer's your manners? What's in your mind now?"

Henry gulped, and pointed to an oak immediately opposite them—a great tree bound about in a robe of ivy.

"Was just considerin' 'bout thicky ivydrum, an' what gude sneyds for scythe-handles her'd make."

"Then you'd best to bide here with your scythe-handles, an' I'll go back-along to the company. I didn't come out to sit an' stare at a ivybush if you did."

"Doan't 'e be so biting against me, woman!" said Collins indignantly. "I be comin' to it so fast as I can, ban't I? 'Tedn' so easy, I can assure 'e. Maybe chaps as have axed a score o' females finds speech come quick enough; but I've never spoke the word to wan afore in all my life; an' 'tis a damn oneasy job; an' I ban't gwaine to be hurried by you or any other."

Sally appeared awed at this outburst. She suddenly realised that Mr. Collins was a man, a big one, a strong one, and an earnest one.

"Sorry I took you up tu quick, I'm sure. I didn't knaw as you felt so deep."

"If I could have trusted pen an' ink, I should have written it out for 'e," he answered, "but my penmanship's a vain thing. I'll have the handkercher out of that pocket you'm sittin' on, if 'tis all the same to you. Theer's a dew broke out awver my brow."

She rose and passed to him a large red handkerchief. Then he thanked her, mopped his face, and continued—

"When fust I seed you, I felt weak by reason of your butivul faace, an' the way you could toss hay an' keep so cool as a frog. An' I will say that the laugh of you was very nigh as fine as a cuckoo's song. Then I got to see what a gude gal you was tu, an' how you scorned all men-folk—'cept Libby."

These words he added hastily, as he saw her colour rising.

"Libby, I do allow, you gived your countenance to, though, if I may say it, ban't no gert sign of love to see a chap in two minds between such a piece as you an' your sister. But I never looked at no other but you—not even when I was up to Exeter. An' if you see your way to keep comp'ny along wi' me, God's my judge you'll never be sorry you done it. I be a man as stands to work an' goes to church Sundays when let alone. An' I'd trust you wi' every penny of the money an' ax for no more'n a shillin' here an' theer. An' I'd stand between you an' your faither, as doan't 'pear to be so fond of you of late as he used to be."

Sally moved uneasily, for he had echoed a recent, dim suspicion of her own.

"Best let that bide," she said. "If my faither likes Margery better'n what he do me, that's his business, not yours."

"'Tis a fault in him, however," answered Henry. "You'm worth ten thousand o' she; an' he'll live to find it out yet. He'm grawin' auld an' tootlish, I reckon, else he'd never set her up afore you."

"She'm a crafty twoad," declared the other gloomily. "I knaw she'm clever'n what I be, but flesh an' blood counts for somethin'. He sees me twice to her wance—Gregory do; an', whether or no, the man's free as ban't achsually married."

Mr. Collins grew warm again, to see the drift of his lady's thoughts, and endeavoured to bring her conversation back to the matter in hand.

"Ban't for me to speak nothin' 'gainst Libby or any other man. An' 'twouldn't be fair fightin' if I said what I'd say wi' pleasure to the faace of un if he was here; but I want 'ess' or 'no' for myself, an' I do pray, my dear woman, as you'll consider of it afore you decide."

"Ban't no need, an' thank you kindly, I'm sure," said Sally. "But you must look some plaace else than me, Henery; an' I'm sure you'll find many so gude, an' plenty better."

He sat silent, staring and sniffing.

"Doan't 'e cry 'bout it," she said.

"I ban't cryin'—merely chap-fallen," he answered, "an' theer's none 'pon the airth so gude as you that ever I see; an' I do wish as you'd take your time an' not be so sudden. I can wait—I can wait if theer's a shade of doubt in your mind. Ess fay, I can wait weeks, an' months, an' years, so easy as a tree, for you to decide. But do 'e take a bit of time. 'Tis cruel short just to say 'no,' after all as I've felt for 'e so long."

She accepted the alternative, half from pity, half from policy. Any hint of an understanding might galvanise the cold-blooded Libby into action.

"Wait then," she said, "an' us'll see what time sends."

"Thank you, I'm sure—cold comfort, but a thought better'n nought. Now, if you'll rise up off my coat I might get 'e a few braave filbert nuts; then us'll join the people."

Sally dusted the coat and helped its master into it. They then returned towards the central festivity, and upon the way, at the bend of a narrow path, came suddenly upon Christopher Yeoland, Honor and her husband, Mark Endicott, with his arm in that of Mr. Scobell, Doctor Clack, and other local celebrities and men of leading in the neighbourhood.

"Lard! how can us pass all this mort o' gentlefolks an' me that down-daunted," moaned Henry; but his companion, secure in her pretty face and trustful of her best gown, felt quite equal to the ordeal.

"So easy as they can pass us," she answered. "They'm awnly men an' women when all's said, an' us be so gude as them, 'pon a public holiday or in church. I mind a time when Squire Yeoland never passed me by wi'out a civil word, an' I shouldn't wonder if he didn't now for all his riches."

She was right. Observing that no parent accompanied her and recollecting her blue eyes very well, Christopher stopped.

"Ah, Sally, glad to see you again. Not married yet—eh? But going to be, I'll warrant. That's your man? Lucky chap. And remember, the day of the wedding I've got twenty pounds for you to make the cottage vitty."

Miss Cramphorn blushed and murmured something, she knew not what, while Henry, now safely past his betters, shook at these bold words. Then the company proceeded, and Myles Stapledon, recollecting when these two had last met, mused upon the nature of the man, while Honor chid him.

"That's the way you'll send your money spinning, by putting a premium on improvident marriages. Ask Mr. Scobell what he thinks of such folly."

"A sentiment. I've always liked Sally. I kissed her once and her father saw me. Myles will tell you about that. Not that she ever liked me much—too good a judge of character, I expect."

Meantime Mr. Collins and his companion passed back to the tents and flags, and as they did so Henry could not refrain from commenting upon the squire's handsome promise.

"Did you hear what the man said?" he asked.

"Not being deaf, I did," answered Sally with evasion. "A wonnerful offer. Twenty pound! An' just for to make a place smart."

"Best to find a maid as won't keep 'e hanging round. 'Tis mere gapes-nestin' for you to wait for me—a wild-goose chase for sartain."

"I hope not."

"Twenty pounds ban't much arter all's said."

"Not to your faither, as he be a snug man enough by accounts; but 'tis tidy money to the likes of me—big money to come in a heap an' all unearned. Not as I'd want it. You should have every penny-piece if you'd awnly—"

"I doan't want to hear no more 'pon that head. I've promised to think of it, an' I ax you not to speak another word till I tell you to."

"'Twas the thought of the money that carried me away like, an' I'll be dumb from to-day, I do assure 'e."

Somewhat later they met Mr. Cramphorn, but it was significant of a lessened interest in his elder daughter that Jonah, instead of reproaching her for thus walking apart with one of the other sex, merely called to Collins and bid him bring his strength where it was needed to brace the tackle of a tent.

CHAPTER IV.
DRIFTING

With return of winter some temporary peace descended upon Myles, and, looking back, he felt ashamed at the storm and stress of spirit that Yeoland's resurrection had awakened in him. For a season, as life returned to its level progress, he truly told himself that he viewed the friendship between his wife and her old lover without concern, because it was natural and inevitable. Honor's very frankness and ingenuous pleasure in the wanderer's company shamed a jealous attitude. Some men, indeed, had gone further and blessed Yeoland's home-coming. Certainly that event was in no small measure responsible for Honor's renewed physical welfare, and the excitement acted kindly upon a temperament that found food in novelty and desired sweep and play of change for her soul's health. Stapledon's wife was well again, and soon she discovered that life could still be full and sweet. Into a sort of lulled contentment he therefore sank, and proclaimed to himself that all was well, that the existence of the three, lived under present relations, was natural and seemly. He checked impatience at the expeditions planned, listened to Christopher's endless designs with respect to Godleigh, advised him and endured from him the old, extravagant conceits and jesting, specious views of life. Yet the glamour was off them now, and they only wearied Myles. He believed at first that Yeoland must be a changed man; but very soon he found no such thing had happened.

Nevertheless, some parity of tastes obtained, as of old, in divers directions. Again they walked for many miles together, each occupied with Nature from his own standpoint; and again they met in the dawn hour that possessed like fascination for both. At such times, under grey winter light, shrewd and searching, what was best in the men stood first, and they almost understood one another; but when they met, smudged by long hours of the toilsome day, and especially when they found each other in common company of Honor, both lacked the former sympathy.

As for Christopher, he heartily appreciated Myles at this period, and found the farmer's common sense a valuable antidote to the somewhat too spacious ideas of Doctor Clack in matters concerning betterment of Godleigh. And not seldom did Yeoland rejoice, with a single eye, that his old love had such a steadfast rock upon which to establish her life.

In his relations with Honor he had been a little astonished to find the fact of her marriage not recognised by his nature, as it was by his conscience.

That Nature could dare to be herself surprised him, when her wave throbbed through his being now and again upon some rare, sweet note of voice or tinkle of laughter. At such emotional moments he complimented the character and heroic attributes of Myles, with a vigour so crude that Honor might have suspected had not she echoed the sentiment from her heart. She never wearied of her husband's praises, and had no discernment as to what prompted Christopher's sudden overflowings of admiration. The man's return, as in the first instance of his own juxtaposition with Myles, served to alter Honor's inner attitude towards her husband. It seemed, in a sense, as she had fancied of old, that these two were the complement each of the other.

And a result was that his wife became more to Stapledon as the weeks passed. Gradually—but not so gradually that he failed to observe it—there came an increase of consideration in small matters, a new softness in her voice, a deeper warmth in her kisses. He marked her added joy in life, noted how she let her happiness bubble over to make him more joyful; and at first he was filled with satisfaction; and next he was overclouded with doubt. He tried to ascertain why her old lover's return should increase Honor's liking for her husband; he laboured gloomily upon a problem altogether beyond his calibre of mind to solve. He failed to see that the subtle change in his wife extended beyond him to the confines of her little world, that some higher graciousness was bred of it, that the least planet of which she was the sun now reaped new warmth from her accession of happiness. He puzzled his intelligence, and arrived, through long fret and care, at an erroneous solution. Utterly unable to appraise the delicate warp and poise of her humours, or gauge those obscure escapements that control happiness in the machinery of a woman's mind, Stapledon came to pitiful and mistaken conclusions that swept from him all content, all security, all further peace. At the glimmer of some devil's lantern he read into Honor's altered bearing an act of deliberate simulation. He denied that this advent of the other could by any possibility possess force to deepen or widen her affection for him; and he concluded, upon this decision, that the alteration must be apparent, not real. Such was the man's poor speed in the vital science of human nature. Next, he strove to explain the necessity for her pretence, with the reason of it; and so he darkened understanding, fouled his own threshold with fancied danger, and passed gradually into a cloudy region of anxiety and gloom. Excuse for speech or protest there was none; yet, unable to discern in Honor's frank awakening to everyday life and her renewed healthful bearing towards all her environment an obvious purity of mind and thought, he suffered his agitation to conquer him. He lived and waited, and sank into a chronic watchfulness that was loathsome to him. His fits of moody taciturnity saddened his wife and astonished her above measure, for it seemed that the old love of natural things was dead in him. In truth, his religion of the Moor—his dogma of the granite and vast waste places—failed him at this pinch. His gods were powerless and dumb—either that, or the heart of him had grown deaf for a season.

His unrest appeared, but the inner fires were hidden very completely. Then Mark Endicott, who knew that Myles was disordered, and suspected the tissue of his trouble, approached him, burrowed to his secret, and held converse thereon through some hours of a stormy night in January.

Stapledon at first evaded the issue, but he confessed at length, and, when invited to name the exact nature of his disquiet, merely declared the present position to be impossible in his judgment.

"We can't live with the balance so exact," he said. "I feel it and know it. Honor and this man loved one another once, and the natural attraction of their characters may bring them to do so again, now that such a thing would be sin."

"A big word—'sin,'" answered Mr. Endicott. "If that's all your trouble, the sooner you let sunshine into your mind again the better. Honor's an Endicott, when all's said, though maybe one of the strangest ever born under that name. I'm astonished to hear that this is the colour of your mind. And the man—queer though he is, too, and unlike most men I've met with—yet he's not the sort to bring trouble on a woman, last of all this woman."

"You prose on, uncle, not remembering what it felt like to feel your blood run hot at a woman's voice," answered Myles with unusual impatience and a flash of eye. "I give him all the credit you desire and more; I know he is honourable and upright and true. What then? Highest honour has broken down before this temptation. He is made of flesh and blood after all, and a man can't live within a span of a woman he loves and be happy—not if that woman belongs to somebody else. I don't assert that his love still exists, yet it's an immortal thing—not to be killed—and though he thinks he has strangled it—who can say? It may come to life again, like he did."

"You judge others by your own honest character; but I'm not so certain. If there is a man who could live platonically beside a woman he loves, that man might be Yeoland. There's something grotesque in him there—some warp or twist of fibre. Remember how well content he was in the past to remain engaged to her without rushing into her arms and marrying her. He's cold-blooded—so to call it—in some ways. I've known other such men."

"It's contrary to nature."

"Contrary to yours, but temperaments are different Don't judge him. There may be a want in him, or he may possess rare virtues. Some are ascetic and continent by disposition and starve Nature, at some secret prompting of her own. I don't say he is that sort of man, but he may be. Certainly his standpoint is far less commonplace than yours."

"I caught him kissing a pretty milkmaid once, all the same; and that after he was engaged to Honor," answered the other gloomily.

"Exactly. Now you would not do such a thing for the world, and he would make light of it. Beauty merely intoxicates some men; but intoxicated men do little harm as a rule. He's irresponsible in many ways; yet still I say the husband that fears such a man must be a fool."

"I can't suppose him built differently to other people."

"Then assume him to be the same, and ask yourself this question: Seeing what he did for love of her, and granting he loves her still, has he come back to undo what he did? Would he change and steal her now, even if he had the power to do so? What has he done in the past that makes you dream him capable of such a deed in the future?"

"I don't say that he dreams that such a thing is possible. Probably the man would not have returned into the atmosphere of Honor if he had dimly contemplated such an event. But I see nothing in his character to lift him above the temptation, or to make me rest sure he will be proof against it. There's a danger of his opening his eyes too late to find the thing which he doubtless believes impossible at present an accomplished fact."

"What thing?"

"Why, the wakening again of his love for her, the returned knowledge that his life is empty and barren and frost-bitten without her. He felt that once. What more natural than that, here again, he should feel it redoubled in the presence of his own good fortune in every other direction?"

"If such a suspicion crossed his mind, he would depart from Godleigh. That I do steadfastly believe. Understand, your welfare would not weigh with him; but Honor's happiness—I feel more assured of it—is still more to him than his own."

"I know—I know; yet how easily a man in love persuades himself that a woman's vital welfare and real happiness depends upon him."

"Now we argue in a circle, and are at the starting-point again. Yeoland believed so thoroughly that she would be happier with you than with him that he actually blotted himself out of her life, and, when he heard she would not marry you while he lived, let it be known that he was dead. Solely for her sake he played that cumbrous prank."

"That is so; yet remember what you told me years ago. Then you honestly believed that this man, from the depths of his own peculiar nature, understood Honor better than anybody else in the world did. You thought that, and you are seldom wrong about people. So perhaps he has come to that conclusion too. If I was the wrong husband for her——"

"I never said such a thing."

"No, because I never asked you; but if it was so, what more likely than that he has discovered it since his return? At any rate he may think that this is the case—though I dispute it with all my heart—and he may feel his sacrifice was vain. Then, what more likely than that he should ask himself if it is too late to amend the position?"

Mr. Endicott's face expressed absolute surprise and some scorn for the speaker.

"Do I hear Myles Stapledon? Where have you sucked poison since last we spoke together? You, who live in the fresh air and enjoy the companionship of natural beasts and wholesome lives, to spin this trash! And wicked trash, too, for what right have you to map out evil roads for other people to follow? What right have you to foretell a man's plan and prophesy ill? Have done with this dance of Jack-o'-lanterns, and get upon the solid road again. Look in your wife's character. No need to go further than that for ointment to such a wound as you suffer from. You have let jealousy into the house, Myles, and the reek of it and the blight of it will make your life rotten to the marrow if you don't set to work and cleanse the chamber again. I know they are happy together; but you've got to face that. I know she's better for his coming, and you've got to face that too. These are subtle things, and if you can't understand them, put them behind you. All this is false fire, and you're in a ferment of windy misery brewed inside you—just wind, because the home-coming of this native has upset your digestion. You ought to feel some shame to harbour such a pack of imps. Time was when a breath of air from Cosdon Beacon would have blown them back to their master. How they got in I can't say; for it's not part of your real character to make trouble. You're like the ploughboy who builds a ghostie with a sheet and turnip and only frightens himself. Get this weed out of your heart at any cost. Burn it out with the caustic of common sense; and trust me, blind as I am, to be quick enough to smell the smoke that tells of fire. I mean in this matter. Honor's only less to me than she is to you. And I know the truth about her as sure as I know the sound of her voice and the things it says, and the secrets it lets out, apart from the words her tongue speaks."

"She's said many a queer thing on the subject of a man and his wife and their relations each to the other. I cannot easily forget them."

"It's her wide, healthy frankness in every affair of life that might set you at rest, if you were not, as I hint to you, a fool."

"If I were a fool, it might. I know she holds the tie lightly. Any conventional sort of bondage angers her. I won her by a trick—not of my hatching, God knows—yet none the less a trick."

"You'd make Job lose his patience—you, that I thought a man of ideas as fresh and wholesome as the west wind! Can't you see this cuts both ways? She's yours till death parts you, so have done whining. You're stirring hell-broth, that's what you're doing, and if you let Honor catch a sight of the brew, there will be some real, live trouble very likely. You, to break out like this! Well, it shows how true the saying runs: that every man, from Solomon down, is mad when the wind sets in one quarter. Now you've found your foul-weather wind, and it's like to blow you into some play-acting if you don't pull yourself up. You're the luckiest man on the whole countryside, if you could only see it so. Be patient, and put your faith in your wife, where it should be, and go your old gait again."

"I'll try your remedy—ignore the thing, banish it, laugh at it."

"Laugh at yourself; if you could only learn to do that, there'd be hope for you. And take another point to your comfort. We're all agreed that Yeoland's no hypocrite, whatever else he may be. Three days since I had speech with him, and your name was on his lips, and he rejoiced that you were his friend and Honor's husband. He does not dream that his return to life has either gladdened her or troubled you. He only sees her now pretty much as she was when he went away. He hasn't seen what you and I have—her sorrows. But, remember that Honor's real happiness rests with you—nobody else—and she knows it, and trusts to you for it. Nobody can ever take your place, and if she glimpses a serious change in you, she'll soon be down in the mouth, and, as like as not, a lie-abed again."

"She has seen a change. She has asked me what was amiss."

"Then stir yourself, and make a giant's effort before she finds out more than you want her to know. I'm glad I spoke to you to-night—wish I had sooner; but it's not too late. You've had tangles to untie in your character before to-day—puzzles to pick—dirty corners to let the light in upon. Who hasn't? And you're not the one to fear such work, I should reckon. So set about it, and the Lord help you."

Myles Stapledon rose and took the old man's hand.

"Thank you," he said. "You've done me good, and I'll try to be worthy of your advice. I don't quite know what this place would be without you, Uncle Endicott."

"Quieter, my son—that's all. I'm only a voice. Words are poor things alongside actions. The great deeds of the world—the things achieved—are not chattered by the tongue, but rise out of sweat, and deep, long silences. Yet I've given you advice worth following, I do think, though, seeing that your blind spot looks like jealousy, what I've bid you do may be harder than you imagine. So much more credit if you do it."

Neither spoke again, and Stapledon, taking the candle, soon went to his bed; but Mark sat on awhile over his knitting in the dark, while the crickets chirruped fearlessly about the dim and dying peat.

CHAPTER V.
A HUNTING MORNING

On such a morning as hunting folk live for, some ten days after the conversation between Stapledon and Mr. Endicott, Christopher, who did not himself hunt, drove Honor to a meet of the Mid Devon. Taking his dog-cart down a mossy by-path at the spinney-side, he stopped not fifty yards distant from where a patch of scarlet marked the huntsman's standpoint. Above was a race of broken clouds and gleam of sunshine from pale blue sky; below spread opaline air and naked boughs, save where great tods of ivy shone; while underneath nervous tails twitched among brown fern and wintry furzes. Then a whimper came from the heart of the wood, and two old hounds threw up their heads, recognised the sound for a youngster's excitement, and put nose to earth again. A minute later, however, and a full bay echoed deep and clear; whereupon the pair instantly galloped whence the music came.

Honor and her companion sat in Christopher's dog-cart behind a fine grey cob.

"They know that's no young duffer," said Yeoland, as the melody waxed and the hounds vanished; "he's one of their own generation and makes no mistake. If the fox takes them up to the Moor, sport is likely to be bad, for it's a sponge just now, and the field won't live with the hounds five minutes. Ah! he's off! And to the Moor he goes."

Soon a business-like, hard-riding, West Country field swept away towards the highlands, and silence fell again.

Christopher then set out for Little Silver, while conversation drifted to their personal interests and the prosperity in which each now dwelt—a thing foreseen by neither three short years before. They had no servant with them and spoke openly.

"My touchstone was gold; yours a husband of gold," said Christopher. "Money he possessed too, but it is the magic man himself who has made Endicott's what it is now."

"Yes, indeed—dear Myles. And yet I'm half afraid that the old, simple joy in natural things passes him by now. It seems as though he and I could never be perfectly, wholly happy at the same time. While I went dismal mad and must have made his life a curse, he kept up, and never showed the tribulation that he felt, but was always contented and cheerful and patient. Now that I am happier, I feel that he is not. Yes, he is not as happy as I am. He has told me a thousand times that content is the only thing to strive for; and certainly he proved it, for he was well content once; but now our positions are reversed, and I am contented with my life, while daily he grows less so."

"He's a farmer, and a contented farmer no man ever saw, because God never made one."

"It isn't that; the work never troubles him. He looks far ahead and seems to know, like a wizard, long before the event just what is going to be successful and what a failure. I think I know him better than anybody in the world, but I can't fathom him just now. Something is worrying him, and he tries hard not to let it worry him and not to show that it does. Partly he is successful, for I cannot guess the trouble; but that there is a trouble he fails to hide. I must find it out and take my share. Sometimes I think——"

She broke off abruptly.

"What? Nothing that involves me? We're the best, truest friends now, thank heaven."

"No, no. Time will reveal it."

For a moment or two they were silent with their thoughts. It struck neither that such a conversation was peculiar; it occurred to neither the man nor the woman that in the very fact of their friendship—of a friendship so close that the wife could thus discuss her husband's trouble—there existed the seed of that trouble.

Christopher mused upon the problem, and honestly marvelled before it.

"I suppose nobody can be happy really, and he's no exception to the rule. Yet, looking at his life, I should account him quite the luckiest man I ever heard of. Consider the perfection that he has crammed into his existence. He prospers in his farm; he has Nestor under his roof in the shape of your wiseacre of an uncle; and he has you! Providence must have been puzzled to find a way to hurt him. And she hasn't hit him under the belt either, for never a man enjoyed finer health. Now where can he have come across melancholy? I suppose it's his hereafter, or non-hereafter, that's bothering him. Yet I should judge that the man was too sane to waste good time in this world fretting because he doesn't believe in another."

"It's a cloud-shadow that will pass, I hope."

"I hope so heartily—such a balanced mind as he has. Now if I began to whine—one who never did carry any ballast—you could understand it. Look ahead and compare our innings. His will end gloriously with children and grandchildren and all the rest of it. And I—but if I painted the picture you'd probably say I was a morbid, ungrateful idiot."

"Very likely; and I should probably be quite right. There's a great duty staring you in the face now, Christo, and nobody who cares for you will be contented or happy until you've tackled it like a man. Don't look so innocent; you know perfectly well what I mean."

"Indeed I do not. I am doing my duty to Godleigh—that's my life's work henceforth, and all anybody can expect."

"But that is just what you are not doing. You're not everybody, remember; and even if you think you are, you won't live for ever. You'll have to go and sleep in real earnest under the skulls with bats' wings, poor Christo, some day, and Myles and I shall be outside under the grass."

"Who is morbid now?"

"Don't evade the point. I want you to think of the thing you love best in the world—Godleigh."

"Well?"

"Godleigh has got to go on. It won't stop because you do—Godleigh's immortal. When a tree falls there, Nature will plant another. Then what is to become of the dearest, loveliest place in Devon after you are gathered to your fathers?"

"I'm going to leave it to you and Myles and your heirs for ever."

"Don't be ridiculous, Christo; you're going to leave it to a rightful heir, and it's high time you began to devote a little thought to him. Don't wait until you're a stupid, old, middle-aged thing of half a century. Then you'll probably die in the gloomy conviction that you leave your children mere helpless infants."

"So much the better for them, for they'd escape the example of their father. But, as a matter of fact, I'm not going to marry. Godleigh's my mother and sister and brother and wife and family."

"Then you'll leave your family unprovided for, and that's a very wicked thing to do. We're growing old and sensible nowadays, and there'll be plain speaking between us as long as we live; so I tell you now that I've thought of this very seriously indeed, and so has Myles. He quite agees with me; and my opinion is that you ought to marry; the sooner the better."

"Don't," he said; "don't go in for having opinions. When anybody begins to cultivate and profess opinions their sense of humour must be on the wane. Keep your mind free of rooted ideas. You were wont to love the rainbow play of change, to welcome sudden extremes as a sign of health and mental activity. Before you married you hated opinions."

"That was before I grew happy, I think. Happiness runs one into a groove very quickly; it steadies our ideas. Now, you won't be perfectly happy until you marry."

"To find her."

"Why, that's not so difficult."

"Never, Honor. There was only one possible mother for my children. You are going over ground that I travelled centuries ago; at least it seems centuries. I told my fib and looked ahead, quite like a son of wisdom for once, and counted the cost, or tried to. Let all that sleep. I shall never know to my dying day how I brought it off, but I did. Perhaps a generous sympathy for unborn boys and girls had as much to do with it as anything else. Candidly and without sentiment, it is time we Yeolands came to an end. For my part I shall die easier knowing that I'm the last of them. I never was very keen about living for the mere sake of living, even in old days, and now I care less than ever. Not that I want to die either; but I go wandering through this great, roaring, rollicking, goose-fair of a world, stopping at a booth here, shooting for nuts or something equally valuable there; and when Dustman Death surprises me, pottering about and wasting my money,—when he puts out his grey claws and asks for his own again, I shall welcome him with perfect cheerfulness."

"Nonsense—and wicked nonsense! You—what?—thirty-two, or some absurd age—trying to talk like Uncle Mark! And Godleigh free! I won't have it, Christo. If ever you loved me, you must obey me in this and find a wife."

"Can't; won't; too small-hearted. I've got nothing to give a girl; and all your fault. Some of me really died, you know, when I pretended that all of me did."

"Then I suppose that it's my turn to go away and perish now? Would you feel equal to marrying anybody if I was dead?"

"Not a parallel instance at all. For you there was a grand chap waiting—a man worth having; else I should not have died, I assure you. In my case there's no grand woman waiting; so if you expire, you will merely be bringing a great deal of trouble upon many excellent people and doing nobody the least good—not even my nebulous prospective lady. No, Myles and I would merely share a mile of crape and live in black gloves for ever. You die! What a thought!"

"Sometimes I wish I had long ago."

"No; you must live to brighten these dull Devonshire winters and strew flowers upon your husband and me when our turns come. Dear old Stapledon! I'm really bothered to know that something is troubling him. I'd tackle him myself, only if you cannot win the truth, I certainly should not. I wish he'd be confidential; I do like confidential men. For my part I haven't got a secret from him in the world."

"He works too hard."

"He does. The man has a horrible genius for making work. It knocks the vitality out of him. I hate this modern gospel that sets all of us poor little world-children to our lessons as a panacea for every evil under the sun. Just look what dull dogs all the hard workers are."

"Well, you've played truant from your youth up."

"Deliberately, as an example to others. But I'm doing any amount of work now. Brain-work too; which is easily the most hateful sort of work. And all for my Godleigh. Yet she doesn't thank me. I see poor Mother Nature stealing about miserably and suspiciously when I go into the woods. She liked me better a pauper. She doesn't know that I'm helping her to make this little corner of earth more and more perfect. She doesn't look ahead and judge how much toil and trouble I am saving her with the ruins of things that must be cleared away—either by her method or my quicker one. She hates axes and ploughs and pruning-hooks, old stick-in-the-mud that she is."

"Treason!"

"No treason at all. Common sense I call it. I'm weary of this nonsense about going straight to Nature. Australia taught me to suspect. She's a bat, a mole; she doesn't know her best friends. She'll sink a saint in mid-ocean—a real saint with an eighteen-carat halo—and let a pirate come safely and happily to some innocent merchantman stuffed with the treasures of honest men, or her own priceless grains and seeds. She'll put back the hand of progress at the smallest opportunity; she'll revert to the primitive if you turn your back on her for an instant; she'll conjure our peaches into wild plums, our apples into crabs, man into—God knows what—something a good deal lower than the angels, or even the cave-dwellers. If we let her, she would hunt for and polish up the missing link again, and huddle the world backwards faster than we spin round the sun. Nature is a grand fraud, Honor. Take the personal attitude, for instance. What has she ever done for me? Did she show me any of her hoarded gold during the month I nearly killed myself exploring in New South Wales? Did she lead me to the water-holes when I was thirsty, or lend me a cloud to hide the sun when I was hot? Has she opened a flower-bud, or taught a bird to sing, or painted a dawn, or ever led the wind out of the east, that I might be the happier? We fool ourselves that we are her favourites. Not so. She is only our stepmother, and behaves accordingly. She knew that the advent of conscious intelligence must be a death-blow to her, and she has never forgiven man for exhibiting it."

"So I'm not the only one in Little Silver who is developing opinions, I see," laughed Honor. "You're growing egotistical, Christo; you're expecting almost too much, I fear. Nature has something better to do than plan your private fortune and convenience, or arrange the winds of heaven to suit a cold in that silly head of yours! Never in my most dead-alive moment did I grow so dull as that. To be cross with poor Nature—as if she had not to do what she is told, like everybody else. To blame her!"

"I don't blame her. I know where to throw the blame of things perfectly well."

"Then you're the only man in the world who does, and you ought to tell everybody and so make yourself famous."

Thus they prattled in the old manner, and, unconscious of difficulty or danger, passed upon their way. Much each saw of the other; much frank delight each took in the other's company; and through the passage of winter to the advent of spring they progressed, coming nearer and nearer to discovery of the secret tribulation in Stapledon's heart that each now innocently, honestly mourned and misunderstood.

CHAPTER VI.
LOVE OF MAN

Mr. Gregory Libby, to whom circumstance denied any opportunity of close investigation, at length came upon a conclusion respecting the daughters of Jonah Cramphorn, and allowed his judgment to be unconsciously influenced by his desire. That is to say he arrived at a mistaken decision because the balance of his feeble, physical emotions weighed toward Sally. She was the eldest and the fairest; he concluded, therefore, that she enjoyed the greater proportion of her parent's regard, and must the more materially benefit under his will in time to come. He braced himself for the crucial question, and it happened that he did so but two days after a very significant symposium at Endicott's, during which Mr. Cramphorn occupied the position of chief speaker, and his daughters were the principal theme of conversation. From discussion upon these primitive maids, and their father's opinion concerning them, discourse had truly ranged to higher subjects; but not before Jonah made definite statements of a sort that deeply moved one among his listeners.

Behind the obscurity blown from a clay tobacco-pipe, Henry Collins sat, round-eyed and wretched. He gasped with most unselfish sorrow for the girl he loved, and committed to memory certain surly assertions of Mr. Cramphorn concerning her, with a purpose to forewarn Sally of the fate her future held. For Jonah spoke definitely and doggedly. He weighed the merits of his own daughters with Spartan frankness, and, arriving at judgment, declared Margery's filial conduct a lesson to Little Silver, regretted Sally's indifference and independence of manners, and concluded with complacent hints that his knowledge of human nature was not wont to be at fault, and that she best able to administer wisely his worldly wealth should have it as a just reward, when he passed beyond need of cottage or savings bank.

These utterances Libby heard too late, but Cramphorn's elder daughter became acquainted with them immediately after they were spoken, thanks to the enterprise of Henry Collins. He felt it his duty to the woman that she should be put in possession of such gloomy predictions, while yet power might lie with her to falsify them.

"Afore the whole comp'ny he said it," declared Henry; "an' he'm a man as knaws no shadder of turning most times. An' he haven't got the wisdom of a mouse neither—not in this matter; so it'll surely happen, onless you fall in wi' his ways more an' knock onder oftener than what you do."

"I've seed it comin', an' he'm a cruel wretch," answered Sally with many pouts. "An' her's worse—my sister, I mean. Sly minx, she've plotted an' worked for it wi' low onderhand ways—cooing to un; an' glazin' at un when he talked, as if he was King Solomon; an' spendin' her pence in pipes for un; an' findin' his book-plaaces to church—'Struth! I could wring her neck, an' 'tis more'n likely I shall do it wan day."

"But he doan't knaw—Libby, I mean—though he's sartain to hear soon; an' your faither won't tell Margery for fear she should give awver fussin' 'bout arter un, when she knaws his will's writ an' signed an' can't be called back. So I comed to say that I doan't care a feather for all his money, an' I loves you better'n ever—better'n better now he'm set against 'e."

"Ess, I knaw all that; and doan't 'e tell this tale to nobody else; an' bid them others, as heard my auld beast of a faither, to keep it in an' tell nobody. Wance Libby knaws, 'tis——"

"All up. Ess, so 'tis, Sally; an' doan't that shaw 'e what fashion o' dirt the man's made of? Do 'e want a chap to marry you for what you take to un in your hand? Do 'e——"

"Doan't ax no more questions now, theer's a dear sawl. I ban't in no fettle to answer 'em, an' I be sore hurt along o' this. A gude darter as I've been tu. An' her—no better'n a stinging long-cripple—a snake as'll bite the hand that warms it. I wish I was dead, I do. Go away, caan't 'e? I doan't want your 'ankersher. Let my tears alone, will 'e? I wish they was poison. I'd mingle 'em wi' her food—then us would see. Go—go away! Be you deaf? I'll scream my heart out in a minute if you bide theer!"

Collins, desiring no such catastrophe, made haste to disappear; and such is the rough-and-tumble of things that chance willed this dramatic moment for the entrance of Gregory Libby. Big with fate he came from hedge-trimming, and shone upon Sally's grief like the sun of June upon a shower. She was sobbing and biting her red lips; and he, with the dignity of toil yet manifested about him, dropped his sickle, flung off his gloves, led Sally behind a haystack, and bid her sit down and relate her sorrow.

"Just gwaine to take my bit of dinner," he said; "so you can tell while I eat. What's the matter? You'm wisht, an' your butivul cheeks be all speckly-like wi' cryin'."

She swallowed her tears, sucked her lips, and smiled through the storm.

"Nought—a flea kicked me. Sit here an' I'll pull down a bit o' dry out o' the stack for 'e."

"Ban't awften them wonnerful butcher-blue eyes o' yourn shed tears, I'm sure," he mumbled with his mouth full; "but we've all got our troubles no doubt. An' none more'n me. I'm that lonesome wi'out mother to do for me. I never thought as I'd miss her cookin' an' messin' 'bout the house so much. An' what's money wi'out a woman to spend it—to spend it on me, I mean?" he added hastily. "I want a wife. A gude woman stands between a man an' all the li'l twopenny-ha'p'ny worrits as his mind be tu busy tu trouble 'bout. I want a useful gal around me, an' wan as'll take the same view of me what mother done."

"You'm a marryin' man for sartain."

"I be. An' I've thought an' thought on it till I got the 'eadache; an' my thoughts doan't go no further'n you, Sally."

"Lard, Gregory dear!"

"True's I'm eatin' onions. I've been figuring you up for years. An' now I knaw we'm likely to be a very fitting man an' wife. You knawed mother; and you knaw me, as ban't a common man ezacally, so say the word."

"Oh, Gregory! An' I thought you was after my sister!"

"She'm a very gude gal, an' a very nice gal tu," said Mr. Libby with his usual caution. "No word against her would I say for money. An' if you wasn't here, I'd sooner have her than any other. A brave, bowerly maiden wi' butivul hands to her, an' a wonnerful onderstandin' way, an'——"

"Ess, but 'tis me you love—me—not her?"

"Ban't I tellin' you so? I say it in cold blood, after thinkin' 'pon it, to an' from, for years. An' I'll tell you how mother treated me, for you couldn't do no better'n what she did. She onderstood my habits perfect."

"God knaws I'll make 'e a gude wife, Greg. An' no call to tell me nothin' of that 'bout your mother, 'cause I'll be more to 'e than she; an' I'll think for 'e sleepin' an' wakin', an' I'll work for 'e to my bones, an' love the shadow of 'e."

"I'm glad to hear you say so, Sally, though mother's ways was very well considered. The thing be to make up your mind as I'm in the right all times, as a thinking man mostly is."

"I knaw you will be; an' a gude husband, as'll stand up for me against all the world, an' see I ban't put upon or treated cruel."

"I will do so. An' 'tis odds if I'll let 'e do any work at all arter you'm wedded to me—work 'cept about my house, I mean."

"No, for 'twill take me all my time workin' for 'e, an' makin' your home as it should be."

"Kiss me," he said suddenly, "an' kiss me slow while I take my full of it. Theer's blood 'pon your lips! You've bited 'em. What's fretted 'e this marnin'? Not love of me, I warn 'e?"

"'Twas, then—just love of you, Greg; an' fear that the fallin' out of cruel things might make 'e turn away from me."

He patted her cheek and stroked it; then her neck; and then her plump bosom.

"So butivul an' fat as a pattridge you be! An' I'm sure I love 'e tremenjous; an' nothin' shall never part us if you say so."

"Then all my tears was vain, an'—an' I'll grow a better woman an' say longer prayers hencefarrard—for thanksgivings 'cause I've got 'e."

"'Tis a gude match for you, Sally; an' I do trust as you'll never make me to regret I spoke."

"Never, never; an' you'll never love nobody else, will 'e?"

"Not so long as you'm a gude wife an' a towser to work. My mind was always temperate 'an sober towards petticoats, as be well knawn."

"Oh, I could sing an' dance for sheer joy, I could! An' so chapfallen just afore you comed. But what's a faither to a lover—'specially such a sour faither as mine?"

"Doan't you quarrel wi' Cramphorn, however," said Gregory; "he'm the last man as I'd have you fall out with."

"Quarrel! I never quarrel with nobody. But he ban't like you—even-tempered an' fair. A wan-sided, cranky man, faither. I be his eldest, yet Margery's put afore me. He can't see through her dirty, hookem-snivey tricks an' lying speeches. I be straight an' plain, same as you, an' he hates me for it."

Mr. Libby's heart sank low.

"Hates you? D'you say your faither hates you?"

"Well, the word ban't big enough seemin'ly. I can tell you now, because we'm tokened, an' my heart shan't never have no secret from you. But he likes Margery best because she foxes him, an' fules him, an' tells him he's a wonder of the world; an' he believes it. An' Collins says as he've awpenly gived out that she'm to have all his gudes an' his money. Why for do 'e give awver lovin' me?"

For Mr. Libby's arm, which was round Sally's waist, fell away from that pleasant circumference, and an expression of very real misery spread over his face to the roots of his yellow hair.

"'His gudes an' his money'?" he asked, in a faint voice, that sounded as though he had been frightened.

"Ess. Why, you'm as if somebody had suddenly thrawed a bucket of water awver 'e! Doan't think I care 'bout his money now. You'll have to make him chaange his mind bimebye. When you'm my husband, you'll have to tackle faither an' see he doan't cut me away."

The man's brain went cold. Desire had vanished out of his eyes, and Sally might have been a stone beside him. He flung away the remainder of his luncheon, and uttered a hearty oath or two.

"'Tis a damned oncomely thing, an', as it takes two to a quarrel, theer's some fault your side as well as his, I reckon. What be the reason as Margery's more to him than you—his eldest?"

"Because she'm a lyin' slammockin' female twoad—that's the reason; an' he caan't see through her."

There was a moment of heavy silence; then Gregory Libby spoke.

"Doan't say nothin' 'bout what we've planned out to-day. Doan't tell nobody. Time enough come Spring."

"Say nought! I'd like to go up 'pon top the hill an' sing out my gude fortune for all ears to hear!"

"No, bide quiet. Us'll let 'em have the gert surprise of it in church. None shall knaw till we'm axed out some Sunday marnin'."

"'Twill bust upon 'em like thunder. I lay Margery will faint if she'm theer."

"An' us'll have the laugh of 'em all."

"'Tis as you please, Greg."

"An' you'll take your oath not to tell?"

"Not even mistress?"

"Certainly not she."

"Nor yet Missis Loveys?"

"So soon tell all Little Silver."

"You might let me just whisper it to my awn sister. 'Twill be a cruel stroke if her hears it fust afore all the people to church."

"If you say a syllable of it to Margery, 'tis off!" declared Mr. Libby, and with such earnestness did he speak that the girl was alarmed, and made hasty assurances.

"Very well, I promise an' swear, since I must. But how long be I to go dumb? Remember, 'tis tu gert a thing for a woman to keep hid for long. You'm cruel, Greg, lovey, to ax it. I'll have to blaze it out soon or bust with it."

"Wait my time. It ban't to be awver-long, that I promise 'e."

"Kiss me again, Greg; an' cuddle me."

"You take your dyin' oath?"

"Ess, I said so."

"Very well; now I must go back to my work."

Presently they separated, and Sally, full of her secret, walked upon air through a golden world, with her hot heart's core aglow, while Mr. Libby bit his hare-lip, employed many coarse words for the benefit of the hedge he hacked at, and put a spite and spleen into each stroke that soon blunted his bill-hook. He was now faced with a problem calling for some ingenuity. He yearned to know how he might retrieve his error, and get well free of Sally before approaching her sister upon the same errand. Where to turn for succour and counsel he knew not. "If mother was awnly alive for ten minutes!" he thought. As for another ancient dame, Charity Grepe, she— publicly exposed as a fraud and delusion by Jonah Cramphorn—had found her occupation gone in earnest, and now reposed at Chagford poor-house. There was none to help the unhappy orphan in his trouble. The matter looked too delicate for masculine handling; and even Gregory had sense to perceive that it would be easy for others to take a wrong attitude before his dilemma and judge him harshly. Then came an inspiration to this lack-lustre son of the soil.

"No pusson else but she heard me tell her," he reflected. "Theer's awnly her word for it, an' I'll up an' say 'tis a strammin' gert lie, an' that she was mazed or dreamin', an' that I wouldn't marry her for a hunderd sovereigns! I'll braave her to her faace, if it comes to that. Folks'll sooner believe a man than a woman most times; an' if I ban't spry enough to awver-reach a fule of a outdoor farm-gal on such a matter, 'tis pity."

CHAPTER VII.
LAPSES

During early spring a new experience came to Myles Stapledon. Physically perfect, he had known no ache or ill until now; but chance for once found him vulnerable. From a heavy downpour upon the land he returned home, found matters to occupy him immediately, and so forgot to doff wet clothes at the earliest opportunity. A chill rewarded his carelessness, and a slight attack of pneumonia followed upon it. For the first time within his recollection the man had to stop in bed, but during the greater part of his illness Myles proved patient enough. Honor ministered to him untiringly; Mr. Endicott was much in the sick-room also; and from time to time, when the master was returning towards convalescence, Cramphorn or Churdles Ash would enter to see him with information concerning affairs.

Then, during one of the last wearisome days in his bed-chamber, at a season when the invalid was somewhat worn with private thoughts and heartily sick of such enforced idleness, an unfortunate misunderstanding threw him off his mental balance and precipitated such a catastrophe as those who knew Stapledon best had been the least likely to foresee. He was in fact forgotten for many hours, owing to a common error of his wife and uncle. Each thought the other would tend the sick man, so Honor departed to Newton Abbot with Christopher Yeoland, and Mark, quite ignorant of his niece's plans, was driven by Tommy Bates to Okehampton. The pitiful mistake had not dwelt an hour in Stapledon's memory under ordinary circumstances, but now, fretted by suffering and as ill able to bear physical trouble as any other man wholly unfamiliar with it, his lonely hours swelled and massed into a mountain of bitter grievance. He brooded and sank into dark ways of thought. Temptations got hold upon him; the ever-present thorn turned in his flesh and jealousy played with his weakness, like a cat with a mouse. Upon Honor's return the man afforded his wife, a new sensation and one of the greatest surprises that experience had ever brought to her.

Unaware of his lonely vigil, she returned home in high good humour, kissed him, complimented him on the fact that this was to be his last day in bed, and remarked upon the splendour of the sunset.

"'At eventide it shall be light,'" she said; "and Christo was so rapt in all the glory of gold and purple over Cosdon, as we drove home from Moreton, that he nearly upset me and his dog-cart and himself. Yet I wish you could see the sky. It would soothe you."

"As winter sunshine soothes icicles—by making their points sharper. Nature's softest moods are cruellest if your mind happens to be in torment."

"My dear! Whatever is the matter? And your fire out—oh, Myles, how wrong!"

"Is it? Then blame yourself. Since my midday meal and before it I have seen no soul this day, and heard no voice but the clock. Here alone, suffering and chewing gall for six hours and more. But what does it matter so you were pleased with the sunset and your company?"

"Then where is uncle? Surely——? I *am* so sorry, dear one. We've muddled it between us, and each thought you were in the keeping of the other."

"Don't be sorry. What do I matter? Where have you been?"

"To Newton with Christo. And he sent you these lovely black grapes. I'm afraid I ate a few coming home, but I haven't spoiled the bunch."

"Eat the rest, then, or fling them into the fire. I don't want them."

"You're angry, Myles; and you have a right to be; yet it was only a dismal accident. We must light the fire, and I'll get you your tea, poor ill-used fellow. It was a shame, but I'm very, very penitent, and so will uncle be."

"I wish I could get out of your way. Such a bother for you to come back to a sick-room; and a sick animal in a house is a bore always—especially to you, who don't love animals."

The woman's eyes opened wide and she stared at him.

"Whatever do you mean?"

"You know well enough. I'm so exacting and my cough keeps you awake at night, and these drives in the fresh air behind Yeoland's big trotter must be such a relief to you. Why don't you ask him to drive you right away—to hell, and have done with it?"

Honor looked at him, then turned her back and knelt down by the fire. Presently she spoke.

"Your thoughts have been ugly company I'm afraid. This is a terrible surprise, Myles, for I know so well how much you must have suffered before you could say such things to me. Will you never understand your own wife?"

"I think I do—at last."

"You'll be sorry—very sorry that you could speak so, and let an unhappy accident be the spark to this. If you had but heard what Christopher said of you this very day driving home——"

"Don't begin that folly. That he slights me enough to praise me—and you listen to him and pretend to think he is in earnest!"

She did not answer; then he sat up in bed and spoke again.

"I'm glad that weakness has torn this out of me. I shall be sorry to-morrow, but I'm glad to-night. Leave the fire and come here. I don't want to shout. You see what you've dragged me down to; you see what a snarling cur with his bone stolen I look now. That's your work. And I'll thank you to put a period to it. I don't live any longer in this purgatory, however greatly your fool's paradise may please you. I'm weary of it. It's poisoning me. Either you see too much of this man or not enough. That is what you have to determine. If too much, end it; if not enough, mend it, and go to him, body and soul, for good—the sooner the better."

"Myles! You, of all men, to be so coarse! Are you mad? Are you dreaming to speak to your wife so? God knows that I've never done, or said, or thought anything to anger you to this, or shadow your honour for a second—nor has he."

"'He!' Always 'he—he—he'—rooting at your heart-strings, I suppose, like a ——. What do you know of his thoughts and dreams? How comes it that you are so read in his life and mind that you can say whether my honour is so safe with him? I'd sooner trust it with my dogs. Then it would be safe. Who are you to know what this man's mind holds?"

"I ought to know, if anybody does."

"Then go back to him, for God's sake, and let me come to the end of this road. Let all that is past sink to a memory, not remain a raw, present wound, that smarts from my waking moment until I sleep again."

"You are weary of me?"

"I'm weary of half of you, or a quarter of you, or what particular proportion of you may still be supposed to belong to me."

"I am all yours—heart and soul—and you know it; or if you do not, Christopher Yeoland does."

"You love him too."

"That question was answered years ago. I love him, and always shall. His welfare is much to me. I have been concerned with it to-day."

"Yet you dare to say you belong heart and soul to me."

"It is the truth. If you don't understand that, I cannot help you. He does understand."

"I lack his fine intellect. You must endeavour to sink to my level and make this truth apparent to your husband's blunter perceptions. I must have more than words. Acts will better appeal to me. After to-day I forbid you to see or speak with Yeoland; and may you never suffer as you have made me suffer."

"I will do what you wish. If you had only spoken sooner, Myles, some of this misery might have been escaped. I wish I had seen it."

"Any woman who loved honestly would have seen it," he said, hard to the end. Then, without answering, she left him; and while he turned restlessly upon himself and regret presently waxed to a deep shame at this ebullition, she went her way and came to tears leisurely along a path first marked by frank amazement. Honor's surprise was unutterable. Never, since the moment of their meeting, had she dreamed or suspected that any imaginable disaster could thus reduce the high standard by which Myles conducted his mental life and controlled his temperament. That physical suffering and a sharp illness should have power to discover and reveal such a secret much surprised her. She remained incredulous that she had heard aright. It was as though she had dreamed the meeting and some nightmare Myles—grotesque, rude, a very Caliban—had taken shape while her mind ran riot in sleep. Yet it was true, for the measure of his lapse from customary high courtesy, was the measure of the months that he had suffered in silence, and the measure of his wrongs. Wholly imaginary she held them; all he had said was the outcome of a nature fretted by sickness and reduced below itself, like a drunken man—this Honor believed; but even so she remained in a stupor of astonishment. To see such a man with his armour off, to hear strange words in his mouth, to watch passion on his face, was an experience unutterably painful. And yet surprise transcended sorrow. She was almost stunned and dazed by this storm of thunder and lightning from a mind whose weather had never promised such a tempest. Now the moody fits and evasive humours could be read a little, for light fell every way. And Honor sat an hour with her thoughts; then passed from first emotions to others deeper and truer. She began to regret the past and blame her blindness. Unconventional enough, she had acted with no thought of any special significance being read into her actions—least of all by her husband. A woman of more common mind and nature had seen the danger and doubtfulness of such relations; but this was her first revelation of it; and the sudden, somewhat brutal disclosure opened her eyes widely indeed. She set herself to see and estimate from her husband's standpoint, to gauge the extent of the justice that had launched his pent-up outburst, and, upon a paltry misunderstanding, loosed these tremendous charges, hugged up and hidden within his heart till now. She ignored the cruel manner of his assault, and felt her heart beat in fear at this shadow of a master passion. Jealousy was its name, and an accident of lonely hours with the demon had suffered it to overwhelm him, tear him, dominate him thus.

The thread of the woman's thoughts need not be traced as she strove with these tangles, and slowly restored the ravelled skein. That Myles would regret this hurricane she knew; that he would ask her forgiveness, and probably desire her to disregard his demands she suspected. Self-control was a garment that her husband could scarcely discard for long, even in sickness; the amazing thing was that it should have proved a garment at all; for Honor always believed it as much a part of Myles as his other characteristics. Meantime she asked herself her duty, and justice spoke, while the woman listened without impatience.

She understood in some degree the strenuousness of many male characters upon the subject of ethics; she conceded that men of her husband's stamp thought and felt more deeply than most women; and she knew that her own sense of proportion, or sense of humour—which often amounts to the same thing—had inclined her, rightly or wrongly, to view all relations of life from an impersonal standpoint, including even those affairs in which she herself participated.

She knew the absolute innocence of her inmost soul with respect to Christopher, and her face flamed here at the thought that her husband had dared to fear for her honour and his own. But she resolutely identified her thoughts with his attitude; she reminded herself that Myles was a bad student of character, and quite unable to see the real nature of Christopher Yeoland, or understand him as she did. Her brain grew tired at last, and pity led to tears; but the nature of the pity was uncertain, and whether she cried for herself, for her husband, or for both, Honor could not have declared with any certainty.

That evening, while Mark Endicott was with Myles and his wife sat alone in her parlour, Christopher Yeoland strolled up to the farm with a parcel forgotten and left in his vehicle. The master of Godleigh stayed for a brief chat, made inquiries after Stapledon, and very quickly discovered that his companion laboured under some secret emotion. Honor thereupon changed her mind. She had not intended to whisper a hint of her tragic discovery, but the other's ready sympathy proved too much for her reserve. Moreover, there was a thought in her that perhaps the sooner Yeoland knew the truth the better. She told him a little of what had happened and attributed it to her husband's great present weakness; yet the thing sounded graver spoken aloud, even in her very guarded version, and Christopher's forehead showed that he, too, held it serious.

"Of course he didn't mean it," she concluded; "and to-morrow he will be sorry for having spoken so. But I'm afraid that dear Myles will never understand that we are different from other people."

"You think we are?"

"I know we are. Surely we have proved that to one another, if not to the world."

"We can't expect people to take us at our own valuation. This row comes appositely in a way. God knows the truth, but all the same, perhaps the position is impracticable. The world would say that Myles was right, and that we were too—too original. Only what's to be done? Of course he can't forbid us to speak to one another—that's absurd. But, for some reason, our friendship makes him a miserable man. He's let that out to-night, poor dear chap."

"I wish I could understand his attitude; but I must make myself understand it, Christo. It is my duty."

"I believe I do know what he feels. It's pride more than jealousy. His mind is too well hung to be jealous, but pride is the bait to catch all big natures. He doesn't like to feel any other man has the power to please you."

"But remember the basis of our friendship. It must make a difference. And I have always been so frank. He knew—none better—what we were each to the other once; and he knows that I am fond of you and always must be so."

"Exactly; and that's not knowledge to make him particularly happy. We have accentuated it of late, and hurt him. He sees perils and troubles ahead that don't really exist—mere phantoms—yet, from his point of view, they look real enough. He cannot see, and so there's probably a growing inclination on his part to kick me out of Little Silver, if such a thing could be done. Yes, I appreciate his attitude, though he can't appreciate mine. It comes to this: my deep content in your society is making him very angry— and worse than angry. He's turning by slow degrees into a volcano. To-day came the first little eruption—a mere nothing. Myles will regret it, and to-morrow bank up the fire again in his usual Spartan way; but he is powerless to prevent the sequel. There may be a regular Pompeii and Herculaneum presently. Your husband is built that way, though I never guessed it. If you were mine, and he was in my position, I should not turn a hair, knowing you and knowing him; but he is different. He doesn't know me at all, and he doesn't know you as well as I do. He must be blind to a nature like yours by the accident of his own personal temperament."

"He understands me, I am sure—at least, I think so."

"Not all round. But that's beside the mark. The question is, What next?"

"No question at all. My whole life and soul must be devoted to making him happy in spite of himself."

"And what must I do?"

She did not answer, and before need of a definite decision and the necessity for action, Christopher fell back upon his customary methods.

"Obviously I must do nothing. Least done soonest mended—a proverb quite as wise as the one I found it on; for deeds make more bother in the world than the loudest words. I shall let Time try his hand. It will probably come out all right when Myles gets well. He's so sane in most things—only there's my volcano theory, I tell you what; I'll speak to your uncle and ask him if he sees any difficulty."

"Can't you make up your mind yourself?"

"No—unless you express a wish. Otherwise I shall go on as I am going. I'll see Mr. Endicott, and when Myles is fit again I'll see him. Yes, that's the road of wisdom. I'll meet him and say, 'Now, old chap, explode and give me the full force of the discharge. Tell me what you mean and what you want.'"

Honor, for her part, found loyalty wakened rather than weakened by her husband's remonstrances. She desired to return to him—to get back to his heart. Christopher wearied her just now, and when Mark Endicott entered from the sick-room, Honor bid Yeoland farewell and hastened to Myles.

Yeoland chatted awhile, shared some spirit and water with the blind man, and then, on a sudden, after private determination to do no such thing, broached the problem in his mind.

"Look here," he said; "I've had a nasty jar to-night, Mr. Endicott, and I'm in no end of a muddle. You know that I'm a well-meaning brute in my way, even granted that the way is generally wrong. But I wouldn't really hurt a fly, whereas now, in blissful ignorance, I've done worse. I've hurt a man—a man I feel the greatest respect for—the husband of my best friend in the world. It's jolly trying, because he and I are built so differently. There's an inclination on his part to turn this thing into the three-volume form apparently. It's such ghastly rot when you think of what I really am. In plain English, Stapledon doesn't like his wife to see so much of me. She only discovered this deplorable fact to-day, and it bewildered her as much as it staggered me. Heaven's my judge, I never guessed that he was looking at me so. Nor did Honor. Such kindred spirits as we are—and now, in a moment of weakness, the man bid her see me no more! Of course, he's too big to go in for small nonsense of that kind, and he'll withdraw such an absurd remark as soon as he's cool again; but straws show which way the wind blows, and I want to get at my duty. Tell me that, and I'll call you blessed."

"What is Honor to you?"

"The best part of my life, if you must know—on the highest plane of it."

"Don't talk about 'planes'! That's all tom-foolery! You're a wholesome, healthy man and woman—anyway, other people must assume so. I'll give you credit for believing yourself, however. I'll even allow your twaddle about planes does mean something to you, because honestly you seem deficient—degenerate as far as your flesh is concerned. All the same, Stapledon is right in resenting this arrangement with all his heart and soul. His patience has amazed me. Two men can't share a woman under our present system of civilisation."

"Which is to say a wife may not have any other intellectual kindred spirit but her husband. D'you mean that?"

"No, I don't. I mean that when a man openly says that a woman is the best part of his life, her husband can't be blamed for resenting it."

"But what's the good of lying about the thing? Surely circumstances alter cases? It was always so. He knew that Honor and I loved each other in our queer way long before he came on the scene. She can't stop loving me because she has married him."

"It isn't easy to argue with you, Yeoland," answered Mark quietly; "but this I see clearly: your very attitude towards the position proclaims you a man of most unbalanced mind. There's a curious kink in your nature—that is if you're not acting. Suppose Honor was your wife and she found greater pleasure in the society of somebody else, and gradually, ignorantly, quite unconsciously slipped away and away from you; imperceptibly, remember—so subtly that she didn't know it herself—that nobody but you knew it. How much of that would you suffer without a protest?"

"I shouldn't bother—not if she was happy. That's the point, you see: her happiness. I constitute it in some measure—eh? Or let us say that I contribute to it. Then why need he be so savage? Surely her happiness is his great ambition too?"

"Granted. Put the world and common sense and seemliness on one side. They don't carry weight with you. Her happiness then—her lasting happiness—not the trumpery pleasure of to-day and to-morrow."

"Is it wise to look much beyond to-morrow when 'happiness' is the thing to be sought?"

"Perhaps not—as you understand it—so we'll say 'content.' Happiness is a fool's goal at best. You love Honor, and you desire for her peace of mind and a steadfast outlook founded on a basis strong enough to stand against the storms and sorrows of life. I assume that."

"I desire for her the glory of life and the fulness thereof."

"You must be vague, I suppose; but I won't be, since this is a very vital matter. I don't speak without sympathy for you either; but, in common with the two of you—Myles and yourself—this silly woman is uppermost in my mind—her and her good. So, since you ask, I tell you I'm disappointed with you; you've falsified my predictions of late, and your present relations with Honor have drifted into a flat wrong against her husband, though you may be on a plane as high as heaven, in your own flabby imagination. This friendship is not a thing settled, defined, marked off all round by boundaries. No friendship stands still, any more than anything else in the universe. Even if you're built of uncommon mud, lack your share of nature, and can philander to the end of the chapter without going further, or thinking further, that is no reason why you should do so. The husband of her can't be supposed to understand that you're a mere curiosity with peculiar machinery inside you. He gives you the credit of being an ordinary man, or denies you the credit of being an extraordinary one, which you please. So it's summed up in a dozen words: either see a great deal less of Honor, or, if you can't breathe the same air with her apart from her, go away, as an honourable man must, and put the rim of the world between you. Try to live apart, and let that be the gauge of your true feeling. If you can bide at Godleigh happy from month to month without sight of her or sound of her voice, then I'll allow you are all you claim to be and give you a plane all to yourself above the sun; but if you find you can do no such thing, then she's more to you by far than the wife of another man ought to be, and you're not so abnormal as you reckon yourself. This is going right back upon your renunciation in the beginning—as pitiful a thing as ever I heard tell about."

"Stay here and never see her! How would you like it? I mean—you see and hear with the mind, though your eyes are dark. Of course I couldn't do that. What's Godleigh compared to her?"

"And still you say that sight of her and sound of her voice is all you want to round and complete your life?

"Emphatically."

"You're a fool to say so."

"You don't believe it?"

"Nor would any other body. Least of all her husband."

"A man not soaked in earth would."

"Find him, then. Human nature isn't going to put off its garment at your bidding. If you're only half-baked—that's your misfortune, or privilege. You'll have to be judged by ordinary standards nevertheless."

"Then I must leave the land of my fathers—I must go away from Godleigh because a man misunderstands me?"

"You must go away from Godleigh because, on your own showing, you can't stop in it without the constant companionship of another man's wife."

"What a brute you'd make me! That's absolutely false in the spirit, if true in the letter. The letter killeth. You to heave such a millstone!"

"You're a poorer creature than I thought," answered Mark sternly, "much poorer. Yet even you will allow perhaps that it is to her relations with her husband, not her relations with you, that Honor Endicott must look for lasting peace—if she's to have it."

"Yet I have made her happier by coming back into her life."

"It's doubtful. In one way yes, because you did things by halves—went out of her life and then came back into it at the wrong moment. I won't stop to point out the probable course of events if you had kept away altogether; that might not be fair to you perhaps, though I marvel you missed the lesson and have forgotten the punishment so soon. Coming back to her, ghost-haunted as she was, you did make her happier, for you lifted the horror of fear and superstition from her. But now her lasting content is the theme. How does your presence here contribute to that?"

"It would very considerably if Stapledon was different."

"Or if he was dead—or if—a thousand 'ifs.' But Stapledon is Stapledon. So what are you going to do with the advice I've given you?"

"Not use it, I assure you. Consider what it means to drive me away from Godleigh!"

"For her lasting content."

"I don't know about that. Of course, if it could be proved."

"You do know; and it has been proved."

"Not to my satisfaction. I resent your putting me in a separate compartment, as if I was a new sort of beast or a quaint hybrid. I'm a very ordinary man—not a phenomenon—and there are plenty more people in the world who think and act as I do."

"Go and join them, then," said Mr. Endicott, "for your own peace of mind and hers. Get out of her life; and remember that there's only one way— that leading from here. I'm sorry for you, but you'll live to know I've spoken the truth, unless your conscience was forgotten, too, when the Lord fashioned you."

Yeoland grumbled a little; then he brightened up.

"My first thought was best," he said. "I should not have bothered you with all this nonsense, for it really is nonsense when you think of it seriously. I should have stuck to my resolve—to see Myles himself and thrash this out, man to man. And so I will the moment he's up to it. The truth is, we're all taking ourselves much too seriously, which is absurd. Good-night, my dear sir. And thank you for your wisdom; but I'll see Stapledon—that is the proper way."

CHAPTER VIII.
THE ROUND ROBIN

Before they slept that night Myles had expressed deep sorrow to Honor for his utterances and declared contrition.

"The suffering is mine," he said; "to look back is worse for me than for you."

His wife, however, confessed on her side to a fault, and blamed herself very heartily for a lapse, not in her love, but in her thoughtfulness and consideration. She declared that much he had spoken had been justified, while he assured her that it was not so.

The days passed, and health returned to Myles; upon which Christopher Yeoland, believing the recent difficulty dead, very speedily banished it from his mind, met Stapledon as formerly in perfect friendship, never let him know that he had heard of the tribulation recorded, and continued to lead a life quite agreeable to himself, in that it was leavened from time to time by the companionship of Honor.

Spring demanded that Myles should be much upon the farm, and the extent of his present labours appeared to sweep his soul clean again, to purify his mind and purge it of further disquiet. All that looked unusual in his conduct was an increased propensity toward being much alone, or in sole company of his dogs; yet he never declined Honor's offers to join him.

She had not failed to profit vitally by the scene in the sick-room, yet found herself making no return to peace. Now, indeed, Honor told herself that her husband's state was more gracious than her own; for there began dimly to dawn upon her heart the truth of those things that Myles had hurled against her in the flood of his wrath. She divined the impossible persistence of this divided love, and she felt fear. She was sundered in her deepest affections, and knew that her peace must presently suffer, as that of Myles had already suffered. Her peculiar attitude was unlike that of her husband or the other man. She saw them both, received a measure of worship from both, and grew specially impatient against the silent, pregnant demeanour of Mark Endicott. His regard for her was steadily diminishing, as it seemed, and he took some pains that she should appreciate the fact.

It grew slowly within her that the position was ceasing to be tenable for human nature, and not seldom she almost desired some shattering outburst to end it. She was greatly puzzled and oftentimes secretly ashamed of herself; yet could she not lay a finger on the point of her offending.

Nevertheless she missed some attributes of a good wife, not from the conventional standpoint, which mattered nothing to her, but from her own standard of right-doing.

Meantime, behind the barriers now imperceptibly rising and thickening between man and wife, behind the calm and masklike face that he presented to the world, Myles Stapledon suffered assault of storm upon storm. He knew his highest ambitions and hopes were slipping out of reach; he marked with punctuations of his very heart's throb the increasing loneliness and emptiness of his inner life; and then he fought with himself, while his love for Honor waxed. In process of time he came gradually to convince himself that the problem was reduced to a point. She loved Christopher Yeoland better than she loved him, or, if not better, then, at least, as well. She did not deny this, and never had. Life with him under these circumstances doubtless failed every way, because his own temperament was such that he could not endure it placidly. He doubted not that his wife went daily in torment, that she saw through him to the raging fire hidden from all other eyes. He gave her credit for that perspicacity, and felt that her existence with him, under these circumstances, must be futile. He then convinced himself that her life, if spent with Christopher, would be less vain. Through dark and hidden abodes of agony his soul passed to this decision; he tried to make himself feel that he loved her less by reason of these things; and finally he occupied thought upon the means by which he might separate himself from her and pass out of her life.

In the misty spring nights, under budding woodland green, or aloft in the bosom of silence upon the high lands, he wandered. A dog was his companion always, and his thoughts were set upon the magic knife, that should cut him clean out of his wife's existence with least possible hurt to her. By constitution, conviction, instinct, the idea of suicide was vile to him. He had spoken of the abstract deed without detestation in Mark Endicott's company, had even admitted the possibility of heroic self-slaughter under some circumstances; but faced with it, he turned therefrom to higher roads, not in fear of such a course, but a frank loathing rather, because, under conditions of modern life, and with his own existence to be justified, he held it impossible to vindicate such a step. And that door closed; he thought of modern instances, and could recall none to serve as a precedent for him. He turned, then, to consider the mind of Christopher Yeoland, and endeavoured to perceive his point of view. Blank failure met him there; but the thought of him clenched Stapledon's hand, as it often did at this season, and he knew that hate was growing—a stout plant of many tendrils—from the prevalent fret and fever of his mind. He worked early and late to starve this passion, but toil was powerless to come between his spirit and the problem of his life for long.

His tribulation he concealed, yet not the outward marks of it. The eyes of the farm were bright, and it was natural that he should be the focus of them all. There came a night when Myles and his wife were gone to Chagford at the wish of others, to lend weight in some parochial entertainment for a good cause. Mr. Endicott was also of the party, and so it chanced that the work-folk had Bear Down house-place to themselves. The opportunity looked too good to miss, and their master was accordingly discussed by all.

"Some dark branch of trouble, no doubt," said Henry Collins. "Time was when he would smoke his pipe and change a thought with the humblest. Now he's such a awnself man, wi' his eyes always turned into his head, so to say."

"Broody-like," declared Churdles Ash; "an' do make his friends o' dumb beasts more'n ever, an' looks to dogs for his pleasure."

"Ess; an' wanders about on moony nights, an' hangs awver gates, like a momet to frighten pixies, if wan may say so without disrespect," continued Collins.

"A gert thinker he've grawed of late," said Cramphorn; "an' if I doan't knaw the marks of thought, who should?"

"Sure a common man might 'most open a shop with the wisdom in his head," admitted Sam Pinsent; and Jonah answered—

"He ban't wise enough to be happy, however. A red setter's a very gude dog, but no lasting company for a married man—leastways, he shouldn't be. Theer's somethin' heavy as a millstone round his neck, an' dumb beasts can't lift it, fond of 'em as he is. The world's a puzzle to all onderstandin' people; yet theer's none amongst us havin' trouble but can find a wiser man than hisself to lighten the load if he'll awnly look round him. Theer's Endicott, as have forgot more of the puzzle of life than ever Stapledon knawed; an' theer's Ash, a humble man, yet not without his intellects if years count for anything; an' me, as have some credit in company, I b'lieve. Ess, theer's auld heads at his sarvice, yet he goes in trouble, which is written on his front and in his eyes. Best man as ever comed to Endicott's tu, present comp'ny excepted."

"Theer's nought as we could do for his betterment, I s'pose?" asked Gaffer Ash. "I've knawed chaps quick to take fire at any advice, or such bowldaciousness from theer servants; but if you go about such a deed in the name of the Lard, nobody of right honesty can say nothin' against you.

Now theer's a way to do such a thing, an' that is by an approach all together, yet none forwarder than t'others. Then, if the man gets angry, he can't choose no scapegoat. 'Tis all or none. A 'round robin' they call the manifestation. You puts a bit of common sense, or a few gude Bible thoughts in the middle, an' writes your names about, like the spokes of a cart-wheel, or the rays of the sun sticking out all around. So theer's nothin' to catch hold of against them as send it."

"Seein' we doan't knaw wheer the shoe pinches, the thing be bound to fail," said Pinsent. "If us knawed wheer he was hit, I be sure auld blids like you an' Jonah would have a remedy, an' belike might find the very words for it in the Scriptures; but you caan't offer medicine if you doan't know wheer a body's took to."

"'Tis the heart of un," said Cramphorn. "I'm allowed an eye, I think, an' I've seed very clear, if you younger men have not, that this cloud have drifted awver him since Squire Yeoland comed to his awn—an' more'n his awn. Stapledon be out o' bias wi' the world here an' theer no doubt."

"I'm sure they'm gert friends, sir, an' awften to be seed abroad of a airly mornin' together 'pon the lands," piped in Tommy Bates.

"Shut your mouth, bwoy, till us axes your opinion," retorted Jonah. "An' come to think on't, seein' the nature of the argeyment, you'd best clear out of this an' go to bed."

"Let un listen to his betters," said Mr. Ash. "'Tis right he should, for the less he listens to men as a bwoy, the bigger fule he'll be come he graws. 'Tis a falling out contrary to all use," he continued. "Missis was set 'pon squire fust plaace; then, second place, he died; an', third place, she married t'other; fourth place, he comed to life; an' fifthly an' lastly, 'pon this thumb of mine, he graws rich as Solomon, an' bides in pomp an' glory to Godleigh again."

"An' they'm awften about together, drivin' an' walkin' for that matter; though God, He knaws I'd be the last to smell a fault in missis," said Jonah.

"Damn bowldacious of the man, however," declared Pinsent.

"'Tis so; an' all of a piece wi' his empty life, fust to last; an' that's what's makin' Myles Stapledon go heavy an' forget to give me an' others 'Gude-marnin'' or 'Gude-evenin',' 'cordin' to the time of day. He thinks—same as I do—that theer's a sight tu much o' Yeoland in the air; an' yet he's that worshipful of his wife that, though maybe she frets him, he'd rather grizzle hisself to fiddle-strings than say a word to hurt her. 'Mazin' what such a wonnerful woman sees in that vain buzz-fly of a man."

"You'm right, no doubt, Jonah," assented Ash. "An' if 'tis as you say, an' we'm faaced wi' the nature of the ill, us might do our little in all gude sarvice an' humbleness towards the cure."

"The cure would be to knock that cockatrice 'pon the head an' scat his empty brains abroad wance for all. Then the fule would have to be buried fair an' square, wi' no more conjuring tricks," declared Jonah Cramphorn.

"You'm an Auld Testament man, for sartain!" admitted Collins in some admiration.

"Fegs! So he be; but these here ain't Auld Testament days," said Churdles Ash; "an' us caan't taake the law in our awn hands, no matter how much mind we've got to it. 'Tis a New Testament job in my judgment, an' us'll do a 'round robin' to rights, an' set out chapter an' verse, an' give the poor sawl somethin' very high an' comfortin' to chew 'pon. Truth to tell, he's a thought jealous of his lady's likin' for t'other. I mean no rudeness, an' if I doan't know my place at fourscore, when shall I? But so it seems; an' the fact thraws un back 'pon dogs an' his awn devices, which is very bad for his brain."

"What's the gude o' texts to a jealous man, whether or no?" asked Jonah scornfully.

"Every gude; an' even a bachelor same as me can see it. Fust theer'll be the calm process o' handlin' the Word an' lookin' up chapter an' verse, each in turn; then the readin', larnin', markin', an' inwardly digestin'; then, if we pick the proper talk, he'll come to a mood for Christ to get the thin end of the wedge in wi' un. An' so us'll conquer in the name of the Lard."

"'Pears to me as a bloody text or two wouldn't be amiss. I'd like to fire the man up to go down-long to Christopher Yeoland an' take a horse-whip to un, an' tan the hide off un. Theer's nought cools a lecherous heart like a sore carcase," growled Jonah, reverting to his Old Testament manner.

Then Mr. Collins created a diversion.

"I won't have no hand in it anyways," he said. "'Tis a darned sight tu perilous a deed to come between a man and wife, even with a text of Scripture, 'specially when you call home how hard 'tis to find lasting work. Us might all get the sack for it; an' who'd pity us?"

"All depends 'pon how 'tis done. Wi' a bit of round writin' the blame doan't fall nowheers in partickler."

"'Tis the wise ch'ice of words such a contrivance do depend on; an' what more wise than Paul?" inquired Jonah Cramphorn. "I read the seventh of Romans to my wife 'pon our wedding night, and never regretted it. He hits the nail on the head like a workman; an' if theer's trouble arter, the chap will be fallin' out wi' an anointed apostle, not us. Ess, I be come round to your opinion, Ash. Us had better send it than not. You wouldn't have had the thing rise up in your head if Providence didn't mean us to do it."

"Might be safer to send it wi'out names, come to think of it," suggested Collins; but Gaffer Ash scorned the cowardly notion.

"Wheer's the weight of that? No more'n a leaf in the wind wi'out names. No sensible pusson would heed advice, gude or ill, as comed so. 'Tis awnly evil-doers as be feared to sign an' seal their actions."

"Us might send it to she, instead of he," suddenly suggested Cramphorn. "Her's more to us, God bless her; an' a woman's better able to brook such a thing. She doan't see how this here do 'pear to other people, else she'd never give the chap as much as 'Gude-marnin'' again. An' her'll be fust to mark the righteous motives to the act. Gimme the big Bible from the dresser-drawer, Tom Bates; an' then go to your bed. Us doan't want a green youth like you in the document.

"A dangerous thing to give advice wheer it ban't axed," mused Pinsent; "an' specially to your betters."

"So dangerous that I'll have no part nor lot in it," declared Henry. "The dear lady's temper ban't what it was, so your darter tells me, Cramphorn; an' you've got a mother an' sister to keep, Samuel, so you'd best to bide out of it along wi' me."

Mr. Cramphorn was turning over the leaves of an old Bible thoughtfully.

"Paul's amazin' deep versed in it, seemin'ly," he said. "'Pears as he was faaced wi' just such a evil when he wrote an' warmed up they Corinthians. Listen to this here. 'An' unto the married I command, yet not I, but the Lard, Let not the wife depart from her husband: But an' if she depart, let her remain unmarried.'"

"Awften had a mind 'pon that scripture myself," declared Mr. Ash.

"An' lower down he's at 'em again. Hark to this: 'Art thou bound to a wife? seek not to be loosed. Art thou loosed from a wife? seek not a wife.' I reckon most men doan't need to be told that last. Then theer's another bracing word further on. Parson Scobell preached 'pon it awnly last month. Ephesians, fifteenth of five: 'See then that ye walk circumspectly, not as fules, but as wise.'"

"Tu strong for a lady," said Mr. Ash.

"Not so, Churdles. I'm the last to say or set a hand to any awver-bitter speech. 'Tis what her wants to awpen her butivul eyes, an' shaw her the right road, same as them 'twas fust writ for. An' here—same chapter: 'Wives, submit yourselves to your awn husbands, as unto the Lard.' Ban't tawld to submit theerselves to young, flauntin' bachelors, you see; an' then it says how women should hold theer awn men in special reverence."

"Theer's the twinge, an' I'd have 'e put that in for sartain," declared Churdles. "If her reverenced un, her wouldn't go about in high-wheeled, cranky dog-carts wi' t'other. Ess, put that down; together wi' any light hint against the lust of the flaish, so long as you can find it set out in parlour language."

Mr. Cramphorn took pencil and paper to his task; and Gaffer Ash, with the help of a round candlestick, drew a shaky circle in the middle of a sheet of foolscap. "Our names will all stick around," he said; "an' in the midst Jonah will set chapter an' verse. Perhaps ten verses might be enough to right the wrong, an' if you'm quick, Cramphorn, us'll get it in a henvelope an' addressed to missis, then slip it off to bed an' leave the manifestation 'pon the table against her comes home."

"More respectful to send it through the post," ventured Collins; and Churdles admitted that it might be so.

"P'raps you'm right theer, Henery. Ess, for sure you be; an' you'm gwaine into Chaggyford wi' the cart fust thing to-morrow, so you can post it theer; then 'twill come wi' all the dignity of the mail," he said.

Jonah finished his pious task and wrote his name; Churdles Ash, who had only learned to write in middle-age, set down a shaky signature, half schoolboy's, half senile in its wavering line; Pinsent wrote a laboured but well-regulated hand, and Mr. Collins also subscribed, yet with such uneasiness that one might have imagined he was signing his own death-warrant.

"Even now I'd like to hear Maister Endicott 'pon it," he murmured. "If he was against it, I'd never willingly countenance the step."

"He'm wan of the family; an' whenever was it knawn as a female gived credit to them of her awn blood for sense?" inquired Jonah. "Why, 'tis last thing they think of. No; us o' the land will send this here for gude or evil. We'm doin' our duty an' shan't be no worse thought of. She'm a wonnerful woman—a queen among 'em at her best—always was so—an' she'll think the better of us for this transaction."

"She'm just the sort to put a bit on our wages if the 'round robin' worked to her betterment—a most grateful woman," said Sam Pinsent, who from doubt had suddenly sprung to the extremity of hope.

"Ess—an' if her didn't, he would, so like as not," declared Gaffer Ash. "If this sets all right an' makes 'em happy an' sensible an' onderstandin', in the name of the Lard and of Paul, how much smoother 'twill be for all parties!"

"An' if all works well an' nobody don't do nothin'," suggested Pinsent, "it might be a question whether us shouldn't send in another to remind 'em of theer well-wishers. However, that's in the future."

"'Twould be like sendin' in a bill, an' not to be dreamt of," answered Cramphorn. "'Tis awnly a small-fashioned mind as would think of such a thing."

Pinsent retorted; but at that moment footsteps and voices warned the company. Pipes were relighted; the Bible was placed in the dresser-drawer; wide innocence sat upon each brown face; and, like lead within the breast pocket of Henry Collins, reposed the 'round robin' destined, as all hoped, to such notable issues.

CHAPTER IX.
RED DAWN

The admonition culled from Paul was duly posted, and henceforth Collins avoided his mistress with utmost care, while Pinsent, fear again overtaking him, did likewise. Cramphorn, on the contrary, itched to hear or see some definite result of his daring, while as for the ancient Ash, he went unmoved upon his way. To tell truth, the missive made an impression as deep as any of those responsible for it could have desired; but they never knew of its results, for the outgrowth of them was swept away by greater concerns. When Honor first received the "round robin," she felt amused; then she became annoyed; and, lastly, she grew anxious. The sort of men responsible for this audacity she understood, and she was aware the action sprang from honest purpose and most laudable intent. Cramphorn, the master spirit, worshipped her with high devotion, and she knew it; for the rest, they had but done as he bid them. The selected quotations, which Honor carefully consulted, were not indeed apposite, yet had this value, that they showed her how present relations appeared in the eyes of an ignorant, though impartial countryside. She was astounded at such an uncharitable and painful mistake; yet, seeing that the error existed, and was probably widespread, the wife felt thankful to know it. She fluctuated between contempt and anger, then finally fell back upon a condition of real concern. First she thought of showing the paper to Myles, but feared that his lack of humour might prompt him to austere treatment of her censors. To speak to Christopher was out of the question, and Honor, after some demur, decided that her uncle should know. From him she expected full measure of sympathy in her embarrassment, but she was disappointed of this hope.

"Very interesting and instructive," said the old man, after his niece had begun in laughter and ended with recitation of every text to which the document referred; "very interesting. So we may learn from the mouths of babes and sucklings."

"I ought to be cross with them. Fancy Cramphorn so greatly daring, despite his feudal instincts!"

"Shows how much and how deeply the man must have felt constrained to act. You say you should be cross. Why? They only try to give you some practical light. There's a great, deep goodwill behind this."

"But it is such nonsense."

"They don't think so."

"Surely you're not going to take it seriously, Uncle Mark?"

"Most seriously; and so do you, though you pretend to laugh—as if I didn't know every note in your laughter, like every note in a ring of bells. It is serious. You cannot defy simple, wholesome usage and custom for ever."

"But who has a right to speak while Myles is silent? If I hurt him, he would tell me. He is quite himself again."

"Shows how little you know him, for all your love of him. You are hurting him, and my ear tells me more than all your senses can tell you. He lives in a dreary hell and speaks out of it. I can almost see his face when I hear his voice."

"I'm always thinking of him."

"Yes, with a moiety of your thoughts. It isn't allowed one woman to make two men wholly happy—else you might succeed. But you're only following the old, stale road and making two men wholly miserable. Any fool in a petticoat can manage as much. That's the foundation your present content is built upon. There's awful wickedness in it, to my mind; and double-distilled sin coming from such as you, because you're not a fool at all, but have sense enough to profit by experience. You must be aware that Myles is a wretched man; and, though you may not think it, Yeoland knows very well he's living in a wrong atmosphere—a mere shadow of happiness. Better far you make one happy, out-and-out, than keep each miserable. One has got to smart, and the sooner you decide which, the better for both."

"That you should ever speak so!"

"You've fallen away much of late—in mind and conduct I mean. Your fine, sharp instincts are grown blunter. You can live this mean, half-and-half life; and you don't understand, or you won't. There's no passion in it, I do think, and I suppose you can go on being fond of two men without disgracing Endicott breed; but I'll speak plainly, since it's vital I should. Men are different. They're not built to go on mooning with a talking doll for ever. Even Christopher Yeoland is made of flesh and blood. A woman may be all mind; a man never is. Now, what are you, and what are you doing? You're a married woman, and you're ruining the life of about the worthiest man I've been happy to meet since my own brother—your dear father—died. End it—if Yeoland hasn't got strength and determination sufficient to do so. Tell him your mind; be true to your husband, and bid the man go—if he is a man."

Honor Stapledon listened to this grave rebuke with a heaving breast.

"You call that justice! You would ask him, after all he has suffered and endured, to go away from his own? You would coldly bid him turn his back on all that makes life worth living for him—Godleigh?"

"Without the least remorse, if he can't stop decently."

"To judge so vilely! If you cannot understand and appreciate the fact that Christopher isn't made of common clay, then the case is hopeless."

"Coarse clay or china clay, he's a callous, cruel devil to do what he is doing; and you can tell him so from me."

"I'm only sorry that you so hatefully misunderstand Christo."

For once the blind man let his anger run over. It had been boiling for many days, and now, before this attitude in Honor, he could restrain the explosion no more.

"Damn Christo!" he said. "Damn him for a poor, white-livered, whole cowardice of curs rolled into one! Your husband's worth a wilderness of his sort, and you ought to know it, and—there, I'll not say more. I blamed Myles first for being jealous of nought; now I blame him no more. Reason is with him. And though this boneless thing doesn't know better, you ought to, if only to credit your stock. What's come to you? What's sapped up all your old sense and self-respect?"

She stared at his wrath as at a new experience.

"I am unchanged," she answered, "though all the rest of my little world is going mad it seems. I have been misled and mistaken, if you are right, though I am not sure at all that you are. Certainly I thought after his illness, and the things he said to me then, that Myles was looking at this matter from my own rational stand-point. He grew sensible again—the old, wise Myles. But if you are correct in this monstrous belief, Myles must have set my mind at rest at the cost of his own peace. Yet could he hide that from me?"

"Not if your eyes were as they used to be. There must be no more rest at any rate—neither rest nor peace—till I'm proved right and the case is righted, or I'm shown wrong, when I'll not be backward in begging for forgiveness. Only remember, it's got to come from you—this clearing up. Myles will do nothing while he thinks your happiness is in blossom; he'll go on silently fretting his soul sour; and t'other will do nothing—that I'll swear to—unless a pitchfork be taken to him. Enough said now. Have it out with your husband, and first put yourself in his place so far as your knowledge of him allows. Look out of his eyes, and try to feel what this means to such a man—ay, or any other man worth calling one."

"I will think of what you say. At least, you are right when you tell me that I have degenerated. Happiness means degeneration, I suppose."

"You're the last leaf of an old tree, and I'd have you live beautifully, and make a good end, and leave a fragrant memory to your children."

"He's the last of his line, too—Christopher."

"That rests with him probably. It is well that he should be if he's no more than appears. But I have done, and am cool again. I'm sorry if I've hurt you. I love you better far than anything in the world, yet you've given me cause for deep mourning of late days."

Honor prepared to speak, but did not do so. She looked at her uncle's wrinkled, grey face and blind eyes, bent down, kissed him on the forehead, and then hastened away without any more words.

While the matter of this serious speech was in his wife's mind, it chanced that Stapledon and the Squire of Godleigh met after the dawn hour, each being led to the same spot upon his homeward way. Neither had seen the other for some weeks, and by mutual exchange of thought, a common subject leaped to the mind of each.

Myles had been upon Kes Tor to see the sunrise; Christopher was returning from a further point; and now in the valley beneath Batworthy Farm they met, where Teign, touched with ruddy gold of the morning, wound murmuring along. Upon one bank the hill rose sharply under silver birch, mountain ash, oak, and concourse of tall pines; to the north more gradual acclivities of shaggy moor extended, and these were broken into leek-green beds of sphagnums, and gemmed with ruddy sundews, where springs opened or rivulets wound with little bubbling whispers to the river. A red dawn scattered the stream with stars and sparks reflected from low eastern clouds above the sunrise; and this radiance, thrown upward from the water, touched the under-leaf of the alders, where they hung above the stream and slashed the shadows with sanguine light. A spirit, sweet, fresh and dewy as any naiad, dwelt here; the place was bedecked with mossy greens and olives, duns and transparent velvet-browns, all softened and swept with the purest opaline blue, by contrast of dawn shadows with dawn fire. Rock shapes upon the river-bed, perfect in their relations of colour and of form, made most harmonious medley of manifold planes. They were touched by sunshine, modelled to the outlines of their mosses by great violet shadows spread between flame-lances from on high, blended by ripple and shimmer of reflected light from the river, broken in mass by the green rushes and tall grasses, by the dancing briar, its point under a waterfall, by the snowy blossoms of great umbel-bearers, and by the majestic foliage of king fern. Teign splashed and spouted crystal-bright through this display of forms and colours, and there was pleasant music of water and murmur of new-born leaves, while red light came and went through the dawn purity, soaked each dingle with misty gold, and chequered the river with many shades of ambers and agates and roses agleam together.

"Sons of the young morning—you and I! This is our hour, and we suck life from the risen day," said Christo, extending a hand to the other as they met at stream-side.

"Rain's coming," answered Myles; "and this splendour will be drowned long before noon."

"Then let us make the most of it. I'm glad we met here. A happy place to talk in, with fair things to fill one's eyes."

"What is there to talk about? I'm afraid our interests are too widely separated."

"Well, that will do for a start. I want to talk, if you'll listen. Frankly, Stapledon, we are not what we might be each to the other. I wish I understood you better. There's hardly a man in the world that I regard more deeply. Yet I know right well you don't echo the sentiment. We grow less intimate daily, instead of better friends. Yet we're bound together in a sort of way by the past, however distasteful that may be to you. At least I should say we must be. And so many common interests—say what you please to the contrary. Both fairly intelligent and intellectual, both prone to probe under the surface of things. What's the barrier? Frankly I have no idea. I thought at one time it might have to do with Honor; and so did Mr. Endicott. He talked to me with amazing vigour and plain choice of homely words. Yes, honestly, he made me feel like a criminal lunatic for about a week. Then, thank God, you recovered your health, and we met, and I saw at a glance that the old man was utterly wrong and had been engaged with a mare's nest. Yet there's a gulf between us, despite so much that we enjoy in common."

"Since you wish to speak of this, I say that there are some things that cannot be enjoyed in common."

Yeoland started.

"You mean that I was wrong, then, and Mr. Endicott right? But don't you see how infernally greedy and unreasonable you are? Either that, or you continue to misunderstand me of set purpose. I gave you Honor for your own; yet you grudge me my place at Godleigh—at the footstool of the throne you share with her. What do I rob you of? Do the birds rob you when they eat the crumbs fallen from your table? I cannot remotely judge of your attitude."

"That is true; but every other man can. And it may be that many do."

"Have you considered that this position you take is in some measure a reflection on your wife?"

"I have not, and if I had, I do not ask your criticism upon that."

"Well, I shall never see how you hold any ground for this ridiculous animosity, Stapledon; but for the sake of argument, you must be conceded a case. What is your exact grievance in English? The thing I have done I can do again: go; but before we imagine you bidding me to do so, or picture me as obeying, out of regard for Honor—before that climax, I say, consider what you are doing in common justice. By banishment you take from me every temporal and spiritual treasure worth living for. As I stand here, I believe I am a happy man—almost; happy in Godleigh; happy in renewed intercourse with Honor; happy—on my oath before Heaven—in the knowledge that she belongs to you. I may be unfinished and unfurnished—only half a man, as Mark Endicott didn't hesitate to tell me; but, such as I am, this hillside is my life, and, if you bade me depart from it and I went, then I should presently die."

Myles lifted his head and looked from under his brows half in contempt, half in dubiety.

"You're a slight thing to turn a man's hair grey—a slight thing on your own showing," he answered. "Can you dissect yourself so glibly and mean it? You parade your own emptiness without flinching. Yet you believe what you say, no doubt; and there may be truth in it, but not all the truth. I can't suppose you utterly abnormal in your attitude towards other people, just because you say you are."

"I say no such thing. It was Endicott who said so. I say that my view of life is very much more exalted and my standards higher than—yours, for instance. If you could understand my plane, you would understand me; but you can't. The æsthetic habit of mind is beyond your percipience."

"Then we can leave it out. You may deceive yourself with big words, nobody else. What are you going to do? That is the question. The fact that my peace of mind and my salvation are bound up in my wife is unfortunate, because I neither wish you to consider me, nor do I desire to be under any further obligation. But Honor is my wife, and, as that relationship is understood by common men, it carries with it definite limitations. She loves you, and never attempts to hide it. Her primitive nature is big enough to find room in her heart for us both; but my still more primitive nature can't tolerate this attitude. I'm not big enough to share her with anybody else, not big enough to watch her happier than the day is long in your company."

"You think soberly and honestly that the world grows too small for the three of us?"

"Little Silver does."

"We might toss up which of us blows his brains out."

"Try to feel as serious as I do, Christopher Yeoland. Try to look at the future of this woman's life, since you have approached me upon it."

"I do so, and I see a life not necessarily unhappy. A woman heroic enough to love two men deserves double share of happiness; don't you think so?"

"I suppose you're in earnest, though God knows it is not easy to argue with such a babbler."

"No, I'm not flippant. It is you who have got the perspective of this thing all wrong. If you were a little older, you would see how absurd it is to try and turn pure comedy into drama. If you were only a better judge of character—can't you understand that I'm incapable of tragedy? There's nothing hurting you, or going to hurt you, but your own narrow nature. When we're all white-headed—the day after to-morrow, or so—when we are all grown into the sere and yellow—you will be the first to laugh, through toothless gums, at this, and say that I was right."

"Well, we won't argue, because there's no solid ground where we can meet as a foundation for any possible sort of understanding. You take such a view of life and its responsibilities as I should have supposed impossible for a reasonable being. We're different to the roots, and, materialist though I am, I recognise, a million times more deeply than you can, the demands of this existence and the need to justify it. Now listen, and then we will part: I tell you that in my judgment as her husband, my wife's ultimate happiness and content and mental health will be more nearly assured if you go out of her life than if you stop in it. I ask you to go out of it. I recognise all that this demand means, especially as coming from me to you. You'll gauge the depth of my convictions that I can bring myself to ask you so much—for her sake, not mine."

"You want me to turn my back upon Godleigh?"

"I do; as that is apparently the only way you can turn your back on Bear Down."

"You have no right to ask such a thing."

"Under the circumstances I consider that I have."

"There is another alternative."

"I cannot see it then."

"You will though, before you sleep to-night. I shall not suggest it to you; but such a level-headed man as you are must presently see it for himself. I say I shall not propose it, because my peace of mind is not at stake. As a matter of fact, you're arguing for yourself now, though you fancy you are speaking for Honor. She's very nearly happy, and would be perfectly so if you were. It is your five-act drama manner and general tragic bearing that make her feel more or less downcast. And I am also happy. Now, consider; if I clear out, you'll be joyous again; I shall be in doleful dumps, of course, and Honor——?"

"Well?"

"Don't you know? She can't help loving us both. She can't alter that now, poor girl. If she knows I'm miserable, she certainly won't be happy.'

"You are making your position clear to me. She is not unhappy now, though my life is dark; but if your peace of mind was spoiled, then hers would suffer too.

"It may appear egotistical, but I think that nearly defines the situation."

"Which is to say that you are more to her than I am?"

"Remorseless logic, but—no; I don't assert that for a second. You are her husband. Such a delicate question should not be raised."

"It is raised, and she must decide it."

"My dear Stapledon, let us have no brutality. Do try to catch a little of her big, pure spirit. We may both learn from her. These earthly wranglings would shock her immeasurably."

"You won't leave this place?"

"Not unless Honor asks me to do so, and without inspiration. Now, good-bye. To think of the sweet air we've wasted in such futilities! You're right about the rain. Look away south."

Yeoland rose from the mossy stone whereon he had pursued this matter, and quickly disappeared; Myles also moved upon his way. Great slate-coloured ledges of cloud were already sliding upwards from the Moor, and it was raining by the time the farmer returned home to his breakfast.

CHAPTER X.
A MAN OF COURAGE

Sally Cramphorn found the secret of her happiness hard to hide, and as the weeks lengthened into months and Libby still bid her hold her peace, yet would give no definite reason for the imposed silence, she grew somewhat restive. He refused to discuss dates, and declared that a year at least ought to pass in order that each should thoroughly understand the other before irrevocable matrimony. Under these circumstances Sally found her engagement fall something flat. She was in no haste to marry, but importunate that the world might learn of her good fortune; and finally, after a decided difference or two upon the question, Gregory realised that definite steps must be taken, and at once. First he thought of telling Sally, with frankness, how he had made a mistake, and was of opinion that, by reason of wide disparity in their dispositions, she could be no bride for him; but, to do Gregory justice, all manner of sincerity he consistently abstained from, and, in the present case, more than a candid bearing seemed necessary. To throw Sally over before her face called for full measure of courage, and any such step, until he was thoroughly established in Margery's good graces, must be highly dangerous. So Libby assured himself. He determined, therefore, first to propose to Sally's younger sister, win to his side the strength of her personality and the bitterness of her tongue, then explain his mistake to Margery and leave her wit to solve and escape from present entanglement with the wrong woman.

For once Mr. Libby acted speedily upon a decision, sought out the other maiden, lured her from the sheltering radius of the farm, and proceeded with his proposal after a plan very similar to that which had conquered Sally.

"It's took me a long time—I may say years—to make up my mind," he said, chewing a blade of grass and glancing sideways at the rather hard profile of Margery; "but I do think as you'm the best maid in Little Silver, cautious though I am by nature. Ess, a wife's a solemn thought, yet you come nearer my fancy than any gal ever I seed or heard tell of, Margery Cramphorn. You've got a warm heart, as would make any man happy, I should reckon; an' to cut a long story short, I've ordained to marry you, if you'm willin'."

For answer Margery began to cry; but she let him kiss her, so he knew that the response was favourable.

"Doan't blubber about it. 'Tis a joyful thing; an' I'm sure I'm mazed wi' gladness to think as you can care for me. An' I hope as your love be big enough to last."

"Always, always, till we'm auld mumpheads—so long as ever I can see an' move an' love—so long I'll do for you an' fight for you, dear Gregory."

"Caan't say no fairer, an' I b'lieve you mean it. An' the whole beauty of married life lies in the woman putting the man fust—so my mother said; 'cause he'm the bread-winner an' must be thought of all times. An' you might remember my mother's ways wi' me—a very gude, comforting, proper woman. I ban't a horse for strength, an' comfort I must have."

"Which you shall have—love an' worship always, dear Gregory; an' I'm a proud maiden to think such a rich man as you could look to me for a helpmate. An' you shan't never be sorry; an' faither do set me higher'n Sally, so come presently I'll bring 'e more'n myself."

"That's no odds. A chap in love doan't heed no such things as them; but theer's wan point as I ban't ezacally clear on touchin' Sally. I can't say nothin' now; but—but next time we meet, I'll tell you how it stands—a mystery like. She'm a gude gal, no doubt, but tu apt to run away with ideas an' misread a man's intentions, an' take for facts things what she've dreamed in her sleep, I reckon. But bide till next Monday, then I'll make it clear. Now we'll just love each other an' tell about marryin'."

"Oh, Greg, I do blush to think of it. An' I've longed for 'e, out o' sight, all these years an' years! Won't her be raw—Sally? Her always thought as she was the favoured piece."

"Ban't seemly in a woman to set her mind 'pon a chap so outrageous. But let her bide. Now, when shall us be man an' wife? An' what fashion wall-hangings would 'e like to the cottage-parlour? For it must be done again, 'cause theer's beastly grease 'pon it, wheer my mother's head got against the wall on Sundays. She used to fall asleep regular in a auld armchair, then roll to the left out o' the chair till the wall stopped her head. Done it for years. An' her recipes I've kept, an' the wan for herby-pie you'd best larn by heart, for 'tis favourite food o' mine."

"I will, Greg. You know how I can cook."

"Wi' a tender-stomached man, same as me, you'll have to put your heart into the cooking."

"So I will then."

He squeezed her slowly until she gasped.

"You'm strong enough, I reckon, however," she said. "Your arm be like a bar of steel around me!"

"'Tis love as hardens the sinews. I've a gert gift for lovin', an' if a man couldn't love the likes o' you, he'd be a poor, slack-baked twoad, for sartain. I'm lucky to get 'e, an' I knaw it, an' us'll be a happy couple, I lay— me a-doin' man's work an' makin' gude money, an' you 'bout the house, so thrifty an' savin' that us shall graw rich 'fore we knaw it, an' p'raps come to keep a servant for you to order here an' theer. An' me wi' my awn hoss an' trap, so like as not, to drive to cattle-shows an' junketings, an' taake my plaace in the world."

"An' I'll sit beside 'e an' look down at the walkers."

"You'll be home-along wi' the childer more like. That's the mother's plaace. But us be lookin' a thought tu far forrard now. Wait till Bank Holiday anyway; then I'll meet 'e quiet by the river—down where Batworthy fishing right ends. 'Tis a private an' peaceful plaace; an' theer you must fix the day."

"So I will then, an' a proud woman I am, an' a true wife I'll make you; Lard's my judge."

"Mother———" began Mr. Libby; but he changed his mind and declared that it was now time to turn homewards.

At Bear Down he left his new love, after cautioning her by all holy things to keep their secret, and, ten minutes later, met his old sweetheart returning from Chagford. Sally was heavily laden and in a bad temper. Indeed Mr. Libby's procrastination seemed enough to try any woman who heartily worshipped him. Now he offered to carry her parcels up the steep hill to the farm, and such unwonted civility soothed her not a little. Presently they rested awhile in the gathering twilight, and Gregory, with cynic satisfaction, kissed Sally's red lips while yet he tasted Margery's caresses. The experience fired him, and a wave of fancied courage held his soul. He told himself that he was the strong, resolute spirit into whose hand destiny had thrust the welfare of these simple maids. He laughed to think what soft wax they were under his control. Then he determined to put Sally out of her misery at once. He began a sentence to that end; but he changed his mind as her blue eyes fell full and honest upon him. After which she travelled the old, weary ground and clamoured for a definite understanding and definite date, superior to all self-respect in her importunity.

"How long be I to go dumb, anyways? An' how long be I to wait? Us doan't grow no younger, an' you'm five-an'-thirty come September. Ban't fair, I reckon, an' theer's more in it than I can guess, for you'm like no sweetheart ever I heerd tell 'bout. So cold as a newt seemin'ly. But if your love's gone poor, then best to say so. If you'm shamed of me or you've changed your mind——"

The opportunity was an excellent one, but Gregory's courage had evaporated. Moreover, there came into his head an inspiration. It occurred to him—while removed from such an event by distance—that it would be an exciting incident to invite Sally to the streamside also, to confront the sisters and clear up the situation once for all. The vision of himself between the tearful twain was pleasing rather than not. He saw himself the centre of an impressive scene.

"I'll play the man," he reflected; "an' set her down handsome afore her sister. 'Tis awnly her word against mine, an' Margery'll believe me quick enough, for 'tis her interest so to do."

Upon this heroic resolution he spoke.

"I doan't say as you'm not in the right, Sally, to ax for somethin' plain. Us'll come to a fixture next Monday, as be a holiday. You meet me wheer Batworthy fishing right do end, down in the valley onder the roundy-poundies on the hill, at three o'clock in the afternoon by my watch, an' us'll settle up 'bout the axing out in church an' such like."

The girl could scarcely believe her ears.

"Really! 'Tis 'most tu gude to be true."

"I mean it. Ess fay, I begin to want a wife 'bout the place."

"I'll come down-long, then, Monday afternoon, rain or shine."

"Very well. An' now I'll bid you gude-night. Mind the spot an' doan't keep me waitin'; but if 'tis pourin' cats an' dogs I shaan't be theer, for I've got to be careful of my paarts, bein' a bit naish, as you knaw."

"Bless 'e, dear Greg; 'tis gert news to me. An' you'll never be sorry for it, wance I'm Mrs. Libby—that I'll swear."

"Theer's awnly wan gal as be the wife for me," he said, and grinned at his own wit.

So they parted; and while Sally went home all gladness, forgetting the weight of her parcels in the lightness of her heart, Gregory moved down the hill occupied with a curious reflection.

"Theer'll be a 'mazin' tempest o' words between 'em, I doan't mind a red rage, but I'm always terrible afeared of a white wan. Sally'll go so fiery as sunset, an' use crooked language, no doubt; but that's nothin'. Awnly I couldn't cross t'other. Her turns ash-colour when her's vexed, an' her tongue's sharper'n a razor. 'Twill be a gert battle to watch an' a very fine study of female character, no doubt."

CHAPTER XI.
THE ROAD TO PEACE

A month after his conversation with Christopher, Myles Stapledon made definite and determined advance upon the road to peace. There came a night when he and his wife lay in bed and a bright moon fretted the wall opposite their eyes with the pattern of the latticed window. The man gazed upon this design as it elongated and stole from left to right; then, conscious that Honor was not asleep, he spoke gently to her.

"You are waking," he said, "and I also. Hear me a little while, dear heart. There's no shadow of anger in what I'm going to say to you. I'm cool in body and brain, and I want to look at your life as it must seem in other eyes—in the eyes of those who love you, though not as I love you. I want to be just—ay, and more than just."

"You are always just, Myles—where you understand. The hard, impossible thing is to be just where we don't understand. You're going to talk to me about Christo; and I'm going to listen. You've a right to speak—which is more than anybody else in the world has, though certain folks don't realise that. I thought all was well, but I am wrong. You hide behind yourself so much—even from me. You are an unhappy man, and you have not told me, but Uncle Mark has."

"I may be considered so. And to know that I am makes you unhappy and Yeoland uncomfortable. I have spoken to him recently. I explained to him that the present position, apart from my personal feelings concerning it, was very undesirable and must be modified, to say the least. He seemed surprised, but quite unprepared to make any suggestion. A plan other than my own proposal he hinted at, but he did not put it before me."

"He can feel deeply too; this must have been a shock and a grief to him."

"At least he recognised that it was so to me. I think he was neither shocked nor grieved himself. If anything, he felt incensed by my attitude. The position is not endurable to me, though you and he see no difficulty. But I must be allowed the decision, and I say that this state has to cease—selfish though that may seem to you."

"Then it shall cease. You could not be selfish if you tried, Myles. I, too, can feel a little. Uncle Mark began what you are going to finish. I'm probably faulty in my intellect, or I should have seen all this sooner. At any rate I know what I owe to you—what a husband you have been to me. I won't talk of duty; I'll talk of my love for you, Myles dearest. That is a live, deep thing at least."

"I never thought to doubt it, or ask proof of it. I knew it was real enough, and believed it immortal until—not doubt—I won't say doubt came—but sorrow, and a cloud, and a mist of the mind that was very chilling to me. I have lost my way in it of late, and have wandered wondering how far off you were in the darkness, asking myself if we were drifting further and further apart, fearing that it was so."

"You have been too patient, and I too blind. And I have loved you more every day, not less."

"It is a question for your decision. I don't like to wound your ear with blunt words; but there must be no more vague misery for want of speech after to-night. Half the wretchedness of life happens because we're frightened to speak out, and make a clean wound, and have done with it. You're my wife, for better or worse—not necessarily for good and all. My heart and soul are wrapped up in your well-being; but I've got to live my own life, not yours; I've got to do the unknown will, and I've no right to let anything from outside come between me and what I believe is my duty. Nothing outside a man can hurt him, unless he suffers it to do so. I must not let these troubles stand between me and my road any longer. I must go on with the light I have—alone, if you say so; but I must go on."

"Alone?"

"If you say so. Self-respect to a man with my outlook is all he has. And I'm losing it."

"To live without me?"

"If you say so. I'm not as conventional as you think, Honor. You made certain promises to me under certain impressions. The fact that the man whom you believed to be dead, when you married me, was not dead in reality absolves you from your undertaking, if you wish to be absolved. So at least it stands in my judgment; and mine is the only judgment, after your own, that you need consider."

"I swore an oath before God!"

"You swore in the dark. Now go back to the starting-point and make up your mind anew. Which of us is to have you henceforth—all of you?"

"To think that I should hear you say that! To know my actions justify the words!"

"I can very easily teach myself to go without; I can never tame myself to share. No man could."

"You have all of me, for ever, and for ever, and for ever. I am your wife."

"Don't let that last accident influence you. Argue as if you were not; argue as if you were free. Second thoughts are often best. You're linked to me by a chain that can quite easily be broken if you desire to break it."

"Your words are blunt, as you said they should be; but you're making the clean wounds you spoke of in my heart. They'll heal if they don't kill. I'd rather die—much rather die than leave you, Myles."

"Consider. Yeoland will be just as ready to accept and applaud your decision as I shall. He, too, realises at any rate that this isn't going on. We don't stand at the end of our lives; rather at the beginning of them. We may have fifty years more of it yet—either together or apart; but not like this."

"The alternatives?"

"We two are the alternatives. Go to him, if you like, and I shall know what to do; or stay with me and abide by my will. What comes afterwards you may leave to me. If you are to be my wife, Honor, you must shut this man clean out of your existence, for evermore, absolutely—never speak his name again, or think it. And for myself I shall be what I have always been—neither better nor worse. I can promise nothing—nothing of the beautiful side of life. No rainbows ever play in my cloudy atmosphere, as they do in his changeful, April weather. I am plain, dull, uninteresting, old-fashioned. I know nothing, and go joylessly in consequence—a cheerless soul with little laughter in me. Sometimes I think the east wind must blow colder for touching me. That's all I have to offer, and you know it by this time. What the other can give you that is better, softer, sweeter for a beautiful woman, I needn't tell you. It's the difference all through the piece between a working farmer and an accomplished gentleman of no occupation—no occupation but to make you happy. And no need to study the world in your choice; no need to think the accident of a human contrivance that makes you my wife should weigh with you. It was under a wrong knowledge of facts that you accepted me, and, in any case, we've gone far beyond paltry conventions and customs. I shall respect you more if you fling away that ring and go to him, than I do at present."

"Can you love me with all your heart and speak so?"

"You know whether I love you."

"And yet you talk so coldly of going on with your life alone."

"The necessity of facing that has been forced upon me, Honor."

"Do you think I am even without a sense of duty?"

"Don't let any trumpery consideration of duty weigh with you. You have to decide what is to become of your life. Consider only your duty to your soul. Your religion—of love and fear and belief in an eternity—should be of service to you here, if ever, for your trust is in a just Being who metes out reward or punishment according to the record in the book. That's a wholesome assumption if you can accept it; but don't let minor dogmas and man's additions interfere with your decision. By your record you will be judged—so you believe. Then create that record; set about it wisely and decide which line of action leads to making of the higher history. If you can justify your existence better with me, then stay with me; if life lived with Christopher Yeoland will offer more opportunities of doing something big and useful and beautiful—as very likely it might, when we consider his money and position and sympathetic nature—then it is your duty to yourself to go to him. Nobody can decide for you; but use your best thought upon it and make no mistake in this critical pass. Look at it every way impartially and distrust even your conscience, for that has been educated by rote, like every other woman's conscience."

"Your speech is very cynical, Myles; but your voice is earnest enough."

"There is nothing ironical in what I say; only the facts are ironical."

"Do you want me to go to him?"

"Yes—if your heartfelt conclusion is that you can live a finer, worthier life so."

"Don't you know I love you dearly?"

"I know you love us both."

"I've never stopped to contrast or compare. I was your wife."

"But I ask you again not to remember that. Decide between us, or decide against us. There's that alternative. I've thought of that for you. Once you said that, as you couldn't have both, you'd have neither. That was in jest; but the course is still open in earnest if the road to your peace points there."

"To leave you. Oh, Myles, how you must have suffered and suffered and thought before you could say these things to me."

She put her arms about him and pressed close to him. The light had stolen round and, one by one, the diamonds of wan silver were disappearing. He showed no responsive emotion, but stroked the small hand on his breast wearily.

"Yes, I have thought a good deal. Will you decide what you are going to do in a week? Is that long enough?"

"How wicked—how wicked I have been in this. To think we can be wicked day after day and never know it! And your patience! And how extraordinary that you had it in you to speak in this cold, calculating way!"

"A stronger man might have borne it longer—into old age, perhaps, as Yeoland said. I could not. I've got nothing much beyond my self-respect. That's the sole thing that has kept me from destroying you, and him."

She thought upon this, but did not answer it.

"Sleep now," he said, after a pause. "'Tis the day-spring nearly. I've wearied you, but it had to be. Speak to me again about the matter in a week. And don't fear me any more. Passion against him is clean passed and gone. Just a gust of nature, I suppose, that makes the males fight in season. I wouldn't hurt a hair of your head—or his."

She nestled closer.

"Why wait a week when there is no need to wait a day, or an hour? I love you—better than anybody in the world; and I'll tell Christopher that; also that I have done great wrong in this matter; and I ask you, Myles, to take me where I shall never see him again—for his good and because I love you with my whole heart—all, all of it. And judge me by what I do henceforth and not what I say now. See how I shall order my life—let that convince you."

He did not speak, but his silence was cardinal—a hinge on which his whole spirit turned.

"You believe me, Myles? You know that I have never spoken an untruth to you."

A sigh rose, and seemed to pass away like an embodied trouble under the first dawn light—to depart like a presence from the man and leave him changed.

"I believe you—I believe you. I wish I could feel a personal God—to kneel to Him and thank Him, and to let my life thank Him henceforth."

"I'm a very wicked woman, and I ought to have lived in the Stone days, for I deserve nothing better than a hut circle and a cruel master to beat me. I should have been kicked about by some old, Neolithic hero with his dogs. I'm not big enough to deserve the love of a man like you, not wise enough even to rate the depth and height of it. But you shall see I can learn still and be single-hearted too. I'll live differently—higher; I'll aim anew—at the sun—I'll—I'll———"

Here she broke down, and he comforted her in his slow, stolid fashion.

"Honor, you are all the best part of me—the best thing that my life has known, or can know. Pray that the time to come may shine brighter seen against gloom gone. I've never doubted your motives—never. I've only lived in torment, because—there, don't be unhappy any more. I could do great things—great things for sheer thanksgiving. I must try to pay the world back in coin for this sunrise. The rest will be easy now you have spoken. Thought can cut the knot that remains, and I will take deep thought for all of us. Nothing is left to hurt us; think of that! Here's a solid foundation to work upon, now that you have decided to be my wife."

"What shall you do, Myles?"

"Think of him, and study how best to take you out of his life with least wound to him. I can be sorry for him now."

"His life is to live as well as ours."

"He must learn how to live it; but not from me. Sleep now, my own woman, again. Leave me to think out the rest. You don't know what this return means to me; I can't find the words to thunder out such a heart-deep thing. I feel as I felt when first you promised to marry me. I am waking out of a long chaos into peace."

Honor answered him, and their conversation presently grew disjointed as slumber stole over her weary brain. She sighed once or twice—the shaken sigh that follows upon tears—then her hand, that held his, relaxed and fell away. But Stapledon did not sleep. A thousand blind alleys of future action he followed, and countless possible operations pursued to barriers of difficulty.

At dawn he arose, and, leaving unconscious rest to repair the fret and turmoil of his wife's mind, pressed on to new problems. For the storm-cloud of his sorrows was touched with light; the ragged soul-garden within him spread smoothed and purged of deep-rooted weeds. He found space for wholesome seed therein, and passing into the air breathed wordless prayers upon the pure morning and opened his heart to the warmth of the sunrise fires.

CHAPTER XII.
PEACE

The day was the first of the week, and Myles, finding that no immediate plan entered his mind under the risen sun, turned homeward to breakfast, then announced a determination to take himself upon the Moor for a tramp alone. Thither he proposed to carry his new-found peace, and, once there, he knew that a final and just decision would reach him from his counsellors of the granite and west wind. After dinner he set forth to spend some hours face to face with the central fastnesses. A dog—his great red setter—accompanied him, and the beast was far less easy at heart than the man, for storm threatened, and since dawn sign upon sign had accumulated of electric disturbances on high. Thunder had growled about for some days, yet night was wont to dispel the gloom.

"Gert bouldering clouds, maister," said Churdles Ash, who met Myles setting forth. "A savage, fantastic sky out Cosdon way, and reg'lar conjuring time up-long in the elements."

Thus this man unconsciously echoed a hoary superstition, that lightning and thunder are the work of malevolent spirits.

But Myles, for once much mistaken, saw no immediate promise of storm. To the north remote banks of low cloud, with edges serrate and coppery, sulked above the distant sea, and all manner of cloud shapes—cumulus, stratus, and lurid nimbus—were flung and piled together, indicating unusual turmoil aloft; but similar threats had darkened several recent noons, and Stapledon, in a mood most optimistic, trusted the weather and foretold the storm would delay for many hours until its purple heart was full to the bursting.

"Exmoor will hold it back as like as not," he said.

Ash, however, believed that he knew better; and it was certain that the red dog did. A silence not natural to the time of day spread and deepened; and the wind came to life strangely at corners and cross-roads, sighed and eddied, then died again.

The farmer, with his thoughts busier than his eyes, strode swiftly onward, for he pictured himself as coming to great definite resolutions at some spot hid in the heart of the heather, bosomed deep upon the inner loneliness, beyond the sight of cattle and the sound of bellwether. He desired to reach a region familiar to him, lying afar off to the south of Cranmere, that central matrix of rivers. Here the very note of a bird was rare and signs of animate life but seldom seen. The pad-marks of some mountain fox upon the mire, or a skeleton of beast, clean-picked, alone spoke of living and dead creatures; sometimes a raven croaked and brooded here; sometimes, from a great altitude above the waste, fell cry of wild fowl that hastened to some sequestered estuary or fruitful valley of waters afar off.

Such stations brought sure content and clarity of mind to this man; they rested his spirit and swept foregrounds of small trouble clean away until he found himself at the altar of his deity in mood for worship. It was only of late that the magic of the Moor had failed him, and now, with new peace in his heart, its power for good awakened, and he knew right well that solution of the problem before him lay waiting his advent in the solitudes.

Over Scor Hill he passed, among the old stones that encompassed each supreme experience of his life with their rugged circle; then, his leathern leggings dusted to yellow by the ripe pollen of the ling, he walked onward over a splendour of luminous pink, crossed northern Teign under Watern, proceeded to Sittaford Tor, and, steadily tramping westward, left man and all trace of man behind him. The unmarked road was familiar, and every gaunt hill-crest about him stood for a steadfast friend. He crossed the infant Dart; he ploughed on over the heavy peat hags, seamed and scarred, torn and riddled by torrents; he leapt from tussock to ridge, and made his way through gigantic ling, that rose high above his knees. Cranmere he discarded, and now his intention was to reach the loneliest and sternest of all these stern and lonely elevations. He beheld the acclivities of Great and Little Kneeset and other mountain anchorites of the inner Moor; he passed the huge mass of Cut Hill by the ancient way cleft into it, and from thence saw Fur Tor's ragged cone ahead, grassy and granite-crowned. Stapledon had walked with great speed by the shortest route known to him, yet suddenly to his surprise a darkness as of evening shadowed him, and, lifting his head, he looked around upon the sky, to regret instantly a preoccupation that had borne him forward with such unthinking speed.

Strange phenomena were manifesting themselves solemnly; and they offered opportunity to note the difference between natural approach of night and the not less natural but unaccustomed advent of a night-black storm from the north. Darkness gathered out of a quarter whence the mind is not wont to receive it. A sudden gloom descended upon the traveller from Cranmere, and under its oncoming the Moor heads seemed massed closer together——massed and thrust almost upon the eye of the onlooker in strange propinquity each to other. A part of the sky's self they seemed— a nearer billow of cloud burst from the rest, toppled together like leaden waves on the brink of breaking, then suddenly frozen along the close horizon—petrified in horror at tremendous storm shapes now crowding above them.

On every side heath and marsh soaked up vanishing day, and were nothing brightened by it. The amethyst of the ling spread wan and sickly upon this darkness; only the granite, in studs and slabs far-strewn, gathered up the light and reflected a fast-waning illumination from the southern sky. One sheep-track, which Stapledon now traversed, was similarly luminous, where the narrow pathway wound like a snake and shone between sulky heather ridges, dark as the air above them. Over this region, now to a timid heart grown tenebrous and appalling in its aspect, pale lightning glared and, still remote, came the growl and jolt of thunders reverberating above distant granite. As yet no rain broke from the upper gloom, and the Moor retained its aspect of sentient and vigilant suspense. All things were still clear cut, and to the eye abnormally adjacent. Like some incarnate monster, that cowered under its master's uplifted lash, the desert seemed; and the granite teeth of it snarled through the heather, and shone steel-blue in the lightning, while a great storm stretched its van nearer and nearer. Yet no breath stirred a grass blade, and between the intermittent thunder from on high, a silence, tense and unbroken by the murmur of an insect, magnified the listening man's heart-beat into a throbbing upon his ear.

Stapledon now perceived from the congested accumulations of the sky that a tempest of rare severity must soon have him at the heart's core of it. He increased his pace therefore, and broke into a run. To turn was futile, and he hurried forward upon Fur Tor, wherein some niche or rocky crevice might offer shelter. Such a spot he knew to the lee of the great hill; and now he stumbled forward, while the black edge of the thunderstorm billowed and tumbled to the zenith, and swallowed up the daylight as it came.

Upon a tremendous gale, still unfelt at earth-level, the clouds hurtled in precipices, in streaming black wisps and ribbons, and in livid solitary patches over the pallor of dying light behind them. Then, half-way up Fur Tor, as he stood panting to regain breath, the wanderer felt the wind at last. A hot puff struck his hotter cheek, then another and another, each cooler and stronger than the first. His dog whimpered and crawled close; there ran a sigh and a shiver through the heath; grass blades and fragments of dead things floated and whirled aloft upon little spiral wind-spouts; vague, mysterious, and solemn—carried from afar, where torrential rains and hail were already churning the mosses and flogging stone and heath—there came the storm murmur, like a tramp of approaching hosts, or the pulsing of pinions unnumbered.

A grey curtain suddenly absorbed and obliterated the purple horizon, and softened the sharp details; lightning stabbed through and seared the watcher's sight, while thunder immediately above his head wounded the ear like discharge of ordnance. He ran for it, having difficulty to see his way.

The vanguard of the wind buffeted him; the riot above his head deafened him; the levin dazed his senses; then by good chance that spot he sought was reached, and he crept into a stony hollow opening upon the south-east—a natural cave among the clatters of the tor, where two masses of stone stood three yards apart, and a block falling upon them from above made a pent-house nearly weather-proof. Growing heather and fern filled the interstices, and the spot resembled a large natural kistvaen of the sort not seldom discovered in the old Moorland barrows, where Stone men laid the dust of their heroic dead.

Hither came the raging spirit of this tempest and looked into the eyes of Myles Stapledon. Then, at the moment of its prime fury, when the very roots of the land were shaking, and its living pelt of heath and rush seemed like to be stripped from its quivering carcase by the hail, did Stapledon pluck a way to peace through future action. Ever curious, he picked up the ice morsels, noted how the hailstones, frozen and frozen again in some raging upper chamber of the air, were all cast in like mould of twin cones set base to base; and then, from this observation, his mind turned to the twin life of a man and woman united indissolubly. Out of the uproar came a voice to him, and where the tors tossed thunder back and forth, until it died among their peaks, the watcher caught a message affirming his own heart in its sudden determination.

The simplicity of his conclusion struck him as sure criterion of its justness; and a mind possessed of one humorous trait, one faint perception of the ludicrous, had been surprised into some ghost of laughter before the idea, had surely smiled—even in a hurricane—before the inevitable contrast between its past long intervals of mental misery and this bald, most unromantic finger-post pointing to peace. True, no decision had been possible before Honor's determination was made known and the nature of the final problem defined; but now, under all this turmoil of sky and groan of earth, from his hot mind came a course of action, right and proper every way, reasonable and just to each of the three souls involved, yet most unromantic and obvious. He stumbled, in fact, upon the manifest alternative alluded to by Yeoland at their last meeting. As the master of Godleigh would not depart therefrom, Stapledon decided that he and Honor must leave Bear Down. That the labour of his brain-toil and deep searching should produce no more notable birth than this mouse of a plan, that the stupendous storm should have uttered no greater thing, appeared small matter to tempt one smile from Myles. Indeed, he forgot the weather and all other questions save this step ahead of him, for upon nearer examination it appeared not at all simple, but both complex and intricate. Retreat was the total of his intention; there appeared no other way to conquer this difficulty than by flying from it. He convinced himself that justice demanded this step, because one must depart from Little Silver, and his interests in that region could by no means be compared with those of Christopher Yeoland.

Justice to Honor faced him; but Bear Down was less to her than Godleigh to the owner, and never had Stapledon known his wife to manifest the patrimonial ardour of the man. Leaving of her old home, therefore, would be no excessive sorrow to her, and the fact that such a course must impoverish them was not likely to count for much with husband or wife. His mind ranged forward already. The fair weather within it laughed at the elemental chaos around him. There was sunshine in his heart, and the whole force and centre of the storm failed to cloud that inner radiance. He thought of the future, and in spirit plunged over seas to the child-countries of the motherland, that he might seek amongst them a new environment for his life and Honor's—a new theatre for work. But from such flights to the far West and South he returned upon these austere regions that now stretched around him, and his heart much inclined to familiar scenes on the fringe of the Moor hard by the place where he was born.

Long he reflected until the night or the storm merged into true dusk, and day closed untimely. The thunder passed, and the rain floods, having persisted far beyond Stapledon's experience of such electric tempests, began to lessen their volume. Yet heavy downfalls steadily drove across the twilight; the wind sank to a temperate gale, and, below him, mists arose from the new-made swamps, and woke, and stretched their tentacles, and crept through desolation round about the footstool of the tor.

A space of five wild leagues now separated Myles from his home, and he stood night-foundered in the very capital of the central waste. Alive to the concern his absence must occasion, he yet hesitated but a moment before declining the ordeal of a return journey. The man was too experienced to enter upon such a hazard. He knew that radical changes had overtaken the low marshes since he traversed them; that the quaking places over which he had progressed by leaping from tussock to tussock were now under water; that great freshets had borne the least rivulets above their banks, and that an element of danger must await any attempt to retrace his way until the morning.

Viewed in the light of his new content, this tribulation looked trumpery enough. He lighted a pipe, regretted his small dinner, and sorrowed more for his hungry dog than himself, in that the great beast was denied consolation of tobacco or the stimulant of an exalted heart.

Mapping the Moor in his mind, Stapledon considered every possible way to food and shelter. He knew more than the actual roads or ridges, streams or natural tracks and thoroughfares of beasts; for the inhabiting spirit and essence of Dartmoor was his—a reward of lifelong service. He possessed some of that instinct of the dogs and birds and ponies born to these conditions. Like them, he rarely erred, yet, like them, he often felt, rather than recognised danger—if danger was abroad; while he knew that widest experience and shrewdest natural intuition are not always proof against those perils that may spring into activity by day or night in these tenantless, unfriended wastes.

Fur Tor stands near the heart of the Devonshire moorland. It is a place not easy to reach at all times, and impossible to depart from under the conditions now obtaining. Water-springs unknown had burst their founts, and the central sponges were overflowing in deep murmurs from the hills. Time must elapse, hours—the number of which would depend upon future weather—must pass by before any possibility of Stapledon's retreat. His mind drew pictures of the nearest human habitations around him and the means by which they might be reached. Five miles away, by the western fork of Dart, was "Brown's house"—a ruined abode of one who had loved the Moor as well as Myles and built his dwelling upon it. Only shattered stones stood there now; but further south, by Wistman's wood of dwarf and ancient oaks, a warrener dwelt in a cabin on the hillside. Yet a network of young rivers and a cordon of live bogs extended between that haven and Myles. Tavy's stream encircled him with its infant arms and wound between him and safety beyond the forest boundaries. Approach to Mary Tavy or Princetown was also impracticable, and, after very brief deliberations, the wanderer decided that nothing could be done until the morning. This conclusion he announced aloud to his dog—a pleasantry indicative of his happy mind, for such an action from Stapledon's standpoint looked a considerable jest.

Soon the man piled stones before the entrance of his hiding-place, filled a draughty gap with fern and heather, and made himself as comfortable as the circumstances allowed. Great content was in his heart, and when, near midnight, the clouds passed, the moon rose and painted with silver the waters spread below, with frosted silver the fog that rolled above them, he deeply felt the silence and peace, their contrast with the frenzy of the past storm; he roamed in thought through the unutterable silence of that moonlit loneliness; and presently he slept, as he had not seldom slumbered on the high land in time past—within some ruined hut circle, or where the wolves, through long, primeval nights, once howled around Damnonian folds.

CHAPTER XIII.
A SOUND OF SUFFERING

Stapledon slept well, and, awakening with the light, found himself strengthened and refreshed. The stiffness consequent on a hard bed soon passed as he rose, stretched himself, strode sharply here and there to restore circulation, and drank of the morning air. Sunlight warmed him, and his thoughts turned homeward. He thought first of descending to Two Bridges and the hospitality that would there await him; but the day was so brilliant after the storm, and in his waking mood he felt so well furnished with strength, that he abandoned this project and determined to tramp back to Little Silver. He tightened his belt on his empty stomach, lighted a pipe, and set his face for home. It was nearly seven o'clock when he started, and, allowing for all reasonable interruptions of progress— incidents inevitable after the storm—he believed that it would be possible to make the shepherd's cot at Teign Head under Watern Tor long before midday.

His road of the previous evening he found quite impassable, and it was nearly nine o'clock before he fairly escaped from the labyrinth of deep waters and greedy bog now spread about Fur Tor. The task of return indeed proved far more difficult than he had anticipated, for the present harmonious contentment of his mind, despite hunger, induced an optimism rare enough in Myles at any time. But experience came to his aid, and he set to work soberly to save his strength for a toilsome journey.

It is unnecessary to describe the many turnings of a tortuous way followed at mercy of the unloosened waters. Chance ultimately willed the man to Watern—a craggy fastness familiar enough to him, yet somewhat removed out of the direct course he had planned. But Teign's birthplace was overflowing, and, to avoid morasses beneath Sittaford, he had tended northerly and so found himself not far from the tremendous and stratified granite ledges that approach the magnitude of cliffs on Watern's crown.

Weary enough by this time, and surprised to find himself somewhat weakened from unusual exertions and lack of food, Myles paused to rest a little while on the northern side of the crags. Here was grateful shadow, and he reposed in the damp rushes, and felt his heart weary and his head aching. His dog similarly showed weariness, but knew the horizon-line easterly hid Bear Down, and marvelled why the master should call this halt, within three miles of home.

Then, pleasantly conscious that the worst of his difficult enterprise was over, Myles Stapledon suddenly heard a sound of suffering. There fell upon his ear reiterated and hollow meanings, that might be expressions of pain from man or beast. Some creature in an extremity of physical grief was certainly near at hand; so he rose hastily, that he might minister to the tortured thing, while his dog barked and ran before him.

And here it is necessary to leave the man for a period of brief hours, for ancillary matters now merge into our main theme at this—the climax of the record.

CHAPTER XIV.
FROM WORDS TO BLOWS

Honor by no means enjoyed such easy sleep as her husband after the thunderstorm; indeed it can scarcely be said concerning her night's rest that it held slumber. The tempest and a belief that Myles was alone in its midst, brought very real terror to her; nor did she win much comfort from her uncle's reiterated assurance that no ill could touch Myles Stapledon upon Dartmoor.

"Return he won't for certain until morning," declared the blind man. "Full of thought he went his way and forgot to raise a weather eye until suddenly surprised by the storm. Its loosened torrents cut him off on the high land and drowned his way home, no doubt; but whatever part of the waste he's upon, 'tis familiar ground to him, and he'll know the nearest way to shelter and doubtless take it."

In his mind, however, the speaker felt a cloud. He was alarmed rather for the storm that he believed might have burst within Stapledon's heart than for any chance accident of sudden tempest from without. Quite ignorant of the last phase of the other's trial; unaware that Myles had passed the point of highest peril and now approached happiness once more, old Endicott only suspected that this man had reached the climax of his tribulation, and believed Stapledon's long and lonely expedition was undertaken that he might wrestle with his fate and determine some final choice of way. Herein he judged rightly, but he knew not the modified enigma that lay before Myles upon that journey to the desert, and remained wholly unaware that the major problem stood solved. Thought upon the matter took Endicott along dark ways; he remembered words spoken long ago; and for once a mind usually most luminous in appraisement of human actions, deviated from the truth. Such a mistake had mattered little enough; for Mark was no harbinger of gloomy suspicions, and never word of his had made sorrow more sad or deepened any wound; but a time came when his conviction, supported by apparent evidence, was confirmed in his own mind; and from thence cruel chances willed that it should escape from him to another's keeping, should hasten night over a life scarcely advanced to its noon.

A morning of almost extravagant splendour followed upon the storm, and the soaked world under sunshine fortified human spirits unconsciously, wakened hopes and weakened fears in the breast of Honor. She walked out before breakfast, and upon the way back to Bear Down met Christopher Yeoland.

He was full of his own concerns, for the lightning had fallen upon Godleigh, slain certain beasts, and destroyed two ancient trees; but, hearing of Stapledon's absence, Christopher forgot his troubles, mentioned various comforting theories, and promised to ride far afield after breakfast upon the Moor.

"He'll probably come back a roundabout way and drive from Moreton," said Yeoland; "but there's a ghost of a chance that he may walk direct, after having put in a night at a cot or one of the miners' ruins. In that case he'll be starving and wretched every way. So I'll take a flask and some sandwiches. Poor beggar! I'm sorry for him; still he knows the Moor as well as we know our alphabet, so there's very little need for anxiety."

But the news of the thunderbolt in Godleigh Park by no means tended to make Honor more content, and she returned home in tribulation despite the sunshine. After breakfast she went out alone, and Christopher, true to his promise, made a wide perambulation on horseback; while others, who had planned no special pleasure for their holiday, also assisted the search, some upon ponies and some upon foot. Yet no news had reached Bear Down by midday, and then Christopher Yeoland arrived, after a ride of twenty miles.

"A good few wanderers I met and accosted—Moor men out to look after their beasts and see what harm last night was responsible for—but I saw nothing of Myles," he said. "Gone far down south, depend upon it. He'll be here in the course of the evening. And it's rum to see the flocks, for the storm has washed them snow-white—a beautiful thing. The hills are covered with pearls where the sheep are grazing. You can count every beast in a flock three miles off."

Yeoland lunched at the farm, then trotted homeward; but Collins and Pinsent, though they had travelled far that morning, set out again after dinner, being privately pressed to do so by Mark Endicott.

Elsewhere, true to his word, the man Gregory Libby repaired to riverside that he might meet Sally and her sister, and settle that great matter, once and for all, at a spot quite bathed in sunlight and little framed to harbour broils, though an ideal tryst for lovers. Libby was first to arrive, and after waiting for five minutes a twinge of fear shadowed his mind. The deed before him looked difficult and even dangerous at this near approach. Gregory, therefore, decided to slink by awhile and hide himself where he might note the sisters' arrival without being immediately observed. They would doubtless prove much amazed each at sight of the other; they would demand an explanation; and then he would come forth and confront them.

He concealed himself with some care, put out his pipe, that the reek of it might not betray him, and settled down to watch and hear from a position of personal safety.

Sally was the first to arrive—very hot and somewhat out of spirits, as it seemed, because the way was rough for a woman, and her green Sunday dress had suffered among the bilberries, while a thorn still smarted in her hand. Libby saw her sit down, ruefully regard her gown, and then fall to sucking at her wounded finger.

There followed a period of silence, upon which broke a slow rustle, and Sally's eyes opened very widely as another woman, cool and collected, appeared within the glade. But Margery also became an embodiment of surprise as her sister rose and the two confronted each other. Then it was that a heartless rascal, from his secure concealment, felt disposed to congratulate himself upon it. He stood two inches shorter than Sally Cramphorn, and he realised that in her present formidable mood the part he had planned might prove difficult to play.

"Merciful to me! What be you doin' in this brimbley auld plaace?" asked the elder girl abruptly.

"My pleasure," answered Margery with cold reserve. "'Pears you've comed a rough way by the looks of you. That gown you set such store by be ruined wi' juice of berries."

"'Your pleasure'! Then perhaps you'll traapse off some place else for your pleasure. I'm here to meet a—a friend of mine; an' us shaan't want you, I assure 'e."

Margery stared, and her face grew paler by a shade.

"By appointment—you—here? Who be it, then, if I may ax?"

"You may not. Mind your awn business."

"I will do, so soon as I knaw it. Awnly it happens as I'm here myself to meet a friend, same as you—an'—an'—is it Henery Collins you'm come to see? You might tell me if 'tis."

"Shaan't tell you nothin'—shaan't underman myself to talk to 'e at all. I'm sick of 'e. You'm spyin' 'pon me, an' I won't have it."

"Spyin' on a fule! Do 'e thinks I care a farthin'-piece what you do or what trash you meet? I'll be plain, anyways, though you'm 'shamed of your company whoever 'tis, by the looks of it. I'm here to meet Greg Libby; so I'll thank you to go!"

"Him?"

"Ess—him. He's a right to ax me to meet him wi'out your leave, I s'pose?"

"No fay, he haven't! No right at all, as I'll soon larn him."

Margery blazed.

"An' why for not, you gert haggage of a woman? Who be you to have the man 'pon your tongue—tell me that?"

"Who be I? I be his gal, that's who I be—have been for months."

"You damn lyin' cat! *Your* man! He'm mine—mine! Do 'e hear? An' us be gwaine to be axed out in church 'fore summer's awver."

"Gar! you li'l pin-tailed beast—dreamin'—that's what you be—sick for un—gwaine mad for un! We'm tokened these months, I tell 'e; an' he'll tell 'e same."

Awed by such an exhibition, and amazed at rousing greater passions in others than he himself was capable of feeling, Gregory sank closer and held his breath.

"'Tis for you to ax him, not me, you blowsy gert female," screamed Margery, now grown very white. "Long he's feared you was on a fule's errand. He knaws you, an' the worth of you. An' he an' faither's friends again, thanks to me. An' he'm not gwaine to marry a pauper woman when he can get one as'll be well-to-do. You—you—what's the use of you but to feed pigs an' wring the necks of fowls for your betters to eat? What sober man wants a slammockin' gert awver-grawn——?"

A scream of agony cut short the question, for Sally beside herself at this outburst, and but too conscious through her rage that she heard the truth, set her temper free, flew at her sister like a fiend, and scratched Margery's face down from temple to chin with all the strength of a strong hand and sharp nails. Blood gushed from this devil's trident stamped into a soft cheek, and the pain was exquisite; then the sufferer, half blinded, bent for a better weapon, picked up a heavy stone, and flung it at close quarters with her best strength. It struck Sally fairly over the right eye, and, reeling from this concussion, she staggered, held up for a moment, then gave at knee and waist and came down a senseless heap by the edge of the water.

Margery stared at this sudden work of her hands; she next made some effort to wipe the blood off her face, and then hastened away as fast as she could. Mr. Libby also prepared to fly. For the unconscious woman at his feet he had no thought. He believed that Sally must be dead, and the sole desire in his mind was to vanish unseen, so that if murder had been done none could implicate him. He determined not to marry Margery, even if she escaped from justice, for he feared a temper so ferocious upon provocation. Gregory, then, stole away quickly, and prepared to perambulate round the farm of Batworthy, above the scene of this tragic encounter, and so return home secretly.

But circumstances cut short his ambition and spoiled his plan. When Margery left her sister, she had not walked far before chance led her to Henry Collins. He was on the way to the Moor once again, that he might pursue search for Stapledon, when Margery's white face, with the hideous wales upon it, her shaking gait and wild eyes, arrested him. He stopped her and asked what had happened.

"I've fought my sister an' killed her," she said; "killed her dead wi' a gert stone. She'm down to the river onder Batworthy Farm; an' if 'twas to do awver again, I'd do it."

He shrank from her, and thought of Sally with a great heart-pang.

"Wheer be she? For God's love tell me quick."

"Down below the fishing notice-board, wi' her head in the watter. She'm dead as a nail, an' I'm glad 'twas I as cut her thread, an' I'm———"

But he heard only the direction and set off running. So it came about that Gregory Libby had not left the theatre of the tragedy five minutes when Collins reached it, and saw all that made his life worth living lying along procumbent beside Teign. One of Sally's arms was in the river, and the stream leapt and babbled within six inches of her mouth. Her hair had fallen into the water, and it turned and twisted like some bright aquatic weed a-gleaming in the sun.

Even as Henry approached the woman moved and rolled nearer the river; but its chill embrace helped to restore consciousness, and she struggled to her side, supported herself with one arm and raised the other to her head.

Mr. Collins praised the Almighty. He cried—

"God's grace! God's gudeness! Her ban't dead! Glory be to Faither, Son an' Ghost—her'm alive—poor, dear, darlin' maid!"

Then he fished Sally from the stream, and hugged her closer to himself than necessary in the act. Next he set her with her back against a tree, and presently she opened her eyes and sighed deeply, and gazed upon Henry with a vacant stare. Then Sally felt warm blood stealing from her forehead to the corner of her mouth, and put up her hand to the great contusion above her eye, and remembered. Collins, seeing that her eyes rolled up, and fearing another fainting fit for her, dipped his Sunday handkerchief in the river and wiped her face.

"A gashly auld bruise, sure enough; but it haven't broke your head bones, my dear woman; you'll recover from it by the blessing o' the Lard."

She became stronger by degrees, and memory painted the picture of the past with such vivid colours that a passionate flush leapt to her cheek again.

"Blast him! The dog—the cruel wretch—to kindiddle me so—an' play wi' her same time. What had I done but love him—love him wi' all my heart? To fling us together that way, so us might tear each other to pieces! I wish I could break his neck wi' my awn hands, or see him stringed up by it. I'll—I'll—wheer's Margery to? Not gone along wi' him?"

"No. I met her 'pon the way to home. She reckons she've killed you."

"An' be happy to think so, no doubt. I sclummed her faace down—didn't I?"

"Doan't let your rage rise no more. You've had a foot in the graave for sartain. Be you better? Or shall I carry 'e?"

She rose weakly, and he put his arm around her and led her away. They moved along together until, coming suddenly above the ridge of the hill, Mr. Libby appeared within two hundred yards of them. He had made his great detour, and was slipping stealthily homeward, when here surprised.

Sally saw him and screamed; whereupon he stopped, lost his nerve, and, turning, hastened back towards the Moor.

"Theer! the snake! That's him as fuled me an' brawk my heart, an' wouldn't care this instant moment if I was dead!"

"'Tis Greg Libby," said Collins, gazing at the retreating figure with great contempt. "A very poor fashion o' man as I've always held."

But Sally's mind was running forward with speed.

"Did you ever love me?" she asked suddenly, with her eyes on the departing hedge-tacker.

"You knaw well enough—an' allus shall so long as I've got sense."

"Then kill him! Run arter un, if it takes e' a week to catch un, an' kill un stone dead; an' never draw breath till you've a-done it."

Mr. Collins smiled like a bull-dog and licked his hands.

"You bid me?"

"Ess, I do; an' I'll marry you arter."

"Caan't kill un, for the law's tu strong; but I'll give un the darndest dressin' down as ever kept a man oneasy in his paarts for a month o' Sundays. If that'll comfort 'e, say so."

"Ess—'twill sarve. Doan't stand chatterin' 'bout it, or he'll get off."

Henry shook his head.

"No, he won't—not that way. The man's afeared, I reckon—smells trouble. He's lost his small wits, an' gone to the Moor, an' theer ban't no chance for escape now."

"Let un suffer same as he've made me—smash un to pieces!"

"I'll do all that my gert love for 'e makes reasonable an' right," said Collins calmly. Then he took off his coat and soft hat, and asked Sally if she was strong enough to carry them back to the farm for him.

"'Tis the coat what you sat upon to Godleigh merry-making, an' I wouldn't have no harm come to it for anything."

She implored Henry to waste no more time, but hurry on the road to vengeance; for Mr. Libby was now a quarter of a mile distant, and his retreating figure already grew small. Collins, however, had other preparations to make. He took a knife from his pocket, went to a blackthorn, hacked therefrom a stout stick, and spoke as he did so.

"Doan't you fret, my butivul gal. Ban't no hurry now. Us have got all the afternoon afore us. 'Tis awnly a question of travellin'. Poor gawk—he've gone the wrong way, an' theer won't be no comin' home till I've had my tell about things. You go along quick, an' get Mrs. Loveys to put a bit of raw meat to your poor faace; an' I'll march up-along. 'Twill be more'n raw meat, or brown paper'n vinegar, or a chemist's shop-load o' muck, or holy angels—to say it wi'out disrespect—as'll let Greg lie easy to-night. Now I'm gwaine. Us'll have un stugged in a bog directly minute, if he doan't watch wheer he'm runnin' to, the silly sawl."

CHAPTER XV.
WATERN TOR

Desperate was the flight, deliberate the pursuit of Gregory Libby. He had started without more purpose than that of a hare at first death-knell from hounds, and now, too late, he realised that by heading directly for the open Moor, his enemy must get the opportunity he needed to make a capture. Mr. Libby indeed was lighter and fleeter than Henry Collins, and at a mile or two the bigger man had stood no chance, but now, with Dartmoor before them, the question was one of endurance, and in that matter Henry held the advantage. He would lumber along in pursuit until dark, if necessary, and it was impossible for the other to hide from him. But the probable result of capture lent Libby wings. He pushed forward, yet wasted precious breath by cursing himself for a fool as he ran. Across the wastes, where old-time miners streamed for tin, he went, and gained a little as he did so. Then it struck him that at climbing his slighter build would win great advantage, so he headed for the rocky foot-hills of Watern Tor. The extra labour told upon Gregory's lungs, however; he had soon been running for half an hour—a performance without parallel in his career—and he found that hoped-for vantage of ground by no means crowned his supreme effort. Henry came along with a steady shamble. He was blowing like a roaring horse, but his huge chest proved equal to the strain, and he grinned to find himself steadily decreasing the gap between his stick and Sally's enemy. Presently the fugitive caught his foot in a rabbit hole, fell, and hit his shins on stone. He groaned and swore, for the accident cost him fifty yards, and quite shook his scanty pluck. His breath began to come hard, and he felt his heart flogging against his ribs very painfully. A mist filled his eyes, and it was lurid and throbbed with a red pulse at every stride. Nervous twitchings overtook him, and his knees and elbows jerked spasmodically. He grew unsteady and giddy, fell again, and then got upon his feet once more. Turning to avoid a bog, and splashing through the fringe of it, he still kept running, but his pace was dwindling to a slow trot, and his force was spent. Now he could hear the other snort within a hundred yards of him.

Then Mr. Collins hazarded a request.

"Stop!" he bawled. "Best to draw up, for I be gwaine to give 'e worst walloping ever you had, an' 'tis awnly puttin' off the hour."

But Libby did not answer. Terror added a last impetus, and he reached the summit of the hill, under those low precipices of granite that surmount it.

Here rises a huge mass of stratified rock, beside which a smaller fragment, the Thirlestone named, ascends like a pinnacle, and stands separated at the summit by a few feet only from the main mass. Moved by physical fear and a desire to get as far as possible from Collins and the blackthorn, did Gregory struggle hither, and over rough granite steps crawled and jumped on to the great crown of the tor. A last effort took him to the top of the Thirlestone, and there, stranded between earth and sky, at an elevation of some forty feet from the turf below, he assumed a very tragical attitude. Frightened sheep leapt away from the granite plateau, and bounded down, sure-footed, from the northern ledges, where they found cool shadows. Bleating, they regained the earth, and so scampered off as Henry, his man safe, stopped to blow and recover necessary energy. For the victim there was no escape; the path to the summit of Thirlestone was the sole way back again. Turning up his sleeves the pursuer advanced from ledge to ledge until only the dizzy aperture between the pinnacle and its parent tor separated him from Mr. Libby. To stride across would be the work of a moment; but Collins felt haste was unnecessary. He sat down, therefore, recovered his wind, and volunteered some advice.

"Best come down-along wi' me quiet. I caan't do what I be gwaine to do on this here gert rock. Us might fall awver an' break our necks."

"If you move a step towards me, God's my witness I'll jump off an' slay myself; an' 'twill be brought home against you as murder," declared Libby. "S'elp me I will; an' who are you to do violence against me, as never hurt you in word or deed?"

"Us won't talk 'bout that. I've got to larrup 'e to the point wheer 'twould be dangerous to give 'e any worse; an' I be gwaine to do it, because I knaw you desarve it—never no chap more. So come awver an' us'll get back to the grass."

"What for do 'e want to bruise a man 'cause a rubbishy gal be vexed wi' un? Females is allus wrong-headed an' onreasonable. You ain't heard the rights, I'll swear."

"An' ban't likely to from such a gert liar as you, I reckon. Come awver, will 'e, an' shut your damn mouth!"

"I'll jump—I'll jump an' kill myself!"

But the other knew his man too well. Even Henry's customary caution did not interfere between him and instant action now.

"You ban't built to do no such reckless deed," he answered calmly. "You wouldn't be in such a boilin' fright of a thrashin' else. I'm sick of the sight of your snivelling, yellow face an' rabbit mouth—lyin', foxin' varmint that you be!"

He strode across the gap, and Mr. Libby, abandoning all thought of self-destruction, merely dropped where he stood and grovelled.

"I'll give 'e money—anything I've got—a gawlden pound—two—five! Doan't—doan't for Christ's love! 'Tis tu hurtful, an' me a orphan, an' weak from my youth. Oh—my God—it'll kill me—you'll do murder if you touch me—it'll———"

At this point, and during a pause in the scuffling and screaming of the sufferer, circumstances very startling were forced upon the attention of both men. Collins had made the other rise and get back to the tor, at risk of falling to earth if he refused the jump. He had then gripped Gregory by the collar, and was cautiously dragging him down the granite ledges to earth, when a strange noise stayed his progress. It was the same sound that had arrested Stapledon upon his homeward way.

"Gude Lard!" exclaimed Collins, dropping the other as he spoke; "theer's somebody groanin' horrid near by. God send it ban't maister!"

They listened, and the mournful cry of suffering was repeated.

It seemed to rise from the heart of the great cliff on which they stood, and while in measure human, yet vibrated with the mechanical resonance of a beast's voice. Collins returned to the summit, crept towards its edge, and peered over where the tor terminated in abrupt western-facing cliffs. Then the mystery was explained, and he saw a dying creature beneath him. Midway between his standpoint and the turf below there stretched a narrow ledge or shelf, weathered out through the centuries, and upon this excrescence lay a mortally injured sheep. The poor brute—probably scared by flash of lightning or roar of thunder overnight—had made a perilous leap and broken both forelegs in its tremendous descent. Now, helpless, in agony and awful thirst, it lay uttering mournful cries, that grew fainter as the sun scorched life out of it.

But Collins, attracted by a barking, gazed beyond, and his eyes filled with active concern at sight of a thing, motionless and distorted as a scarecrow, upon the rocks and turf below. Beside it a red setter sat and barked. Then the creature rose and ran round and round, still barking. Collins knew the broad shape below, and the brown, upturned face. He nearly fell forward, then turned, leapt to safety, and, forgetting the other man, hastened down to earth.

And there he found Myles Stapledon, unconscious if not a corpse. Upon his open eyes was peace, and the Death that must have looked into them had lacked power to leave there any stamp of terror or impress of fear. He had fallen backwards and so remained, supine. No visible violence marked his pose, yet a general undefined distortion pervaded it.

"God's holy will!" murmured the living man to himself. "An' he heard the same cry as us did, an' quick to end the sorrow of the beast, tried to get to un. Cruel plain; but 'twas no job for a gert, heavy piece like him. An' he slipped, an' failed backward on the bones of his neck 'fore he could say the words."

Libby shivered at the other's elbow.

"Be you sure he'm truly dead?" he asked

"The gen'leman's warm, but the faace of un tells death, I be feared; an' his niddick's scatted in somethin' awful. But the dog do think he's alive by the looks of un; an' such things is awften hid from us an' shawed to beastes."

"Please God he've enough heat in un to bring back life."

"It may be so. Anyway, 'tis for us to be doin'. I'll bide along wi' un, an' you slip it back quicker'n you comed. Run for your life, or his'n, to the farm, an' tell what's failed, an' send folks here an' a man 'pon a hoss for a doctor, an' bid 'em bring brandy."

Collins spoke with extraordinary passivity. He received this tremendous impression with grief indeed, but no shock. Fear before any plain, daylight event, however horrible, his nature was incapable of suffering; only the night unnerved him.

"Go!" he said. "Doan't stand starin', an' keep out of Missis Stapledon's way, but see the men. An' tell Pinsent, or the bwoy, to bring a gun along wi' 'em. 'Twas his dyin' deed to try an' put thicky sheep out of sufferin'; an' I'll see 'tis done my awn self, for respect of the man."

Gregory answered nothing, but departed. In the excitement of this event he forgot his own pending discomfiture and escape. But he remembered these things half-way back to Little Silver. Then he had time for personal satisfaction.

"'Tis a ill wind as blaws gude to none," he thought.

And the other ordered the body of his master in seemly pose, and placed a pillow of fern under the battered skull, and sat down and waited. Not all the mellow sunset light could bring warmth to the face of Myles Stapledon. An evening wind blew over the Moor; the mist, generating and growing visible at close of day, stole here and there, and spread silver curtains, and wound about her familiar playthings of granite. She hid the heath, and transformed the stone, brushed by the living, and glazed the placid eyes of the dead.

With profound respect, but no active emotion of sorrow, Henry Collins sat and watched; yet bitter mourning did not lack, for the great red dog still ran up and down, nosed his master, then lifted up his voice and howled as the cold truth struck into him. His wonderful eyes imaged a world of misery and his face showed agonies far more acute than the moonlike countenance of the man.

But Collins had come correctly to the truth, and, in his speech, accurately described an incident that here, upon thresholds of renewed hope and peace, had ended the days of Myles Stapledon.

At sudden cry from a brute in pain above him, Myles climbed Watern, realised the sheep's sad plight, and immediately essayed to throw it down, that its miseries might be ended. But at unguessed personal disadvantages, from a protracted fast and recent physical exertions, the man over-estimated his strength, nor took account of the serious difficulties attending such a climb. Half-way to the ledge, he grew suddenly giddy, and, for the first time, realised that though he might descend, return must be for him impossible. A desperate effort to get back proved futile; he slipped, struggled, slipped again, and found his hands and arms powerless to serve or save. And then he heard the unexpected Message and knew that his hours were told.

Now he slept where he had fallen, below the unchanging granite. His life was done with; its tribulations and sunrise of new hope alike quenched. Yet no pang of mental sorrow marked his dead face, and physical suffering was likewise absent from it. The man lay calm of feature, contented of aspect. His eyebrows were arched and normal, his hands were unflexed. One had guessed that he made no effort to question the mandate, but rather, in a phrase of Aurelius, had yielded up life with serenity complete as His who issued the discharge.

CHAPTER XVI.
THRENODY

"In all my life, and long it has been, I never met a particular good man, nor yet a particular bad one. Maybe each sort's rare as t'other, for black and white mixed is the common dirt-colour of human nature. Yet—him—him we've laid to his rest—I do think he was good. He was better than sight to me—that I know."

The men in Bear Down kitchen were clad in black, for that noon they had buried their master, not without tears. He lay in Little Silver churchyard beside his wife's father; but Honor had not attended the funeral.

"Ess, a very gude, upright man, I think. A man as stood to work in season, and never bid none do a job what he couldn't have done better hisself," said Churdles Ash mournfully.

"A man of far-seeing purposes, as allus carried through whatever he ordained; an' could tell when rain was comin' to a day," added Samuel Pinsent. He knew of no higher praise than that.

"An' so soft-hearted wi' the beasts what perish that he comed by his death for a silly auld sheep. Who but him would have thrawed away life on such a fool's errand?" asked Cramphorn bitterly.

"No other man for sartain, sir," answered the boy Bates.

"Very fine to bring it in death by misadventure," continued Jonah, "an' I'm not saying 'twas anything but seemly so to do; but all the same, if the maister had lived an' come off wi' a mere brawken leg or arm, I'd have been the fust to tell un as he was riskin' his life in a fule's trick, even if he'd been a lighter built an' spryer man."

"A plaace as looks much easier than 'tis," said Tommy Bates. "I climbed it next day an' done it easy gwaine down, but 'twas all I could do, hangin' on by my claws like a cat, to get up 'pon top again."

"'Twas playin' wi' his life, I say, an' though he'm dead, worse luck, theer's blame still falls against un. What do 'e say, maister?"

Mark Endicott's face wore a curious expression as the question reached him. The blind man had preserved an unusual silence before this tragedy, and while the real explanation of Stapledon's death was accepted by all, from Honor to those amongst whom the farmer was no more than a name, yet Endicott had at no time discussed the matter, though he exhibited before it an amount of personal emotion very rare from him. The sudden end of Myles had aged Mark obviously, shaken him, and set deep currents surging under the surface of him. Even his niece in her own stricken heart could find room for wonder at her uncle's bitter expressions of sorrow and self-pity before his personal loss. After the first ebullition of grief, when tears were seen to flow from his eyes for the first time in man's recollection, he relapsed into a condition of taciturnity and accepted the verdict brought at the inquest with a relief not understood by those who observed it. He kept much alone and spoke but seldom with Honor, who rarely left her room through the days that passed between her husband's death and burial. Out of the darkness of his own loss Mark seemed powerless to comfort another, even though she might be supposed to suffer in a degree far keener than his own; and the men of Bear Down, noting his attitude, whispered that old Endicott was beginning to break up. Yet this was but partly the case, for private convictions and an erroneous conclusion before mentioned were in the main responsible for the blind man's great concern; and the impossibility of sharing his burden with any other at this moment weighed heavily upon him. Spartan he still stood under the blow and that worse thing behind the blow; but the night of his affliction was darker than a whole lifetime of blindness, and the signs of it could not be hidden. The man began to grow aged, and his vigour and self-control were alike abating a little under steady pressure of time.

Now each of the toilers assembled there uttered some lament; each found a word of praise for his dead master.

"The auld sayin' stood gude of un," declared Churdles Ash. "'The dust from the farmer's shoes be the best manure for his land.' Ess fay, everywheer he was; an' no such quick judge of a crop ever I seed afore."

"Never begrudged a chap a holiday, I'm sure," declared Pinsent.

"Would to God it had been t'other," growled Mr. Cramphorn. It was a vain desire that he had openly expressed on every possible occasion, and once to Christopher Yeoland's face.

"Don't wish him back, lads," answered Mark Endicott. "His life's work was done nearly perfect—by the light of a poor candle, too; an' that's to say there was a deal of pain hidden away deep in it. For pain is the mother of all perfect work. He's out of it. We that have lost the man are to be pitied. We cannot pity him if we're good Christians."

"A cruel beast of a world 'tis most times," declared Cramphorn, as he lighted his pipe. "Takin' wan thing with another, 'tis a question if a man wouldn't be happier born a rabbit, or some such unthinking item."

"World's all right," answered Ash. "You'm acid along o' your darters. 'Tis the people in the world makes the ferment. 'Twas a very gude plaace when fust turned out o' hand, if Scripture's to count; for God A'mighty seed it spread out like a map, wi' its flam-new seas an' mountains an' rivers; an' butivul tilth—all ripe for sowin', no doubt; an' He up an' said 'twas vitty."

"Ah! Awnly wan man an' wan woman in it then—wi'out any fam'ly," commented Jonah. "The Lard soon chaanged His tune when they beginned to increase an' multiply. Disappointing creations all round, them Israelites. God's awn image spoiled—as they be to this day for that matter."

"Pegs! an' us little better'n them judged in the lump. Take I—as'll be next to go onderground by the laws of nature. What have I to shaw for all my years?" asked Ash sadly.

"You've done a sight o' small, useful jobs in your time—things as had to be done by somebody; an' you've worked no ill to my knowledge. 'Tis somethin' to have bided on the airth eighty year an' never woke no hate in a human breast," said Jonah. "Very differ'nt to the chap that mourned in his Lunnon clothes at the graave-side, an' cried his crocodile tears into a cambric 'ankersher for all to see," he added.

"They was real, wet tears, for I catched the light of the sun on 'em," said Tommy Bates. "An' he shook grevous at 'dust to dust,' as if the dirt was falling 'pon him 'stead of the coffin."

"He'm gone since—drove off to Okington, they tell me; an' Brimblecombe says he be off to furrin paarts again to roam the world," murmured Samuel Pinsent.

"Like the Dowl in Job, no doubt," declared Jonah; "though 'tis question whether he'll see worse wickedness than he knaws a'ready—even among they Turks.

"The man stopped in the yard till the graave was all suent, an' smooth, an' covered to the last turf, however," answered Collins; "for I bided tu, an' I watched un out the tail o' my eye; an' he was cut deep an' couldn't hide it even from me."

"No gude for you to spit your spite 'gainst him, Jonah," summed up Churdles Ash. "It caan't be no use, an' 'tis last thing as dead maister would have suffered from 'e."

There was a silence; then Collins spoke in musing accents, to himself rather than for any listener.

"Really gone—dust—that gert, strong frame—an' us shan't see the swinging gait of un, or the steady eye of un, nor hear the slow voice of un calling out upon the land no more."

"Gone for ever an' ever, amen, Henery," answered Ash. "Gone afore; an' I like to be the fust to shaake his hand, in my humble way, t'other side the river."

"An' his things a mouldering a'ready," whispered Tommy Bates with awe. "I found the leggings what he died in behind easy-chair in the parlour, wheer he wus took fust; an' they'm vinnied all o'er."

Jonah Cramphorn nodded.

"'Tis a terrible coorious fact," he said, "as dead folks' things do mildew 'mazin' soon arter they'm took off of 'em."

The talk fell and rose, flickering like a fire; then silence crowded upon all, and presently every man, save only Mark Endicott, departed; while he was left with a horror of his own imagining, to mourn the last companion spirit his age would know.

BOOK IV.

CHAPTER I.
THE PASSAGE OF TWO YEARS

Upon the death of Myles Stapledon great changes marked the administration of Bear Down. The event stood for a landmark in the history of the farm, and served as an occasion from which its old, familiar name of 'Endicott's' fell into disusage; for the place now passed into alien hands, and from it departed the last of the old stock, together with not a few of those whose fortunes had been wrapped up with the farm for generations.

Honor determined to leave her home within a month of her husband's death. To roam awhile alone seemed good to her, and, for a space of time that extended into years before her return, she absented herself from Devon. Her farm had appreciated much in value of late years, and a tenant for it did not lack long; but the new power brought new servants, and certain of the older workers took this occasion to retire from active service. Churdles Ash went to live with an elderly nephew at Little Silver; Mr. Cramphorn also resigned, but he continued to dwell in his cottage at Bear Down and was content that Sally and Margery should still work upon the farm. Collins, promoted to deputy headman, took his life with increasing seriousness—a circumstance natural when it is recorded that matrimony with Sally Cramphorn had now become only a question of time.

Mark Endicott also left Bear Down for a cottage at Chagford, and Mrs. Loveys accompanied him as housekeeper. This great uprooting of his life and necessary change of habits bewildered the old man at first; but his native courage aided him, and he unfolded his days in faith and fortitude. From Honor he heard erratically, and gathered that she drifted rudderless amid new impressions now here, now there. Then, as the months passed by, into the texture of her communications came flashes or shadows of herself, and the blind man perceived that Time was working with her; that her original, unalterable gift of mind was awakening and leavening her life as of yore.

Humour she still possessed, for it is an inherent faculty, that sticks closer than a spouse to the heart that holds it from puberty to the grave. It wakens with the dawn of adult intelligence, and neither time nor chance, neither shattering reverse nor unexpected prosperity can rob the owner of it. Earthly success indeed it brightens, and earthly failure it sets in true perspective; it regulates man's self-estimate and personal point of view; enlarges his sympathies; adjusts the too-staring splendours of sudden joys; helps to dry the bitterest tears humanity can shed. For humour is an adjunct divine, and as far beyond the trivial word for it as "love" is, or "charity." No definition or happy phrase sums it correctly, or rates it high enough; it is a balm of life; it makes for greater things than clean laughter from the lungs; it is the root of tolerance, the prop of patience; it "suffers long and is kind"; serves to tune each little life-harmony with the world-harmony about it; keeps the heart of man sweet, his soul modest. And at the end, when the light thickens and the mesh grows tight, humour can share the suffering vigils of the sleepless, can soften pain, can brighten the ashy road to death.

In the softness of the valley air lived Mark Endicott, and still knitted comforters for the Brixham fishers.

His first interest was Honor and her future. Of these, he prophesied to those few who loved her and who came to see her uncle from time to time. To Mrs. Loveys, to Ash, to Jonah Cramphorn the old man foretold a thing not difficult of credence. Indeed, eighteen months after the death of her husband, a letter from Honor, despatched at Geneva, came as confirmation, and informed Mark that she had met Christopher Yeoland there.

"They will part no more," said he when the letter was read to him; and he was right.

An interval of six months separated this communication from the next, and when his niece wrote again, she signed herself "Honor Yeoland." The missive was tinctured with some unusual emotion, and woke the same in Mrs. Loveys as she rehearsed it, and in Mark as he listened. "I am just twenty-seven," said the writer. "Do not tell me that it is too late in life to seek for a little happiness still. At least I know what Myles would think."

But the deed demanded no excuse in her uncle's judgment, for he had long anticipated it, and was well content that matters should thus fall out.

And a few months later, when August had passed again, the master of Godleigh and his lady returned home. Special directions prevented any sort of formal welcome, and the actual date of their arrival was only known to a few. Through a twilight of late summer they came, unseen and unwelcomed; and one day later, upon a fair afternoon in mid-September, Honor, escaping from the flood of new cares and responsibilities, slipped valleywards away to traverse the woods alone and visit her uncle at Chagford.

A chill touched her heart as she proceeded, for in these dear glades, at Doctor Clack's command, the woodmen had been zealous to help Nature during the preceding spring. Wide, new-made spaces innocent of trees awaited her; light and air had taken the place of many an old giant, and raw tablets of sawn wood, rising in the vigour of bramble, and refreshed undergrowths were frequent beside her path. Then, at a familiar spot, no pillar of grey supporting clouds of mast and foliage met Honor's eyes. Instead there opened a little clearing, created by one effort of the axe, with the frank sky above and a fallen column below—a column shorn of branch and lopped of bough—a naked, shattered thing lying in a dingle of autumn grasses and yellow, autumn flowers, like, yet unlike, the old nest of memories.

And this fallen tree, so unexpected, came as right prelude to the matter that awaited her beside it. The beech of her joy and sorrow was thrown down, and its apparition awakened in her heart none of that gentle and subdued melancholy she anticipated. Rather, such emotions were smothered in active regret at its downfall. And now a howling, winter storm descended upon her spirit—a tempest very diverse from the silver-grey, autumnal rainfall of placid sadness that here she had foreseen and expected.

The stricken tree struck a chord of deeper passion than it had done beheld in prosperity; whereupon, looking forward, Honor found herself not alone. Close at hand, in a spot that he had favoured through the past summer, sat Mark Endicott with his knitting; and a hundred yards away, beside the river, a boy, successor to Tommy Bates, stood with his back turned watching the trout.

Mark sat in the sunshine with his head uplifted.

There was speculation in his face, but his hands were busy, and the old wooden needles flashed in white wool.

She watched him a moment, then her eyes caught sight of something nearer at hand.

CHAPTER II.
NO AFTER-GLOW

The object that had attracted Honor's attention was an inscription carved upon the fallen beech tree. Ignorant of the interest awakened by that ancient work of Christopher's hand, when the same came to be discovered by woodmen, she glanced hurriedly at the initials and love-knot, now weathered and toned by time and the tree's growth; then she produced a little pocket-knife, and, not without difficulty, erased the record of her husband's red-letter day in a vanished summer.

Mark Endicott sat within ten yards of Honor while she worked; but he continued unconscious of her near presence, for the song of a robin and the music of Teign muffled the small noise she made. Moreover, the blind man's own voice contributed to deaden all other sound, for, following his ancient use, he thought aloud. This Honor discovered, hesitated a moment, then, her task upon the tree completed, listened to Mark Endicott.

There are blind, dark forces that spin the fabric of man's day and night from his own emotions and sudden promptings. In thoughtless action and unconsidered deed; in impulse born of high motive or of low, they find their material, weave our garments; and, too often, led by destiny, steep most innocent white robes in poisoned blood, as Deianira that of Hercules. Thus they fashion man's black future out of his sunny past, breed his tears from his laughter, his enduring sorrows from fleeting whims, and tangle him soul-deep in networks of his own idle creation. Our secure hour is the signal to their activities; they sleep while we are watchful; they wake when we enter upon our pleasures and seek for joy.

Moved by a sentiment that herself might be the object of his thoughts, and her heart yearning to him as he sat there alone, Honor gave heed to the slow voice and listened to Mark Endicott's oral musings upon the time that was past. Fitfully he spoke, with unequal intervals of silence between the sentences. But his thoughts were of a piece; he dwelt upon a theme that he could now endure to handle—a theme rendered familiar to his mind by constant repetition and convictions rooted beyond power of further argument. Of Honor indeed he had been thinking; for the sound of her voice and the touch of her hand he had greatly longed. These were numbered first among the few good things left to him; but from reflection upon his niece he had now passed to her dead husband, and he spoke and thought of Myles Stapledon. His voice, though he communed with himself, was so clear that no word escaped the listener; and every utterance came as cloud upon cloud to darken her day and deepen her night henceforward.

"A man good in the grain—frugal—industrious—patient—yet the one thing needful denied him—held out of his reach. Maybe faith had made him almost a hero—maybe not. Anyway, there was strong meat in the rule he set himself; and he didn't swerve even to the bitter end of it.... Strange, strange as human nature, that his way of life could reach to that. Yet I heard the words upon his lips; I heard him say how self-slaughter might be a good, high deed. And certain 'tis the Bible has no word against it. Little he thought then—or I—that he'd take that road himself....... And the foundations of his life so simple as they were. His pleasures to find out flowers and seeds in season, and the secret ways of wild creatures. To think that 'twas only the Moor, and the life of it, and the moods of it, that he sucked such iron from. 'I will lift up mine eyes unto the hills, from whence cometh my help.' That it should have been help to do such a thing as he did! All a big mind turned to ruination for lack of faith..... Close touch with natural things taught him the killing meaning of selfishness; for everything in nature is selfish but Nature's self. Out of the innocence of barren heaths, the honesty of the sky, the steadfastness of the seasons and the obedience of green things to the sun—out of all these he gathered up the determination to do a terrible deed....... 'Twas all they taught him, for Nature's a heathen. Yet a wonderful departure; and the heart of him held him up at the last, for his face was happy, his eyes at peace, so they said. 'Twas a glimpse of that life to come he could never believe in here that made his eyes at peace. God spoke to him I doubt. Yet never a glimmer of promise did he see, or a whisper of hope did he hear in this life. And he gave up the only life he knew for her—died brave enough, to the tune of his own words spoken long, long since.... And the suicide of him not guessed, thank God. Even she couldn't see—so quick as she is. The dust was flung in her eyes by a kind angel. Yes, surely she was blinded by some holy, guardian thing, for his great nature was understood by her. She had sense enough for that."

He shook his head for a space, then fell into silence again.

He had uttered his conclusion—this old, wise man—in the ear of the soul on earth most vitally involved. He had been for long years a voice that conjured some sense out of his own darkness; he had lightened the difficulties of others; he had spoken not seldom to the purpose and won a measure of love and respect; yet here, by same flaw of mind, or by the accident of blindness; by weakness that hinted approaching senility, or by mere irony of chance, he had taken a wrong turning and missed the transparent truth concerning Myles Stapledon. The dead man's own past utterances were in a measure responsible; and upon them Mark had long since built this edifice of error; he had lived in the belief for two years; had accepted it as life's most tragic experience, to be taken by him in silence to the grave.

But now this opinion crashed into the mind of Honor Yeoland, and she reeled before it and was overwhelmed. Up into the blue sky she looked blankly, with a face suddenly grown old. For an instant she fought to reject the word; for an instant she had it in her to cry out aloud that the old man lied; then the life of Mark Endicott—the sure bulwark of his unfailing wisdom and right judgment rose before her, and she believed that what he said was true. Not in her darkest hour had the possibility of such an event entered Honor's thoughts. Agony she had suffered at Stapledon's death, and the mark of it was on her face for ever, but he had left her for the last time at peace to seek a course that might maintain peace; he had departed full of awakened content to find the road to new life, not death.

Yet this utterance under the woods made her uncertain of her better knowledge; this remorseless, unconscious word, thrown by a voice that had never spoken untruth, was, as it seemed, a blind oracle above appeal from human suffering, an inspired breath sent at God's command to reveal this secret in her ear alone. The glare suddenly thrown upon her mind she held to be truth's own most terrible white light; and she stood helpless and confounded, with her future in ruins. At least some subdued Indian summer of promised content with Christopher had seemed to await her. Now that, too, was torn away and whelmed in frost and snow; for Myles had killed himself to give it to her; Myles had not believed her solemn assurance, but, convinced that she still placed him second in her affection, had set her free. With steady heart and clear eye he had gone to death, so ordering his end that none should guess the truth of it. And none had guessed, save only this ancient man, whose judgment within Honor's knowledge was never at fault.

She believed him; she saw that her present state, as the wife of Christopher, could only confirm him in his conviction; she pictured Mark Endicott waiting to hear how, all unconsciously, she had followed the path Myles Stapledon marked out for her when he died. And then she looked forward and asked herself what this must mean.

A part of her answer appeared in the old man who sat, ignorant of her presence, before her. He—the instrument of this message—had spoken his belief indeed, but with no thought of any listener other than himself. She knew Mark Endicott; she was aware that he had rather himself suffered death than that this matter should have reached her ear. Loyalty to him was not the least part of her determination now. He must never know what he had done.

Neither could she tell her husband for a kindred reason. Such news would cloud his mind for ever, and lessen all his future joy in living.

Before the loneliness of such an unshared grief the woman's soul rose up in arms, and, for one brief moment, she rebelled against her lot, told herself that the evangel of evil had spoken falsely, determined with herself to reject and cast aside this thought as a suspicion unworthy, a lie and a libel on the dead. But the unhappy soul of her was full of the fancied truth. Had she possessed power to turn deaf ears and reject this theory as vain and out of all harmony with her own knowledge of Myles Stapledon, Honor's state had been more gracious; but it was beyond her mental strength to do so. Understanding the dead man no less and no more than her uncle, she read new subtleties into the past before this bitterness, credited Myles with views that never existed in his mind at all, and concluded with herself that he had indeed taken his own life that she might be what she now was—the wife of Christopher Yeoland.

Therefore her own days stretched before her evermore overshadowed until the end of them, and her thoughts leapt whole abysses of despair, as the revelation gradually permeated her being. Seed was sown in that moment, as she stood with the blue sky mirrored in her brown eyes, and a growth was established, whose roots would keep the woman's heart aching till age blunted sensibility, whose fruits would drop gall upon her thirst while life lasted. Unshared darkness must be her portion—darkness and cruel knowledge to be revealed to none, to be hidden out of all searching, to be concealed even beyond the reach of Christopher's love and deepest sympathy. He indeed had her heart now, and knew the secret places of it; therefore, in a sort of frenzy, she prayed to God at that moment, and called upon Him to show her where she might hide this thing and let it endure unseen.

The boy by the river had not observed Honor, and her uncle remained ignorant of her presence. She turned, therefore, and departed, lacking strength at that moment to speak or hearten his desolate life with the music of her voice. She stole away; and in the woods, returning, her husband met her and rejoiced in the accidental encounter.

"Good luck!" he cried. "I'd lost half myself the moment you disappeared, and had made up my mind to mourn unobtrusively till you came back to me. Why hasn't outraged Nature sent a thunderbolt to suppress Courteney Clack? I might have known that desperate surgeon would have prescribed amputation upon most shadowy excuse."

"He has been very busy."

"And done absolutely the right thing, viewed from standpoint of forestry; which makes it impossible to say what one feels. But forget all that. Home we won't go yet. Come and see the sunset."

A promise of great aerial splendours filled the sky as the day waned, and Yeoland, to whom such spectacles were precious as formerly, hastened upwards to the high lands with his wife by his side.

Together they passed through the wood of pines above Godleigh, then, pursuing their way onwards, the man caught a shadow of sobriety from Honor, being quick at all times to note the colour of her thoughts. The fact that she was sad called for no wonder where they then stood, for now in her eyes were mirrored Bear Down's wind-worn sycamores, ripe thatches, whitewashed farm-buildings, and grey walls. The relinquished home of her forefathers lay there, and she had now come from visiting the last of her line. This Christopher supposed, and so understood her demeanour.

Overhead a splendid turmoil of gloom and fire waxed heavenwide, where wind and cloud and sinking sun laboured magnificently together.

"I know every strand in your dear thoughts, love; I could write the very sequence of them, and take them down in shorthand from your eyes."

She smiled at him. That favourite jest of his had been nearly true until now. Henceforth it could be true no more. It was not the picture of home and the thirsty, shorn grass lands spread around it that made her soul sink so low. Even Christopher henceforth was outside the last sanctuary of her heart, and must so remain. There had come a new sorrow of sorrows, to be hidden even from her second self—a grief not to be shared by him, a legacy of tears whose secret fountains he must never find.

She held his hand like a child, and something of her woe passed into him; then he knew that she was very sad, and suspected that her unhappiness had source in deeper things than the renewed spectacle of her home. He instantly fell into sympathy; but it was only a little deeper than that of an artist. What she felt now—walking where Myles Stapledon had so often walked—he could readily conceive; and it made him sad also, with a gentle, æsthetic melancholy that just fell short of pain. For him and for Honor he believed that a future of delicate happiness was spread. These clouds were natural, inevitable; but they scarcely obscured the blue. So he argued, ignorant of that anguish in the mind of his wife. For her the anticipated summer of peace appeared not possible. Now her future stretched before her—ghost-haunted in sober truth. Here was such a mournful twilight as broods over all personifications of highest grief; for her, as for those Titan figures—each an incarnate agony—who pace the aisles of olden drama, there could be no removal into the day-spring of hope, no departure into any night of indifference. Only an endless dusk of sorrow awaited her. Western light was upon her face; but not the glory of evening, nor yet the whole pageant of the sun's passing, could pierce the darkness of her heart.

They stood upon Scor Hill above the Moor; and Christopher spoke—

"This was his god—poor old Myles! This was a symbol to him of the Creator. A great, restful god, yet alive and alert. A changeless god—a god to pray to even—a listening god."

"He would have given all that he had to know a listening god," she said.

"And yet who is there but has sometimes seen his god, moving dimly, awfully, behind the veil? A flash—a divine gleam at higher moments. We fall on our knees, but the vision has gone. We yearn—we yearn to make our crying heard; but the clay comes between. That was his case. You and I have our Christ to cling to. He sweetens our cup of life—when we let Him. But Myles—he walked alone. That is among my saddest thoughts—among the very saddest thoughts that Nature and experience bring to me."

"The earth is very full of things that bring sad thoughts."

"Yes, and a man's heart still more full. There are plaintive sorrows I could tell you about—the sadness of hidden flowers, that no human eye ever looks upon—the sadness of great, lonely mists on lonely lands; the sadness of trees sleeping in moonlight; the sadness of a robbed bird; the eternal sadness and pathos of man's scant certainties and undying hopes. How wonderful he is! Nothing crushes him; nothing stills the little sanguine heart of him, throbbing on, beating on through all the bitter disillusions of this our life from generation to generation."

Far below them, in fulvous light of a wild sunset, the circle of Scor Hill appeared. Concerning the memories its granite girded, Christopher knew little; but, at sight of Watern's crest, now dark against the flaming sky, he remembered that there lay the scene of Stapledon's end, and regretted that he had come within sight of it that night. To him the distant mountain was a theatre of tragedy; to Honor, an altar of sacrifice.

Without words they waited and gazed upon the sky to witness after-glow succeed sunset. Over the Moor a vast and radiant mist burnt under the sun and faded to purple where it stretched beneath the shadows of the hills; and the earth, taking this great light to her bosom, veiled herself within it. All detail vanished, all fret of incident disappeared, while the inherent spirit of the place stood visible, where loneliness and vastness stretched to the sunset and heaved up their huge boundaries clad only in a mystery of ruddy haze. Particulars departed from the wilderness, save where, through alternate masses of gloom and transparent vapour, carrying their harmonies of orange and tawny light to culmination and crown of fire, there twinkled a burn—twinkled and tumbled and flashed, under mellow drapery of air and cloud, beneath flaming depths of the sunset, and through the heart of the earth-born mist, like a thread of golden beads. Here colour made a sudden music, sang, and then sank back into silence.

For heavy clouds already reared up out of the West to meet the sun; and amid far-flung banners and pennons and lances of glory he descended into darkness. Then the aspect of earth and heaven changed magically; day waned and grew dense, while a great gloom swept over the heath and rose to the zenith under a cowl of rain. Dim radii still turned upon the clouds where light fought through them; but their wan illumination was sucked away and they died before their shafts had roamed full course. The cry of the river rose and fell, the rain began to whisper, and all things merged with unaccustomed speed into formless chaos of twilight.

"No after-glow—then we must look within our own breasts for it—or, better still, each other's breasts," said the man.

But neither heart nor voice of the woman answered him.

THE END

Milton Keynes UK
Ingram Content Group UK Ltd.
UKHW020754200524
442968UK00006B/804

9 789357 962643